902759209 8

Please return/renew this item by the last date shown.
Items may also be renewed by the internet*

https://library.eastriding.gov.uk

* Please note a PIN will be required to access this service
- this can be obtained from your library

D1350471

HOTEL ST KILDA

HEAVEN'S DOOR

MICHAEL KNAGGS

Matador
9 Priory Business Park
Kibworth Beauchamp
Leicestershire LE8 0RX, UK
Tel: (+44) 116 279 2299
Fax: (+44) 116 279 2277
Email: books@troubador.co.uk
Web: www.troubador.co.uk/matador

ISBN 978 1784620 493

British Library Cataloguing in Publication Data.
A catalogue record for this book is available from the British Library.

Typeset in Aldine by Troubador Publishing Ltd
Printed and bound in the UK by TJ International, Padstow, Cornwall

Matador is an imprint of Troubador Publishing Ltd

For Carol

'Pride goes before destruction
and a haughty spirit before a fall
Sometimes there is a way that seems to be right
but in the end it is the way to death.'

Proverbs 16

'A week is a long time in politics.'

(Attr. Harold Wilson)

Three months is a lifetime.

CHAPTER ONE

Week 1; Monday, 23 March…

The detective inspector replaced the desk phone on its cradle and looked across at his sergeant.

"Come in, number three."

"Sir?"

"That's the third one …" he checked his watch "… in twenty-two hours who's agreed to come and talk to us. Almost as if they were conferring, don't you think, given their intransigence over the last five weeks?"

"Do we pick him up or is he going to claim fifty quid for a taxi?"

The DI snorted a laugh. "I think we play it softly-softly for the moment. I offered to bring him in – he said he'd make his own way later today."

"And the other two?"

"Should be here late morning unless they change their mind again. They told me they were coming yesterday afternoon."

"Should we chase them up, do you think?"

"Not sure. We don't want to seem to be pushing too hard, but the worry is they could easily choose to disappear again. I mean, there's nothing in it for them really, is there?"

"Revenge, I suppose?" offered the sergeant.

"That's true, but revenge usually takes a different form in these cases, doesn't it? I still don't understand why three unconnected people – well, seven, I suppose you'd have to say – would chose to do it this way. Anyway, let's just leave them for now and see what happens over the next couple of days."

The two men were sitting across the desk from each other in the

DI's office, which was small and modern. The beech-finish desk was L-shaped, incorporating a PC work station on the short leg of the 'L'. Down one side of the room was a line of matching cabinets and on the wall on the opposite side was a large screen with a back-projection facility for the computer and which doubled as a dry-wipe board.

The senior man clicked a few keys on his keyboard and the screen came to life. He got up from his tilt-and-swivel and stretched, then stepped over to the collage of images and words on the screen. He was of average height and build, and untidily dressed in a grey suit which had seen better days. His thinning grey hair made him look older than his forty-two years.

"So, what have we got so far?"

★

Two days later
Week 1; Wednesday, 25 March…

"Welcome aboard, as they say."

The large man in the dark blue uniform smiled and extended his hand to each of the two visitors as they walked up the ramp at the rear of the vessel.

"Thank you, Captain …"

"Oh, I'm not the captain. Calum Nicholson at your service, Chief Prison Officer at Lochshore. Captain McLeod is on the bridge doing his final checks. I'll take you to see him later."

The man who had spoken to Calum was tall, in his mid-forties and distinguished-looking, with a mane of steel grey hair. He was well-dressed in a short reefer coat worn over an expensive lounge suit, shirt and tie, and shining black brogues. The other man was much smaller, around average height and in his mid sixties. He wore a thick waterproof coat over a round-necked fisherman's jumper and, with his grey beard and woolly hat, looked much less out of place preparing to enter the bowels of a ship than his companion.

"Lawrence Harding," the tall man introduced himself, "Parliamentary Under-Secretary of State for Prisons, and this is Mike Needham, chief designer of Alpha. We are here *only* to observe and absorb – nothing else. And we're very grateful to you for finding time to show us round."

Calum checked his watch. "You're very welcome, but I'm afraid we don't have long. We start embarking at seven, so that gives us just thirty-five minutes. Please ask any questions as we go round."

He turned and they followed him onto the vessel, stopping just inside.

"The ship is a specially-modified passenger ferry," said Calum, "previously used to take people to some of the most beautiful places imaginable. Back then it was called *Spirit of St Columba* and where we're standing now was the vehicle deck. Now it's known as PTV1 – short for prisoner transfer vessel one."

In front of them were two walkways. Calum took them along the one on the port side.

"What we have are one hundred and fifty separate, two-metre-square cabins, each with three solid metal walls and one outward-facing wall with steel bars and a sliding door. The cabins are linked together in four lines – two lines of forty back-to-back down the centre of the ship and a line of thirty-five on both this and starboard sides. As you can see, each line sits separately on rail tracks so they can be moved on and off the vessel like a giant flexible cage on a fairground ride. This and the other gangway run the length of the deck between the outer and central line of cabins on either side."

"Amazing," said Mike Needham, looking round like a little boy in a toy shop. "I can't wait to see the link-up to the lifting platform, especially how it's done in heavy seas or high winds."

"Well, speaking personally," said Calum, smiling, "I hope you *don't* get to see that on this trip – the heavy seas and high winds, I mean."

Lawrence Harding was peering into one of the cabins. Calum continued.

"Each cabin has a bench along one side, a small swing-out table, like those on passenger airlines, and a TV monitor." Calum was pointing out the furnishings. "And behind the plastic curtain across the corner there's a chemical toilet and small wash-hand basin. A bit basic and spartan, but it's just for a single one-way trip of twenty or so hours."

"And the television," said Lawrence. "What's that for?"

"Not for Sky Movies, I'm afraid. We'll be showing them a training film during the second half of the trip. A thirty-minute programme on a continuous loop, covering aspects of life on Alpha. Not sure myself whether it's a good idea. More likely to scare them than educate them, I reckon."

"But they've had their training already, haven't they?"

"That's right, but the thinking is that it's all a bit unreal at that stage."

"A *bit* unreal." Lawrence raised his eyebrows.

"Well, whatever. At least it's something for them to look at if they want to."

"And meals?"

"Once we've got them installed they'll get trays with coffee, a cereal bar and sandwiches. We slide them under the doors of the cabins."

"But they'll get other meals?"

"Three today and breakfast tomorrow morning. Although I can't imagine many of them having much of an appetite, can you? Let's go up here."

He led them up some metal stairs and along to the monitoring centre on the deck above, where they would be able to observe proceedings on the array of CCTV screens. Calum took them over to a map on the wall.

"Here's where we are now." He pointed to the map. "After we leave Loch Fendort we go round Kerrera into the Firth of Lorne and head north-west through the Sound of Mull. From there we'll cross the Hebridean Sea and skirt the southern tip of the Bishop's Isles, before heading north-west again into the open Atlantic for a further sixty miles. That will take us twenty miles south-west of here." He pointed to the island group which represented the farthest outpost of the British Isles. "The entire trip is planned to take around twenty-two hours, so we should be there around seven tomorrow morning."

"Will I need any seasick pills?" asked Mike.

"You'll have to ask the captain," Calum smiled. "I've been too scared to ask him myself."

★

The first fifty yards of the walk passed calmly enough. After all, the young man was in a familiar building where he'd been moved around frequently during the past three weeks. He knew this was different, of course, but it was only when they reached the outer double doors that this awareness surfaced in the form of violent panic.

The doors were open and fastened back. The metal walkway stretched ahead in a straight line. Along and round the quayside the lights shone brightly in the early morning gloom and were reflected in the still waters of the harbour. The ferry, two hundred yards away and looking huge against the flotilla of smaller boats, was facing directly away from them with its rear ramp lowered. The walkway split into two just before it mounted the ramp and disappeared into the stern of the vessel.

He was no more than average height, slim and wiry with long fair hair, wearing a baggy grey jogging suit over a black tee shirt. The two security officers he was handcuffed to were huge men in dark blue uniforms, with hard faces and short cropped hair. As the prisoner stepped through the doorway, the sight of the vessel and the cold morning air hit him at the same moment. He lunged at the man on his right causing him to crash heavily against the rail of the walkway and slump to the floor. He kicked wildly at him, karate-style, with the heel of his foot, the steel bracelets tearing at the skin around his wrists as he tried to pull himself free. The second officer gripped him round his chest from behind, squeezing hard as his colleague scrambled up and grabbed his flailing legs.

"Needle – now!" he yelled as they held him still.

The prisoner screamed at the sudden stab of pain in his thigh as a third man stepped forward and jabbed the syringe hard into the muscle. The guard holding the prisoner's legs turned to the medic.

"Tell Gally to show them all that thing – or the biggest one you've got – and make sure they know you're going to stick in them if they don't behave themselves and walk nicely for us. How long will this take?"

"About four or five minutes; should last for up to six hours. I'll tell Gally, but it's supposed to be a fall-back measure, that's all."

"Just tell him!"

He turned back to the writhing young man.

"Settle down, son," his colleague was saying. "Don't make it even rougher on yourself."

"You're breaking my fucking arms, you fucking bastards!" he spat the words out at them.

"I'll break your fucking neck if you try anything like that again," the other guard shouted.

They eased him onto the walkway, laying him face down and moving his arms so they could rest naturally at his sides. His rapid breathing slowed as the relaxant did its work. After a few more minutes they helped him to his feet and guided him along the walkway and into the vessel, locking him into his cabin.

★

It was 7.55 am. The man got out of his chauffer-driven BMW at the Members' Entrance in New Palace Yard and breathed in the fresh March morning air as he gazed up at the ancient walls of Westminster Hall, which still retained some of the original building dating back a thousand years. He waited until the first of the sixteen strokes which counted down the hour sounded in Elizabeth Tower close behind him before pushing his way through to the entrance foyer.

The man was tall and slim, with broad shoulders and an upright military bearing. He was impeccably dressed in an expensive light grey suit, a shirt which matched the colour of his twinkling pale-blue eyes and a navy and yellow striped tie.

"Good morning, sir."

He beamed down at the prime minister's diminutive, freckled PA.

"Morning, Shirley, you look lovely today, as always."

"You're in Committee Room 14."

She escorted him in silence to the meeting room on the first floor. It was exactly eight o'clock.

Committee Room 14 was set out with a table on a dais at one end and three rows of facing benches down each side. Along the outside wall, were a number of leaded windows reaching almost to the ceiling. The room was also known as the Gladstone Room and around the other walls, above the wood panelling, was a series of paintings showing parliamentarians who served during his terms as prime minister.

"Ah, the Home Secretary; at *last*."

Andrew Donald was seated on his own at the table on the dais, with the thirty members who represented the top level of his government occupying the seats closest to him. With the exception of the man who had just spoken they all rose to their feet as Tom Brown entered the room.

"And good morning to *you*, Prime Minister."

He took his seat on the dais next to Andrew – the signal for the others to sit down – and opened his briefcase to remove a red leather-bound folder, which exactly matched those in front of each person in the room. The thirty-two attendees opened the folders in perfect synchronisation.

"As you know," said Tom, "we've made remarkable progress against the NJR targets. In fact, we've met them all."

★

Andrew brought the meeting to a close one hour later and the members began to close their folders and open their briefcases. Tom rose to his feet to stem the exodus.

"If I may, Prime Minister, whilst we're all together, could I just share a thought as to how we might move on from here?"

★

The prison doctor stood behind the consultant, looking over the woman's shoulder at the pale, thin figure she was examining. The room had bare white walls and contained four beds lined abreast with a small cabinet at the side of each. Just one of the beds was occupied. After a few minutes they both walked away to the corner of the room. The consultant spoke in a low voice, almost a whisper.

"Very slight deterioration over the last couple of days but significant all the same, I'm afraid. We need to get him weighed again. Not a lot else we can do except make him comfortable. And they can take his name off the door in there – he won't be going back."

"We'll need to move him from here if that's the case," said the doctor. "He can't stay indefinitely in the hospital."

"I'll arrange that," said the consultant, looking at her watch. "Ten-fifteen. Might even get him in somewhere today if I can catch someone right away."

"Thank you, but I don't think we can move that quickly at this end. I'll start the ball rolling right away but we'll need approval from on high, given who he is – well, *what* he is. Although he doesn't look much of a danger to anyone now, does he?"

"Shame. This is one of the good guys, whatever the official record will say about him."

They left and the duty nurse pulled the curtain around the bed.

★

"I wish you wouldn't spring things on me like that, Tom. I don't like being backed into a corner."

Committee Room 14 was empty except for the two men. The prime minister was an inch or so taller than Tom, with a bulky frame, and a round face under dark brown hair which was combed to the side with a ruler-straight parting. As always, he was fashionably dressed in an Italian suit and silk shirt and tie, and carried his surplus weight well.

"I just felt with all the positive feedback we are about to give," Tom replied, "this would pre-empt anyone saying, 'Okay, so far so good, but what next?' We don't want to look like we think the job's done …"

"The job *is* done, Tom. The job being the successful implementation of the New Justice Regime. What happens next *within* that regime is part of the new process of law."

"I can't see how this can possibly hurt us, though. It was in our manifesto, so no-one can say …"

"Actually, it wasn't *part* of the manifesto, if you remember. It was *mentioned* in the manifesto as a future possibility – no more than that."

"So you're saying … well, what exactly? The Cabinet agreed to go with it. They're expecting it now. Are you going to reconvene?"

"No, we're going with it and if the whips do their job in the intervening four hours or so, we won't get the wrong reaction from at least *our* side of the House this afternoon. But you've got Latiffe to thank for that – *he* swung the meeting, not you. And if the initial reaction of our own cabinet members is anything to go by, this could knock the shine off the massive positivity of the NJR feedback."

"Then why did you …"

"Agree to it? Because in principle it's the right thing to do. It's just the timing I'm not entirely comfortable with. And the spontaneity, if I'm honest. No testing of the water."

"And how did you propose to do that, Andrew? The usual way? Leak it through the press and prepare a disclaimer just in case? And this time it would have to be me that resigned, I suppose?"

Andrew glared at him. "Don't get carried away with your own importance, Home Secretary. That was *not* what I meant, and you know it!"

"Yes, my apologies," said Tom. "I guess I've never lost the cavalier instincts which brought us to power. We seemed to be another Party then."

"We *were* another Party," said Andrew. "We were the fucking *Opposition* Party trying to become the government! Can't you understand the difference?" He rose from his seat to signal they had finished. "Look," he added, "*I'll* raise this in the House at the end of your report. You just finish as planned after the feedback. That way I can cut off any discussion today and leave it for debate next Monday. Any more surprises?"

"None, Prime Minister. Oh, except that I was going to call for special prayers tomorrow for the Exiles. That's if …"

"As you please," said Andrew. "But let's not forget that those bastards are getting exactly what they deserve and exactly what we promised them."

★

Calum checked the time on the large wall clock in the monitoring area. It was 12.55 pm and they were exactly three hours into their journey.

"Well, gentlemen," he said, turning to his two guests, "time to call on the captain, I think. You can ask him about the weather," he nodded at Mike Needham.

They climbed the stairs to the deck and Calum noted that the wind had increased and the waves were slightly higher than before. Captain Douglas McLeod waved for them to join him on the bridge. Calum and Douglas were very much alike in appearance. Both large men in their early fifties, with broad muscular shoulders and arms, and barely any surplus weight in the places it normally starts to accumulate at that age. Even their uniforms were similar – both dark blue, although Douglas's sported white flashes on the cuffs and shoulders. He also had the captain's compulsory full grey beard.

Calum introduced Lawrence and Mike.

"So you're the guy who designed Alpha," Douglas said, smiling at the smaller man. "Have you seen it in situ at all?"

"I've spent most of the last two years of my life on it but I haven't seen the finished article fully functional yet."

"Well, you're in for a treat," said Douglas. "And talking about a treat…"

He pointed across to the island on their left no more than a mile away. Two rows of brightly coloured houses were reflected in the calmer water of the bay. A dozen or so small boats languished in the harbour along with a large ferry taking on vehicles and early season tourists. Above and behind the houses stood a sandstone hotel, which looked like an old castle, and beyond that some low tree-covered hills.

"Tobermory. Beautiful, isn't it?" he said. "And that," he pointed ahead, "is Ardmore Point, northernmost tip of Mull. After that, well, it's more or less the Atlantic Ocean. We'll be slowing down when we get into open sea, but we're right on schedule."

"Mike wants to know if it's likely to be rough," Calum said, with a faint smile.

"No, smooth as a mirror," said Douglas, smiling back in a way that left the three men wondering whether he meant the exact opposite.

★

"Afternoon, Tom."

Tom looked round with a start. He was sitting out on the Terrace, having just finished a cold lunch of smoked salmon and salad, and was staring absently out across the river. The generously proportioned figure of Gerald Portman, ex Home Secretary, now Shadow Chancellor, beamed down at him and gestured towards one of the empty chairs next to his table. "Do you mind?"

"Not at all," said Tom.

"Le jour de gloire est arrivé, n'est-ce pas?" Gerald was of medium height, but everything else about him was larger than life. He carried most of his weight in front of him, stretching the material of his pinstripe suit and white shirt. His tie and his general manner were as flamboyant and pleasing as ever.

"Not sure how glorious it is," replied Tom, who had been picturing in his mind the scene on the transfer vessel and coming up with some uncomfortable images.

"I thought this was your dream, Tom. Not having second thoughts, I hope. I mean, it's a bit late …"

Tom laughed.

"Not a chance, Gerald. After you completed the easy bit, I have nothing but smug satisfaction for the way we finished the more demanding part of the job. But it would be churlish not to acknowledge your contribution. So if *you* want to call it glorious, I've no objection."

Gerald chuckled.

"That's more like it, I thought you'd gone all melancholy for a moment." He stood up. "Well, I guess you weren't sitting here all alone on the off-chance you'd get picked up by a Shadow Cabinet Minister. You must have a few things still to think about. And anyway, it's bloody cold. So I'll leave you in peace and go and finish rehearsing my spontaneous one-liners."

Tom laughed.

"Go, by all means, but please not on my account. I can't do any more now in the next half-an-hour. If you like, I'll send for a hot water bottle and a blanket, and we can go in together in a few minutes."

"Okay, I'll be brave," he said, sitting down again.

CHAPTER TWO

"Mr Speaker, Members of the House. Today is a historic day in the annals of British law and British government. A day which represents a landmark in the age-old conflict between good and bad, right and wrong."

Andrew looked up and around at the array of dark suits and white shirts representing the standard uniform of the House, interspersed with the pastel colours and brighter shades of many of the women members.

The Commons Chamber is much more austere than that of its Lords equivalent and the rest of the Palace of Westminster. The oak panelling is plain and the benches, as well as other furnishings, are green. The windows are of plain rather than stained glass. The Chamber is also surprisingly small; far too small, in fact, to accommodate the 650 or so members whose right it is to attend, even when including the galleries high above and behind the main seating where the government and Opposition benches face each other across the floor of the House. Due to the prevailing level of members' absence from the House, this restriction is not normally a problem, except on occasions such as Prime Minister's Questions, major debates and Budget Day, when MPs will stand at the sides wherever they can find the space.

Andrew noted with satisfaction, if not surprise, that today the Chamber was packed to capacity, as was the public gallery to his right, with its glass security screen separating the members from the watchers.

"Three years ago," he continued, "an incident occurred on a

residential council estate in the London Borough of Marlburgh. It was, sad to say in those more violent times, not so remarkable in itself even though it involved the slaying of three young men. What *was* remarkable, however, was the chain reaction it set in motion across the country and, more recently, in continental Europe as well. We are here today to reflect on what are, in effect, the ultimate consequences of that incident. But let us be clear; the existence, and initial success, of the New Justice Regime has not just happened as the result of some natural chemical process; it has involved an enormous – and courageous – effort, on both sides of this House, to achieve it.

"So, Mr Speaker, having already stolen more of my colleague's thunder than I intended, I ask the Home Secretary, the Right Honourable Tom Brown, to address the House with the main item from the Orders of the Day."

Tom rose as Andrew sat down.

"Mr Speaker. Thank you, Prime Minister. And please don't worry; I have plenty of thunder left."

There was a ripple of amusement on both sides of the House.

"During the course of the next forty minutes or so, I will share with you details of the financial impact to date of the New Justice Regime, its influence on crime figures around the country, and plans for further developments going forward. I am also delighted to be able to report on the favourable feedback we have received during that period from our European partners following some intense debates centred around Human Rights when we first unveiled our plans. As you know, they have since not only accepted our new provisions as complying with redrafted EU requirements, but many member states have actually *adopted* them – or derivatives of them – to deal with comparable issues in their own countries.

"However, this is *not* an occasion for unreserved triumphalism. Because the first point I will cover in this report is something we all hoped could be avoided – the expulsion of the first group of Life Exiles. As I speak, one hundred and fifty offenders under the new legislation are leaving these shores behind and heading into the Atlantic to Platform Alpha for a very different and totally isolated future. We must accept that this necessary act represents, if not a failure in the system, at least an indication that we still have some way to go."

He paused and looked around the chamber to see members on both sides of the House nodding their agreement.

"Between the hours of 7.00 am and 9.30 am today," Tom continued, "these one hundred and fifty young men embarked on a prisoner transfer vessel at the Lochshore high security facility on Loch Fendort. As you know, we have a senior Home Office representative on board monitoring proceedings and he has been reporting progress to me at regular intervals since the operation began. They left the loch at 9.55 am and when I received the last report from the vessel – at 1.15 pm – they were just leaving the northern end of the Sound of Mull on their way to their final destination. I have been assured that they are on course to arrive at the appointed time of 7.00 am tomorrow morning.

"The House is aware of the logistics involved at that stage and I do not propose to go into great detail again. But very briefly, they will disembark onto the satellite platform and will be transferred from there across to the main platform. It is expected they will all be in situ by 10.00 am tomorrow. I will, of course, be pleased to address any queries and provide further details if necessary during the session arranged for questions at the end of this report."

Tom paused, lowering his head. There was complete silence. He looked up, sweeping his gaze slowly around the Chamber.

"I have asked Mister Speaker if the Chaplain would break with tradition and include these people in our prayers tomorrow, if the House agrees."

There was a hushed but almost universal, "Hear, hear" from all areas of the Chamber.

"Thank you," said Tom "I hope we can break with another tradition and have a full turn-out for those prayers."

He swept his eyes round the silent Chamber before continuing.

"It is only natural that we should feel sympathy for the ones who have fallen by the wayside, but the story of the twelve months of the NJR is one of unparalleled success. The country gave this government a clear mandate twenty-one months ago when it elected us on the promise of reclaiming *all* localities for the benefit of their communities. There would be pain – we made that very clear – in order to achieve this and we would need to be strong when that pain manifested itself in our own and other people's suffering.

"We, this government, this House and this country, have kept faith with that notion in pursuit of our collective vision of the future. So let there be compassion, but no shame; let there be some sorrow, but much rejoicing; let there be awareness of the sacrifices, but no deflection from the goal. And, most of all, let there be *no turning back*."

There were more cries of "Hear, hear" this time, loudly and enthusiastically from the government side of the House, but also accompanied by nods of assent from the Opposition, notably Gerald Portman, who seemed to be nodding from the waist with the whole upper part of his body. Tom continued.

"So let us consider how life has changed since the New Justice Regime was officially launched exactly three hundred and sixty days ago today."

★

At exactly 3.40 pm, Tom concluded his address, to enthusiastic shouts from his own Party and more-than-polite murmurings of support from the Opposition benches. Gerald Portman even engaged in a silent mimed hand-clap as the Home Secretary sat down.

The Speaker addressed the House.

"The next item on the Orders of the Day is Questions to the Home Secretary. Can we proceed in the customary *orderly* way?"

Several MPs on both sides of the House raised their hands. The Speaker nodded towards Gerald Portman, who rose deliberately to his feet, beaming around the Chamber.

"Mr Speaker. Our thanks to the Home Secretary," he boomed, "for that succinct and informative report, from which we can all take, I think, considerable comfort and much satisfaction – not to mention a degree of self-congratulation. I would like to ask the Home Secretary, however, if the government has any plans for the provision of more carrots in the treatise of the issue of urban disorder, to supplement the plethora of sticks being applied to the problem.

"The excellent work – and tangible results – achieved by the previous government was intended as a long-term contribution to addressing this challenge by providing the perpetrators with meaningful choices. It was never meant to be the 'quick fix', which his NJR sets out to be. Can he assure us that, in all the excitement with which he has thrilled us over the last year or two, he has not abandoned the concept of establishing alternatives to the lives of crime and disruption which many of our young people seem to be born into and who simply follow what must appear to them to be a predetermined path?"

Tom was on his feet before Gerald had even started to sit down.

"Mr Speaker, I thank the Right Honourable Member for his question. First let me say that there is nothing wrong with a quick fix. If something needs to be fixed – can be fixed – properly fixed – and *permanently* fixed – then the quicker the better, I say. So if he says the NJR is a quick fix, then we thank him for his compliment. The point he makes about carrots and sticks I would answer by reminding him of the many times members of this Party congratulated the previous government on their actions in tackling the issue of crime on the streets by providing those choices he mentioned.

"However, it is our contention that enough is enough – for the time being, at least. What I mean by that is that the efforts of the previous government went as far as they could in providing those choices. We have provided the *incentive* to adopt those options. It is right that the carrot comes first, then the stick. I'm tempted to say it was almost like teamwork." He smiled broadly around the House. "If not a football team, working together, then a relay team, working in sequence. But interdependent in the pursuit of success."

Tom sat down and several other members raised their hands. A tall elegant woman in her early fifties on the Opposition side, catching the eye of the Speaker, was next to rise to her feet.

"Mr Speaker, could the Right Honourable gentleman, the Home Secretary, explain the rationale behind the timing of the transportation of the Exiles to Platform Alpha? Why has it been necessary to travel overnight when, if my understanding is correct, the vessel is capable of making the journey within daylight hours?"

Tom stood up again.

"Mr Speaker, let me first correct the Right Honourable Member's *mis*-understanding. The scheduled transit time from

Lochshore to Alpha is twenty-two hours, so the journey could *not* be completed in daylight. PTV1 is *theoretically* capable of covering the distance in less time, but only at the expense of the comfort of the passengers and the efficiency and safety of the vessel.

"The choice of today's departure time was to ensure we will be disembarking the prisoners as close as possible to seven o'clock tomorrow morning. Ideally, around five o'clock would be the optimum time, as this is when it would be most easy to handle them with minimum risk of resistance and possible violence. However, we felt it important to ensure it was daylight when the operation took place, and 7.00 am was chosen for that reason, sunrise being at around 6.45.

"If this seems a rather clinical – even cynical – approach, we have been advised at every stage of the process by a team of psychologists. They assure us that this will be less stressful for the prisoners themselves. When I say less stressful, of course, I am speaking in relative terms – this, I am afraid, will be a very traumatic experience for them and any physiological advantage to be gained, for the sake of *all* parties, must not be ignored.

"Also, and perhaps more obviously, it will provide the maximum amount of daylight for them to acclimatise to their new surroundings, as much as will be possible in such extreme circumstances, and to familiarise themselves with the facilities on Alpha. And similarly, it is for this reason that we have chosen to place them on board at this time of year – the earliest opportunity, in fact – with daylight increasing and the weather improving from this point onwards."

Tom sat down as the same person rose to her feet.

"And once they are on board, we simply leave them there to get on with it?"

There were groans and loud sighs from the government benches and some head shaking on the Opposition side. This time Tom rose much more slowly and with some drama. Before he answered the question he turned to the government benches shaking his head with overstated exasperation. Turning to the front, he looked across at Marian Dunnett, Member of Parliament for Easterby and Bexham.

"Mr Speaker, we have heard on many, *many*, occasions the Right Honourable Member's concerns over the issue of expulsion. Given the importance and volume of business we have to get through today, I wonder whether this is the appropriate time – if indeed there *is* an appropriate time – to hear a re-run of those oft-stated views. I have outlined in detail on numerous occasions the facilities, which are in place to service the residents of the platform – the accommodation, leisure facilities, medical support, etc.

"For example, as you know each prisoner has had a chip surgically – and *painlessly* – implanted in his chest close to the heart. Each chip contains a micro-transmitter, which will send information in a continuous stream, via the main transmitter on the satellite platform, to the Exile Data Centre in Lochshore, where the monitoring team will check a range of health indicators and respond accordingly. These transmissions can also be used to identify the person's exact location on the platform.

"There are many more examples I could give, but the *simple* answer to your question is – *no*, we do not just leave them to get on with it. And I trust that addresses your *only* query on the issue and hope that it is not, as has previously been the case, the wedge used to keep open the door for the customary flood."

The murmur of amusement from the government side was this time drowned by a burst of protests born of simple loyalty from the Opposition benches. Tom raised his arm in a plea for quiet and went on.

"Mr Speaker, I repeat, I will answer all questions put to me – this is not a day for evading issues. If the Opposition feels that the House's time is best served by an impromptu review of the rationale and morality of the NJR – and this element of it in particular – then so be it."

He sat down.

Ellen Gormley got to her feet before Marian Dunnett had time to respond. Ellen was a petite, almost fragile-looking woman in her mid forties, whose appearance belied a toughness and determination which had seen her re-elected unopposed as her Party leader after their election defeat. She had a pleasant face, but with penetrating steel grey eyes which she turned on the Home Secretary.

"Mr Speaker, I know we are all aware of the significance of today in terms of what has been hailed as a new era for this country. And we are also mindful that this new beginning comes at a cost. That cost includes the way we have chosen, as a free democracy, to address the issue of the small problematic minority of now lost souls. If any members on either side of this House have – and choose to articulate – continuing concerns in the light of today's events, then we should allow them that freedom and view their thoughts with tolerance, rather than ridicule and impatience. As we stand together, as separate parties or, as has been the case in many instances recently, as a united House, it is incumbent on us also to reflect inwardly as free-thinking individuals with conscience and compassion."

The Leader of the Opposition sat down as members on both sides of the Chamber stood to show their appreciation of her remarks. Tom rose to his feet.

"Mr Speaker, I thank the Right Honourable Lady for so succinctly capturing the mood of the House, and I stand admonished by her words. It is quite proper that we are conciliatory in our reaction to diverse viewpoints in such poignant circumstances, but can I just restate this government's intentions so there is no mistake. Let me compare the matter of expulsion *in principle* to the widespread use of speed cameras on our roads. The ultimate objective of these cameras is to *stop* people speeding. It is not to *catch* people speeding. Otherwise, we would not warn people where these cameras are; we would not allow the AA and Bartholomew's to print road atlases showing the location of all cameras across the UK. And I believe it is easy to adopt that simple principle in these circumstances. The reason for the new powers of arrest and detainment; the purpose of the new sentencing options; the existence of Platform Alpha – these are not there so we can banish large numbers of people from our society. They are there to stop people behaving in such a way as to make that necessary.

"If the absolute ideal was a realistic goal, our target would be to have zero Life Exiles, zero offenders in deferred centres for assessment – indeed zero people in detention at all. But this is the *real* world, and we can only strive to minimise the numbers who have to be treated in this way. I think that is a goal we can all embrace."

There was general approval of the point, on both sides of the House. Tom continued.

"I do feel, however, that by focusing too much on that point –

important though it is – we risk missing the opportunity to rejoice on behalf of the many whose lives have changed so much for the better as a result of the brave steps we have taken on their behalf. Mr Speaker, might I humbly suggest that, in the interest of expediency in the limited time available, we move on from this one aspect of the report, to the other items covered."

The Speaker smiled benignly. "My thanks to the Home Secretary for his generous advice on how to manage the House during this sitting, and – on this occasion – I concur with his suggestion."

★

As the session neared its end, Andrew rose to his feet.

"Mr Speaker, I thank my Right Honourable colleague, the Home Secretary, for his excellent report on the New Justice Regime, but much more so for his enormous contribution towards our achieving it. History will judge this period with the all-knowing benefit of hindsight, but I believe it will recognise not only the political giants who brought it about, but also the unprecedented maturity of this House in performing as a unit to make it work.

"Before we finish, Mr Speaker, I have one item to add; an item which I believe we should debate at the House's next scheduled sitting on this matter on Monday, following the Justice Committee's meeting on Friday."

★

"Right, all eyes on the screen, please."

The detective inspector addressed the fifteen people leaning against walls and slouching on chairs in the major incident team room. Most were clutching polystyrene cups and a few were gnawing at bacon rolls and hot-dogs they'd picked up at the mobile kiosk on their way in for the afternoon briefing.

The DI loaded a disk into the laptop on the table in front of him and the ceiling-mounted projector threw an image onto the large white board on the end wall of the room.

"CCTV footage from Delaware" he said, as the grainy picture showed a countdown from five to zero. He clicked on the screen to

20

pause the show. "This is an edited extract from around one hundred and twenty hours from each of two cameras. The extract only lasts about fifteen minutes, but if you watch the timeline in the bottom right hand corner you'll see that it spans a period of five days starting just over two weeks ago. I'll talk you through it as we go."

He started the show, and the picture burst into life.

"That's our guy there," said the DI, pointing at the screen. "Watch carefully."

★

Calum sat in the monitoring area with his deputy, Gally McPherson, and the two observers. He had his back to the window and was trying to ignore the messages from his stomach telling him the weather was deteriorating. He called Douglas on the intercom.

"Where are we now? Are we still on schedule?"

"Just rounding Barra Head into open Atlantic. About to change course for final destination. No problems."

"Does that mean we *are* on schedule?"

"Absolutely."

He turned to the others.

"He said, no problems."

"We heard," said Gally. "It depends how you define problems." He nodded towards the screens.

The guards were serving the final meal of the day and it was clear that the simmering tension was growing. Bars were being rattled and abuse yelled at the officers. Calum checked his watch.

"We've got all the bad guys back at full throttle," he said. "The shots will have worn off by now. Shit!"

As he spoke, one of the prisoners was seen to kick his food tray back into the aisle. Another appeared to spit at one of the guards, setting off a chain reaction. Several on the starboard side unzipped their trousers and urinated into the gangway, aiming for the guards near by.

Calum jumped to his feet. "Stay here, Gally. I need to get down there. You know what to do." Gally nodded.

By the time he got down to the prison deck, a full riot was in progress. TV monitors were being ripped off the walls, fold-out tables pulled from their brackets and benches from their supports. The cabins were designed so that none of these items could fit through the bars to be used as weapons against the officers and this seemed to fuel the anger and frustration.

The prisoners next turned their attention to the chemical toilets, many half full with prisoners' excrement, vomit and urine. They emptied them under the doors or through the bars into the gangways. Some pulled their wash-hand basins from the walls, fracturing the inlet pipes and sending water spouting into the air and across the cabins. On the starboard side, the prisoners were making a concerted assault on their line of cabins, holding onto the bars and swinging in unison back and forth, eventually dislodging the line from its rails.

The guards ran up and down the gangways between the lines of cabins, shouting threats and appealing for calm, but helpless to influence the prisoners' actions. There was a genuine risk that some of the rioters might succeed in damaging the cabin doors to such an extent as to make them insecure.

Calum unclipped a small loud hailer from his belt.

"All officers leave the deck!" he shouted above the cacophony of yelling and screaming.

The guards gathered at an assembly point at the top of the stairs.

"Right," said Calum. "Geordie and Greg …" He turned to two of his biggest colleagues, both a couple of inches taller and wider than himself. "Come with me, lads."

★

The two observers stared at the screens as the three officers burst back onto the prison deck and headed straight for one of the main protagonists on the starboard side.

"Want to get out, do you?" Calum yelled, loud enough to ensure as many as possible could hear above the din.

"Just open that fucking door, and see what happens," the prisoner yelled back

"That's exactly what we're going to do. It's your lucky day – you can go home. How about that? Just one problem – you're going to have to swim for it. I'm sure a hard bastard like you won't mind that. Get him out, lads!"

22

Lawrence and Mike watched in disbelief as Calum unlocked the door and slid it open with a metallic crash. The two huge men rushed into the cabin, yelling loudly.

"Come here, you twat!"

"You're dead, you little fucker!"

The prisoner, suddenly wide-eyed and trembling, crouched down against the back wall, hands covering his head. He was no more than medium height and slightly built. The officers towered over him; one reached down and grabbed him by the hair, pulling him to his feet.

"Hey, you can't do this, you bastards. Fuck off and leave me alone! Get the fuck away from me!"

They cuffed him roughly as he screamed, with one wrist secured to each of Calum's two men. Other prisoners started shouting at the guards. Calum turned to them as they dragged the squealing man up the steps towards the upper deck.

"Who's going to find out?" he yelled through the loud hailer. "What're you going to do, write to your MP? But, don't worry, we're not going to throw him overboard on his own." He pointed to one of the other prisoners. "You're going with him!"

Calum followed the others up the steps, disappearing from the monitor screens.

"Really, I can't just stand by and …" Lawrence got to his feet and turned towards the door. Gally was standing with his back to it blocking the doorway. Calum's deputy was slightly bigger than his boss with a barrel chest and immense shoulders and upper arms. His face showed the scars of conflict collected over years of working with the hardest and most violent criminals north of Hadrian's Wall.

"That's exactly what you're going to do," he sad, quietly.

"But he can't just …"

"He can do what he likes," said Gally. "He's in charge, after all."

"Yes, but I represent …"

"The Home Office, yes, I know. But aren't you here – let's see if I've got this right – 'only to observe and absorb – nothing else'?"

Lawrence raised his eyebrows.

"How did you know that?"

"Same way you know about this." He nodded towards the screens. "I saw it on the tele."

Five minutes later, Calum and his two officers burst noisily through the metal door back onto the prison deck. It was completely silent.

Tom said goodnight to Reggie Greyburn, the Chancellor, and Gerald Portman and left the Members' Lounge, checking his watch as he stepped out into New Palace Yard. Paul Webster opened the rear door of the silver BMW.

"Nine-thirty," he said. "Christ, Paul, where has the day gone?"

"Don't know, sir," his Special Branch driver replied. "But did it go *well*?"

"It certainly did, Paul, thank you."

Tom sat back, with just the slightest sense of anti-climax and checked his mobile for any messages. There were plenty, but he scanned through the list of names to pick out any from Grace Goody. There was just one.

"Who's a clever boy, then? I'm very proud of you."

Tom smiled and texted back.

"Go on, I bet you say that to all attractive, charismatic MPs."

The reply came immediately.

"I don't know any."

Tom laughed out loud as he responded.

"Well thanks a lot! Speak tomorrow. Night."

"Night."

He lay back in the seat and started to check the rest of the texts. There was one from his wife, which he certainly did not expect. His first thought was that it must be some sort of emergency – Jack or Katey, perhaps. But when he opened it the content was much more surprising than anything he might have guessed.

"Saw you make your speech today. Surprised how it affected me. Must talk asap. Mags x."

Tom read the text several times, confused by the 'x' at the end; a symbol which seemed to him totally incongruous in the context of their current relationship. He lay across the back seat with a sigh and drifted off to sleep. He was awakened twenty minutes later by the opening of the nearside rear door. It was a couple of seconds before he realised where he was.

"Thank you, Paul," he said, handing him his brief case and turning in his seat to sit for a further few seconds, his feet out of the car, collecting his thoughts. The text from Mags came back to him and he looked across to the porch door just as it opened and his wife stepped out and down the steps to the driveway. Tom got out of the car.

"What time tomorrow, sir?" asked Paul, handing back his briefcase.

"Early, I'm afraid," said Tom, his eyes on Mags as she walked towards him. "Press conference at eight followed by one-on-one with the lovely Sylvie. Let's make it six-thirty again. No rest for the wicked, eh?"

"No, sir," said Paul, with a chuckle. "*They* won't be getting any rest – there's a storm out in the Atlantic. Goodnight, sir."

"Goodnight."

Mags moved very close to him. Without speaking, she reached up and kissed him – on the cheek, not the lips, but a tender, affectionate kiss. She turned, took his hand, and led him up the steps and through the outer porch into the house. The hall was large and high, with a wide staircase rising to a half-way landing. There were heavy oak doors off it to a number of rooms and a couple of wing chairs on either side of the entrance with small round-topped side tables next to them. Mags took his case from him, placing it on one of the tables.

"I got your text," said Tom.

Mags wrapped her arms around his neck. She placed her mouth against his, kissing him softly at first but with increasing firmness. They did not break away from each other when the kiss ended, but stood for a full minute, pressed together in their embrace.

"Mags, I …"

"Shall we have a drink?" she said, finally, in a whisper. "And then *I've* got a speech to make."

She led him by the hand into the front sitting room, and then walked over to the drinks cabinet.

"JD?" she asked.

"Talisker, please," he said, sitting at one end of the sofa, ignoring his favourite chair near the window, except to throw his jacket onto it.

Mags's golden blonde hair fell loosely onto her shoulders framing her perfect features. She was wearing high platform heels and a loose chiffon dress, pulled in with a matching belt around her slender waste, which lifted the hemline just above her knees. Tom recognised it as the one he always told her was his favourite. She poured two large whiskies and joined him on the sofa, placing the glasses on the low table in front of it and sitting close to him, but far enough away so that she could turn to face him.

"We need to talk," she said.

Tom grinned at her.

"What?" asked Mags, frowning and smiling at the same time.

"I just knew you were going to say that."

They both laughed, probably for the first time – together – in over two years.

"This is serious, Tom-Tom," she said.

"I'm sorry, Mags. But to be honest, you've made me a bit nervous. I'm not sure what I've done to deserve this."

"Deserve what?" she said.

"This," and he leaned forward and kissed her again. She kissed him back, more passionately this time.

"First," she said, pushing him gently away and becoming more serious, "my speech. I just want to say that … I love you – I mean *really* love you – so *very* much – and I've never stopped. I realised today that that has never changed."

He leaned forward to respond.

"Don't say anything yet," she held up a restraining hand, "I'll take questions later," she added, half smiling. "I've said a lot of hurtful things recently – well more than just recently, I guess. I think we've both been at fault, but I know that I have been the main culprit. I've been deliberately blind. I've refused to listen, refused to bend, refused to show any sort of empathy or understanding or support …"

Mags's voice broke and she lowered her head, not able to continue for a few moments. Tom took both her hands in his.

"I'm a bit emotional, to tell the truth," she said, gripping his hands tightly and still looking down at her lap. "Not because I'm sad, but because… well … I'm suddenly happy. At least I will be if you can feel the same about me as you used to and start loving *me* again. It's like I've walked out of a fog into the sunlight – God, how dramatic is that!" She looked up at him through glassy eyes, half-laughing, half-sobbing. "I feel a bit idiotic, actually, like a love-struck teenager asking you not to pack me in."

Tom looked back at her.

"Go on," said Mags, through her tearful smile. "I'll take questions now."

"And not before time!" said Tom, making her laugh. "I've *never* stopped loving you Mags – I thought you knew that – not for a single heartbeat. But I thought I'd lost you. I really did. You said as much last night, remember?" His own voice was trembling as he finished.

They fell together kissing with a passion he had thought would never return. This was a time for gentleness and tender words, but he felt his body responding to the closeness in a way he neither intended nor wanted right now. He pulled himself away slightly to regain control. Eventually they broke off the embrace and sat closer together on the sofa, Tom's arm around her and Mags's head buried into his shoulder. They reached for their drinks and sipped them in silence for several minutes, each simply delighting in the other's closeness. Tom was amazed at just how wonderful he felt. Less than twenty-four hours ago they had been squaring up to each other over a broken coffee mug in the kitchen.

"But Mags, why ..." he asked, at last.

"It was watching you this afternoon, like I said in my text," she answered. "I've never heard you express yourself in those terms before. It put my own views together with yours and helped me understand that they were *not* mutually exclusive, that they *could* exist together. It also made me realise what an easy option I've always taken – spouting my own ideas without any attempt to come up with compromises or alternatives. You've had to do that. It never occurred to me that you felt anything but contempt for the people you were putting away. I'm not saying they don't deserve our contempt, but they *do* warrant our sympathy and prayers as well. It was a revelation for me, hearing you say those things, and after you'd finished, as the day wore on, it seemed to have more and more significance – for us, I mean." She hesitated. "I'm not explaining this very well, am I?"

"You're doing fine, darling. And if I didn't share these thoughts with you before, then it's my fault you didn't understand, isn't it? And to be honest, Mags, it's only very recently that I've been thinking in those terms, so I guess it's a case of us coming together on this, rather than just you changing your mind. I think that's better, don't you? That we've *both* accepted the other's position."

She moved even closer as he looked at the time on the wall-clock in front of him – 11.30 pm. He guessed that the vessel might almost be there by now, until he remembered what Paul had said.

A storm in the Atlantic…

★

The rumbling in Tom's stomach brought them both back to reality.

"When did you last eat?" asked Mags.

He looked at the clock again. It was twenty minutes past midnight. "Yesterday," he said.

"Yes, I know that." She nudged him in the ribs. "But *when* yesterday?"

"One-thirty – eleven hours ago. God, I'm such a hero for the cause."

Mags laughed. "Stay right there; I'll make you something."

"No, I'm coming with you," he said. "Not letting you out of my sight from now on."

He followed her through to the kitchen, standing behind her with his arms around her waste as she made him a sandwich. He sat at the breakfast bar and ate it ravenously whilst Mags went through to the sitting room, returning to lean seductively in the kitchen doorway, their two glasses pinched together between the thumb and forefinger of one hand and the half-empty whisky bottle swinging from the other.

"What shall we do now?"

"Can't think of a single thing," said Tom, smiling. "Well perhaps just one."

Tom finished his snack, and, after setting the security alarm and switching off the lights, followed Mags up the stairs.

"Oh dear," said Tom, as they entered what had been for nearly two years Mags's separate bedroom. "I seem to have left my pyjamas in the other room."

"Sorry. No time for Tom-Tom to get jim-jams," said Mags.

They both became silent, as if they had suddenly grasped the significance of the moment. Tom was the first to speak.

"Where are the children?" he asked. "I'd forgotten all about them."

"No lectures tomorrow morning; staying over with friends."

Tom smiled. "Good."

CHAPTER THREE

Douglas's cabin was large, rectangular and traditionally appointed, with an old-fashioned oak desk and upholstered captain's chair on castors at one end and a large table with six similar chairs – minus the padding and castors – at the other. The walls were covered in paintings of sailing ships and the wall-to-ceiling shelves along one side of the room were filled with ancient books, ornaments and other sea-faring memorabilia.

Calum had called the meeting to update Lawrence and Douglas on the status of the prison deck, and to discuss any likely schedule changes.

"Well, if it wasn't a shit-hole before, it is now," said Gally. "The deck's just covered in the stuff – *and* puke and piss. And as far as we can see, there's no way of cleaning this up, and lurching about like we are, it's moving all the time, slopping everywhere. We've got broken glass from the smashed monitors in it as well – mostly just in the cabins. The only good thing," he added, with feeling, "is they're suffering more than we are. Most of them have nowhere to sit or lie down, and they're honking all over with the stench and the movement of the ship."

"Even so," said Lawrence. "You have to feel for them a bit. I mean given their circumstances …"

"*You* feel for them if you want to," said Gally, leaning across the table. "And while you're doing it, remember it was your Home Office that put them there."

"Okay, Gally," said Calum.

"Well, perhaps Mr Harding would like to step into a couple of plastic bags and go down there and help. I don't like our guys having to do this, boss, and certainly not without the gear to do it safely. Perhaps as part of his feedback, the man from the ministry can recommend we get protective clothing."

They all looked at Lawrence, who didn't speak.

"What about the plumbing?" asked Douglas. "How bad is that?"

"We've had to turn off the water supply to the cabins on all but the port side central line because of the ruptured inlet pipes," said Gally. "Not possible to isolate individual cabins within a line. Needless to say, there's no way we can consider any repairs while the cabins are still occupied. In any case, the whole deck would need to be sluiced and disinfected first."

Calum turned to Douglas.

"How are we doing with ETA? Any change?"

"We're close to falling behind, I'm afraid. I've slowed down to minimise the effect of the worsening weather on the prison deck. We speed up, we'll feel it more. Headwinds are force eight now." He looked at the brass wall clock. "Five after one. I thought we'd be much closer by now, but we could just still make it for seven."

There was silence for a few moments.

"I guess we should get our friend back down below," said Calum.

They looked out through the glass panel in the cabin door. It was pitch dark outside except for the halo of light which the vessel itself was shedding onto the spray and rain which encircled them. Below them, at the bow of the ship, a bedraggled shape was handcuffed to the rail. As they watched, a wave crashed against the bow, shooting spray upwards and over the deck.

"He could die of hypothermia if he stays there much longer," said Douglas.

"Well, we wouldn't want that, would we?" said Gally, getting to his feet. "I'll put him back in his cabin. Unless you'd like to do it, Mr Harding. You could apologise for the inconvenience as well."

★

Tom awoke once in the night at around 3.00 am and slipped from the bed, retrieving his mobile from the pocket of his trousers, on the floor of the bedroom, and setting the alarm for 5.00 am. He got back into bed, squeezing closely up against Mags, pulling her arm over him and putting his around her.

★

Douglas and Calum stood on the bridge together, shuffling their feet and occasionally shrugging their shoulders to keep warm as they watched the early light of dawn picking out the heights of Hirta and Soay, lying about three miles off their starboard bow.

"Land ahoy!" said Douglas, and Calum smiled. The sight of the island group, albeit through a fine swinging curtain of spray and mist, which offered a quick look then snatched it away again, was somehow comforting after a dark and turbulent few hours, even though it was only there to be passed by and left behind.

"And then there was none," said Calum, as it disappeared again. "At least the weather's improving. That's the last time I ask you if we're in for a pleasant trip."

Douglas laughed. "I just thought you had enough to occupy your mind without worrying about the weather."

"And you were dead right there."

They were silent for a few moments.

"Have you been through the checklist with Alpha Control yet?" asked Douglas.

"Yes, and everything's okay. You'd think with two hundred and thirty-odd items to cross-check, at least one isn't going make it. But, thankfully, not this time; they all passed with flying colours. So we're cleared for docking when we get there." He stamped his feet and shrugged again. "I don't know about you, Captain, but I can't wait to get back to Lochshore. I didn't appreciate what a nice place it was until now."

"Aye to that."

A few minutes later, as visibility improved, they saw the first rays of the sun, rising astern above the mist, alighting on the top of the massive construction ahead of them. The uppermost part of the superstructure reflected back the pale light and the sight of their objective squeezed a gasp of wonder from both men. With most of it still in mist and partly below the horizon, what they saw looked like the top of a giant cube, breath-taking in its size and emerging like a ghostly mirage out of a seemingly empty world.

"Go and get Mike," said Douglas. "He'll never forgive us if he misses this."

★

Tom awoke thinking about Grace Goody. It was not a consciously driven thought; but she was the first person in his mind as he reached to switch off the alarm on his mobile.

He turned to where he expected to see Mags asleep beside him. She was not there. He sat up, the sudden movement reminding him that he had consumed nearly half a bottle of malt the previous evening. At that moment Mags appeared in the doorway carrying a breakfast tray.

"Good morning, Home Secretary. Can I press you to a hot muffin?"

"What are you doing awake at this time?"

"When you'd gone back to sleep, I checked when you'd set your alarm for, and set mine for ten minutes before."

"Well, it's very much appreciated and …"

"Oh, don't thank me," she said, placing the tray on his bedside table. "I have an ulterior motive."

She was wearing the same short, loose robe she had worn the night before last when she had confronted him in the kitchen. Now she pulled it slowly apart and placed her hands on her naked hips, thrusting one forward in a seductive pose. She was wearing nothing underneath except a very small pair of briefs. She dropped her arms and, with a shrug of her shoulders, the gown slipped to the floor. She lifted up the duvet and crawled over him to her side of the bed.

"Don't let it get cold," she whispered, slipping her tongue into his ear.

"Some chance," he replied, already breathing heavily, and rolled on top of her.

They made love a second time as they showered together before going down to breakfast, soon hearing the sound of tyres on the gravel driveway.

"Six-thirty already," said Mags. "God, couldn't Paul be late just once?"

Tom went back to the bedroom, put on his tie and jacket and returned to the hall, picking up his briefcase from the table where Mags had placed it eight hours before. They kissed passionately again for nearly a full minute before Tom turned to leave.

"By the way, are the kids back tonight?" he asked.

"I'm going to invite them formally to have dinner with their parents," replied Mags.

"Do you think they'll come? When was the last time the four of us sat down to a meal together?"

"It's the only way they'll get fed," said Mags. "I'm sure they'll put in an appearance even if it's just out of curiosity. It would be great if you could get back so we could have a chat beforehand."

"You mean prepare ourselves for Question Time? Yes we should, I guess."

"So will you make it? What's your day looking like?"

"Well, got a date this morning with Hanker the Anchor. I'll ask her to be gentle with me …"

"And I suppose you'll be flirting with her, as usual – in front of millions of people?" said Mags.

"I *never* flirt with her," said Tom, "I just respond in kind to *her* flirting with *me* – simply out of courtesy. I don't understand how anyone can fail to see the difference."

Mags grabbed him by the lapels of his jacket. "Just watch it," she said, "or no more hot muffin in bed for you!"

Tom laughed. "After that I'm meeting Tony for an exclusive. He wants to do a more personal insight into what the last year has meant to me." He smiled at Mags. "That's going to be a lot different to what I would have told him yesterday at this time."

"I hope you're not planning to go into too much detail."

Tom laughed again. "Okay, I won't mention the muffins. Anyway, this afternoon there's a debate in Westminster Hall; session ends at five, so if I can get away straight after that I can get back by, say, six-thirty to six-forty-five. That okay?"

"Fine. I'll arrange dinner for eight."

Tom opened the front door. It was raining heavily. He gave his wife one more kiss and went down the steps. He stopped at the bottom and turned back to her.

"Listen, how do you fancy getting away for the weekend? Set off as early as possible tomorrow evening and go somewhere far away. Get a cottage in the Yorkshire Dales or Peak District. Just the two of us."

"That would be wonderful; let's do it."

"Doing it is exactly what I had in mind," said Tom, looking up at the sky. "If it's anything like this we'll have to stay in bed all the time."

"Now just you stop that and go to work," said Mags, putting on a serious face.

Tom grinned then walked to the car through the pouring rain.

"Morning, Paul. Wonderful day, isn't it?"

"Morning, Home Secretary. And actually, it's lashing down."

"Yes, I know," he said, and settled into his seat.

★

Tom was jolted awake by the rapid deceleration of the car. He looked up to see Paul waving his arms at a vehicle that was attempting to turn right out of a side road and had blocked their lane. He checked his watch – 7.05. He had a sudden feeling he'd forgotten something. Then he remembered and stared at his phone, not knowing what to do.

His indecision was resolved by the sound of its ring tone – the thumping intro to Police's *Every Breath I Take* – which made him jump as it interrupted his thoughts. He looked at the display and hesitated for several moments; Sting was already into the lyrics before he touched 'Answer'.

"Hi!" he said, in a rather high-pitched and exaggeratedly cheerful voice.

Grace paused before she spoke. "Okay, what have I done? You're five minutes late phoning me – I've aged about the same number of years in that time just worrying about it."

"Sorry," said Tom, "I was nodding off in the car. The phone woke me up."

"Well don't worry. At least you don't need any beauty sleep."

"I think you'll find that's my line," he said.

"You're right. I was lying. You need all you can get."

"You can be very wounding at times, you know. And after all I've done for you."

"*For* me," said Grace, in her sexiest voice, "but nothing *to* me – yet."

"Now, Ms Goody," he said. "You know I'm the champion of family values and all that. You can't expect me to compromise my position, surely?"

"Wow! We've never got around to discussing actual *positions* before, compromising or otherwise. This is most encouraging!"

"Anyway, what have you got lined up for today?" he asked. "A few knee-cappings, a bit of horse-whipping?"

"Just the whippings. I could fit you in …" she hesitated as if she was checking a list, "… just after lunch, if that's convenient."

"Oh damn, what a shame," he replied. "I've got to change my library book today."

"Something wrong?"

"No, why do you ask?"

"You just sound a bit different," she said.

"In what way?"

"Not your usual wayward self. Almost respectable. Not sure I like that." There was silence for a few seconds. "Not had another row with Mrs T-hyphen-B, have you? Has she given you a written warning or something? An ultimatum?"

"Not an ultimatum, no. Well … nothing … really," he almost stammered over his response. "No, nothing at all."

"There must have been *something*; I can tell there must have been something."

"Well, yes, a sort of clearing the air. That's all."

"Gave you a bad time, did she?"

"No," he answered a bit too quickly, instinctively in defence of his wife. "Not really. Well, not at all, actually."

"I see." Grace's voice was suddenly hard. "So we're all friends again, are we? Never stopped loving you for a moment, darling, and all that."

"Grace, I can hardly refuse when my wife wants to talk to me, can I? And I can't insist that she only says nasty things. All she said

36

was that she appreciated my asking for prayers for the Exiles today. That's all. Nothing else."

Grace was silent for a long time. When she spoke, the hardness had left her voice, and her tone was flat and neutral. "You've never promised me anything, Tom. If you and Maggie get back together again – you know what I mean – then you don't owe me an explanation or apology. I'm not going to create a fuss or anything. There's enough going on in my life right now. When you think about it, we don't have anything to lose, you and I. Just the obscene phone calls."

"Nothing's changed, Grace," he said. "Look, we've arrived now; got to go and get sorted for the press conference. When can I call you? Sometime between midday and two would be good."

"One o'clock then." Her voice was quiet and soft.

"One o'clock," he repeated.

★

"Hi, Grace, how are you?"

"Okay," she replied. "And guess what. I think Brown has settled his differences and made his peace with his wonderful, hyphenated wife. Isn't that *marvellous*?"

"Well, actually, I think it is. Like someone's just removed the fuse from a powder-keg, don't you think? The party's champion of the family unit. Wouldn't help the cause much if he split with his wife. It appears that he's a giant step away from his kids already. Good news, I'd say."

There was silence for a few moments.

"I guess," said Grace, sounding thoroughly miserable.

"Oh, come on, Grace. You're not getting too close are you? It's a job, that's all."

"I guess," she said again, ending the call.

★

The three men on the bridge watched with breathless awe as they approached the gargantuan structure in the hazy early morning light.

"Your turn to give us the tour, Mike," said Calum. "How the hell does this thing come to exist?"

37

It was so massive that they all thought they had almost reached it long before they were anywhere close, and the platform just grew and grew before their eyes, drawing them towards it until the wonder gave way to a collective feeling of unease.

"Well, you can see now what it *was*," said Mike. He pointed to its four giant cylindrical columns. "It started life as an oil and gas production platform, the largest off-shore installation the world had ever seen."

The door behind them opened.

"Morning," said Lawrence. "Nearly there, I guess. Christ!" His eyes opened wide as he saw their destination in front of them. "That's … frightening."

"You're just in time for the lecture, Mr Harding" said Douglas. "Go on, Mike."

Mike nodded a greeting to Lawrence and continued.

"Each column has a diameter of eighty feet and rises 300 feet above the waterline. The area they support used to be the platform's production deck, now what we call the main recreational deck, which is one hundred and sixty yards square, that's just over five acres."

"And what's below the waterline?" asked Calum. "Not that much, I'm told."

"Certainly not as much as you might think. The columns extend down a further hundred feet to a huge pontoon – like an enormous square dough-nut – which joins them together below the surface like the deck does above it. The whole thing is what's called a semi-submersible design, which provides a lower centre of gravity and more stability."

"It couldn't look *less* stable if you ask me," said Lawrence. "Why doesn't it bounce about?"

"Well, it's anchored by sixteen deepwater chains and a number of wire mooring lines. And in case you're still not convinced, it was originally designed to survive a once-in-a-hundred-year storm, and withstand the hurricanes and ocean currents of the Gulf of Mexico. That's where it had been in operation for its working lifetime, until your friend at the Home Office acquired it."

"Amazing," said Calum. "So tell us how it got from being that to being this."

"I'm glad you asked," said Mike, "because what I've told you so far had nothing to do with me."

They smiled and Mike continued.

"By the time your lot had won the election," he nodded at Lawrence again, "I'd already presented the basic design. It was nothing special, really; just an apartment complex designed to fit on a five-acre site. The big challenge was timescale. Mr Brown – bless him – had promised everything would be in place in eighteen months. It meant that every week counted."

"So they dumped everything they didn't need in the sea on the way over?" said Douglas, with a smile.

"Not quite, but it saved us two weeks, which was the time it took to get it from the Gulf to here. You would have loved that, Douglas. You probably know we used the *Mastodon* to bring it across, the largest heavy-lift vessel in the world. If you ever get chance to see that … Anyway, while we were in transit we removed the twin drilling derricks from the production deck. We dropped them onto rafts and floated them back to the Gulf along with everything else on the deck."

"You were on board?"

"That's right. Once we'd cleared the deck, my job was to get it ready for the accommodation. In the end, we missed our final deadline by just three months, but it was still an amazing achievement."

They looked ahead at the huge box-like structure, tapering slightly inwards as it rose above the main deck. They were close enough now to make out windows in the sides and a collection of wires, panels and masts on the top,

"There are eight hundred identical apartments completely surrounding the main deck to a height of ten storeys, eighty on each level, twenty along each side. So the whole encloses the deck like the sides of a box. It means there's no way off the deck except back into the accommodation block."

"What are those things sticking out from the sides?" asked Calum, pointing to a number of large metal sheets secured at various angles to the walls of the block.

"Wind deflectors," said Mike, "They move in response to changes in wind direction. Just a precaution more than anything, to reduce the impact of the wind on the flat surface of the walls."

"And all that stuff on top?"

"Solar panels and aerials. And, of course, the security fence. I can absolutely guarantee nobody's going to get over that."

★

Half a mile from the platform, PTV1 slipped inside the ring of fifty-five massive wind turbines that formed a circle round the platform spaced at 100-yard intervals around the circumference.

"Just about the biggest challenge of all was powering the thing," said Mike. "And for me probably the highlight of the whole project."

"How big are these things?" said Lawrence, craning his neck to look up at the closest one.

"Three hundred and fifty feet from the surface to the top of their towers and five hundred feet to the tip of a vertical blade. Biggest we could get and, along with the solar panels and wave energy converters, more power than we need. So we'll be supplying the NTS and the MOD on Hirta once we're set up to do it, and we can store any surplus. There's talk of getting a cable to the Long Island in the future. I guess that will depend on how many platforms we end up with out here."

They could now clearly see the receiving floor, which was suspended thirty feet below the main deck.

"That's the only point of access onto the main structure," said Mike. "You get across to it from the satellite platform. There's no other way onto it. Except by parachute, I suppose," he added.

At exactly 7.25 am, they passed underneath the massive construction and docked with the lifting deck of the satellite platform. This secondary structure comprised a huge single column, with a 120-foot-square cross-section, rising vertically out of the sea next to the main platform to the level of the recreational deck. Seen from above, it formed the points of an equilateral triangle with two of the columns of the main platform. It was secured to each of these by steel girders every twenty feet of its full 300-foot height. The satellite platform was essentially a lift-shaft from sea level up to the level of the receiving floor. The thirty feet of the column above that comprised a two-storey service building housing a medical centre, communications facility and the control hub for the wind farm, solar panels and wave power modules.

Douglas McLeod, edged his vessel skilfully between two enormous projecting arms, positioned at sea level and sticking out from the lifting deck like the blades of a giant fork lift truck. He cut his engines, and, along with Mike Needham, made himself comfortable on the bridge to watch.

The arms, designed to hold the vessel steady during the process of disembarkation, clamped its sides like the beak of a monstrous bird. One hundred and twenty horizontal steel rods slid out from each arm to hold the vessel along its full length, all with sensors at the end to ensure that the lightest pressure necessary was applied to avoid any possibility of crushing the hull.

Once held and locked in place, the computer on the service platform took over control of the disembarkation process. They watched as the vessel's front ramp was lowered onto the lifting deck. The four parallel lengths of track on the vessel linked and locked with corresponding tracks on the ramp. The left-hand track on the ramp continued straight ahead whilst the others curved into it through a series of points, so that just a single track left the ramp to link with the lifting deck. On the deck itself, the track coiled round in a spiral to accommodate the full length of up to forty cabins.

A series of red warning lights along the length of the track changed to green.

"That's telling us that we're ready," said Mike. "It means the vessel, ramp and platform are locked together. More than locked, in fact; it means they are now, to all intents and purposes, a single rigid structure, which can move with the swell or air turbulence without effecting the unloading operation."

As he spoke, the port side line of cabins emerged from the PTV onto the lifting deck, curving round and stopping under cover of its low-profile arched roof, like that of an aircraft hanger or engine shed.

CHAPTER FOUR

"Thanks, Paul. See you later."

"Have a good day, sir."

Tom eased himself out of the car and made his way to Peel Building where the press conference was being held in one of its large meeting rooms. The government press officers had already started shepherding journalists into their designated places after they had passed through the security checks, observing the hierarchical protocol for recognising the main media channels and dailies in the seating plan.

The headquarters of the Home Office occupies Number 2 Marsham Street in the City of Westminster. The site comprises three buildings connected by a multi-storey bridge, forming part of a corridor, known by the occupants as 'The Street', which runs the full length of the buildings. The whole complex is light and airy with many open plan areas and offices, and incorporating natural greenery in three central atria and a number of tiny interior parks.

The conference started promptly at 8.00 am, with Tom seated at a table covered in a red velvet cloth with three microphones on small stands facing him. Across the table from him was a three-deep semicircle of reporters and seventeen TV cameras. Along each side of the room were around a dozen photographers. Tom was flanked at the table by Paul Webster on one side and one of his Special Branch colleagues on the other. At the back of the room, behind the journalists, a further six officers lined the wall, relaxed but attentive in stand-at-ease positions.

One notable absentee from the media group was Sylvie Hanker, former Breakfast News anchor and currently the BBC's chief political reporter, who was watching it all unfold on a TV monitor whilst supervising the arrangements for her one-to-one interview with Tom in his office, due to start in just under an hour's time.

★

"Tuesday, 24th March, 6.05 pm, Delaware." The detective constable consulted her notebook. "Subject was observed walking towards Mansfield Road and was approached by one Darren Hargreaves, who is well known to us. Brief conversation ensued, developing into quite an argument. It looked like it was going to kick off, in fact, and a few other people looked like getting involved. Anyway, it all calmed down and Hargreaves left."

She looked up from her notes. She was in her early thirties; average height, with dark hair cut very short, and was smartly dressed in a black trouser suit.

"Left where?" asked the detective inspector.

"Went back across the road and down a side street." She checked her notes again. "Mill Street, it was."

The DI, in his everyday grey suit, stood up and paced back and forth behind his chair.

"So with this, we've got twelve separate incidents, eight different people, six on camera and two live."

"And the phone calls, sir."

"And the phone calls," he repeated.

"Including the guys who are coming in tomorrow to talk to us."

"If they ever show up." He turned to his colleague. "So, what do you think?"

"I think it's building up nicely."

He sighed and stretched.

"Nicely is not the word I would use."

★

"Sylvie!" Tom opened his arms wide as he entered his office and the reporter turned towards him. Her mouth twitched a little with just the ghost of a smile, but there was no preamble, no pleasantries,

43

just a formal handshake without the usual proffered cheek – or lips, as was more often the case.

"Sylvie?" Tom frowned, holding on to her hand. She pulled it away with some discomfort and embarrassment.

"They're waiting to do the sound checks," she said, not meeting his eyes. "Ten minutes to go…"

They faced each other in large wing chairs in the corner of Tom's office across a low table on which Sylvie had placed, immediately in front of her, a single sheet of A4. The technicians finished fitting and testing the radio microphones and the lighting engineer adjusted the filters on the spot lamps. Two cameras were positioned to pick up each of Tom and Sylvie face-on with a third to cover a side shot of both. The actual interview was being broadcast unedited but with a five minute delay, and was being picked up by CNN, most European channels and BBC World Service radio.

"Ready, folks?" The director stood behind the side camera and counted down. "Four, three, two, one, *go.*"

The camera zoomed in close on Sylvie who smiled into the lens. In her late-thirties but looking much younger, she was just above average height, with a trim figure accentuated in all the right places. Her hair was dark blonde in a simple style, just long enough to frame her face, which was round and pretty with full lips and deep brown eyes. She was wearing a dark blue trouser suit over a cream shirt, a change from her usual short dress or skirt.

"I'm here in the office of the Home Secretary, Mr Tom Brown, to talk to him about his recent first review of the New Justice Regime and put to him questions raised by his speech to the House yesterday. Many of you will have seen the Home Secretary's morning press conference, which finished just a few minutes ago," she turned towards Tom. "So, we are very grateful for your giving up more time at what must be a very busy period."

Tom nodded, without smiling, and said nothing. Sylvie hesitated for just a moment.

"Home Secretary, I will not ask you to go through the full list of items again. You've done that twice in the past twenty-four hours. I'd like to focus on one aspect of your report or rather an issue, which arises from it. I think you know which one I'm referring to?"

"Well, it could be any number of things, I suppose. For example, how was it possible to achieve so many of the changes in so short a time? And under that umbrella question, of course, there are so many individual success stories, I guess you could pick any half-dozen and still barely scratch the surface. Where would you like to start?"

"As I said, Home Secretary, I think you know which one I mean; the one which the prime minister announced at the conclusion of your report and which made most of the headlines yesterday evening and in this morning's papers."

Sylvie paused. Tom waited for her to continue.

"Okay ..." She spoke very slowly. "What I want to talk about is the use of expulsion for convicted dealers in hard drugs."

She paused. Tom said nothing, his expression completely neutral.

"This was unexpected, to say the least, and something I believe the prime minister is not totally comfortable with."

Tom raised his eyebrows in an expression of mild surprise.

"Would you like to respond to that, Home Secretary?"

Tom shrugged. "Well, I can't speak for the prime minister, of course, although it seems unlikely, don't you think, that he would say something at such an important meeting as yesterday's – or at any meeting, in fact – that he didn't agree with. So I'm not sure in what context he said those or similar words, but it would certainly *not* have been the context in which you've just implied they were spoken."

"His very words were ..."

"But what I will say, if this helps you out, is that being 'comfortable' in the sense of safe, cosy, relaxed, et cetera, was not what the overhaul of the justice system in this country was all about. To make the sort of changes we have seen involves a level of risk – *calculated* risk – *acceptable* risk – but risk all the same. And that comes with a certain level of *dis*comfort, at least in the short term."

"Well, we agree on something, then – we three – you, me and the prime minister – that changing the laws for drug sentencing is a risk. Is that what you're saying?"

"That's what *you're* saying, but ..."

"Because it seems that in just a few short sentences yesterday the government changed the whole concept and rationale for expulsion; a concept which was extremely radical when it was proposed and which the public bought into on the basis of the very specific circumstances under which you explained it would be applied. To use your own words at the time, Home Secretary" – she picked up the sheet of paper from the table in front of her and read from it – "'the introduction of facilities such as Platform Alpha will provide a place for serially disruptive elements of our society whose presence adversely affects the community as a whole and individuals within it. These facilities will offer both an alternative environment where they can no longer pursue their extreme antisocial tendencies and, at the same time, a significant deterrent for their doing so. They are *not* designed for criminals in the literal meaning of the word, in the sense that they need not have committed a specific crime. Their banishment will be on the basis of their consistent rejection of the communities in which they live.'

"That statement could not be any clearer. I repeat, *your* words – *'these facilities are not designed for criminals'*. My understanding is that dealers in hard drugs *are* criminals. Or are you going to surprise us again, Home Secretary, with the news that this government will be decriminalising cocaine and heroine?"

Tom drew in a deep breath.

"Everything you quoted from your notes was absolutely correct at the time it was stated. This change is an extension to the use of expulsion to address another – you might say the *next* – priority issue that is affecting the safety and security of our streets. Like a Pareto analysis, you tackle the biggest thing first, and then when that's sorted, you move onto the biggest of the things that remain.

"And let me remind you that this comes under secondary legislation, which, as you know, enables the government to make changes using powers conferred – in this case in the Act of Parliament which includes the NJR Directive – without going through full parliamentary procedure. The debate on Monday is merely a vehicle to enable the members to air their views, but is *not* a stage in an approval process. This extension, in fact, was in the Party's manifesto, which was embraced by the largest majority of voters in any election for over ninety years. So I hardly …"

"Except that it wasn't actually *part* of the manifesto, was it, Home

Secretary? It was *mentioned* in the manifesto as a possibility for the future. I think that's true, isn't it?" Tom thought the words sounded surprisingly familiar.

"Well, if we're playing with semantics, then I think it's true to say that today *is* the future in relation to when that statement was made. So, however it was included in the manifesto, what we have done is consistent with our promise."

"Very well, but let's recap on the distinction between those currently qualifying for exile status and a convicted criminal, because that is where this change is *inconsistent*. The principle is that someone may find themselves exiled if they continuously or repeatedly disrupt their communities. It is all about *behaviour*, is it not?"

"That's right, and exactly what we promised …"

"I think that is clear to everyone. Mr John Deverall put it very succinctly in his famous – and oft-quoted – speech from the dock." She read again from further down the same sheet. "He said 'the fundamental question should not be are they guilty or not guilty? It should be would society be better or not *without* these people in it? If the answer is 'better', then it is the law's duty to make it so by removing them.'" She looked up from the sheet. "Whether one agrees or not with the *means* of removing them, the argument for doing it is perfectly logical."

"So are you saying," said Tom, shuffling in his chair, "that such a rationale should *not* apply to dealers in illegal drugs? Is there *any* doubt, in fact, that society – the world – would be better without these people?"

"Well, you've asked two different questions there, Home Sec …"

"Well, give me two different answers, then."

"Alright, answer to the second one – of course, the world would be better without them. Okay? Your *first* question – I paraphrase – should the 'better or not' criterion apply to them? Well, collectively, yes, but individually, no."

Tom leaned forward in his chair.

"Let me ask a different question at this point, Home Secretary. Are there any contingency plans in existence that would allow you to retrieve Exiles from the off-shore facilities – like Platform Alpha – once they have been put there?"

47

Tom paused.

"No," he said. "This was a decision taken to ensure that such a step was irreversible and we have made this very clear to the public from the beginning. We felt it was essential that offenders – or *potential* offenders – were aware of the finality of this step. Their actions would, in effect, seal their fate *forever*. But I will say again that we envisage it will apply only to a very small …"

"You don't have to justify your reasons to me, Home Secretary, or, it seems, the electorate. It *was* made perfectly clear at the time; people knew what they were voting for. But that was based on the certainty of the people on Alpha *deserving* to be there. 'Long term extreme disruption and intimidation in their communities' – another one of your quotes. Long-term – incessant – unrelenting – never-ending – you've applied all these adjectives at some time or another. But adding illegal drug dealing only makes sense if those same two essential criteria are met."

"Which two?" Tom asked.

"Well, one – the *certainty* that they should be there. That is not always absolute in a 'guilty or not guilty' situation – that's the flip-side of the point John Deverall was making. And two – will these also be *long-term* offenders, and if so, what constitutes long-term? My understanding is that much of the hard drugs scene is now with very short-term dealers, who can quickly make a lot of money but must, for their own safety and freedom, get in and out of the market very quickly. Are you proposing to put, say, first time offenders on Alpha?"

Tom leaned back.

"Well …"

"And one last point, Home Secretary, will you be extending the guidelines for setting the dates for trial? Currently, the period from charging someone under threat of expulsion to their actual trial is two weeks. This seems just about manageable in a situation where there is an accumulation of evidence over a long period of time prior to the charge being made. But for drug dealers in a more traditional criminal trial, surely this would be far too short, given the finality – the *irrevocability* – of the sentence."

Tom waited a few moments before answering.

"Well," he said, "let me address that last question right away.

Although you have chosen to home in on one element of the NJR, that of expulsion, the changes were designed to address every aspect of the law and justice system. And this specifically included taking out of it time-consuming, over-administrative and, hence, unnecessarily costly functions across the whole judicial process. These included long delays in bringing people to trial, delays that bred inefficiencies and over-elaboration in preparing those cases for the courts. The two-week period you referred to is a guideline, not a rule, although we have encouraged magistrates and the CPS to stick with the recommendation as much as possible.

"As I'm sure you are aware – like everyone else – this period can be extended by the courts at the request of either counsel providing they can substantiate that request with genuine expectations that such an extension will add value to their case – or both their cases. In exceptional circumstances, a further period of up to six weeks may be granted if the court believes this would be necessary to benefit the cause of justice. So in the specific example you cited – that of drug dealing – it may be necessary in some cases – perhaps in many cases – to provide more time to ensure the right conclusion is reached. But by setting a very short period as the official guideline, this will keep the focus on concluding each case in the most cost-effective and time-efficient way."

He waited for a response, which was not forthcoming, so he continued.

"If I interpret your other comments correctly and can summarise them simply, you seem to be saying that with a traditional criminal case, it is possible to make a mistake – where evidence for and against is being weighed in order to make a decision. You are, quite rightly, contrasting this with the situation where a record of an extended history of wrongdoing has been compiled to arrive at a conclusion. Your argument being that if we banish someone in the former category and later discover a mistake has been made, then it is too late; whereas in the latter case, it is virtually impossible to get it wrong."

Sylvie gave him a brief smile.

"That is exactly right, Home Secretary, thank you for putting it so succinctly."

"Then we come back to the question of risk. The hard drugs market is a festering global sore. Many third world countries are virtually controlled by cartels whose members are getting unimaginably rich by peddling misery to all parts of the world, and doing so with a ruthless, sickening contempt for the lives of the users themselves *and* the people who are part of their own business empires. That situation can only prevail if the supply chain to the end users can be maintained. Break that chain anywhere down the line and the market folds.

"That, of course, is a massive over-simplification. The whole structure needs to be dismantled eventually to rid the world of this insidious malady. But *anything* that can be done to chip away at the issue will help, and taking the last-stage suppliers off the streets would be a big step – more than just a chipping away, in fact. There is a lot of support already in place for the end-users, so we are ready to deal with the fall-out of depriving them of the source that fuels their addiction. And now we believe we have a more effective means of deterring these street criminals who predate on that dependency, and we intend to use it.

"To your point about making mistakes, then I accept we need to apply the most extreme diligence to reach correct decisions to rid ourselves of the right people. But in any serious conflict, there may well be innocents caught in a crossfire. There may well be collateral victims. Such possible eventualities are the calculated – the *acceptable* – risks I referred to before."

"That would all sound perfectly fine, Home Secretary, if it hadn't just appeared out of left field as a sort of knee-jerk, if I can put it that way."

"Jackie Hewlett, the then Shadow Home Secretary, made the point in a speech in the House of Commons nearly *three years ago* – on the 21st July, to be exact – so how this can be termed a 'knee-jerk' is beyond me, quite frankly. She told the country on that day that our proposals for dealing with the people who terrorise our streets could be extended to cover other offenders, and of half a dozen examples she quoted, drug dealers were at the top of that list. Since that time, the previous government has decriminalised the selling of soft and recreational drugs, *and* removed the *taking* of hard drugs as a crime. We totally agreed with those steps, as we showed in the way we voted, and that left a clear route open to tackle the *selling* of hard drugs. This is part of our plan to do just that."

"But I must say, Home Secretary, taking it in isolation …"

"Is the wrong thing to do." Tom leaned forward suddenly in his chair causing Sylvie to instinctively retreat further back into hers. "It is totally misleading to take this one item out of context, ignoring the impact of what has been achieved over the past two years or so. Were it not for the fact that we have delivered on all fronts – against the most challenging agenda and timescale for change ever seen in British politics – we would not be justified in proposing this extension of the qualifying criteria for Exiles. But we *have* delivered …"

Tom clenched his right hand in front of him and began counting, opening out his fingers one by one.

"Increased the number of police officers across the country by 12%, at the same time reducing the amount of lower value administrative work; enhanced powers of arrest and retention; introduced trained, paid jurors serving a period of up to three years; installed a series of police hubs across the country and established Fast Reaction Teams for deployment across traditional police area boundaries to enable resources to be moved quickly into priority areas; reduced – *already* – the cost to the community of vandalism and social disruption by 35% – and bear in mind that around 75% of police time is spent dealing with these sorts of issues.

"That cost saving plus the introduction of the loan tax for high earners is already easing the burden of the implementation costs of the NJR, which we *know* will have a positive financial payback, albeit over the long term. And possibly the most remarkable achievement of all, establishing the first of the offshore platforms, fully functional and, as we speak, receiving its first Exiles, just twenty-one months after the votes were counted at the last election. There are far more points than I've got fingers – *and* toes.

"These were all commitments we made in our manifesto – most of which our critics doubted we would *ever* meet, let alone in the very short timescale we set ourselves. Making expulsion work for convicted hard drug dealers is a relatively small challenge – albeit with an element of risk – compared with our catalogue of success to date."

He leaned back in his chair. Sylvie did not respond for several seconds and when she did she spoke slowly and quietly.

"The saying goes, Home Secretary, that if your favourite tool is a hammer, there is a danger that the entire world will start looking like a nail. Isn't the danger in your case that you'll be wanting to put *everybody* into exile; that it will become the routine catch-all for all criminals?"

Tom looked at her with deliberate incredulity and shook his head very slowly.

"Two things, Ms Hanker. One – the saying actually goes 'if the *only* tool you have is a hammer …' and we have many tools. And, two, if you yourself had listened to what I've said *twice* in the last twenty-four hours, you would know that what I want is to put *nobody* into exile, not everybody."

★

The leading rider raised his arm to slow the small convoy of three vehicles as the gates opened ahead of them. He pulled to the side to let the main vehicle through and turned his motorcycle through a tight half-circle, positioning himself on one side of the opening, facing the way they would leave. He reached for his radio to report their arrival exactly on time at 10.00 am, as the second rider took up the same position on the other side of the entrance.

The gates closed with a loud clunk as they locked together automatically.

The security ambulance was a standard emergency vehicle with an extra skin of steel down each side and an additional pair of heavy metal doors at the back. It was completely black. The driver reversed it to within a couple of yards of the hospital wing's rear entrance. The police officer in the cab next to the driver got out and opened the back doors. Three more men jumped down to join him and form a short corridor of two each side, facing outwards, holding their semi-automatic Heckler & Koch MP5s in readiness; a needless precaution under the circumstances, but instinctive standard procedure.

The patient was wheeled from the building and raised into the vehicle on the chairlift. The prison doctor climbed in with him along with the same three officers and both sets of rear doors were closed, the outer one locked from the outside. The gates opened to allow it to leave and the two bikes tucked in, one leading and one behind, for the short journey to West Smithfield.

★

"I guess it was a bit too much to expect to get them together at such short notice."

"Well, to be fair, Jack's actually got a careers forum – so it's not even a social engagement. Katey's going to a movie with Jason."

"Well, we can't compete with that …"

"*But*," Mags interrupted, "they both suggested tomorrow night. I said yes, but that sort of scuppers our plans to get away for the weekend, unless we go early Saturday."

"Tomorrow's fine with me, if you're okay to postpone our bid for freedom. I think I'd rather wait until we can get away for longer."

"Great. I'll tell them. See you later."

Tom put his phone away then checked the time. It was just after 12.40 pm. Twenty more minutes…

★

"He's quite comfortable, but there is no prospect of his making any sort of recovery."

"I knew he was terminally ill, of course," said Tom. "But I didn't realise it was that close. I saw him only a couple of weeks ago." He was speaking from a quiet spot at the very north end of the Terrace, leaning with his back against the parapet under one of the ornate lamps.

"I guess we'll never know what it is," said Grace. "No-one seems to have any information about the condition – or if they do they're not saying anything. I've been getting weekly updates on him for some time, but it came as a real surprise to me that he's this close to the end."

Tom felt a lump in his throat at the thought of losing his best friend a second time. His mind went back to the shock of hearing of Jad's death in action over five years ago, and then, three years later, the joy of discovering he was alive. Followed by the sadness and frustration he had experienced since then, with his friend's

53

confinement after the killing of the Bradys, and then his failing health.

"Are you still there?"

"Yes, still here. Sorry, Grace, mind wandering. What about the press? Are we doing a release?"

"No," said Grace. "I think it could be dangerous to advertise the fact he's out of prison. We've got a guard with him outside his room at Bart's all the time, and a couple more positioned close by, but he's still news – or would be if this got out. I'm worried there'd be some ill-conceived attempt to spring him or something. And, of course, he may still be a target for some sort of retribution."

"Yes, understood," said Tom. "But I assume he can still have visitors?"

"Of course, but if you're thinking of going – I assume you will – then you need to do it on the quiet."

"I could go in disguise," said Tom, with a forced chuckle.

"I've got a canary suit you can borrow," said Grace.

"You remember that?"

"Of course. I thought it was going to be my grand entrance on to the political stage."

They both laughed.

"Well as it turned out, you didn't need it."

They were both silent for a few moments.

"Listen," said Tom. "Are you going to be around at about five-thirty? Perhaps we could have a drink together; in the Members' Bar or on the Terrace. I'd like to have a chat, if that's okay."

"Not a very private place to have a discreet conversation."

"Well, it'll be just about dark on the Terrace. I'm sure we'll find a suitable corner," said Tom. "And if we can't, we'll head off somewhere else. Can't be late home, but this is important."

"But not as important as not being late home?" asked Grace.

Tom sighed.

"Sorry," said Grace. "See you later."

He ended the call and sent a text to Mags. 'As kids have stood me up am staying for meeting this eve so can promise early finish tomorrow. Love you lots x'

CHAPTER FIVE

Calum watched with Gally from the deck as the port-side line of cabins left the vessel for the second time with the starboard prisoners on board. The final act, he thought; he could feel his mood changing for the better.

"How long do you reckon?" he said, checking his watch. It was 1.20 pm.

"An hour, top-side, I'd say; two-fifteen latest. Unless Harding wants to pop over and tuck everybody into bed."

"He's only doing his job, Gally. I can't imagine he *wants* to be here. I'm sure he'd much rather be back in Westminster slaving over a hot secretary."

Gally laughed. "So would I, come to think of it."

They watched the line of cabins roll onto the lifting deck where it curved round into its loose spiral. The rail linkage decoupled automatically and the prisoners started their two-minute ride up to the level of the main platform receiving floor.

"Talk of the devil," said Gally.

Lawrence Harding walked across to them.

"Nearly over," he said. "What exactly happens when they all get on board."

Calum pointed up to the receiving floor.

"Once they get onto that, all doors along the length of the carriage are automatically unlocked to allow them to leave their cabins. Then the carriage reverses onto the lifting deck and the tracks lift up like a drawbridge to isolate the receiving floor. There's only one way off the floor – a metal stairwell taking them up to the main recreational deck Once they're all up there, the stairwell is closed of, so there's no going back."

"And what then? How do they find their way around?"

"Well, they've been told plenty of times," said Gally. "Including every thirty minutes on this trip up to the time they chose to smash their monitors."

"Everyone's been provided with a laminated plan of the platform indicating where their own accommodation is sited," said Calum. "They've been given a swipe card for access and when they first use it, they're asked to enter a four-digit number into a key pad on the door which can be used for access in future if the card is lost or stolen."

"And, if I remember correctly," said Lawrence, "they each have their own apartment comprising a living room, including a kitchen area with cooking and washing facilities, and a small bedroom with ensuite shower, WC and wash basin."

"You *do* remember correctly," said Calum. "Ironically, in many cases, it's a lot better than the accommodation they left behind. The cupboards in the kitchen area are fully stocked with food and toiletries, which can be replenished from a central storage facility situated in the pontoon, which itself will be re-stocked from the satellite platform. The sharing and distribution of these items is the responsibility of the Exiles themselves, so it's anybody's guess how that will work out."

Lawrence nodded, seemingly deep in thought.

"Just one more question, Calum. If, when they get onto the receiving floor, they simply refuse to get out of their cabins, what then?"

Calum paused for just a moment.

"We encourage them," he said.

"How exactly?"

"You don't need to know that," said Gally, with a broad grin. "It might spoil your report."

Lawrence turned to him, eyes flashing.

"I can always ask the Home Secretary!"

"Go ahead. We don't tell him everything."

★

Just under an hour later, at 2.15 pm, when the port cabins had been locked in position on PTV1, Douglas ordered his crew to raise the ramp and prepare for departure. Ever since they had left Lochshore over twenty-eight hours ago, he, like everyone else currently on board, had been looking forward to this moment. Now, as with so many things eagerly awaited, he felt a sense of anticlimax, and of sadness. The remoteness of Alpha seemed to him so much greater now that human beings were occupying it. The thought of his part in their fate swamped any sense of relief he hoped and expected to feel.

★

Calum and Gally sat together in silence in the forward observation lounge awaiting contact from Alpha Control with verification of the safe arrival of the Exiles.

"Any time now," said Calum, checking his watch for the fourth time. "How long does it take to count up to a hundred and fifty and make a phone call to the Home Office?"

"Perhaps the Home Secretary's tied up at the moment," said Gally. "Probably by his own hot secretary."

The two men laughed, half-heartedly, and looked out beyond the bows towards their port of return; neither wanting to be up on deck watching the platform receding astern.

★

"Delivery for Mr Deverall."

Jad smiled across at the man in the doorway. His visitor was a sprightly sixty-something in a formal suit, shirt and tie and carrying a brown leather briefcase. Jad swung his legs out of bed and sat up. The official 'Voice of Older People' – appointed by Jackie Hewlett in her role as Diversity Minister – and best-selling author of *The Meek's Inheritance* – shook his hand warmly and seated himself in the armchair next to the patient's bed.

"This is the moment you've been waiting for," said George Holland, taking a book from his briefcase and handing it over. "Hot-off-the-press copy of the second edition. Just feel it; it's still warm."

Jad laughed. "So is it like one of those puzzles where you have to spot six differences?"

"Only two," said George. "The *Foreword* is different, of course – your new text replacing the speech from the dock – and two additional chapters reviewing the impact to date of the New Justice Regime."

"Well, thank you very much. I feel very privileged."

"And so you should," said George, getting to his feet and checking his watch. "Look, John, I'm sorry this is a flying visit, but I have a meeting. I just wanted to get this to you as soon as possible. After all, it wouldn't have happened without you. I can never thank you enough."

"You're very welcome," said Jad, "but don't give me that crap about a meeting. More likely a book-signing at Waterstones."

"Rumbled," said George. They laughed and shook hands again. "See you soon."

Jad got up off the bed after his visitor had left and sat in the same armchair, picking up the book from his bedside table and reading the hand-written message inside the cover.

'For John Deverall, my hero and friend. With best wishes from George Holland'

He turned the page to read the dedication – the same as in the first edition. The words brought tears to his eyes.

'For, and in eternal memory of, my beloved Irene.'

★

Tom entered the Members' Dining Room just before 5.30 pm. Grace, as usual, was surrounded by people – all male. It was hardly surprising; she looked her usual stunning self in a white shirt under a formal charcoal suit with a skirt which finished about six inches above her knee. The suit was close-fitting enough to show off the curves of her figure, and today her hair hung loose, in contrast to its usual style – pulled back from her face in a bun or pony-tail. Her dark eyes shone behind the heavy-rimmed glasses. She smiled across at Tom and, after a suitable delay in order to wind up her conversation politely, she excused herself. They ordered drinks at the Members' Bar and moved out onto the Terrace.

It was not yet dark, but quite cool. Even so, there were a lot of people on the Terrace, in twos and larger groups, sipping their drinks and chatting. They strolled to the Speaker's Residence end of the Terrace, sitting at a table well away from the others. Neither spoke until the steward arrived and placed the drinks on their table.

"So, how was your day?" asked Grace. "Sorry to be the bearer of such bad news about Deverall," she added.

"Yes, it's a real shock," he said. "I've not been able to think about much else all afternoon."

"Really!" she said. "Something else that's more important than us."

Tom rolled his eyes and sighed. "Come on, Grace. Tell me what's wrong, for goodness' sake."

"You really don't know?" she said, a little too loudly. A couple of people turned to look at them, and then turned immediately away. Grace sipped at her drink, looking across to the River.

"What I do know," said Tom, "is that we agreed to have a drink and a quiet chat, and I got the distinct impression that we were *both* looking forward to it. It seems it was just me."

They both remained silent for a while observing the activity on and across the Thames as more and more people poured out of their places of work. Grace sighed, and turned to look at him. Her eyes were cold and intense.

"Look," she said, "cards on the table, I had the distinct impression that we were heading for some sort of relationship – albeit extremely slowly. Clearly, I got it all wrong and it was never your intention. I just completely misread the signs – you know, your making improper suggestions to me on a daily basis for the last two years, looking up my skirt and down my shirt during all that time, and doing it deliberately so I'd *know* you were doing it. Easy for a girl to get the wrong idea, don't you think?" The words became more and more intense as she all but spat them out. She looked away again.

"But we *do* have a relationship," he said, lamely. "We've always been very close, and we always will be."

"Oh, for Christ's sake!" Grace almost shouted, turning quite a few more heads this time. "You know exactly what I mean," she added, lowering her voice. "Don't hide behind semantics; you're not on your high horse in the fucking House now!"

Tom placed his hand over hers, oblivious to the eyes still watching them from further along the Terrace.

"Grace," he said, "what on earth do you think has happened? What have I done?"

She was quiet for a long time. When she spoke, the anger had gone and she was perfectly calm; her voice was very matter-of-fact, in contrast to the words it conveyed. "The fact is, Tom. I'd been thinking recently that I might be falling in love with you. But I've just decided not to. And now I'm leaving."

She made as if to get up but Tom held on to her hand. There was a long silence before he spoke.

"We both need to get out of here and go somewhere we can talk about this," he said, gripping her hand more tightly.

There were a few people murmuring now, still looking at them. Tom shouted across to one of them.

"Barry, could you get Martin, please."

"Okay."

Tom's colleague placed his drink on one of the tables and disappeared into the building. Tom was watching Grace closely, still holding her hand. She did not move; even to pull her hand away. Barry reappeared with a tall elegant man in grey striped trousers and a white jacket.

"Oh, Martin," said Tom. "Miss Goody is feeling a little unwell. Could you let us out through the library, please, so we can avoid the crowd round the tea room?"

"Of course, sir," he replied. "Can I get Miss Goody anything before you leave? Brandy or something?"

"No thank you, Martin," Grace put in, recovering some of her poise. "I'll be alright, but I'd just rather not face a barrage of well-wishers, if you don't mind."

"No problem, ma'am."

He pulled a bunch of keys from his white jacket pocket and they followed him off the Terrace into the library. Tom shouted over his shoulder to his colleague, loudly enough for his voice to carry.

"Thanks, Barry. I'll get Grace home; I'm sure she'll be okay."

"Probably hypothermia," said Barry, feigning an exaggerated shiver. Tom smiled and followed Grace through the library and down the corridor to the Members' Entrance. He was speaking on his mobile as he walked.

"Paul, can you stand by, please?"

Once outside, they walked through New Palace Yard towards St Margaret's Street, Grace a few yards ahead of Tom. She stopped before reaching the gates, out of earshot of the police guard on duty. Tom stopped beside her.

"I've called Paul," he said. "He'll take us somewhere where we can talk."

"My office," she said.

"Is that wise?" asked Tom. "What about your place?"

"That's a lot less wise," she said. "Security will clock us going in, and linked with that little episode on the Terrace, we'll be an item in time for the morning papers."

"Okay," he said. "I'll get Paul, or would you rather we just picked up a cab?"

"We'll walk," said Grace. "Along the River."

"Okay," said Tom. "You sure?"

For an answer, Grace set off through the gate, acknowledging the nods of the police guard, and turned right for the few yards to Bridge Street. There was a cluster of about half a dozen photographers on the corner, who quickly started taking pictures of the two as they walked past. Tom gave his usual beam and wave and Grace managed a relaxed smile. They went along to Victoria Embankment and turned left, walking slowly and in complete silence, heading north, up the River. They turned off the Embankment into Richmond Terrace and were just 100 yards from the entrance to the Main Building when Tom broke the silence.

"Grace, wait a minute, before we go in."

"What?" She turned towards him, her eyes betraying no emotion whatsoever.

"What you said back there. It took me by surprise. I didn't know what to say. Of course I'm attracted to you – how could I not be? You're … you've got … everything. But I guess I'd always thought it could never … you know … be more than a fantasy for both of us. I suppose I've been careful not to let my feelings go further than that. But I couldn't stand it if there was any bad feeling between us. Our friendship means so much to me – I mean, more than friendship…"

His voice tailed off.

"Friendship?" said Grace. "Friendship? Do you make twenty references a week to *all* your friends about shagging them? No, Tom, it can't ever be the same again now, can it? My fault. I shouldn't have said what I did back there."

She looked away again.

"Do we really have anything to say to each other?" she said, turning back to him, now with a look of defiance.

Tom looked into her eyes and put his hands on her shoulders.

"Yes, we do," he whispered. "Let's go in."

★

Grace sat down at the workstation-cum-desk in her compact modern office which featured white walls and ceiling and a huge picture window overlooking the Thames directly opposite the London Eye. She had been a relative unknown when Andrew appointed her to the newly-created function of Ministerial Director of Justice, a role in which she was charged with expediting the transformation of government policy into operational effectiveness. The position exercised considerable influence, if not direct authority, over the machinery and resources of the police and judiciary services. In addition it had strong links to domestic-based operations of the armed forces, which was the rationale for her being allocated a base in the Headquarters of the Ministry of Defence – known as the Main Building.

It was a job in which she had quickly proved her worth in the rapid deployment of the NJR's new powers, an achievement which was as much her own personal triumph as it was the officially-spun 'team effort.'

"So, what is it we have to talk about?"

"About us, of course," said Tom.

"It seems there is no 'us'," replied Grace.

"There is and there always will be," said Tom. "Grace, you *know* that I have strong feelings for you; feelings I've struggled to keep under control. We've grown so close over the past few years." He shook his head in exasperation. "I just don't know how we've got to this state in just a few hours. I'm not sure what I've done wrong and what you want me to do next."

"Do next?" Grace echoed. "Okay, Superman, here's what you can do next. Get up there into the stratosphere, or whatever, and orbit the Earth in reverse a few times. I understand from the movie that this will turn back time by an hour or so. To just before we sat down on the Terrace would be fine. *That's* what I want you to do next. Other than that, there's nothing, thank you."

"That's very amusing, Grace, but not very helpful," said Tom. "I am trying to understand why, since you called me this morning, we have suddenly become strangers. Worse, in fact, more like enemies. I'm assuming this is all because last night I had my very first civilised conversation for nearly three years with my wife, without getting clearance from you beforehand. This, of course, makes me an evil philanderer and you a jilted lover, the victim of heinous two-timing and monstrous insensitivity. That's it, isn't it?"

Grace was looking down at her hands, clasped together on top of the desk.

"Okay, Grace. Let me ask you one question at a time. Am I right in saying this all stems from my talking with Mags last night?"

Grace did not answer.

"Tap once on the desk for yes and twice for no," he said.

Grace remained silent.

"For the sake of expediency, I'll assume that's a 'yes'. Next question – apart from what I briefly told you this morning, do you know anything about the content of mine and Mags's conversation last night?"

Grace said nothing. She was still looking down at her hands. Tom reached across and separated them, tapping twice with her right hand on the desk.

"That's a no, then," he said.

Grace still showed no sign of softening.

"The next one needs more than a yes-no answer, I'm afraid. What precisely do you think went on last night between Mags and me?"

She looked up and straight into his eyes, leaning forward a long way across the desk.

"You fucked her!"

Tom leaned back in the chair and looked in shock at Grace whose eyes continued to blaze into his.

"And what if I did!" he shouted back. "Next question – what the hell has it got to do with you?" He got up from the chair and began to pace round the room. "Look, Mags and I had a grown-up, friendly – yes, friendly – chat last night. For the first time for God knows how long, we had a pleasant, civilised" – he searched for a suitably bland word – "encounter without yelling at each other. It seems to have stabilised the relationship – a bit. I thought that's what everyone in the Party wanted, for Christ's sake. The Family Values Champion of the World behaving like he actually means it."

"God, that's exactly what *he* just said."

"Sorry? What did you say?" he asked.

"I said" – she hesitated – "that's what they all think."

"No, that's not what you said."

"Okay. What I said was, 'that's … what he says'. Andrew – and everybody else in *the Party*. You're right, it is best for *the Party*. And it's *the Party* that's important, isn't it? Not the living, breathing people in it. So I'm sure our Leader will be ecstatic about you and Maggie getting all lovey-dovey again. And his sheep will all be bleating in unison!"

"For God's sake, Grace. 'Lovey-dovey!' Is that how far we've descended in this argument?" He breathed in deeply. "We've got to sort this out," he went on. "We both have a meeting tomorrow with the Justice Committee. We can't go into it like this."

"Give me some credit," said Grace, calming down. "I'm not exactly going to bring this up under any other business, am I?"

She sighed, momentarily looking hurt and vulnerable again. Then she seemed to recover quickly, staring at him evenly.

"Look, I need time to think. So just to help me know what to think about, answer me this simple question. My turn, after all. I want an honest answer – I want you to swear on your children's lives."

"Christ, Grace, I'm a politician. You can't put me in a position like that." He realised his response would have been funny if he hadn't been deadly serious.

"Just the one question," she went on. "Do you feel the same way about me now – tonight – as you did when you sent me that text on your way home *last* night? Remember, on your children's lives."

Tom hesitated. "Yes," he said, looking away.

"You're too much of a boy scout to be a half decent liar," she said quietly. "The answer is no, and you just showed a fairly cavalier attitude to the welfare of your kids."

Tom was silent, still not meeting her eyes. She stood, turning half to the door and extending her arm, inviting him to leave.

"You've given me what I asked; something to think about," she said. "Goodnight."

Tom walked to the door, then stopped and turned back towards her. She had her back to him, appearing to be moving some papers around on her desk.

"Grace," he said, "did you *really* mean …?"

"Goodnight."

★

"All of them gave the same two phone numbers, but they're pay-as-you go with false IDs – so we can't confirm the names. And it must be a closed client list, because no one's answering when we call. Must be ignoring anyone not on their contacts list."

"Can't we just track down the phones? I thought we could do that now."

"Some sort of blocker, sir, or so the IT bods say. Must be some techie involved who knows what he's doing – or she's doing."

"Okay, thanks, sergeant." The Detective Inspector was pacing again, this time backwards and forwards in front of his team in the MIT room. Fifteen pairs of eyes were following him all the way, like spectators watching a tennis match played in slow motion. "Not sure we need to confirm their IDs anyway. I can't think how they could be any other than the same guys."

He turned to a tall young man in jeans and leather bomber jacket. "Bradley, statements?"

"Taken, sir. All pretty much identical and consistent with the calls."

"And the mug shots…?"

"They picked them out. Right away."

The senior man sighed and stopped pacing for a moment.

"Okay, thank you. Anything else, anyone?"

A large, bulky man wearing a replica of his boss's suit raised his hand.

"One more of the magnificent seven coming in tomorrow morning, guv. Sounds like he's got an interesting tale to tell. Claims he's been to the house and left a calling card."

"And then there were four," said the DI. "I suppose we should be delighted. Good work, you lot. Have a nice evening – what's left of it. Then let's get back to it early in the morning."

★

"There's absolutely nothing wrong," said Mags.

"Well, Katey seems to think there must be," said Jack. "And I have to say, once she'd mentioned it, it got me thinking. It's a bit unusual, isn't it? All of us sitting around the same table. So I thought I'd give you a call back in case we should be psyching ourselves up for a big announcement or something?"

"Such as what?" asked Mags.

"You're having a baby, is that it?"

Mags chuckled to herself. "I'm not sure, come to think of it," she said, "just let me check the calendar. No, everything seems okay …"

"Divorce, then?"

"Now you've gone and spoilt our surprise!"

"What!"

"Oh, my little wolverine! Look, there's no mystery at all. I just thought it's about time we had a nice family dinner together – if that doesn't sound excruciatingly boring. All three of you need reigning in a bit and food was the only suitable bait I could think of."

"Good choice, in that case," said Jack. "It works for me. Until tomorrow then."

"Until tomorrow; eight o'clock."

★

"Your niece is here, Mr Deverall."

The nurse opened the door to announce his second visitor. The attractive young woman who entered the room was tall, with a full figure and dark-brown hair which hung in curls onto her shoulders.

"Hi, Vicky," said Jad, checking his watch. "Seven-thirty; right on time."

Corporal Barrowclough smiled but said nothing until the nurse had left, closing the door behind her.

"Am I supposed to call you Uncle John or Uncle Sir?" she

whispered. "Anyway, I thought you were supposed to be lying down," she added, sitting in the other chair at the foot of the bed.

"Just thought I'd better make an effort for our first date in my new pad." He gave her a mischievous smile.

She shook her head and wagged her finger at him. "Now you're not to get over-excited."

They both laughed.

"Have you brought the book for me?"

"Oh, yes." She reached into her shoulder bag, pulled out a battered copy of Charles Dickens' *David Copperfield* and handed it to him. He opened the back cover and noted the mini-disk taped inside. "Why did you want that one, by the way?" she asked.

"What do you mean?"

"Well, that particular book. I can't imagine why you'd want to read something as dry as that."

"I beg your pardon, young lady," he chastised. "You are speaking about possibly our greatest-ever writer. This is a classic of its time. Nay, a *timeless* classic."

"Well I stand corrected and admonished," she said. "I just thought it's not the sort of book to cheer you up and help you get through the day. I would have thought something like *The Complete Works of Winnie the Pooh* would be much better. With the same appendix, of course."

Jad laughed. "Anyway, I've got another one to read," he said, picking up George's book and handing it to Vicky. "The first copy," he said. "Makes me feel very important."

"Well, you *are* very important," said Vicky.

"Certainly the focus of resources, if that's a reflection of importance. I've just been thinking, Vicky, just how much I screwed up – all over the place. Responsible for God knows how many innocent deaths and one young guy crippled for ever – probably worse than dead. And everyone still thinks I'm a big hero. How can so many people be wrong?"

"Hey," she said, "where did this come from? Mike's fine now. And whose deaths?"

"Well, my mother's. How's that for a start? It couldn't get any worse than that, could it? Then the Bradys..."

"The Bradys!" Vicky almost shouted, incredulously. "Now come on, sir. They were responsible for your mother taking her life. Taking theirs was the best thing you could have done – and not just for her."

"Murdering three kids was such a fine, heroic thing, was it?"

"Yes, as it turned out, and you know that's true. And they weren't kids. Anyway, who are the others?"

"The lady on the third page," he said, nodding towards the book she was still holding in her other hand.

Vicky opened the book and read the dedication.

"Mrs Holland just stepped in front of her husband at the wrong moment, didn't she? I don't suppose she was actually intending to sacrifice her life for him; it was just instinctive. And anyway, how can that *possibly* be your fault?"

"Well I set the whole thing going, didn't I? If I hadn't shot the Bradys, the gang wouldn't have gone looking for revenge, and Irene Holland would be alive today."

"Now really, sir, you can't take the credit and the blame for *everything* that's happened since then. Thousands of free-thinking people have made their own feelings known since that happened. Millions – in fact, tens of millions – if you count all the voters. You'll be claiming next that you put Andrew Donald in Downing Street single-handedly. And that will really annoy me, because I voted for him and I want some of the credit! Sir."

Jad smiled. "Out of the mouths of ..." he quoted.

"I'm not a babe," Vicky interrupted, pouting, "and I'm certainly not a suckling."

"Do you know what a suckling is?"

"Not exactly, I just know that I'm not one."

Jad laughed again. "Well whatever you are, Vicky, you've brightened my day."

"The pleasure was all mine, sir," she said. "Anyway, I must go so you can get your rest. Start reading Mr Copperfield; I'm sure you'll soon get off to sleep."

She stood up, placing George's book on his bed, "I'll see you again soon," she said.

"*Very* soon would be even better."

"Go on, I bet you say that to all your nieces."

★

Mags heard the tell-tale creak of the main gates and was already at the front door when the car crunched to a halt on the pebbled drive. The moment she saw Tom get out of the car she experienced that same euphoria that she had felt on each of the many times he had returned home on leave from active service. It was as if he had just fought his way back again from oblivion.

She rushed into his arms, almost catching him off-balance as he said his goodnight to Paul. They clung together for a long time then she eased back out of their embrace and smiled.

"Well, if that was Hanker the Anchor's idea of foreplay, I'd hate to get on the wrong end of her aggression."

Tom laughed. "I just assumed you'd phoned her and warned her off," he said.

"It did cross my mind …"

They kissed again briefly then walked up the steps to the front door together.

CHAPTER SIX

Week 1; Friday, 27 March…

"The meeting concludes that the stretch goals set for the Crown Prosecution Service at the onset of the New Justice Regime have been met and, in some cases, exceeded, and I think that the Justice Committee can take some satisfaction from its own involvement in that process." The chairperson checked his watch. "Meeting ends at 4.23 pm and, on behalf of the committee, I'd like to thank the Home Secretary and the Ministerial Director of Justice for their attendance and participation today."

The distinguished figure of the Right Honourable Sir Ian Beecham, in a navy pinstriped suit, white shirt and dark grey tie beamed at Tom and Grace and then at the other members of the group. The words barely registered with Tom, who had spent the best part of six hours failing to make eye-contact with Grace in spite of her sitting directly opposite him.

Committee Room 15 of the Palace of Westminster was set out in its usual format with a top table and five others arranged in an open horse-shoe in front of it to accommodate the fourteen members of the Justice Committee and their two guests. One seat on the top table was occupied by Sir Ian and the other, currently vacant, was for any witness called to provide information and answer questions. In the centre of the horse-shoe a young man in a light grey suit and a full black beard sat at a small table taking notes of the meeting on a laptop. The room itself was ornately wood-panelled and the green leather-upholstered chairs each bore the crown and portcullis insignia of the Houses of Parliament.

The members stood to allow their guests to leave first. Grace thanked Sir Ian and set off quickly along the corridor, with Tom almost running to catch her.

"Grace, for God's sake," he said, grabbing her arm then releasing it immediately as the rest of the group left the committee room behind them. Grace took the opportunity to rush off again, with Tom calling after her.

"What about Deverall? You said we could talk about that."

Grace stopped. She half turned towards him.

"Speak to Georgia," she said, and then disappeared into the Upper Waiting Hall.

★

Tom and Mags were waiting for them in the hall. Tom wore a pale-blue lounge suit with open-necked purple shirt and Mags a black off-the-shoulder dress.

Their dinner guests came down the wide staircase together, side by side, Jack in a cream linen suit and black tee shirt, leading his sister slowly and very formally with a raised, out-stretched hand, like a royal couple joining a reception in their honour. Katey wore a short, pale blue evening dress, very low at the front, with a white velvet choker, and sparkling white tights above blue stiletto-heeled shoes. Tom observed that his daughter seemed less enthusiastic about the comic charade than her brother, but at least she was there, he thought, and that was the main thing. She even managed a brief smile when Tom bowed and Mags curtsied as they reached the bottom of the staircase.

The dining room was large and airy, the only furniture being the oak table, four dining chairs and an antique sideboard. Three walls were plain white and displayed a number of Mags's paintings. The other comprised floor-to-ceiling windows overlooking the side garden.

Mags served the meal which passed with polite, rather than relaxed, conversation. As they finished their coffee, Katey raised her wine glass and tapped it with her teaspoon in a request for silence.

"As Bob Cratchit famously said, 'I'll give you…'" she held out her glass towards Mags, "'the founder of the feast.'"

"The founder of the feast," echoed Tom and Jack.

Mags smiled.

"If my recollection of *The Christmas Carol* is correct," she said, "then the founder of the feast should be your father. He paid for it."

"Not so," put in Jack. "Your recollection is *in*correct, Mother. Father, as I see it, in the context of this impromptu dramatisation of the well-loved Dickens classic, is Bob Cratchit himself. The founder of the feast, then – his employer, Ebenezer Scrooge, in the story – must be the prime minister."

"If you don't mind," said Tom, "I think I'd rather drink to Ebenezer Scrooge."

They all laughed, and he raised his glass again.

"All together, then," he said. "One, two, three …"

And – all together – they shouted. "Ebenezer Scrooge!"

Tom replenished their glasses and they sat in silence for a while.

"So, Mum," said Katey, "when are we going to hear what all this is about?"

"What's all what about?" said Mags.

"Well," said Katey, "why are we here, suddenly, all together, acting in this very civilised way? There's got to be something, hasn't there? This is the first time since my seventeenth birthday that the four of us have been in the same room together, behaving ourselves. What's that, eight months?"

"And *that's* exactly the reason, Katey," said Mags. "It's *because* it's been so long. I thought it was about time we showed that we *could* behave ourselves when we're together. That's all. Don't you like it when we don't fight? Would you rather we argue all the time?"

"Hey, I don't make the rules," said Katey, raising her hands in her mock gesture of surrender. "You and Dad set the rules *and* the standards, especially when it comes to arguing and fighting. So what's happened?" She turned to Tom, her mouth smiling, eyes challenging. "Home Secretary, will you take the question?"

"No, *I'll* take the question," said Mags, determined to keep Katey and Tom apart for as long as possible. "Your father and I have discussed our differences and have reached an understanding. We have concluded that our views," she added, carefully selecting her words in an increasingly official tone, "albeit still at variance on some fundamental issues, are not mutually exclusive and are capable of parallel existence. Going forward, we feel that, notwithstanding the aforementioned differences, a level of reciprocal tolerance will enable us to work together for the benefit of the family unit."

"Hear, hear!" cried Tom, spontaneously; with genuine appreciation. Jack added a brief round of applause.

"Wow!" said Katey. "That must have been some discussion to bring about Mum's complete surrender so quickly. So how are you going to do it, Dad? You know, keep your side of the bargain?"

Tom said nothing, returning the questioner's look with a blank stare. After a brief, silent stand-off, Katey went on.

"I mean, how are you going to dismantle the NJR so soon after the government has wasted all that money in implementing it?"

Again, no response.

"Because, in spite of Mum's wonderful speech just now, I know for a *fact*," Katey continued, volume increasing, "that that would be the *only* way you and Mum could get anywhere near a truce. Otherwise, all the bitterness and fighting over the past three years or so would have been pointless. A waste of time. And totally irresponsible, in the context of good parenting."

Still Tom did not say anything.

"Well?" she said, getting angry now. "Do I have to submit all this in writing?"

"No," Tom spoke at last. "I'm just waiting for a question worthy of an answer."

There were loud 'here-we-go-again' sighs from both Mags and Jack.

"I see, same game," said Katey. "Don't have an answer so it must have been a shit question!"

There was silence for a moment. Then Tom laughed out loud, looking affectionately at Katey and shaking his head.

"God, Princess," he said, "you are bloody good when you get going. I just wish I could have you on *my* side occasionally."

He looked at Mags and then Jack.

"Don't *you* think she's good?"

They were both beaming. Katey shrugged in resignation and rose from the chair.

"Okay, if I am to be scoffed at and ridiculed for trying to find out why my parents have suddenly and inexplicably decided not to kill each other, then I think I'll leave you and …"

"Oh, come on, Katey," said Mags, "please don't spoil it. It means a lot to me to have the three people I love most with me right now."

"Yes, short-one," put in Jack. "They'll start picking on me if you disappear."

Katey hesitated, looking at Mags. "That's a cheap trick, Mum, saying that, trying to make me feel bad." She hesitated, just a moment, and then sat down again. "However, it worked," she added, glancing across at Tom. "Anyway, I guess that would be no way for royalty to behave."

They sat in silence for a few moments. Tom got up, picked the wine bottle from the ice bucket and examined its contents.

"Nearly finished," he said. "Shall I open another? Katey? Jack?"

"Yes, sure," said Jack, looking at his sister who half nodded, half shrugged.

"And what about the chef?" asked Mags.

"You're on the Talisker with me," he said.

"I suppose resistance is pointless."

There were smiles all round. Tom dispensed the wine and whisky and resumed his seat.

"And now, back to Katey's question..."

"Haven't we got past that?" asked Jack.

"No, certainly not," said Tom, now seriously. "What your mum said before – and said so eloquently – was absolutely right, but if that doesn't meet Katey's data requirements, then I think she deserves a fuller explanation. I'd like to think that the fact we're all here tonight means that we care about each other both as individuals and collectively as a family. In which case we need to be open and honest and trust each other's good intentions."

He looked across at Mags who smiled .

"Okay, Princess, ask away."

★

"Thanks for a great evening, you two," said Katey as she rose to go to bed around midnight. "I've really enjoyed it, and I didn't think I would to be honest. It's great to see you both like this, loving instead of fighting. I actually thought the 'what's all this about?' might have been you announcing a separation. How wrong can you be?"

There was a catch to her voice as she spoke and a hint of wetness in her eyes as she kissed first Mags and then Tom, wrapping her arms around him and holding on for a long time.

"Come on, short-one," said Jack. "I'll read you a story if you like just to make it a perfect ending."

He kissed Mags and hugged his father, and then they both left the room.

Tom and Mags smiled at each other and held hands in silence for a while across the table.

"I've been thinking," said Tom. "I need to go to Lochshore very soon. If I can arrange it for, say, the middle of next week, we could perhaps stay up there somewhere and have Friday to Sunday together, possibly part of Thursday as well. What do you think?"

"That sounds wonderful," Mags said. "You don't want me at Lochshore, though, do you?"

Tom thought for a moment. "No," he said, "but if we can arrange a separate itinerary for you and a travelling companion for a couple of days, we could still travel up together."

"Great. I wonder what Hugh Jackman's doing next week."

"He's busy; I've checked."

"Oh, well, what the hell. I'll do it anyway."

★

Week 1; Saturday, 28 March…

Tom was up early, going down to breakfast at 6.30 to give himself plenty of time before his weekend driver picked him up to take him to the constituency office in Marlburgh for his Saturday surgery. He took his toast, coffee and juice into what they called 'the morning room', a huge conservatory overlooking another large pond and a range of bird-feeders in the side garden. At seven o'clock he looked up in surprise to see Katey in the doorway, coffee cup in hand. She was wearing a short pink robe and a pair of flip-flop slippers. Her hair was un-brushed and wild.

"Okay to join you?" she said, in a hoarse voice and with her eyes struggling for focus.

"Of course." Tom moved round the table and pulled out a chair for his daughter. She sat down heavily, not quite fully awake.

"Are you working today?" she asked, the words competing with a wide yawn.

"Leaving in half-an-hour," said Tom. "Want to come and play boss and secretary?" he added.

"I'd love to, but I'm meeting Jay at eleven. Got to report back on last night. He figured you might be going to bar me from seeing him."

"You're kidding me, aren't you? Why would he think that?"

"He thinks you don't approve of him. Actually, *I* think you don't approve of him as well."

"That's not so, Princess, honestly. He's a nice guy and I like him. That's the truth. But don't forget, I'm your dad and it's my job to be unreasonably protective and to resist anyone wanting to whisk away my little girl. And anyway, you're only seventeen and he's the only boyfriend you've had. You can't …"

"Mum tells me that she met you when she was seventeen and never ever wanted to be with anyone else. In fact, you may be interested to know she told me that only a couple of months ago, years after you two fell out and before you made it up again. She's never wavered in all that time. So what's wrong now with being in love at seventeen?"

"But that was totally different …" Tom began.

"Why was it so different? Because you were white and rich?"

Tom was silent for a few moments before replying.

"I'm sorry you feel like that, Katey. In your report to Jason, tell him I'm happy that my daughter is in such good hands. I know he looks after you really well."

Katey looked at him with sudden tenderness and tears came to her eyes. "Thanks, Dad," her voice trembling. "You can't know how much that means to me."

She rose from the chair and put her arms round him, holding him for a long time. He could feel the warmth and wetness of her tears on his neck and struggled to keep his own emotions in check. They broke from the embrace and her wet face smiled at him with an expression he had not seen for too many years. Then she turned to leave with a whispered, "See you later. Love you."

"Come in!"

The DI was already pacing round the office when the sergeant entered. The man was around ten years younger than his boss, medium height, stocky and with close-cropped fair hair.

"Something you might actually *want* to hear for a change, sir."

"Bring it on. God knows I need it."

"We can't find any link at all to the death of the Johnson kid. Different gangs, different locations. No reason to believe there's any connection."

"Except for the obvious one."

"Well, yes," said the sergeant, "but that could be coincidence."

"As you know …"

"You don't believe in coincidences."

"That's right." He paused. "But in the absence of anything else bringing succour to my life at the moment, I'll waive my beliefs for now and accept this morsel of solace."

"Very poetic, sir, if I may say so."

Both men smiled and were silent for a while.

"Will we go to strike on this, do you think?" the sergeant asked.

"Certainly. Have to."

"In which case, I'd like to apply for a transfer to traffic; at least on a temporary basis."

"No vacancies. I've already asked."

They smiled again.

"Don't worry," said the DI. "I think the big guy's going to use one of his Farts for the main event."

"Excellent decision," said the DS. "I always had a feeling they'd come in handy."

The senior man raised his eyebrows.

"In spite of everything you've said to me about them?"

"Well, I can waive *my* beliefs as well, can't I?"

They laughed this time.

★

"Bit of a detour this morning, Joe."

77

Tom's Saturday driver opened the rear door of the BMW.

"Okay, sir. Anywhere exciting?"

"Well, not so now, but it's where all the excitement started. I'll join you up front, if that's okay."

"Okay with me, sir."

Tom put his briefcase in the back and slipped into the front passenger seat. They set off for the office in Marlburgh with the back-up vehicle, as always, following fifty yards behind. As they neared their destination, Tom directed Joe down a road off to the right.

"Short diversion," he said. "Every so often I like to remind myself of where it all kicked off."

They turned again at Cullen Hall shopping mall onto the main road through the estate.

"When they created this constituency five years ago," said Tom, "they stuck together some of the best and worst neighbourhoods imaginable. Some of the highest priced properties outside the City itself, along with one of the worst FSIAs in Greater London."

"Cullen Field Estate?"

Tom nodded.

"Weren't you Princes and Marlburgh's first Member of Parliament, sir," Joe asked.

"That's right." He pointed to a road off to the left. "Just down there is the Wild Boar, where John Deverall went to find the Brady brothers. Just turn in here and then first right."

The manoeuvre brought them onto a minor road which left the estate and soon reached a dismal area consisting of old factories and warehouses.

"Right, stop here, Joe, across the end of this street." He pointed down the cul-de-sac towards the iron gates across the end. "That's where they cornered him and that's where he killed them."

He sat in silence for a full minute looking down the street, then turned to his driver.

"Right, Joe. Let's get to work."

Tom's constituency residence was the top floor of a large three-storey Edwardian detached house on Westbourne Avenue, a quiet leafy street overlooking a small park on the opposite side of which was Parkside Police Station. The constituency office was at the other end of the same road.

Jenny Britani, Tom's PA, was seated in the reception area, laying out numbered cards to hand out to the constituents to establish the order for the meetings. Jenny was a small, attractive, twenty-something Somali, with an irresistible smile, large laughing eyes, and dark brown hair in natural tight curls. She was wearing a short yellow dress and black leggings – her Saturday gear – as she called it – in contrast to the smart two-piece trouser suits she wore through the week.

Tom checked his watch; it was 8.35 am.

"Jenny, shouldn't you be crashed out and hung over somewhere? It's Saturday morning, for goodness' sake."

"And good morning to *you*, Home Secretary," she replied. "There's really nowhere I'd rather be. I thought you knew that."

He laughed.

"Well, it's very much appreciated, but I'll say what I say every week; you really don't need to be here this early. However, it's nice to see a happy, smiling face at this ridiculous time on a weekend."

"Not just *any* happy, smiling face, I hope," said Jenny, frowning.

"*Your* happy, smiling face, I mean, of course."

"Well that's alright then," she said.

Jenny brewed tea and toasted a couple of bagels, and they shared their usual Saturday morning second breakfast together.

"By the way," said Tom, "I've decided to run away from home."

Jenny was wide-eyed.

"Nothing exciting," Tom went on, "Just a state visit to Lochshore and then a few days' holiday in Scotland. Hopefully, Tuesday to Sunday next week. And before that, if possible, a visit to St Bart's. I'll just need you to apply your brilliance for me over the next couple of days to arrange it all."

"Well, as I've said before, Home Secretary," said Jenny, eyes now twinkling. "Brilliance I can do any time; it's just for miracles that I need a bit of notice."

They both laughed, Tom almost choking on his bagel.

★

His last constituent meeting finished at 3.30 pm and they went over the proposed arrangements for Tom's trip again.

"I've left a message with Georgia to call me early Monday to arrange for you to see Mr Deverall. I assume you'll touch base with the PM to sort it with him. I'll circulate the usual list this afternoon so they'll pick it up Monday morning latest."

"Thanks, Jenny. Now don't you stay too long; take a couple of hours off at least."

He waved her goodbye as Joe pulled up outside.

★

All flat and nearly-flat surfaces in the family lounge – sofas, chairs, floor, and two large coffee tables – were covered in OS Explorer maps for the west of Scotland from Glasgow north to Cape Wrath, including the Inner and Outer Hebrides. Mags was kneeling on the floor, sitting back on her heels, adding another possible venue to an already extensive hand-written list attached to a clip-board.

"Wow," said Tom. "I was thinking more of a visit rather than an invasion."

She smiled up at him and he dropped down beside her, putting an arm round her shoulder and kissing her on the lips. Their mouths opened, tongues pressing together. Tom eased her onto her back and rolled on top of her, crumpling one of the maps. Mags pushed him off.

"Not here, not now," she said, in a loud whisper. "Katey's back, and anyway, you're creasing my Trossachs."

"Oh, my goodness!" said Tom. "I'm so sorry; I had no idea …"

Mags giggled and held him tightly to her, winding a leg around the back of his thighs.

Katey walked in and gasped in pretended horror.

"What on Earth is going on here?" she demanded, glaring down at them, hands on hips.

"Just trying out a new map-reading technique," said Tom.

"Yes, well I think I'll make myself scarce," said Katey, "before you start practicing roping yourselves together. Have you mentioned it yet, Mum?"

"Not yet. I've not had chance – as you can see!"

Katey laughed, and turned and left the room.

"See you both later."

Tom pushed himself away, frowning at Mags.

"Mentioned what?"

"Well, I told Katey we were going away and she asked if they could have a party …"

"And you said you'd check with me first?"

"Not … exactly …"

"You said 'no'?"

"One guess left …"

"You said 'yes'?"

"You got it! Well done!" Mags clapped her hands.

Tom sat up.

"Listen, Tom. You know what she's like – exactly like you, come to think of it – she can always remember, word for word, what we say to her. When she asked me I started to say, 'Well, I'm not sure it's a good idea … I don't think Dad will want you to …' and she said, 'Dad won't mind. Last night he was very clear that we should be open and honest and trust each other – his very words, in fact…' And you did say that, didn't you, darling?"

"What I said was 'trust each other's *good intentions*', to be precise."

"Well, I'd like to hear you try to argue the difference with Katey. On second thoughts, I don't want to be anywhere near when you try to argue the difference …"

"Okay, point taken."

"So it's okay?"

"What, the party? I guess it will have to be. Although …"

"Come on, Tom-Tom. They didn't even have to ask us, you know. They could have just arranged it without us even knowing. We owe it to them to say yes for that alone."

"You're right. But I'm not taking security off. They'll have to come and go under the watchful eyes of the men in black. That's the deal. And it might be best if you tell Katey that. I don't want to push my luck." He paused, and then laughed, shaking his head. "Listen to me! I sound like the kid instead of the parent!"

"Well, you are a big kid, really," said Mags, wrapping her arms around him. "Fancy some more map-wrestling?"

★

"What about this?" said Tom, holding up the DVD. "Been some time."

The movie *X-Men* had a particular significance for them.

"Well, if I can't have him in the flesh next week, I guess that will have to do."

"Even so, you must admit it's a bit tame," said Tom, "compared to our own little drama at the Première. You screaming in agony in the back of a taxi with Jack trying to escape."

"I'm still not sure I've forgiven you yet for dragging me out before the movie had finished."

"Well it's a good job I did …"

"Oh, I'd have managed somehow. Kept my knees together or something."

"I doubt it. You always have trouble keeping your knees together when Hugh Jackman appears on the screen."

"Just you retract that statement or you're in big trouble, my lad," said Mags.

Tom laughed. "And the first thing you said when you held our little baby boy – *three minutes* after we'd arrived at the hospital, incidentally – was … well, can you remember?"

"I don't have to remember; you tell me every time we watch the movie. 'Oh, my little wolverine'."

"Yes, 'oh, my little wolverine'. God knows what the nurse must have thought."

Tom slipped the disk into the player and started the movie. They lay together on the four-seater sofa in the large family room at the rear of the house overlooking the pond. Fifteen minutes into it, the sound of Police punctuated the entertainment. Tom checked his mobile and recognised the number.

"Hi, John, hold on a second," said Tom, unravelling himself from his wife. He held the phone away from him. "John Mackay. I'll take it through there."

As he was nearing the end of his conversation with John, the warning bleep on his phone alerted him to another incoming call. When they'd finished speaking he checked the new number. It looked vaguely familiar but was not on his contact list. He phoned back.

"Hi, Tom." A woman's voice. "It's Sylvie here."

"Sorry, Sylvie who?"

"Oh, come on, don't give me a hard time."

"*Me* give *you* a hard time. God that's a bit rich."

"You *are* teasing me, aren't you? We're still friends, right?"

"You tell me, Ms Hanker. You're the one who changed the rules."

"Well, it wasn't me, actually. I was told by the big guy – the *very* big guy – Sir Brian, no less – not to give you an easy ride. His exact words, in fact, were 'the *usual* easy ride'. So, I'm very sorry, but I was just following orders, guv, as they say."

"And you didn't enjoy it one bit, I could tell."

"Well … it's the way I am with everyone else *except* you – usually."

"Anyway, it's not like the Director General to be that hands-on, is it? *And* to take a political stance. In fact, I don't think he's allowed to do that. You should interview him, Sylvie, and put that to him. And don't hold back."

She laughed. "In fact, it wasn't actually his idea. An even higher authority had pressed him to make sure I gave you a tough time. And don't ask me who, because I couldn't possibly reveal my source. Even if I knew who it was."

"Okay, I won't ask. Anyway, what makes you think you gave me a tough time. I thought I won hands-down."

"Only because I let you."

Tom laughed. "Alright, we're still friends. But I'll be thinking of ways you can make it up to me."

"So will I. In fact, I've thought of a few already."

He laughed again. "Can't wait to hear them. Bye, Ms Hanker."

"Bye, Home Secretary."

He walked back through to where Mags had paused the movie and was flipping through a walking magazine; part of the impressive anthology she had assembled that afternoon.

"So, what did our favourite Chief Superintendent want?" she asked.

"Well, a career in politics, apparently. He's just given me feedback and advice on the next phase of the NJR, which" – he held up his hands to deflect any response – "I have no intention of even *thinking* about let alone discussing tonight. Not when there are more important things to get my mind – and my arms – around."

Mags laughed, throwing the magazine to one side. They resumed their previous close formation on the sofa and Mags restarted the movie.

"Oh, by the way," said Tom, "you're off the hook. My ex-favourite interviewer called just now to apologise for last Thursday. It seems it wasn't you who phoned her to warn her not to come on to me, but somebody else. Her boss had instructed her to give me a going-over, but Sylvie reckons *he'd* been told himself by – she said – 'a higher authority'. So, who do you think?"

"Andrew." It wasn't even a question.

"Yes, I reckon so. God knows what he's playing at." He twisted round to look at Mags. "And anyway, who cares? All I care about is this bloody film ending so we can get on with something else."

"Shall I fast forward it?"

"Now you're talking."

CHAPTER SEVEN

Three days later
Week 2; Tuesday, 31 March…

They were sitting on the two bedside chairs facing each other across a low table on which there were two mugs of coffee and a plate of biscuits.

"Tell you what," said Tom. "You never did tell me the full story of how you died."

"I thought old Barrington Henshaw told you."

"He told me that you had to assume a new identity and so they faked your death, but you were going to fill in the details. Am I still not to be trusted with military secrets? Perhaps when I'm Minister for Defence…"

Jad laughed. When he first arrived, Tom had been shocked by his friend's appearance. He had lost a lot of weight in the few weeks since they had last met whilst he was still in Pentonville, but Jad seemed as bright and positive as ever.

"So what do you want to know?"

"Well, everything you can tell me, I guess.

"Okay. You know already that it happened when we were on a mission in the Kush – exact same place where I missed taking out el Taqha, in fact. There were only two of us in the group who knew the real objective of the mission – me and the patrol leader – Malc Randall. The hit was real; the guy was a senior mover and shaker with the insurgents, but in reality, we could have used a Predator UAV for that one. The Hellfires have an accuracy of plus or minus a couple of yards. What you *don't* get with an unmanned aerial vehicle, of course, is someone to tell you they've hit the right guy and that he's dead. So we used that as the reason for the ground hit."

Jad was silent with his thoughts for a long time.

"So how did it work? Your faked death?" Tom prompted.

"Two explosive charges had been laid in this sort of basin-shaped area beyond a bend in the gully. They'd put a body of the same height and build as me, dressed identically, over the charges in a position so that it would be unrecognisable after the blast. I just had to be at the front of the group at the point when we reached the turning. I went ahead – round the bend and out of sight – to investigate a noise I said I'd heard. Malc held the group back to give me time to place some personal items on the body and set the timer on the detonator with a twenty second delay. Then I just jumped into a jeep, about fifty yards past the basin, and it drove me away."

"Simple as that. So what went wrong? How did the corporal get hurt?"

Jad was silent again for a while.

"I guess we'll never know for certain why, but only one of the charges went off at first. Theory is they were wrongly wired – in series rather than in parallel. So setting the timer could have caused a second twenty-second count-down to the other charge. I don't understand really; it doesn't sound all that likely, but something went wrong, and from what Malc said later it was around twenty seconds between the explosions. By that time, Mike Hanson had gone charging in to the basin to see what had happened to me. I was sitting comfortably in the back of a jeep and he was getting blown to pieces."

Jad's voice broke as he finished the story and he dropped his head into his hands.

"But it wasn't your fault, Jad, surely? If it was set up wrong ..."

"No, no-one has ever even hinted that it might have been, but you know what it's like. He was a great kid – big, good looking, brilliant at his job ..."

"Well, he's got a new job now, thanks to you. A new life."

"You know what I keep thinking about, Tom? He always wanted to try out the second rifle. We each carried two – an Accuracy as the main weapon, and a Barrett M82 as back-up if we couldn't get close enough. Most powerful sniper rifle in the world; twice the range and a much heavier bullet than the Accuracy – capable of bringing down a helicopter with a single shot – or so it says on the tin. It became a sort of joke between us; he'd always act disappointed if we got into a good position – you know, comfortably within range." He paused and shook his head. "And for whatever reason, I can't stop thinking about that. The fact that he'll *never* get to try it. Just so sad…"

"Not for the guys in the helicopter," said Tom.

Jad smiled. "No, I guess not. You only see one side, don't you?"

"That's the side that was paying us, though, wasn't it?"

Tom looked at his watch and got quickly to his feet.

"Got to go, Jad. Really sorry to rush off, but I've got a beautiful woman waiting for me and a plane to catch."

Jad got up as well. "Give Maggie my love, and come back soon, ol' pal o' mine."

The two men embraced.

★

Paul eased the BMW through the special security check-point at Terminal 1 and up to the door leading into the lobby of the small VIP lounge. Tom was met by two aides from his extensive Civil Servants' empire, who escorted him inside. Matty Jaynes and Cheryl Webber looked as if they'd just stepped off the front cover of an up-market fashion magazine.

Matty strode forward. He was a couple of inches taller than Tom with classic features and a perfect build. His hair was quite long, almost jet black, and combed back in a modern style. His flashing smile revealed teeth that were gleaming white and impossibly even.

"Home Secretary," he said, "I'm Matty; this is Cheryl. We're here to help you with everything through the next few days. Anything you or Maggie want …"

"Nice to meet you, Matty," said Tom. "And you too, Cheryl," his voice softer and more sensual.

He shook hands with both of them, gripping Matty's strongly in an impromptu display of alpha-male-ism, and then almost caressing Cheryl's. She was as perfect as her male companion, with a dark complexion and shining chestnut hair framing a beautiful, smiling face. She wore a short, pale blue dress, which was flared below the waste and swung enticingly around her legs when she moved on her four-inch heels.

"This way, Mr Brown," she said with a dazzling smile, extending an arm to indicate the entrance to the inner sanctum of the VIP lounge with its lush carpet and velvet-effect wall covering.

Mags was seated in an enormous bucket-chair near the floor-to-ceiling windows which looked out onto the Cessna Citation executive jet just below them. Jenny was sitting in a similar chair close to her, running through the itinerary for the week. She rose to vacate the seat as Tom approached, but he waved her to sit down again, pulling over the leather tilt-and-swivel from the computer desk near the wall.

"Would you like a drink, Mr Brown?" Cheryl asked, the smile hardly moving as she spoke.

"Coffee would be great, White, no sugar, please, Cheryl. And do call me Tom."

Mags gave a silent, knowing giggle. Cheryl brought over the coffee, almost curtsying as he flashed a thank-you smile, and then joined Matty on a sofa behind them.

"Are we all set, Jenny?" Tom asked.

"I've been through it all with Mrs Tomlinson-Brown."

"Absolutely," put in Mags. "Don't make Jenny go over it again; I'll cover everything with you on the way if necessary. You've been great, Jenny. We really appreciate all the arrangements you've made for us, and at such short notice."

"Well, you'd already done all the hard work, finding the place and everything," Jenny replied.

"God, listen to the pair of them," Tom said to Matty and Cheryl, over his shoulder. "Talk about mutual admiration."

They all laughed. A few minutes later the door opened and the Flight Officer entered. Tom rose to greet him. Captain Josh Wilcox was his regular assigned pilot on all his official flights and the two men had become close friends since Tom's Cabinet appointment. Josh was tall and slim, in his late thirties, with close-cropped greying hair. The short sleeves on his white pilot's shirt showed off tanned and muscular arms.

"Ready to board," he said, shaking Tom's hand and kissing Mags and Jenny on both cheeks. He flashed a sparkling smile across at Cheryl and nodded neutrally to Matty.

They all stood up. Jenny passed a document case to Tom.

"Lunchtime mail, and a note from Georgia," she said.

Mags gave her a hug and an affectionate peck on the cheek, saying "thank you" again, and then they left her and followed Captain Wilcox down the short flight of stairs to the tarmac and across the few yards to board the jet. Near the plane two stocky men – Tom's security escort – looked around with darting eyes and habitual anxiety, then followed the long shapely legs of Cheryl Webber up the five steps into the aircraft.

★

Two men sat side-by-side at one end of the large table in the small meeting room of the Lochshore Security Centre. Gordon Sutherland, Westminster Member of Parliament for Argyle and Bute, and Calum Nicholson were on a conference call, preparing for their following day's meeting with the Home Secretary. Also on the call, at different locations, were the other four people who would be attending the meeting

"Do you think we should just add it on?" asked Gordon. "I mean, the Home Secretary has had a copy of the agenda already."

"Well, you're seeing him tonight, aren't you?" said Eleanor Morrison, his counterpart in the Scottish Parliament. "You can agree it with him then. In fact, let him suggest it. One thing is certain; we won't get through the meeting without discussing it."

"Okay," said Gordon. "I'll let him bring the subject up."

★

The passenger cabin of the Citation Sovereign had eight seats, arranged in 'club' formation so that its normal payload could be accommodated in two groups of four. A further seat at the front of the cabin, adjacent to the integral rosewood drinks cabinet, faced inwards with its back to the fuselage. Tom and Mags sat across from each other in two of the rear group of seats, with Cheryl, Matty and the two security guards in the front set.

Chuck and Simon were almost identical in size and shape, just under six feet tall with broad shoulders, barrel chests, and necks which were the full width of their heads. They were also dressed the same, in mid grey suits, white shirts and dark blue ties. Simon was in his early thirties – the younger by about ten years.

Once airborne, Mags moved forward to talk to them, leaving Tom to check the contents of the document case presented by Jenny. The three men almost banged their heads together in a race to stand and offer her a seat, Simon winning and moving to the spare seat at the front.

Tom didn't get as far as checking his mail. The message left him by Georgia, from Grace, stopped him in his tracks. Jenny's hand-written note said:

'Georgia phoned to confirm that Ms Goody has approved your trip to Lochshore. However, Ms Goody asks that in future you request approval in advance.' Jenny had added, 'Sorry – I didn't know we needed to do that.'

"You're not the only one," said Tom, loudly enough for everyone to hear. They all turned to him. "Sorry," he said, lightly, returning their questioning looks. "Just talking to myself. First stage of madness, so they tell me."

Mags got up to join him again in the seat opposite.

"Anything wrong? You can tell me, I'm a doctor."

He smiled at her.

"Yes, doc, I've got these shooting pains," he whispered, rubbing his groin, the noise of the engines preserving the privacy of their conversation.

Mags smiled, opening her eyes wide, then becoming serious again.

"Really," she asked, "is there anything wrong? I just get the feeling this is all going too well."

"No, honestly. Just somebody chucking their weight about and getting ideas…"

"Above his station?" she prompted.

"*Her* station, actually," he said.

"Who? Not the perfect Grace Goody, surely?"

"Er, no, not her," he said.

"Of course, it couldn't be," said Mags. "I mean, her station is as high as a human being can go. There isn't anything above it, is there?"

"Anyway, about these shooting pains," said Tom, dropping his voice again.

"Shall I ask Cheryl if she's got a first aid certificate?" Mags whispered back. "Actually, she looks like she might be a trained masseuse."

"I wish," he said.

They both laughed.

"Listen," said Tom. "Are you sure you'll be okay for the next couple of days?"

"Of course. You don't really think I'm likely to get accosted in broad daylight on the mean streets of Oban, do you?"

Tom smiled.

"No, but I don't like leaving you on your own."

"I won't be on my own; I'll have the afore-mentioned lovely Cheryl for company. But you're right," she added, frowning and seeming to reconsider. "Much better if I had Matty with me all the time."

"Then it would be Matty I'd worry about being accosted," he said.

They smiled at each other.

"I'll be fine. I've got my dark glasses and any number of credit cards. I'll easily blend in with the tourist set. Come to think of it, I'll be part of the tourist set, anyway. And *then*," she leaned forward, tapping his knee, "just you and me and flickering candles and Talisker whisky and a peat fire, with, most probably, a soft sheepskin rug in front of it …"

"Is there no electricity in this place? I hope there's at least a generator for the tele, otherwise Chuck and Simon will be watching *us* all night."

She stopped tapping and smacked him hard on the leg just as Josh joined them from the cockpit.

"Ladies and gentlemen, we are approximately forty-five minutes from touch-down and will be crossing the Scottish border in ten minutes. I suggest you celebrate this event in an appropriate way by helping yourselves from the selection of single malts in the drinks cabinet. I'd love to join you, but … I'm driving."

Matty and Cheryl did the honours, administering refreshments all round and discovering that a half bottle of The Macallan contained exactly six measures, providing each recipient was prepared to go the few extra millilitres.

Tom returned the papers to the document case.

They touched down at Glasgow International Airport exactly on time and taxied to the waiting Bell 430 executive helicopter. Transfer between the two aircraft took only a few minutes, and then they lifted off for the sixty-mile journey to the Heliport at North Connel; estimated flight time twenty-five minutes.

The manufacturers of the helicopter boasted in their brochure of 'an interior rivalling any business jet' and it was difficult to argue with that as they settled into their luxurious leather seats and Mags kicked off her shoes to wriggle her toes in the deep-pile carpet. The six cabin seats were in three pairs, the middle pair back-facing, forming a group of four. Tom and Mags occupied the two forward seats. When they had cleared the airport, one of the pilots left the cockpit to serve refreshments, Tom and Mags this time taking coffee and the rest of the entourage following their example with silent disappointment.

They hardly spoke during this second stage of their journey, due at least in part to the increased buffeting by the wind as they ventured further north into the unsettled weather, which had persisted since PTV1's maiden voyage the previous week.

Mags closed her eyes and, in spite of the turbulence, seemed to doze off, though when Tom gently took her hand he felt a telltale squeeze. He thought back to her earlier remark about it all going too well, and he did have an uneasy feeling about something, though he couldn't identify what it was. He closed his eyes and drifted off to sleep, still holding his wife's hand.

They landed at North Connel, a few miles from Oban, at exactly four o'clock. Two vehicles, both Range Rovers but of very different vintage, were awaiting them on the tarmac. As they alighted they were approached by two men. A tall, impeccably dressed young man in his late twenties wearing an expensive suit stepped forward and extended his hand to Tom.

"Welcome to North Connel, Home Secretary." He nodded to the rest of the group by way of extending the greeting. "I'm James Stewart, representing Mr Gordon Sutherland, the Westminster Member of Parliament for Argyle and Bute. Mr Sutherland will be your host during your stay, Home Secretary. He apologises for not meeting you personally, but everything's had to be rushed through at very short notice," he added, without a trace of irony.

The second man, shorter by a good few inches than James and older by about twenty-five years, was similarly dressed but looked decidedly uncomfortable in formal attire. His bronzed, smiling face and rugged features also contrasted sharply with the younger man's pale complexion and formal manner. He stepped forward.

"Hi, I'm John Bramham, manager of the Eriska Hotel, and I really can't tell you what a privilege it is to be receiving you and your companions as guests." He addressed Mags, and then turned to Tom. "Only sorry you won't be joining us, Home Secretary."

"I only wish I could, John," Tom said, shaking his hand.

"Well, we're open all year, Home Secretary," he said, with a smile. "Maybe next time."

"*Definitely* next time," Tom replied. He kissed Mags. "Now be good and don't give this gentleman any trouble," he said. "And don't let that Cheryl lead you astray."

They laughed as James ushered Tom, Matty and Chuck into the shining brand-new vehicle and set off on the thirty minute drive to Lochshore.

"Can I sit in the front?" asked Mags, like an excited child, as the rest of the party prepared to board the second vehicle for the five-mile trip in the opposite direction to the Isle of Eriska.

"Only if you promise to sit still," said John, with twinkling eyes, "and you let me take this tie off."

★

"Anything you want to add, Tom? I guess there must be something."

Gordon Sutherland, Calum Nicholson and Tom had just shared a delicious dinner, served in the small meeting room they would be using the next day. Its wood-panelling and floor-to-ceiling book shelves, along with the long sideboard, antique oak table and dining chairs, gave the impression of a room in an old Scottish castle.

Over coffee and malt, Gordon was running through the proposed agenda. His host was a stocky, round faced man of around Tom's age. He had the typical fair complexion and red hair of his native Scotland and was dressed in a tweed jacket with muted tartan tie as if to deliberately reinforce the image.

"No, I think you've hit all the right spots; looking forward to the tour of the facility and the transfer vessel."

Gordon seemed slightly surprised, pausing after Tom had answered as if inviting him to reconsider.

Tom shrugged. "No, that all looks fine," he said.

CHAPTER EIGHT

Tom looked again at the bedside clock. It was 2.15 am. His constant checking was not making the time go any faster. Since turning in just after midnight feeling relaxed and contented, and ready for sleep, his earlier feeling of apprehension had suddenly returned, and this time he was able to identify its source.

It was Jack and Katey's party. Nothing specific; just a vague feeling of unease, but enough to repel the sleep he was expecting to overtake him as soon as his head hit the pillow.

He got out of bed, putting on a lightweight fleece over his tee shirt, and went through into the small kitchenette which was part of his suite of rooms to make himself a coffee; totally the wrong thing to do, he told himself, for someone trying to get to sleep. He settled himself at the small table in the sitting room and set up his laptop to check his emails.

He knew from experience that he only received about ten percent of the number sent him; the rest were filtered through Jenny, who diverted them to his group of Under-Secretaries. He opened each of the twenty-two that had reached him; mostly they were for information or just 'yes-or-no' answers. In addition, there was one from Jenny herself; one he didn't understand.

He yawned and stretched and checked the time. It was 4.00 am, and his shot of caffeine was wearing off again. He shut down the laptop and went back to bed, soon falling into a shallow sleep.

★

"Right, so we all know what we're doing?"

The detective inspector addressed the six members of his major incident team who were gathered round the desk in his office. They all nodded.

"Okay, good, but just let's be clear on a few points of protocol," He counted on his fingers. "One, we are there to watch and learn, not to act. Two, we need these guys on our side, so let's not get into any sort of turf war or demarcation issues. Three, following on from that, any difference of opinion, *they* decide – okay? Bradley, I'm looking at you."

The others laughed and the young man in the leather jacket shrugged his shoulders, wide-eyed with innocence.

"And four, you meet back with them before you report to me."

The others looked at each other. "Why's that, guv? We're not being transferred are we?"

The DI smiled. "I should be so lucky. Let's not forget who and what we're dealing with here. It's a question of loyalty. I'm not sure how I'd be feeling if I was one of those guys. They just want to know what's going to happen. And anyway, more to the point, we don't have a choice. Okay?"

They all nodded.

He checked his watch. "Seven fifteen. Time for breakfast." He went over to the window and looked outside. "When does the bacon butty wagon get here?"

"Not until eight, sir."

"Okay, Plan B. Canteen."

★

"Excuse me, Mr Chairman – Gordon – but, as we all know – at least, perhaps, all except the Home Secretary – there is one other item for the agenda, and I feel it would be appropriate to start with that."

Eleanor Morrison was an attractive woman in her early forties, with neatly-cut auburn hair and large hazel eyes, which for most of the time were intense and challenging. Everyone looked first at her and then at everyone else, with eyes darting from face-to-face as if trying to read people's reaction.

They were in the room where they had dined the previous evening and Gordon had established himself as the chair for the meeting, sitting at one end of the table directly opposite where he had shown Tom to his seat.

"Well?" Tom said.

Gordon gave Eleanor a withering look then turned to Tom.

"I'm afraid we have some bad news. Something which we assumed you must have been made aware of, but, well, it seems you possibly haven't and we've been waiting to get more information before we …"

"For God's sake, Gordon, what is it?" Tom's voice was louder than he had intended.

"We've had our first fatalities on Alpha."

Tom felt his neck and scalp go instantly cold, the same sensation he had when waking, frightened, from a very bad, very real dream, or being surprised by a sudden shock in a tense movie. The anxious faces around the table were all turned to him.

"When?" His voice was barely above a whisper.

"Monday, early morning. Two of them. It seems …"

"Monday?" Tom almost shouted. "Early morning? What do you call early?" He looked at his watch. "Before nine-fifteen, would you say?"

"Confirmed about that time …"

"Confirmed about …! So earlier than that? That's two whole days, for God's sake. Haven't you told anyone?"

"Yes, of course. The MDJ; Monday afternoon."

"And why would Ms Goody need to know before me?"

"Well, I suppose we assumed she'd …"

Allan Macready, the Secretary of State for Scotland, leaned forward in his chair. He was a large, thick-set man in his early fifties, still with a mop of black hair and a slightly greying beard. "Home Secretary," he boomed. "If our decision not to discuss the incident with you before this meeting is contrary to what you would have preferred, I ask you to at least accept that we acted, collectively, with the best of intentions. Gordon has explained that the MDJ was informed just a few hours after it was brought to his attention and we were keen to have a full picture before we released further information, be it to you or Ms Goody first. Or both at the same time," he added, with a trace of sarcasm.

"As you were in meetings or in transit the whole of yesterday, it seemed logical to wait until now for a full discussion. And if I can be so bold as to suggest, it may be more appropriate that you look elsewhere for evidence of tardiness in the communication. I am sure you will recognise the impracticability of our being charged with informing *all* interested parties of *every* development on Lochshore and Alpha. Perhaps we need to discuss at this meeting – under any other business, let's say – just how many people we need to contact, and in which order."

There was silence around the table when he finished and all eyes were on Tom. He was remembering Jenny's email; 'Anything I need to do about the Alpha thing?'

"Of course I accept that you acted with the best of intentions, Allan. How could I think otherwise of the people I know around this table? I would, however, for the foreseeable future at least, like to be made aware of all issues – *all* issues – relating to Alpha just as soon as they occur. And I ask that you accept that my reaction today was born out of shock at the event rather than criticism of the messengers, even if it sounded that way."

The whole company relaxed, most with audible sighs of relief.

"Accepted," said Allan. "And the bad weather has meant that Alpha has been virtually inaccessible for the past two days, so there's no chance at all that the media will have been able to get out there."

"The media?" Tom looked round the table, checking if he was the only one who didn't understand the point Allan was making. "What has the media got to do with it? What the hell is there to see out there?"

Allan looked across at Gordon who continued.

"It's bad, I'm afraid, Tom. We're not sure why, whether it was a fight and they were trying to get away, or they just flipped or there was a concerted attempt …"

"For goodness' sake, Gordon, you can tell me. I've been in the army like you, remember. There's nothing much …"

"The two of them are impaled on the razor wire at the top of the superstructure."

"Jesus!" said Tom.

"We couldn't understand what was happening on Sunday night, just before midnight," said Stephen Beresford. The Head of the Scottish

Prison Service was tall, with broad, muscular shoulders and chest, a ruggedly handsome face and close-cropped brown hair. "We were monitoring them on the IDTS ... Individual Data Tracking System," he added in response to Tom's quizzical look. "These two had moved upwards and away from the main group. Obviously climbing from the recreation deck up the outside of the south side accommodation block. Must have been bloody good climbers to do that."

"Or bloody desperate," put in Eleanor.

"Possibly, I guess," said Stephen.

"Almost certainly," she insisted, "given what happened next."

"We tracked them to the top of the block and assumed they would just come back down. Then we noticed a few of the others starting to climb up after them. Whether they were chasing them or trying to save them, we'll never know."

"Well, one of the two was the nephew of a High Court judge," said Eleanor, "so we can hazard a guess."

Tom looked round the table at the heads nodding in agreement.

"And then?" he prompted.

"They just kept going higher. On the screen it looked like they were flying. The digital lattice of the platform only goes as high as the top of the superstructure. The security fence is on top of that. So we realised they must be on the wire."

He stopped speaking again and swallowed, as if painfully reliving that moment.

"It's deadly stuff; razor sharp – well it would be, wouldn't it? – with lethal barbs ..." His voice tailed off.

Gordon took over again.

"As Stephen said, that happened about midnight. By around ten in the morning the IDTS indicated that they were both dead. They hadn't moved since about fifteen minutes after they went on to the wire."

Tom was silent for fully half a minute.

"Ten hours," he said. "Would we expect someone to die that quickly in those circumstances?"

"The thing is, Tom," Allan again, "we don't *know* the exact circumstances. The weather was atrocious; around zero, but with the wind – force eight – and rain, perhaps sleet ... Even so, we thought it was a bit quick, as well."

"It's possible, of course," said Eleanor, "that if there had been a fight, they might have been injured, bleeding perhaps. That could have been a factor."

"Has anyone been able to get out there to see?" asked Tom, looking round the table.

"Yes, I have." Donald McClure, the Head of Grampian Police, spoke for the first time. He was a tall man in his early fifties, slim and athletic-looking, with bright eyes and slightly receding grey hair. "We took a chopper out there Monday early pm. Just about made it there and back. Couldn't get too close, but close enough. Not pretty. Bad start."

"It was after Donny returned and confirmed the incident that I informed the MDJ," said Gordon. "*Immediately* after," he added.

"Plans for getting them down?" Tom looked round the group again.

"Not decided yet, Home Secretary," said Eleanor, formal and clipped. "This falls outside any 'what-ifs' in the NJR handbook."

"Quite," said Tom. He paused. "Look," he said, "as Donny says, this is a bad start. This will undoubtedly activate a lot of critics of the NJR," he turned to Eleanor, who pointedly returned his look, "but we are charged, through the wonder of democracy, to carry out the wishes of the populace. And taking accountability for dealing with these situations, irrespective of our personal views, is what we are paid a lot of money to do."

He continued to look at Eleanor who finally nodded briefly and looked away, more in surrender, he thought, than agreement.

"I do think Eleanor is right, though," he continued. "It seems appropriate to deal with this prior to addressing the rest of the agenda. Almost unthinkable that we don't, in fact."

The others nodded as Tom got to his feet.

"And now if you'll excuse me, I need to make a couple of calls. I'm sure you understand."

He rose and left the room before anyone had time to speak or move.

★

"Hi, Tom. Everything okay?"

"No, everything is most definitely *not* okay! Who informed you about the Alpha incident? I take it you have been informed."

There was a brief pause as Jonathan Latiffe, Minister of Justice and Tom's most senior direct report, got over his surprise at the question.

"Yes, of course. The MDJ informed me. Why?"

"And when was that?"

"Tuesday morning, really early. Around seven, seven-fifteen."

There was silence for a few moments.

"Home Secretary," Jonathan went on, "is anything wrong? Ms Goody said you had a meeting and would I attend at Downing Street. Should I have got in touch to check?"

"Of course not," said Tom. "That was absolutely right, I did have a meeting. It's just that it was one that could have been postponed. There's just been a cock-up. You won't believe this, but I've only just been made aware of the incident. Two bloody days after it happened! Not your fault, Jonno, but I should have been informed *first*. Even before the MDJ. And I certainly should have been at that meeting."

"I'm really sorry, sir."

"I'm not sir, I'm still Tom, and you don't have anything to be sorry about. As I say, it's just a cock-up, and it certainly won't happen again. I can promise that! I suppose everybody assumed somebody else would tell me. I guess we need to put out a full press statement and get someone in front of the cameras. That probably *will* be you, and the sooner ..."

Jonathan interrupted, with a voice full of apprehension.

"That's already been taken care of, Tom."

"Oh, for fuck's sake!" Tom exploded. "Well, it doesn't go out until I've okayed it! Is that clear enough?"

"What I mean is it's already out there. It was communicated in the House yesterday afternoon, and I gave a press conference immediately afterwards. I assumed you would have seen it. In fact, when Jenny told me it was you just now, I thought that's what you were phoning about, you know, with some feedback. And, of course, it's front page in the nationals today."

★

Mags and Cheryl were enjoying a Full Scottish Breakfast. They had occupied the bar until the early hours, along with John Bramham and Simon, and a group of eight Munro-baggers, seven of whom were male. They were on their way to South Ballachulish from where they planned on tackling the two separate 1,000-metre peaks of Scorr Dhumuill and Scorr Dhearg the following day.

The girls chatted about what had been an exceptionally pleasant evening, during which they were subjected to a barrage of comments, which became more personal and flattering as the evening unfolded. Only Simon, along with Rachel, the eighth member of the climbing contingent, failed to whole-heartedly enter into the high spirits, both annoyed and dismayed at their respective competition. However, they had later made amends for this initial disappointment in Rachel's room, where they shared first their grievances and then the king-size bed.

The climbing party, minus Rachel, were occupying a table for breakfast at the end of the dining room farthest away from Mags and Cheryl. They were being typically hung-over-noisy and were clearly discussing their previous evening's company. Their conversation was frequently punctuated by bawdy laughter, followed immediately by all seven turning towards them and waving cheekily.

"God," said Cheryl, "I don't know about 'if looks could kill'. If looks could *strip*, we'd both be sitting here in just our trainers."

Mags laughed.

"Yes," she said. "Not sure about those two Munros. If you asked them right now which twin peaks they'd prefer, I reckon it would be mine or yours."

Cheryl almost choked on the piece of toast she was eating.

"Mrs Tomlinson-Brown!" she scolded, laughing through a fit of coughing. "Are you allowed to say things like that?"

"Only when they're true."

They both laughed again, and looked across at the party, who returned their attention with a collective expression of puzzlement, clearly wondering why the joke was suddenly on them.

From where she was sitting, Mags saw Simon and Rachel appear and stop briefly just outside the entrance to the dining room. They exchanged a brief kiss, which quickly developed into a more passionate embrace. Then another brief kiss and Rachel entered the room to raucous cheers and applause from her companions.

"Overslept," she announced, her head bowed in a failed attempt to hide the deep blush on her cheeks.

Attention was deflected from her as Simon entered a few moments later, looking suitably flustered and apologetic. He looked around the room searching for Mags and Cheryl. He blushed as well, the colouration looking completely out of place on the rugged features above his muscular frame.

He walked across to the girls' table.

"Morning, ladies. Sorry I'm …"

"No apology required, Simon," said Mags. "Did you sleep well?" Her eyes were wide and innocent. Cheryl failed to turn her snigger into a sneeze.

"Not bad," he said, smiling in surrender. "Bed was a bit lumpy."

The girls laughed and Mags waved him to sit down as the climbing party rose to take their leave with loud goodbyes. Rachel smiled across at Simon and blew him a kiss, to his heightened embarrassment.

"She's a nice girl," said Mags. "Will you see her again?"

"Probably not," he replied. "But I hope so."

"We didn't score, by the way," said Mags.

"I'm glad to hear it," he said, with an air of officialdom. "That's why I'm here; to make sure that sort of thing doesn't happen."

They all laughed.

Mags turned to catch the waiter's attention. He was over by the window clearing plates from the table of an elderly man who was reading the morning paper. Her eyes were drawn immediately to the two-inch-high headlines on the front page.

★

"I'd like to go out to Alpha this afternoon."

They turned in their seats to face him, laptops were closed and mobiles put away. There was a shuffling, an exchange of anxious glances and a few brave headshakes, but no-one spoke.

"Is there a problem?" asked Tom.

"To what end?" asked Gordon. "What could that possibly achieve?"

"No 'end', Gordon. Just because I *want* to," returned Tom. "Look, I put that bloody great thing out there, and I put those people on it. And I am here at Lochshore, an hour away from it. I would just like to be in a position – given those circumstances – to provide the prime minister with a first hand report. I think he'd expect that, don't you? And he's entitled to expect it."

Gordon shook his head.

"We'd need to get clearance …"

"You've got it!" snapped Tom. "From the Home Secretary."

"Home Secretary, with respect, you're not the one …" Eleanor picked up the head-shaking habit.

"If you really want to show respect," interrupted Tom, his voice now threateningly calm, "you'll pick that up," he nodded to the phone in the centre of the table, "and instruct someone to start getting a helicopter ready." He looked at his watch. "We take off in one hour."

He stood in preparation to leave the room; the others rose quickly to their feet.

"Donny," he turned to the senior policeman. "I'd like you to come with me. Oh, and incidentally," he looked at the faces around the table, "*I* can fly a helicopter; so if it just so happens that there aren't any pilots available … that won't be a problem!"

He turned and left the room, heading back to his office. This time Matty, who had been sitting quietly in the room with James away from the meeting table, followed him out.

"Are you okay, Home Secretary? Can I get you a coffee – or something stronger, perhaps?"

Tom relaxed a little and smiled at him.

"I'm not ready to drown my sorrows yet, Matty, especially if I've got to drive that bloody chopper."

Matty frowned.

"Yes, I see what you …"

"It was a joke, Matty. You don't really think they'd let me loose with one of those, do you?"

Tom looked at the dejected expression on his young colleague's face.

"I guess I was a bit rough on them in there," he said. "Do you think? No-one here's done anything wrong – it may turn out that no-one anywhere's at fault. Just an accident of timing or something." He paused. "I will have that coffee, please. Get yourself one as well and bring them both in here. Thanks, Matty."

The young man left the room looking a bit brighter. Gordon had been waiting outside the door and entered as Matty left.

"Leaving in fifty minutes," he said, stiffly, and turned to leave.

"Thanks, Gordon," said Tom. "Look, I'm sorry this hasn't worked out, but cut me a bit of slack today, will you? I'm just feeling a little bit like a victim at the moment. And when you get the opportunity, will you tell that smug bitch to wipe the smirk off her face, or I might end two really promising careers – hers and mine – by doing it for her."

Gordon chuckled.

"Okay to both those requests," he said. "Incidentally, we're all coming for the ride, except James and your guy – Matty, is it? Not enough room for them. Is that alright?"

"Fine. Make sure Eleanor gets the seat nearest the door in case there's an emergency and we have to jettison something quickly."

Gordon chuckled again.

"Will do. Oh, and bad news, I'm afraid. We've got a pilot; so you'll have to sit in the back with the rest of us."

★

Mags made an excuse and left quickly to pick up a copy of the paper from the reception desk, then shortly afterwards made her way back to the dining room. John Bramham, Cheryl and Simon were waiting for her. John was wearing a sea captain's cap; the other two were smiling.

"Your transport awaits, ma'am," said John. "Just a brief walk. Please follow me."

Mags, who was expecting a ride into Oban, looked enquiringly at Cheryl, who tilted her head to one side and opened her eyes wide in a 'wait-and-see' expression. They followed John, single-file, down a narrow path from the hotel to a sheltered anchorage and a gleaming cabin cruiser. The *Wave Nymph* was a luxurious sixty-footer, fitted out with every conceivable gadget and appliance, and featuring a heated observation deck with leather seats and a fully stocked cocktail cabinet.

"Best I could do," said John. "Off-season and all that."

"Brilliant!" said Mags.

★

The EC135 lifted off from the Lochshore helipad at 11.30 am and headed north-west towards the Sound of Mull. The pilot and his seven passengers filled the police helicopter to capacity and Tom could not help contrasting this with yesterday's luxurious accommodation in the Bell 430. On the other hand, he thought, it seemed appropriate to experience some discomfort to accompany the trepidation they all felt at the prospect of what awaited them at their destination.

As they cleared the island of Kerrera and headed across the Firth of Lorne, Tom, on the right hand side of the aircraft, looked across at Eriska and wondered what Mags was doing and – much more importantly – how she was feeling right now. He noticed a cabin cruiser making its way round the southern tip of Lismore, heading towards Mull. A small charter, he guessed, taking a group of early tourists for a quiet day's trip. How he wished he was down there with them.

★

Looking up from the cruiser, one of the passengers was wondering if the police helicopter had anything to do with the 'HORROR ON ALPHA' described on the front page of the *Daily Record*. She watched it recede from view ahead of them along the Sound.

"Craignure ahoy!" someone shouted, pointing ahead to port. "Change here for Torosay Castle!"

CHAPTER NINE

"The distance from Lochshore to Alpha is one hundred and seventy miles," the pilot announced as the EC135 headed out across The Minch. "Our optimum cruising speed is one-fifty-five but with this wind speed and direction, we'll be averaging no more than about one-thirty. Total estimated journey time eighty minutes; our ETA, then, about sixty from now."

As they reached the open sea and gradually left behind the islands of Coll and Rum to their left and right, respectively, the conversation flagged and the group became silent for a long time. At their cruising altitude of 6,000 feet, Tom estimated that their horizon was over 150 miles away, but the visibility was such that they could only see for a few miles.

The flight was relatively smooth, but as Tom looked around at his travelling companions, he couldn't help wondering about the wisdom of such a senior group all travelling together in these circumstances, straight out over the Atlantic. There would be quite a flurry of bi-elections if this went down.

"There she is." Gordon broke the silence and the others leaned forward in their seats to peer ahead. But he was pointing over to the right at the far western outpost of the British Isles. He turned to Tom.

"Just how did you manage to persuade the National Trust of Scotland to let you use that? I would have thought they'd be dead against it."

"Well, we weren't initially planning an off-shore hotel," said Tom. "In fact, we were looking at putting the Exiles on Hirta. That really *was* a non-starter – double status World Heritage Site and all that. But the MOD already has it on a long-term lease for the missile tracking. That's been discontinued now, of course, and there was talk of removing the military altogether. So it sort of suited the Trust our using it as a base for supplies and services. It means a presence all year on the islands, utilities provided and maintained free of charge; *and* all the power they need – again free – from the wind farm. Most of the new storage is underground, anyway, so the only blot on the landscape is the same blot, the existing MOD buildings."

"So, everybody wins?" said Allan.

"Not everybody," Eleanor was pointing ahead.

"There she is," said the pilot, swinging the helicopter to the right and then left so that all the passengers could have the first sight of their destination still twenty or so miles away. "Hotel St Kilda!"

The spectacle drew gasps from all on board, and a quiet but distinct whimper from Eleanor. Tom felt his stomach churning.

"Officially called 'Life Exile Detention Centre Alpha'," the pilot went on, like a tour guide. "Referred to in writing as LEDCA, and verbally simply as Platform Alpha."

Tom remembered how the national dailies had had a field day, each coming up with their own name for it. Paradise City, Sea View Guest House, the Lost World of Atlantic, Fort Deverall, House of the Setting Sun and others, before they had collectively adopted it as Hotel St Kilda.

"I still can't believe how you managed to pull it off," said Allan. "I mean, how you managed to get the platform without any money to buy it with."

Tom smiled as he thought back to his trip to Düsseldorf with Grace and Reggie Greyburn, the Shadow Chancellor at the time; their meeting with the board members of Pet Euroleum, majority owners of the platform, and the incredible deal they had pulled off, exploiting the desperation of the multinational to offload their assets during the oil shortage crisis. And what a leap of faith it had been for both parties; for the oil company, anxious enough to do business with an Opposition Party months away from an election, although long odds-on favourites to win it; and for the Party itself, committing the new government – albeit *their* government – to enormous expenditure within days of their gaining office.

Tom thought also about his relationship with Grace at the time of the meeting. How secretly excited they had both been at the prospect of the brief time away together; and how Reggie had decided to turn in early the night before the meeting leaving him and Grace together in the bar with time to themselves and anything possible. In the end nothing much had happened; some 'accidental' brushing together of legs under the table accompanied by exaggerated apologies and mischievous laughter; Tom escorting Grace to her room at some time after 1.00 am; Grace opening her door with the cardkey and turning to face him; their standing toe-to-toe, with the open doorway behind her, both wondering what to do next, like school kids on a first date. Why hadn't he just pushed her into her room and done what they had both wanted? Instead he had placed his hands on her shoulders and reached forward as if to kiss her on the cheek, stopping a few inches from her face. Grace had turned her head slightly so their lips had met. No more than a brushing together, minimal contact, but by far the most significant moment in their relationship up to that point.

"Did you get much sleep?" Tom remembered asking the next morning.

"No," was the reply, with obvious regret, "but more than I actually wanted."

With the EC135 approaching directly towards the platform, it was difficult for the passengers to see it clearly – except by straining to look through the cockpit – until the pilot lost height and circled a hundred feet or so above it.

At that altitude, they were closer to the two lifeless figures on the security fence than were the people on the recreation deck below. As the chopper approached, a dozen or so sea birds that had been perched on the bodies or close to them on the wire rose and then flew down towards the waves, circling around the platform as if waiting for their chance to return. But even with the harrowing human drama to digest, the initial impact of the situation was dominated by the gigantic size of the platform and its absolute isolation. The fickle weather conditions had drawn a curtain over St Kilda again, and it was possible to believe that this was the only thing that existed on the planet.

The lines of razor wire, twenty-five in all, ran in parallel lengths round the full circumference of the superstructure, attached to vertical metal posts at six-foot intervals, creating an impassable fence thirty feet high.

The two lifeless forms were in identical positions, each with one arm and one leg stretched out ahead of the other, snared immovably as they attempted to climb either to safety or freedom. It was as if they had been crawling, single file along the ground, then frozen and turned vertically upwards through ninety degrees. The head of the leading figure hung forward, chin on chest, while the other's had fallen back and slightly to one side and was facing the sky.

As the Eurocopter drew closer still, the work of the sea birds could be clearly seen; eye sockets devoid of their contents and flesh plucked and hanging from faces and limbs.

"Can we go now?" asked Eleanor, her voice trembling. "What are we doing here anyway?"

"Yes," said Gordon, "let's head back."

"How can we get them down?" asked Tom.

"Our problem," Calum replied, with absolute authority, "but rest assured, we'll keep you informed."

No one spoke as the helicopter climbed away from the platform for the return.

Calum broke the silence. "Once the weather settles down a bit more – could be a few days yet – we'll get someone onto the fence from a chopper. We'll attach a line to each body in turn and cut the wire around them. Then we'll lift them off. Needs to be pretty still to do that though. Don't want to be sending someone else the next day to cut the winch man free."

"And the fence itself. Can we fix that?" asked Gordon.

"First things first. The fence can wait."

★

Matty was seated at the desk, a half empty polystyrene cup of coffee in one hand and his phone in the other. His laptop was open in front of him. Tom thought his relaxed manner and impeccable appearance seemed at odds with the drama going on around him. He got to his feet quickly as Tom entered.

"Hi, Matty," said Tom, waving him to be seated again. "Finish your call, but I need to make a couple myself from here pretty urgently."

"Yes, of course," said Matty, sitting back down. "Speak later," he said in to the phone, ending the call and getting to his feet again immediately. He almost ran to the door.

"Can I get you something to drink, sir?" he said, turning back as he opened it.

"No, I'm fine. Can you get in touch with James, though, and both stand by. We should be resuming the meeting very shortly."

"Okay, right away."

He closed the door behind him.

Tom picked up the receiver and entered a number.

"Hi, Shirley. Is it possible to speak to the PM right away?"

"He's in a meeting at the moment."

"That's not what I asked, was it?" he said.

"No, sorry, Home Secretary. What I mean is, do you want me to interrupt him, or can it wait?"

"Right now would be really good."

"Just a moment, please."

Thirty seconds of silence.

"Can he phone you back on that number in five minutes?"

"No, that's okay. I'll hold until you can put me through," said Tom.

"Okay, sir. I'll put you on silent hold."

Tom checked his watch. Andrew's voice ended the silence three minutes and forty seconds later.

"Tom, couldn't this have waited? I'm due at the Palace in less than an hour. I'm just preparing for it."

"*Not* in a meeting then?"

"No, but Shirley said what I told her to say, so don't get snotty with her. So what's important enough to upstage the reigning monarch of our country?"

"Well, let's see if I can think of something. Oh, I know, what about the deaths on Alpha?"

"What about them? That's old news, isn't it? Unless we've had some more."

"It's not old news, actually!" Tom erupted. "Not to me, it isn't. I only found out a few hours ago. Two days after it happened!"

111

"And? What's your point?" Andrew exploded back. "Is that what can't wait? Someone in *your* department fails to let *you* know what's going on, and you have to run to the PM. Thank goodness I've got nothing to do right now. I'll get onto it right away!"

"Right, Andrew," Tom said, regaining his composure. "Point taken. That is not what I want you to do. It's just that I arrived here this morning to find out that just about everyone in the country knew about this but me. Pretty embarrassing, to say the least. Humiliating, in fact. Just trying to find out what went wrong and I thought I'd start with the guy who knows everything." It was said with humour, rather than sarcasm.

"Okay, just a minute," Andrew said. "Shirley, get on to HRH and tell her the meeting's back on again."

Tom allowed himself a brief chuckle. "It's not good, though, is it? Something like this happening just a few days after …"

"What isn't good?" Andrew interrupted. "The fact that somebody died on Alpha?"

"Yes, but the circumstances … I've just been out there and …"

"You've *what*?!"

"I've been out to Alpha to see the damage. I thought as I was at Lochshore …"

"For Christ's sake, Tom! What do you think you've achieved by doing that? Are you planning to do that *every* time someone dies? If so, you'd better move up there permanently. We're putting eight hundred of the bastards on that platform, and what do you think their average life expectancy's going to be? Two, three years?"

"Jesus," Tom said. "Do you genuinely think that's all the time they'll have? We've never discussed it in those terms before."

"Listen, Tom. If they're *lucky* it'll be only two years or so. They're not there to learn a trade or get experience of the great outdoors. So what's the big deal? It was you who used the words – 'we need to be prepared to sacrifice part of a generation for the long term good'. That was way back at the very conception of the NJR, possibly even before then. And I said it was fantasy, remember? You must have gone over the scenarios when you worked through this thing. We are not all going to fall apart every time someone dies on Alpha. That's what's supposed to happen. We *put* them there to die!"

Tom took a few moments.

"Look, Andrew, I'd better come back tomorrow. Mags will have had a couple of days. She'll understand."

"Tom, I absolutely *insist* that you don't change your plans. Haven't you heard a word I've been saying? What has happened on Alpha is the norm. The *new* norm, I admit, but the norm all the same. This is what it's going to be like; what we have accepted. Hang on a minute..."

Tom could hear keys clicking on a keyboard. When Andrew spoke again, he was obviously reading from his screen. "'It is only natural that we should feel sympathy for the ones who have fallen by the wayside' – blah, blah, blah – 'the country gave this Government a clear mandate twenty-one months ago when it elected us on the promise of reclaiming *all* localities for the benefit of their communities'. Any of this sound familiar? Here's the really good stuff – 'there would be pain – we made that very clear – in order to achieve this and we would need to be strong when that pain manifested itself in ours and *other people's suffering*. We, this Government, this House and this country, have kept faith with that concept in pursuit of our collective vision of the future. So let there be compassion' – like that, do you? – 'but no shame; let there be some sorrow, but much rejoicing; let there be awareness of the sacrifice, but no deflection from the goal. And, most of all, let there be no turning back'" Andrew paused, then, "Great speech, don't you think? Can't for the life of me remember who made it."

Tom remained silent.

"Are you still there?"

"Yes," said Tom. "And you're right; that was a great speech."

Andrew snorted a laugh.

"So get yourself off to wherever you've planned to take Maggie – or where she's planned to take you, if what Jenny tells me is correct. You can sort out the communication cock-up when you get back. In the meantime, we take this seamlessly in our stride. The least fuss the better. And we will *not* be releasing to the press that you went out sightseeing in the Atlantic. Understood?"

"Understood."

"I just wish you hadn't, Tom."

★

"Just to let you know," Andrew said when he was put through to voicemail, "I've just talked to Brown. He's pretty mad about being circumvented in the communication, but it seems it was a good decision. God knows what he would have made of it. He talks about what's happened as if it's a major disaster, like it's a real shame these guys have to suffer at all. I don't know whether this is Maggie's influence or what. But he needs watching, closely. Whether we like it or not, for the time being anyway, he can still swing public opinion as easy as rocking a cradle. If he says the wrong thing we could have another bloody Dunkirk out there."

★

"Sorry about that," Tom said, joining the group in the meeting room. The table had been cleared of laptops and papers to accommodate a cold banquet plus bottles of wine and jugs of fruit juice and iced water.

"Wow, that looks good."

Matty and James were already circulating with coffee and tea. Matty raised his pot, catching Tom's eye.

"Thanks, Matty."

Tom looked towards Gordon.

"Should we review the agenda – again," he said, "to make sure we get through everything? Am I right in assuming we are all okay until tomorrow lunchtime? If not, then I'm the one who's twisted the schedule out of shape, so if anyone was planning to leave this evening, or earlier tomorrow, then please don't change your plans."

"I think we're all here for the duration," Gordon replied, looking round and acknowledging the nods from the group. "Do we need to discus this morning before we move on? I think we've all been very moved by what we've seen, and if anyone wants to comment on it, then it's probably better now so it's not preying on their mind as we cover the rest of the agenda."

He made a point of not looking directly at Eleanor, but it was she who spoke anyway.

"Not from my point of view," she said, "if I was the one you had in mind, Gordon. As you all know, I have been an opponent of the NJR all along, but it is here and working and, as Tom said, it is what the majority of people want. I think we need to move on – not just with the agenda, but with the understanding that Alpha is a bad place and it's that by design. Every day on the platform will be absolute hell for those on it. We just have to get our minds round that. 'Horror on Alpha', as the *Daily Record* put it this morning, is not news, it's just fact."

★

"Look," Mags said, "before you say anything, I've heard about the deaths. I am sorry about what has happened, but the subject is not for discussion as far as I'm concerned. We can talk about it next week if you want to, but I'd rather just leave it. This is the new reality, and if you and I are going to move forward, we have to accept what we can't change."

Tom was silent for a moment.

"It's a good job you're not here right now," he said. "I just might squeeze you to death."

"You could try, big boy, but I'm no push-over, you know."

"So what sort of a day did …"

"Absolutely brilliant! And guess where I've been."

"Oban, I expect …"

"No, not Oban; guess again."

"Mull?"

"Oh, you're not supposed to guess *right*!" said Mags. "Okay, then, but where on Mull, do you think?"

"I'm not saying in case I guess right again."

"Well, back to the cottage where I stayed thirty-five years ago. There, what do you think of that?"

"Gardener's Cottage?" said Tom. "Wow, I bet that was great."

"And we went there on a *train*! I can't wait to tell you all about it – in real time, probably."

"Well, you'll *have* to wait, I'm afraid, my darling. I've got less than twenty minutes to shower and change for dinner. But I really do want to hear about it."

"Okay, until tomorrow then. I've had a fantastic time, Tom-Tom. I feel really guilty, actually. I bet your day's been absolute … shite."

"Succinctly put, and one hundred percent accurate. But that's for another world. For the next few days it's just you, me and the sheepskin. And I promise you can then tell me absolutely *everything* about today – including what Cheryl was wearing," he added.

"Just watch it, you," said Mags.

They both laughed.

"Love you," said Tom.

"Love you, too."

★

The Alpha incident was not mentioned again. The atmosphere at dinner was relaxed and enjoyable; all business put to one side.

"That was absolutely excellent, Gordon," said Tom, as they finished the meal.

"Thank you, although I feel I must apologise for the repeat of the starter and dessert …"

"Not at all, that was the highlight – the two highlights – for me. Take this down, Matty – 'the Home Secretary respectfully requests that a year's supply of haggis and clooty dumpling be sent to his house with immediate effect'. That should do it."

Gordon laughed. "Well, I hope you'll also approve of some more local produce I have lined up." He went across to the long sideboard at the end of the room and took out a bottle each of Oban and Tobermory single malts.

The evening ended with an impromptu sing-a-long of traditional Scottish songs. Tom's participation was somewhat limited, but he observed with amusement as the others became involved with each new song in a sort of 'sing-off'. They all started loudly with the better-known part and then one by one dropped by the wayside as the song progressed into greater obscurity, until just a single voice remained to deliver the final verse or verses.

Although no-one was officially scoring, Tom reckoned it was a two-way tie between Donny and Calum for first place. There was applause all round as he announced the result and presented each with their medal – one of the pewter coasters which resided in a stack on the same sideboard.

The drinks, singing, applause and general laughter reflected the overall good mood of the gathering – albeit assisted by the flow of malt whisky – but left each one feeling slightly guilty in the early hours when they turned in to bed, and more than slightly fragile the following morning when they turned up for the final session.

CHAPTER TEN

Week 2; Thursday, 2 April…

"Thank you, Calum. Excellent tour," said Tom, shaking the Chief Prison Officer's hand before they all went back to the meeting room. "The whole place does you a lot of credit. When do you think you'll get PTV1 back in service?"

"Shouldn't be too long. Seven to ten days, they tell me. Well in time for the next group in six weeks time. Although we'll be reviewing the design of the rails before then to avoid the same thing happening again. And the toilet facilities as well," he added. "I assume you heard about our dirty protest."

Tom nodded. "I'm sure you'll get it right. Very impressive."

"Thank you, Home Secretary."

★

The meeting concluded on time at noon. After handshakes all round, and a polite kiss from Tom on Eleanor's cheek, James again loaded his charges into the Range Rover, including Chuck – who no-one had seen since they arrived nearly two days ago – and set off for North Connel.

Already approaching the helipad from the opposite direction, Mags and Cheryl were gushing all over John Bramham as he drove them to their rendezvous.

"It's been absolutely amazing, John," said Mags. "We really can't thank you enough. The tour of the Castle and the cottage … well, it was just … brilliant. Although I guess it meant more to me than Cheryl and Simon …?"

"Not at all," said Cheryl. "It was all superb. If this is work I'm going to get as much overtime as I can," she added.

They all laughed and Simon nodded his agreement.

Tom kissed Mags as they all met at the helipad. He gave Cheryl a gentle peck on the cheek, and shook hands with John and Simon.

"My wife's had far too good a time," he said, solemnly, to John. "You'll be hearing from me."

"I hope so," John replied. "You said something about definitely staying here yourself next time."

"And I meant it," said Tom. "As soon as we can."

They said their goodbyes; Mags and Cheryl each gave John a hug and Simon, in an uncharacteristic show of humour, pretended he was about to do the same. John stepped back in mock horror and the two men exchanged a smiling handshake. They climbed into the Bell 430 again, taking the same seats they had occupied two days ago, and lifted off for their flight to the remotest part of the British mainland.

★

"Firstly, let me thank Alan – I can call him that now, along with lots of other names I've only been able to use behind his back …"

The huge frame of David Gerrard dominated the familiar room, with its collection of work stations and its floor to ceiling white panels along the length of one wall. At a fraction under six-and-a-half feet and with a muscular frame to match, he stood half a head taller and seemed to be about a foot wider than anyone else present. He paused for the laughter to subside, as Chief Superintendent Alan Pickford wagged an admonishing finger at him.

"Let me thank him," he continued, "for waiting until I retired before banishing this young lady to another destination. As you know, she was one of only two officers nominated by Heather Rayburn, our Chief Constable, as a candidate for the new Flexible Response Teams.

"Quite honestly, I don't think I could have faced the prospect of losing her as a colleague – and my best friend – whilst I was still working here. I am, of course, delighted that she now has the chance to enhance her career with this prestigious move to Guildford, but

I'll always remember her as the Marlburgh lass here at Parkside who brightened my days in the final few years of my career. And I'll never forget the contribution she made to my own modest success during that time.

"It's a privilege to be asked to be the one to say, on behalf of everybody here, au revoir and good luck to you, and to present these gifts from all your friends. It's been a pleasure to know and work with you, Joannita Cottrell, and if you don't keep in touch, I'll report you missing to the police – and how embarrassing would *that* be?"

Jo rushed, tearfully, into his arms and they hugged for a long time. She was just above average height, with the natural curls and colouration of someone of mixed Caribbean and White British ancestry, and a pretty, friendly face, currently streaked with mascara. Detective Sergeant Omar Shakhir eventually tapped David on the shoulder.

"Excuse me, mate, there's a queue here, you know."

Jo turned and embraced Omar, and the queue duly moved forward, each with the same genuine expressions of affection.

"And now," said David to the room in general, "I suggest we all adjourn to the Wagon and Horses, and provide Alan with the platform to demonstrate the limitless spending power of a Chief Superintendent."

Laughter and the wagging finger again.

★

"How did you find this place, Maggie?" asked Cheryl as the Bell approached.

The FarCuillin Lodge on Knoydart was arguably the most isolated dwelling in the UK. Situated on the western slopes of Glen Guseran, it would normally be reached via a barely-passable trail off the narrow single-track road from Inverie, the only village on the peninsula, which was the normal stepping-off point for visitors to this remote area, and could only be accessed by boat – usually from Mallaig. The other means of reaching the region was by a sixteen mile walk through and over some very challenging terrain. That's if you didn't have the use of a helicopter, and didn't know the owner of the lodge itself.

"Well, I didn't actually find it, as such," said Mags. "I just knew it was here. It belongs to Sir Iain Ballard-McGregor. He was a close friend of my father when they were at Oxford together. Sir Iain went on to be big in the Arts and my dad in international property development, but they've remained life-long friends."

"But why would he want a place this far out?"

"Well I think he just loves Scotland, and the wilder the better."

"And it doesn't come any wilder than this," added Tom. "And that's official – you can check the guidebooks."

The Bell dropped slowly down towards the helipad, a hundred yards from the Lodge. The landing place itself had been chiselled out of the rock to create a horizontal area in the side of the Glen. The overall effect was of a natural looking, if unusual, small plateau in otherwise uneven terrain. The rugged beauty of the surroundings remained uncompromised. All seven people alighted from the aircraft, and the pilot quickly unloaded Tom and Mags's holdalls and cases. After saying their goodbyes, the rest of the party boarded the Bell again, which lifted off to take them to Inverie.

'Lodge' had seemed a rather grand title for what appeared to them at first sight to be an exact replica of an old traditional single storey croft, sporting a thatched roof and small slits of windows. It looked, from a distance, as if it had been there for hundreds of years. It was only close up that the illusion became evident. Although it resembled a typical croft in shape, it was a very much larger, two storey building. Perched on the glen side, and seen from a distance, as it usually was, with no common objects close by to measure its proportions against, there was no reason to assume it was anything other than what it was designed to look like.

The upper floor of the Lodge comprised a gallery at the back and each side of the property with bedrooms and bathrooms off it, leaving the ground floor completely open plan with a kitchen-dining area at one end and an enormous fireplace at the other, in front of which were three leather sofas in a u-formation and a large sheepskin rug. They looked appreciatively at this last item, and then at each other, with smiles as wide as the limits of their faces would allow.

"Right, let's do a recce," said Mags. "I want to see what the view's like across to Skye." They changed into their walking gear and boots before climbing the rocks behind the Lodge and picking out the jagged teeth of the Cuillin Ridge which had inspired its name from the Scottish folk song, *The Tangle o' the Isles*.

"Beautiful they may be," Mags said, "but the far Cuillin isn't pulling me away right now. This is exactly where I want to be."

They scrambled back down again. Tom fired up the oil-fuelled generator and the radiators which served the gallery area soon heated the upstairs. Mags lit the fire and stoked it up for a long burn from the pile of logs stacked at the edge of the hearth. Together they cooked themselves a simple meal, accompanied by a bottle of Australian Chardonnay and followed by a Talisker or two. After making love, with almost desperate passion, on Mags's sheepskin rug, they lay peacefully in front of the roaring fire. They were both naked except for Tom's boxer shorts and Mags's small pair of briefs.

Tom had been quiet for a long time.

"What if we just gave everything up and moved here permanently?" he said. "I don't mean *right* here, to this place, but somewhere way out. We could keep the apartment in SW1, and even something smaller near Etherington Place. We could concentrate on developing the business, but at arm's length. Perhaps Jack would be interested …"

Mags placed her hand gently on his lips to slow him down.

"Hey, whoa there," she said, with a chuckle. "That's a wonderful idea, darling, really it is, but let's not get ahead of ourselves. I would just *love* to do that, but we can't abandon Katey and Jack right now."

"Well we wouldn't be *abandoning* them, as such. Anyway, I don't want to think about the reality; I just want to enjoy the dream."

"But I suppose it doesn't *have* to be a dream," said Mags, pushing herself up on one elbow. "We could do it; we really could. That's if you *really* want it, and you're not just living this moment. Why couldn't we? I mean we could live here half the time, during the summer – or perhaps the winter when there are no midges – and …"

This time it was Tom's restraining hand.

"Hey, whoa there."

Mags pretended to bite his fingers.

"Spoil sport," she said.

"No I'm not," he replied. "Let's agree right now that we *will* do it! We'll do it in … five years' time. Katey will be through Uni, and independent. Jack will be okay. Look, it's a plan. We don't have to think any more about it right now. But let's agree we'll do it – and *mean* it!"

They lay together in silence with their separate thoughts on the adventure until Tom drifted off to sleep. Some time later Mags nudged him.

"Hey, Rip Van Winkle! Where's your stamina?"

She got slowly to her feet and pulled him to his.

"Come on, Tom-Tom, best get to bed. Got to bag a Munro tomorrow."

"We are not going anywhere *near* Ladhar Bheinn," he said. "It's too far away, too difficult and I don't want you getting over-tired for the serious stuff later. Anyway, from what Cheryl tells me, you've already bagged a few Munro-baggers."

"That girl cannot be trusted with a secret. I'm going to pick up guys on my own next time."

"Which will sort of put her at a loose end, I guess," said Tom, studying his fingernails.

"Not on your life, mate!" said Mags, dragging him towards the staircase. "Time for one more?"

Tom swept her up in his arms and crouched down in front of the fire, rolling her back onto the rug.

"Right, you've asked for this!" he said.

"Help, help, get off me, you beast," she whispered.

★

Week 2; Friday, 3 April…

Tom knew he had to get them down. In spite of what had been said about the new normality of the situation, he had put them there and he needed to act. Not only that, but the previous night, as he and Mags had drifted off to sleep, the nagging apprehension about Katey and Jack's party had returned. The unsettling thoughts about his children were, in his tired mind, somehow inextricably linked with the Exiles trapped on the wire,

Even so, it was good to be going into action again. He glanced down with affection at his uniform with its random four-colour design. DPM – Disruptive Pattern Material – the camouflage worn by just about every land-based or land-bound member of the UK and Commonwealth Armed Forces. He reached up to feel the lovat-green beret and traced his finger around the cap-badge with its upward-pointing sword insignia of the Special Boat Service. Whatever the seriousness of this mission, his spirits were lifted by a feeling of being back where he belonged.

The men wearing the same battledress waiting for him near the rumbling Super Lynx helicopter were all familiar to him; the group he would have chosen for every mission given the chance to make his own selection. They all had nicknames, of course; it was almost unthinkable that someone should be known by their given name. In fact, the use of nicknames was actively encouraged. It helped preserve the anonymity of personnel in the Special Forces, whose real names were never officially released into the public domain.

"Hey, Blisters! How's the feet?" shouted Tom, embracing the smiling, stocky soldier who almost crushed him with his powerful arms. Anthony 'Blisters' McNaughton, at the end of the most brutal day, with bits of him held in place by straps and bandages, would only ever complain about the soles of his feet and how they could never provide him with boots which properly fitted him.

A shadow engulfed both men as the massive figure of Idobu Bondi, a native-born Nigerian, loomed over them. He slapped Tom on the back, almost knocking him down, his face shining with pleasure.

"Chalky!" said Tom. "Christ, are you still growing?"

The big man stepped forward and hugged him. Someone had once pointed out that every unit had to have a 'Chalky', and as there was no-one in theirs called White, Idobu would have to do. Chalky eventually released him and Tom, gasping for breath looked wide-eyed at the next man stepping forward to greet him.

"I don't believe it," said Tom. "I thought you'd have been shot dead by a jealous husband by now!" The two men embraced. Gary 'Anything' Henderson – known as 'A.T.' for short – had been named for his legendary reputation when it came to targeting someone to sleep with.

"They tried, Tuber, but they missed. Big advantage being not much of a target." He was no more than average height, slim and wiry, and by far the smallest of the group.

Standing next in line was the baby of the team; the last one to join the group and the wildest of them all. A fiery, red-haired young Scot with the physique of a champion body-builder. Even so, Terry 'Big Mac' McQueen had earned his nickname through his addiction to burgers rather than his size and ancestry.

"See *you*, Jimmy!" said Tom, with the widest of grins, prodding him in the chest.

"That's the worst fucking Scottish accent I've heard since I watched *Brigadoon*, Major … sir."

They all laughed, happy to be together again. Then, behind them, Tom spotted another figure, this one in the sand-coloured beret of the SAS with its inverted sword insignia.

Tom gasped. "Sweet! Sweet Deverall! What the hell …? You look great. What happened – miracle cure?"

Jad laughed.

"Nothing was going to stop me," he said. "Not from the chance of one more mission with you."

They embraced, and then the whole six-man team boarded the Lynx. Blisters and Big Mac seated themselves at the controls; the rotors engaged. The others settled comfortably and naturally into their seats and after two minutes of intensifying noise the two 1120-shp Rolls-Royce engines seemed to throw them into the sky. The nose dipped and the helicopter raced away, quickly reaching its maximum speed of around 180 mph.

It seemed to Tom that he had never been away. None of them appeared to him to have changed at all; even Jad looked completely restored to his former self. The banter in the cabin was so familiar that Tom could almost speak the words before he heard them from his comrades. He had almost forgotten the grim purpose of their mission when he was suddenly snapped out of his nostalgia.

"Target dead ahead! Three miles! Positions!" shouted Big Mac.

Tom looked out of the side window but could see nothing except dense swirling mist.

Chalky and A.T. moved quickly on Big Mac's command to the door on the left side of the aircraft, sliding it back and subjecting the cabin to the intense cold of the Atlantic weather. They unclipped the pintle-mounted heavy machine gun from its restraining brackets just forward of the door, and swung it round on its rotation arm through 180 degrees, securing it against the bulkhead in its attack position aiming outwards through the opening. Settling behind it, Chalky adjusted trajectory and sights.

"Check ATS!" Big Mac again.

"Missiles ready." Blisters responded.

Tom looked anxiously around the cabin trying to understand what was happening, wondering why they would need machine guns and air-to-surface missiles. Before he could speak, Big Mac's voice cut across his thoughts.

"Circling Alpha now. Port side."

Tom, seated on the left-hand-side of the aircraft, looked out of his window. The mist had parted revealing the structure five hundred feet or so below them. Except it was not the structure. It was nothing like it. It was more like a house. A large house in extensive grounds. There were lawns and ponds and fountains, and people running and shouting. Rock music coming from somewhere. *His* house! He had never seen it this close from the air before, but it must be his house.

Then the mist took the image away, and a voice brought him out of his day-dream.

"Closing at same altitude as target. Circling first to confirm."

Tom looked across from his window. There it was, the security fence. About twenty feet of it sticking up out of the dense mist below with the two figures impaled upon it. But this was not at all as he remembered the scene from less than two days ago. In fact, the figures were not impaled; they were clinging to the wire in desperation. One of them was actually waving at the Lynx. And as the helicopter moved closer to them in decreasing circles, Tom almost fainted with shock.

The people on the wire were known to him; very well known. On the smaller of the two he saw the pale blue dress and white tights, torn and streaked red with blood from the wounds inflicted by the wire and the sea birds; the face turned towards him, the white-blonde hair blowing wildly above it. The eye sockets were not empty, and the eyes burned into him with a furious hatred. The waving figure, also ragged and bleeding, the pale clothing all but ripped completely away, gazed at him with a pleading expression. The gashed mouth formed the words in slow motion, inaudible above the roar of the engines, but unmistakable nonetheless.

"Please … help … me … Dad!"

Another barked order from the cockpit and then the deafening sound of the machine gun, just a couple of feet away from him. He watched the two figures jerking violently in their death throes as they were repeatedly hit, their screams loud enough to compete with the rotors and the gun.

"*Noooooo!*"

Tom was yelling in his agony of guilt and despair. He turned desperately to Jad for some sort of explanation, some rationale. But his friend was now lying on the floor of the Lynx. His beret had gone, he was covered by a sheet and his pallor and the thinness of his face had returned to how Tom remembered it just a few days ago.

"Better this way, Tom," he said, tears in his eyes. "You said so yourself, or at least you thought it. They're the lucky ones; just a few days of torment, and then death…"

"*Noooooo!*"

Tom shouted again, lurching forward. Restraining arms were round his shoulders, a voice was calling his name.

"Tom! Tom!"

A woman's voice.

"Tom! Darling! What's wrong? Please, *please*, wake up!"

He was sitting up staring at a blank wall. The bedclothes had been thrown off and he was soaking wet with sweat. Mags was hugging him tightly from behind, her arms vice-like round his chest, both controlling and comforting, and her head on his shoulder pressed against his cheek. He was shaking and breathing heavily, but after a couple of minutes he began to relax.

"Bad dream," he said.

"No! Really?" said Mags.

He lay back and she kissed him on the forehead, stroking his cheek and temple for a long time until he fully recovered. "Do you want to tell me what it was about – as if I couldn't guess?"

Tom did not reply at first. When he did it was in a voice trembling with pretended terror.

"Well, I was chasing Cheryl down this corridor," he said. "She was throwing her clothes off as she ran and I was shouting after her, begging her to put them on again. She turned a corner…"

Mags stopped stroking his cheek and roughly grabbed and twisted his ear.

"And when I followed her round, there she was, stark naked, waiting for me! It was horrible. I guess I just panicked and shouted out."

"What a remarkable coincidence," said Mags. "I just had the same dream about Matty and this group of Munro-baggers chasing me. I was running down this corridor throwing off my …"

Tom turned to her and rolled her onto her back slipping one of his legs between hers.

"Right, you've asked for this," he said.

"What again? But I haven't told you how my dream ended yet."

★

Tom was awoken by Mags slipping into bed beside him, holding a mug of coffee. He lay quietly watching her as she sipped her drink, unaware that he was awake. He marvelled again at how beautiful she looked; how she never looked anything less under any circumstances, dressed for a ball or just emerging from a long, deep sleep. He placed his hand on her bare midriff under the duvet, causing her to start and almost spill her coffee.

She smiled across at him.

"Morning, Tom-Tom. No more nasty dreams?"

"Morning, darling. No more nasty dreams."

"You never told me what it was really about," she said, suddenly serious.

"Just what you thought, I guess. A hangover from Wednesday. You know, the images of the platform …"

That was as much as he wanted to say.

"Poor you," she said, putting down her mug and snuggling up against him. They lay like that for a long time.

★

Week 2; Saturday, 4 April…

The land-line phone ringing on her bedside table woke Mags up. She grabbed at it, clumsily juggling with the handset for a few moments before pressing it to her ear.

128

"Oh, hi!" she said, turning to Tom, who was blinking himself awake. "Katey," she mouthed at him.

"Just thought I'd phone to confirm that we've come through all the excitement completely unscathed," said Katey.

"That's great," said Mags. She gave a 'thumbs-up' sign to Tom with her free hand. "Good time?"

"Yes, really good. Must have had about two hundred round all together. And live music, no less. Mickey got us this singer and one of the bands he manages. Lilli Bo-peep and Abattoir Ratts. I know them, actually. Really nice guys and they were absolutely brilliant, and did it for nothing – well they didn't charge *us* anything, anyway."

"That's fantastic," said Mags. She checked the time. "It's only nine-thirty. That's very early for a morning-after-party call. You actually woke us up."

"Sorry about that. It went on 'til about three o'clock, but nobody misbehaved. And Dad's heavies played it really low key, although there seemed to be more of them than usual. I don't know whether he'd drafted in reinforcements. But they behaved impeccably – tell him – didn't throw anybody out or beat anybody up or anything. Oh, except they did frog-march somebody back *in* when they thought he'd given them a false name or something; but it wasn't a problem. Jack seemed to thoroughly enjoy himself as well, although I haven't seen him yet this morning. Or Megan."

"Megan! I see. Is this serious with Megan, do you think?"

"About as serious as my big brother can get, I reckon. Mind you, they had a bit of a fall-out last night. I think the singer has quite a thing for Jack and – well, you know what they're like – he didn't exactly discourage her. It must be pretty serious though, because he said he was going to bring her round to meet you both. She's really nice; you'll like her."

"I'll look forward to that. Is Jason there?"

"No, he went home quite early – around midnight. Their house was broken into on Thursday during the day. They did about half-a-dozen other houses down their street at the same time. His mum's really shaken up so he didn't want to leave her alone all night."

"Oh, that's a shame; poor woman. Did they take much?"

"Well, sadly, they don't have much to take, but it doesn't seem there was anything missing."

"Oh well, I guess that's something to be thankful for – nothing stolen, I mean. Did everyone turn up who you were expecting?"

"Yes and a hell of a lot more. Well, actually, Mickey himself didn't show his face. Surprising, because he'd helped arrange it – I mean the band and that. No doubt we'll find out why when we see him. I don't expect the Home Secretary will be too disappointed at his absence," she added. "Is he there?"

"Yes, right beside me. Where else would he be? But don't worry; he can't hear what you're saying."

She looked at Tom, with wide conspiratorial eyes.

He laughed.

"Give Katey my love," he mimed, then got out of bed and went downstairs.

"Anyway, what have you two been doing to make you sleep this long?" asked Katey. "And remember, I'm your daughter. I'm not expecting too much detail."

Mags laughed.

"Well, put it down to the soporific properties of the Chardonnay and Talisker, and the expending of so much energy hiking."

"And then there's the map-reading, of course," said Katey. "I saw last weekend how much that was taking out of you both."

Mags laughed again.

"By the way, Dad sends his love."

"Thanks. What do you have planned for today?"

"More walking, hopefully. It's beautiful here, Katey. We must *all* come some time – including Jason – and, who knows, perhaps Megan as well."

"Who knows? Anyway, must go and get dressed. Love to Dad. Bye, Mum."

"Bye."

She put down the phone just as Tom arrived carrying a tray.

"Right," he said, handing Mags her coffee and slipping back into bed beside her. "I'll just drink this and then I'm ready for anything. And I mean absolutely *anything!*"

"Well drink up quickly, then," she said. "And don't worry about burning your lips. I know exactly where you can cool them down."

She took Tom's free hand and pulled it down under the duvet.

"Perhaps we should stay just like this until the helicopter picks us up," he said.

"That's tomorrow," said Mags, smiling broadly.

"I know, but we could always put it back a couple of days."

★

Week 2; Sunday, 5 April…

The large man drumming his fingers on the desk looked very different in his dark grey suit, lilac shirt and purple-and-white striped tie. So much so that he seemed almost like an intruder in his own office, sitting in his own chair.

"So what have you got that's important enough for me to miss my weekly appointment with God?"

"I'm sorry, sir. It could have waited. When I called I didn't expect you to come straight away."

"Not a problem, Inspector. There are enough decent baritones in the congregation without me. You might have to write me a note, though, so my wife doesn't think I've just skived off."

The DI laughed.

"So, do tell."

"Just feedback from the op, sir. Or more to the point, *no* feedback from the op."

"Meaning?"

"No action at all – well, none observed. There was an issue with one camera, but we think we know why. Nothing sinister or suspicious."

"So what does this tell us?"

"Precisely nothing, I suppose. Which is a lot better than *something* that we didn't want to hear. I think we've had enough of that."

"And the targets?"

"Visible virtually all the time, sir. Fully accounted for. No time out worth recording."

"You're right; no news *is* good news on this occasion."

"Even so, not surprising, I suppose, given the level of surveillance. Not that I want to put a damper on it …"

"Well you just *did*. But you're right, of course. It doesn't actually change anything."

CHAPTER ELEVEN

Week 3; Monday, 6 April…

Tom sat at the breakfast bar in the kitchen, laptop open, trawling through his emails when his mobile pinged with an incoming text message. It was from Jonathan Latiffe. He checked his watch – 6.45 am.

'Please call. Alpha again. Stuff to know.'

Tom topped up his cup from the cafetière on the worktop then perched on a bar stool again to make the call. Jonathan answered immediately.

"Hi, Tom. Just felt you ought to know what you'll be walking in to today. They tried earlier this morning to get them down off the wire, but when the chopper got close, it came under attack from some of the guys. A few had climbed up to the top of South Block and started throwing stuff at it. They had to get away fast."

"So they haven't got them down yet?"

"Right. They figured there was no point in trying again straight away. Thought exactly the same would happen."

"They did the right thing," said Tom. "Any one hurt?"

"No, but I think the crew were pretty shaken up."

"I'm not surprised," Tom. "Look, Jonno, you can fill me in on the details when I get in. Are you okay to meet me at around nine?"

"Yes, I expected you'd want to. Jenny was holding everything until after your meeting with the PM at ten-thirty. So there's space on CT."

"Good. What about the press?" asked Tom.

"Well, the mission was around five this morning – that's the best time, when everyone's at their lowest …"

"I know the theory well," said Tom.

"Well, it seems for these guys it *is* just a theory. Too early to be sure about the press – only happened a couple of hours ago. But seems unlikely at that time in the morning."

"Had any contact or comments from the PM or Grace about the deaths since we last spoke?"

"No, except it was Grace who told me about the rescue attempt, just a few minutes before I sent you the text. She asked me to bring you up to date right away. And I think she's planning to be at your meeting with Andrew, or at least for part of it."

He ended the call and entered his 9.00 am meeting with Jonathan on Corporate Time, and then his mobile sounded again. It was Jenny.

"Hi, Jenny. How are you?"

"I'm fine, thank you, Home Secretary. And you? Did you have a good time?"

"It was absolutely great. And thanks again for making the arrangements – and on a Sunday. I guess I owe you a day off in lieu for that."

Jenny laughed.

"So put me out of my misery," he said. "What do you have to tell me? I can take just about anything except the news that you're looking for another job."

She laughed again. "Well you can relax, then. As if I would ever do that. It's just to let you know that the press gang is gathering outside. They've been checking that you are back at the Street today, so I'm afraid you must be the target. I guess they'll want your comments on Alpha."

He looked at his watch – 7.15 am.

"You're at work already? Do you *enjoy* making me feel guilty?" he said. "Anyway, thanks for the heads-up. By the way, I've spoken to Mr Latiffe this morning and I'm meeting with him at nine o'clock. Just so you don't send him away if he gets there before me. Looking forward to seeing you again very soon."

"That's exactly what I was going to say, Home Secretary!"

Mags appeared, yawning in the doorway, just as the gravel crunched outside signalling the arrival of Tom's car.

"Oh no!" she said. "Paul's here already. No time for a quickie."

"Tell you what," said Tom. "You can fondle me while I'm cleaning my teeth."

"You really do spoil me, don't you?"

★

Guildford Centre of Justice was a huge new complex, which included a range of facilities located in buildings around New Station Yard, a massive rectangular courtyard. The Centre had been developed to reflect Guildford's status as one of the NJR's regional hubs. Dominating the site, opposite the main vehicular entrance to the courtyard, was Guildford New Station, the police headquarters for the South Thames Division covering the area bounded by the Metropolitan Police District to the north, the M3 to the west and the English Channel to the south and east, and which housed the region's Flexible Response Teams.

In his palatial office on the second floor, Chief Superintendent John Mackay rose from his chair to welcome his new recruit. John was a large man who carried just a little too much weight around his middle, although his light athletic movements belied his fifty-plus years.

"Detective Inspector Cottrell," he said, beaming and extending his hand. "Welcome aboard. Delighted to have you on the team."

"Thank you, sir," said Jo. "I'm very happy to be here."

He gestured for her to sit down.

"Before we start," he said, "have you had breakfast? I don't suppose you have."

"No, sir, but I don't usually have much, just coffee and toast. I managed half of that this morning before I set off."

"Must have been an early start; so let's put that right. I can really recommend the toasted teacakes. Let's rustle up a plateful before we get down to business. Okay?"

"Definitely, sir," said Jo, with a relaxed smile.

John pressed a button on the desk phone and a voice crackled on the loudspeaker.

"Yes, sir?"

"Alice, can you get us some coffee and teacakes, please, right away."

"I've got them standing by in the canteen, sir."

John laughed. "Am I that predictable?"

"Consistent is a better word," Alice replied.

He laughed again as he released the button.

"But predictable is more accurate," he said to Jo, who was still smiling.

★

"Good morning, Tom. Welcome back."

The prime minister's private office at Number Ten, or his 'inner sanctum' as he liked to call it, was a functional room lacking the opulence and grandeur of the rest of the famous address. It featured an antique wooden desk with red leather inlay covered by a glass top, and, behind it, a well-upholstered swivel chair of similar vintage. In front of the desk, and facing it, was a pair of wing chairs a couple of feet apart and turned slightly in towards each other. A huge sideboard occupied one side of the room and floor-to-ceiling book shelves the other. In front of the book shelves was a low, circular glass-topped table between two armchairs. A single, plain chandelier hung from the ceiling.

Grace was already seated in one of the wing chairs and looked as though she had been there for some time. Evidence of that was a nearly empty coffee cup in front of her on the corner of Andrew's desk. Her eyes met his, betraying no indication of either her mood or her feelings towards him.

"We felt it was important that you were up to date with the Alpha situation," said Andrew. "*Especially* after what happened last week," he added.

"Jonathan told me about the aborted attempt to get them off this morning," said Tom.

"Splendid!" said Andrew, waving him to the vacant wing chair. "So we're all friends again at the Home Office. I'm so pleased. Grace, do you want to bring the Home Secretary *even further* up to date."

"Yes, of course." She turned to Tom, with the same dispassionate expression. "We'll be making a further attempt in a couple of days' time depending on the weather conditions. We'll use two choppers this time. If we've got personnel on the superstructure we'll send in a Wildcat first to strafe the roof of South Block with live ammo, so they'll be clear that we mean business. If that doesn't send them back straight away, we'll get in as close as possible and aim directly at them with a second machine gun loaded with blanks, using a hailer instructing them to climb down. If needed, we'll fire a few blank bursts to simulate the start of an attack. Once they've retreated, the second chopper will go in and release the two on the wire."

"Sounds good," said Tom, thinking how eerily similar it sounded to his own dream attack on the platform. "What happens if that doesn't work?"

"Then they'll withdraw," said Grace, "and we'll look for a Plan C. But any third attempt is likely to feature live ammunition in both machine guns."

"In the meantime," put in Andrew, "let's hope Plan B works. Thank you, Grace."

Grace rose from her chair.

"Yes, thanks, Grace," said Tom, standing up.

Their eyes met briefly again.

★

"My main concern, Tom, is that you may be incapable of taking a step back from what is now a done deal."

After Grace's departure, Andrew had ordered coffee and croissants and the two men had moved away from the desk to occupy the arm chairs which faced each other over the low table where the refreshments had been placed..

"The NJR is no longer a hands-on priority for the Home Secretary," Andrew continued. "Yours is a leadership role, not even a management function. You've done the job – defined the future state and facilitated our getting there. That's what leaders do – not dash around in helicopters interfering in other people's work."

"I think that's very harsh, Andrew. If it *is* a done deal …"

"It *is*, Tom, there is no '*if*' …"

"Okay, point taken, but let me put it another way, then. *If* my hands-on involvement with the NJR *is* finished, then it's only *just* finished. Until the feedback to the House last week, you seemed perfectly happy with what I was doing. And my impression – and other people's – was that the speech itself went well. So what other things have led you to this conclusion?"

Andrew was silent for several moments.

"Let me turn this around, Tom, and ask *you* a question. Do you honestly feel you can now turn away from the new regime and leave it with Latiffe – and Goody, I suppose? That's what you need to do, and what I *insist* that you do. They are more than capable of taking the reins, and you will just screw up their jobs if you don't back off."

Tom leaned forward, but Andrew held up his hand to stop him and continued.

"And you asked about other things. I just have an uneasy feeling about your attitude towards certain elements of the NJR itself. The opening to your speech in the House – the bit about the prayers – was way over the top on the sympathy side. To be fair, you got away with it, but that could have been interpreted as an expression of doubt – wondering if it was really okay what we'd done. We can't afford that. And then there's this knee-jerk reaction in charging off to Alpha to see those bastards on the wire. Given what nearly happened to that chopper this morning, we could have lost the Home Secretary and the Scottish Secretary plus a couple of MPs all in the same pointless exercise. So tell me, *are* you having second thoughts on some of the provisions?"

"Absolutely not! And, as I said, I think that's harsh, drawing that sort of conclusion from two minor incidents after more than three years of my unswerving pursuit of this new justice system. Here's an example within this timeframe that you've chosen *not* to mention – my extending the provisions to hit drug dealers, *and* in the face of some opposition. It was on *my* insistence that it went through, with your backing, of course. I hardly think that points to a softening of my commitment to the overriding principles. But …" it was Tom's turn to raise his hand to stop Andrew jumping in, "I will admit that it will be a wrench to hand over the reins to Jonathan. However, it's a challenge that I will meet, so you need have no worries about that. Okay?"

Andrew paused before responding.

"Whatever we decide, Tom," he said, "I want you to be comfortable with it. So, if you're telling me right now that you can leave Latiffe alone to manage this, then that's great. We'll give it a go and review it again in, say, three months. In the meantime, we won't say anything more about it. Okay?"

Tom nodded.

"*However,* that's just one option," said Andrew, leaning forward. "But here are a couple of others I'd like you think about. *Either* … we detach Home and Justice again and Latiffe gets full Cabinet status, and this time Police Reform goes with Justice, rather than shared. You stay Home Secretary. And you can't say Jonathan doesn't *deserve* a full Cabinet role based on his support as a Shadow Minister.

"*Or* … we focus you on the current real biggy – Security and Counter Terrorism, and make you Minister of State. That would mean shunting Ruby Weller to one side, of course. I could try to get the role up-graded to Cabinet level, but frankly, I'd rather not, and I'm not sure I could anyway. That would mean a step back, but we can position that carefully. We'd say we were focussing you on where your strengths lay, ex Special Forces, wealth of practical knowledge, et cetera. We would make it absolutely clear that it's not a question of demotion."

"Even though it would be," Tom said.

"Well, yes," said Andrew, "in hierarchical terms, but not in the context of visibility or salary, if I get my way. This could, in fact, *raise* your profile again. You're a campaigner, Tom; an agent for change. The NJR's all about the status quo now; a *new* status quo – if that's not a contradiction in terms – but, all the same, a maintenance job."

Tom did not reply.

"Look, let's leave it for now, but please think about those options. Let's get together again in, say, ten days time – a week on Thursday – and let me have your thoughts. And, as I said, if you want to stay as we are for now, then we'll review it after three months. Okay?"

Tom nodded and rose from his seat, taking the prime minister's offered hand.

★

"Same again all round?" Jack asked the five people sitting with him in the Cross Keys beer garden. The large open area behind the pub was crowded with young people clustered around the dozen or so wooden tables. A number of unhealthy-looking potted plants in a variety of tubs, were dotted around between the tables, all hung with strings of lights. Music could be heard from inside in the public bar, the whole creating an unlikely party atmosphere for a Monday lunchtime.

"Yes please," said Jason, pushing his empty pint glass across the table towards him.

"He means 'no thanks'," said Katey, standing up and grabbing Jason under the arms, pulling him to his feet.

Jason stretched and sighed in resignation, smiling broadly. Just nineteen and a fraction under six feet, he was slim and broad shouldered, with a handsome face which featured shining eyes and a wide smile. His hair was short and styled, but retained some of the natural curl which was his Kenyan birthright.

"We're leaving," said Katey. "Come on, you're taking me to the movies."

"I love it when you beg," said Jason.

The others laughed.

"See you later," said Katey, over her shoulder, as they walked away, arms around each other.

The group had met up on Monday lunchtime as usual. They were reviewing Friday's festivities and sharing claims about the amount each of them had drunk on the night.

"Tell you what," said Jack, "if this random sample of six is typical – consumption-wise – of the wider population, then I haven't a clue where all the booze came from."

"Well it can't be truly representative, can it," one of the two girls present pointed out, "because one of the sample wasn't there at all."

"Okay, Jade, sample of five," said Jack, turning to Mickey Kadawe. "Yes, come to think of it, you haven't come up with an excuse for not attending. Have you got an absence note or anything?"

"Now don't try and embarrass me, Jack," said Mickey. "You know I don't like parties …"

The other three jeered.

"Oh no. I forgot," said Jade.

"Come on, Mickey. I'm serious," said Jack. "What could possibly have been more important than spending an evening with a bunch of beautiful women? Like Megan and Jade, here."

He waved an arm towards the girls. They were similar in appearance; slim, with long blonde hair tied back in ponytails and wearing tight denim jeans and loose tops over tee shirts.

"Yes," said Jade. "Come on, tell us."

"Unless, of course," put in Megan, "it was because of just *one* beautiful woman somewhere else."

"Okay," said Mickey, raising his arms in a gesture of surrender. "Guilty as charged. It wasn't a date, though; it was someone over from Jo'burg, a friend from my mysterious past. I gave her a lift to Heathrow and her flight was delayed for a couple of hours. So I stayed with her to keep her company. It was after eleven-thirty when I got back. I was far too wasted to start boogying at that time."

"What do you think?" Jack asked the girls. "Do we believe him?"

"Mmm…" Jade wasn't sure.

"Slightly more believable than him not liking parties, I suppose," said Megan.

"That settles it, then," said Jack. "You're off the hook, Kadawe. Just this once. So, I ask again, same all round?"

"My turn," Jade raised her hand. "Sex equality, and all that."

"I accept," said Jack. "Just because I'm a rich kid, doesn't mean I have any pride. Double whisky and lemonade, please."

"Same here," said Mickey. "In fact, make it a treble. Oh, and some crisps as well…"

Jade stood up.

"Okay, that's two halves of Stella. And what would you like, Megan?"

"Orange juice, please."

Jack and Mickey looked at each other and shrugged in mock disappointment.

"Worth a try," said Mickey.

★

Jo had an excellent first day, spent mostly in the company of her new boss. He had an easy charm which made her feel both relaxed and attentive as he showed her round the Centre, introduced her to her colleagues and went through the fundamentals of her new position,

140

in particular the differences from her previous experience as an Area Detective Inspector.

"I think the biggest challenge," he said, "will be integration with the local Forces. Everyone is aware that you people are, in effect, an elite group. As Tom Brown put it, you are to the police what the SAS is to the army, the SBS to the navy. And, like that analogy, we take only the best from the main Force.

"The big danger, of course, is in the breeding of resentment. Because where the analogy with the Special Forces breaks down is that you won't be doing anything different from what the Area Force is doing. You are there to help, to provide additional manpower, and special qualities and skills. You'll build respect and gain your acceptance over time, with positive contributions and excellent results. I have absolutely no doubt about that. But I think it could be rocky to start with. I think you might feel you're piggy-in-the-middle between the law and the lawless for a while; hopefully not for long.

"One way we've mitigated these concerns," he went on, "is by keeping accountability – and hence over-riding authority – with the local Area Forces. So wherever you work, anywhere in the UK, your assignment boss will be a local DCI or, more likely, Detective Super. That way, the focus – and the credit – will stay within the area."

"And what about the blame, sir?" Jo was relaxed and confident enough to make a joke. "If things don't go to plan."

John laughed.

"We'll make sure they get that as well."

★

Tom watched the gates slowly open as Paul turned off the lane and their escort car sped away. Mags was waiting for him on the porch.

"What are you smiling at?" she said.

"I'm just happy to be coming home to the world's sexist woman."

"Well, I know *that*. But there's something else. It's sort of satisfied going on smug, I would say."

"That's an excellent description, actually. Because, after a meeting with Andrew which was full of the unexpected, including an attack on my ability to do my job, the greatest surprise of all is how little I care about what he said. I've been thinking about the plans we made on the rug in front of the fire in Knoydart, and wondering whether five years is too long to wait."

Mags smiled at him. "Well, we should talk about that – but later perhaps. In the meantime, I've been thinking about the other things we did on the rug in front of the fire in Knoydart."

She took his hand and led him inside.

★

Tom looked at the clock on his bedside table – 11.30 pm. He could hardly have been asleep for more than a few minutes. He gently untangled himself from Mags, trying not to disturb her.

"What's wrong?" she said, blinking herself awake.

He swung his legs out of bed.

"Has Jack come in?"

Mags sat up. "I don't think so."

He got up to check, looking along the corridor towards Jack's room. Katey's head appeared, peering out from her own room further along and looking back towards him.

"Did you hear something?" she asked.

"I thought I did. A mobile, was it? I thought it might be Jack's."

"It wasn't his phone," said Katey. "I didn't recognise the ring tone."

"He's not back, is he?" asked Tom. "I thought he was out tonight."

Tom knocked on Jack's door. No answer. He opened it and they both went in. There was no one there. The bed had been half-made after the previous night, but it was clear that it hadn't been slept in since.

Mags appeared in the doorway.

"What's going on?"

"We thought we heard a phone," said Katey.

"Should we check downstairs?" asked Mags.

"I'll go," said Tom. "You two wait here in case it rings again."

Ten minutes later he was back.

"Nothing," he said. "Anyway, if it was a phone, it was definitely up here. I must have dreamt it."

"It must have been *something*," said Katey. "We can't both have dreamt the same thing."

"Well, whatever it was, there's nothing we can do," said Mags. "Night, Katey." She gave their daughter a brief hug and they all went back to bed.

Tom and Mags wrapped their arms around each other and Mags was asleep again within a couple of minutes. Tom lay awake for a long time.

★

Two days later
Week 3; Wednesday, 8 April…

"No sign of life."

The voice crackled over the radio. The Wildcat dropped low to make sure, dipping into the huge box formed by the accommodation blocks round the sides of the platform, and out of sight of the second aircraft.

"Okay to go." The same voice, as the helicopter rose into view again, climbing vertically to hover a few hundred feet above the highest point of the fence.

The EC135 moved in below it, the winch man already descending towards the bodies on the wire. When he was level with the highest one, he signalled to the chopper which moved him laterally until he could reach the lifeless form. He slipped a harness onto the body, securing it under the arms and crotch, then unclipped a pair of heavy-duty wire-cutters from his belt and got to work.

He needed only half a dozen cuts to release him from the wire, and they swung away from the fence as the Eurocopter pulled clear and started to hoist them up. He turned his head away from the horrifying sight hanging closely in front of him, the shredded remains of the young man's face only inches from his own. A crew man pulled the body into the helicopter and released the harness.

"You okay?"

The winch man swallowed and nodded; and set off down again.

★

143

"A call box! Who the hell uses a call box these days?"

"Well, apart from people who don't have a mobile or a house phone, sir, anyone who wants to get rid of the phone afterwards. You just walk away from it," said the DI. Today it was his turn to be sitting down watching someone pacing the room. A large man in a senior officer's uniform.

"Yes, silly question."

"We found the box, lifted some prints; hundreds of them, in fact. So, don't hold your breath, sir. There's nothing we can use."

"Doesn't matter anyway. It's the message we need to focus on, not the caller."

"Yes, sir."

"And that was very specific."

"Yes, sir."

They were both silent for a moment. The senior man stopped pacing and leant on the back of his chair. He spoke slowly, choosing his words carefully.

"Right. We've been very diligent with this, Harry. Very meticulous, very critical, treating with suspicion every bit of evidence as it's come in. More so than in any normal case – and for good reasons. But that stops *now*, with this latest piece in the puzzle. From this moment it *is* a normal case and we do what we do as well as any bunch of cops anywhere. We go by the book and get a result. I want you on target two; I'll get one of the FRTs to take target one. We'll go early next week."

"With respect, sir, should we wait?"

"I know what you mean, but in spite of what I've just said, I want one more trawl through everything we've got. And there's no reason to think anything will change between now and then."

"Very well, sir."

They were silent again for a while.

"Have you seen the movie *Journey to the Centre of the Earth*?"

"Yes, sir. Brendan Fraser wasn't it?"

"Actually I was thinking of the earlier one – end of the fifties, I think it was. James Mason and Pat Boone." He sat down and leaned forward with his elbows on the desk. "There's a scene at the end where they're sitting on this huge stone dish with a volcano under them about to erupt. Well, right now *I* feel exactly how *they* must have felt."

The other man laughed.

"But they survived, didn't they, sir."

The big man across the desk smiled.

"That's true, I suppose. But it must have been bloody hot on there before they got spewed out into the open."

★

Week 3; Thursday, 9 April…

The climate in John Mackay's office was very different to that of a few days ago.

"Just one question, sir. Why me?"

"Because you're new, Jo – four days new. You've no history here. You might not think so, but it will be easier for you than for any of the others."

Jo was silent for a while.

"I hope it's not true," she said, at last, half to herself.

"I'm one-hundred percent with you there," said John.

Neither spoke for a full minute.

"Do we have to do it like this, though?" she asked. "I mean, given who we're dealing with."

"It's *because* of who we're dealing with that it's essential we do. The MO is set out very clearly in Section 7 of the NJR Directive. And what if we didn't? With the evidence we've got to date, if we subsequently fail because we didn't follow procedure, think of the ramifications; the accusations of a cover-up. No, the best case scenario is … we do it by the book; we've got it wrong; there's no case to answer."

Jo sighed again, shaking her head.

"When, sir?"

"Five days from now. Next Tuesday. 5.00 am."

"And the other party?"

"The same."

145

CHAPTER TWELVE

Five days later
Week 4; Tuesday, 14 April…

Tom was awoken by the sound of loud banging and a ringing bell. Mags was already sitting up in bed, shaking with alarm and looking at the strobing blue lights on the bedroom curtains.

Tom instinctively checked his watch, as if the disturbance might be justified by the hour it was taking place. Three minutes past five. He grabbed hold of Mags, pulling her close to him, whilst his mind raced to take in what was happening. The banging was someone knocking hard on the outer front door and the continuous ringing was the doorbell being pressed in and held. There were voices outside; he went quickly to the window, fractionally pulling back one of the curtains to look out.

Four police cars and two police vans were parked on the drive, line-abreast in a fan formation, each vehicle pointing towards their front porch door. A number of dogs were jumping down from the back of one van, their excited barking quickly silenced by the louder barked commands of the dog-handlers. Three police officers, including a woman in plain clothes, were at the top of the porch steps and a dozen others were milling around, looking up at the bedroom windows for signs of a response to their presence. The twitching curtain was spotted by a couple of the officers who pointed it out to the rest. The woman walked back down the steps, looked up at the window and raised a small loud-hailer to her mouth.

"Mr Tom Brown! Home Secretary! We need to speak to you now, sir!"

"Katey!" Mags gasped. "It must be Katey!"

"It can't be …" Tom started, going back to her and holding her again.

"Oh, God! Please no!" Mags clung closer to him.

"Mags, it can't be anything like that. There's half the bloody Force out there. I'll go and see what's going on. Probably got a call to say someone's snooping around. It's not about Katey; trust me."

Tom left her again to open the window.

"Okay, I'll be right down," he shouted. He quickly pulled on his dressing gown and opened the bedroom door. Jack was outside in just his boxer shorts, hand raised, about to knock.

"What the hell's going on?" he asked.

"I'm just going to find out," said Tom.

He raced down the stairs, deactivated the house alarm and unlocked the inner front door and outer entrance door to the porch. The woman officer held up her ID badge in her right hand and a printed sheet of A4 in her left.

"Detective Inspector Cottrell, sir, Guildford CID." She lowered her badge and thrust the other document forward. "I have a warrant to search this property with immediate effect. Please let me in."

"Search the house! For what exactly?"

"Please let me in, sir. We have a warrant to search this property," she repeated.

"Yes, you've already said that, and I've already said 'for what?'"

"Please let me in, sir."

Mags and Jack were watching and listening from the mid-stair landing. Mags had put on a long bathrobe and Jack's arm was round her shoulders; she was still trembling with anxiety as she shouted down.

"Tom, what? Katey?"

Jo heard the question.

"Nothing to do with your daughter," she said quietly to Tom.

"It's not about Katey," he shouted up to Mags, stepping back a little from the doorway. Jo edged on to the threshold.

"They want to search the house," he added. He turned back to Jo.

"I'll ask again," he said, this time with the hint of a threat in his voice. "What are you looking for?"

Jo stood her ground, now just inside the porch door. Mags and Jack had descended to the hallway.

"I didn't want to have to say this, sir, given that it might sound a bit facetious, but under Section 7 of the NJR provisions – I quote – 'the police shall have the right of access and search in such circumstances as they think appropriate given a weight of evidence, as set out in the notes to Section 7 below'…"

"Yes, you're right," Tom interrupted, "it does sound facetious."

"'*Without* the requirement to disclose either the details of that evidence or the purpose or objects of their search'. I believe you wrote those words, sir, or at least you approved them. So I say again, please let me in."

Tom sighed and stepped back.

"Very well, Inspector …?"

"Detective Inspector Cottrell, sir. Thank you." Jo walked through the porch and into the hallway. She nodded to Mags.

"Mrs Tomlinson-Brown, I won't take up any more of your time than is necessary, but I need to search the whole of the property, including outbuildings if necessary. And I'd like to start right away."

Jack turned and went back up the stairs.

"Follow him, Sergeant," said Jo. "You know where to start."

Tom watched as she followed the sergeant up the stairs, with a dog-handler and his long-haired cocker spaniel immediately behind.

Mags turned to Tom, anger now taking over from anxiety.

"This is outrageous!" she shouted. "Don't they even know who you are – *what* you are? This is the Home Secretary!" she yelled after them, and to the other officers now filling the hallway. "Your *boss!*"

"Let them get it over with, Mags," said Tom. "It's some sort of mistake, obviously," he said loudly for all to hear. "I can't wait to see all the red faces in a few minutes time."

As he spoke he was heading up the stairs after Jo and the others.

"Inspector Cottrell," he shouted, "refresh my memory. Is there anything in the provisions that prevents me accompanying you on your search? Perhaps I could help by pointing out the most likely places where the arms and explosives are stashed."

Jo ignored him. She and her two colleagues were focused on following Jack, who turned off the upstairs corridor into his room, locking himself in. The dog sniffed enthusiastically at the bottom of the door.

"Please open the door, Mr Tomlinson-Brown," said Jo, banging on it with the palm of her hand.

"Just a minute!" Jack's voice from inside. "Just making myself decent."

"Don't worry about that. You'll do as you are, thank you. Open up, please. *Now!*"

Tom had arrived at the door.

"Can't you give him a couple of minutes, for God's sake, just to get dressed? Here, you can start in our bedroom. The handgrenades are in the top drawer of the dressing table and the rocket launcher is behind the wardrobe."

"That is neither funny nor helpful, sir. We are just doing the job *you* gave us. Now this door is about to be opened, either by your son, or by us."

"Jack, open this bloody door, will you. This is not helping ..." Tom added his weight to the request.

"Just a couple of minutes ..."

"*Now!*" Tom and Jo shouted in unison. They could hear a shuffling inside, like things being moved around.

"Okay in there," Jo shouted, "stand away from the door; we're coming through it now!"

She signalled to one of the officers further back along the corridor. He stepped forward carrying a two-handled battering ram and positioned himself ready to swing it at the door. Tom stepped across it facing the officer and shouting over his shoulder.

"*Jack, open this fucking door!*"

The movement inside ceased and the door opened. Jack was still dressed in just his boxer shorts. Jo looked him up and down.

"Why, Jack. You must be the slowest dresser in the world," she said.

She looked around the room. A wardrobe door was open and in front of it was a sports holdall into which had been stuffed a large number of magazines. There were a few more of the same still inside at the bottom of the wardrobe. It was clear that Jack had been removing them from there.

"What exactly were you doing?" asked Jo.

149

"Nothing," said Jack, "just tidying up …" His voice tailed off.

All eyes were on the spaniel, which was half into the wardrobe giving little yelps and vigorously wagging its stubby tail. Its front legs were scraping at the pile of papers as if trying to dig through them.

"Easy, Jilly; good girl; sit."

The dog handler pulled her gently back. One of the other officers knelt and peered into the wardrobe. He turned to Jo.

"SOCOs, ma'am?"

Jo nodded, removing her radio from her pocket.

"Andy, bring them up, please."

Tom looked across at his son who was sitting on the bed, elbows on his knees and head in hands staring unfocussed at the floor a couple of feet in front of him. Tom turned to Jo who looked back at him with eyes full of sadness.

"Home Secretary, we'll need to spend some time in here. In the meantime, I suggest that you and Mrs Tomlinson-Brown and Jack get dressed. I can't allow anything to be touched in this room. I'm sure you can find Jack some clothes from somewhere. Constable Marsh, here, will accompany you." She nodded towards one of her officers. Her voice was suddenly gentle and kind.

He and Mags dressed and went downstairs to the front sitting room off the large hall, Constable Marsh remaining outside the door.

"This is unbelievable!" Mags was shouting. "Can't you just throw them out, for God's sake? Charge them with trespassing or something!"

"They're just doing their job, Mags."

"Oh, of course! Their bloody job! Trampling all over people; abusing their new powers!"

Tom sighed, recognising the old barriers being raised. Jack entered the room, looking sheepish and avoiding their eyes.

"Well, Jack," said Tom. "Anything to say at this stage?"

Jack looked at him briefly and then turned away again.

"Sorry," barely audible.

"Sorry!" shouted Tom. "You wouldn't like to tell us sorry for what, would you?"

Mags turned on him.

"There's no point in shouting at Jack!"

"No point in …! Have you any idea what this is about? Would you like to enlighten us, please, Jack, or would you rather we just listened in when you explain it to the police?"

"Explain what to the police?" Mags stared at Tom, eyes blazing in anger.

"Look, I'm really sorry," said Jack, the calmest of the three by a long way. "I was going to get rid of them."

Tom wrinkled his brow.

"Get rid of them? Get rid of what, exactly?"

"The magazines. The porno mags, for God's sake. It's not like they're hardcore or anything. I can't believe …"

"For Christ's sake, Jack! How long have you lived on the planet Earth? This isn't about bloody lads' mags. They don't send trained dogs to sniff out pornography – hard *or* soft. But can you think of something they *do* use sniffer dogs for? I'll have to rush you on this one, I'm afraid!"

Mags gasped. "Drugs!" Her voice was a hoarse whisper. "Jack?" She turned to her son.

Jack laughed mirthlessly. "Drugs! There are no drugs in there. I had the last of the paracetamol on the morning after the party …!"

"You think this is a joke?" shouted Tom. "Perhaps the dog's mistaken!"

"It is if it thinks there are any drugs in there," Jack shouted back, losing his cool. "I can't believe you think that of me. Thanks a lot, Dad."

Mags began to cry. Both Tom and Jack went immediately to console her. Jo Cottrell appeared in the doorway. They all turned towards her.

"I'd like you all to come with me, please," she said.

Jo led them up the stairs and along the corridor to Jack's room. She stepped aside to let them through the door.

Half a dozen officers in white hooded overalls and surgical gloves were gently searching through drawers and picking items from shelves. The wardrobe door was still open and the police sergeant waved his arm in a gesture inviting them to look in. The magazines had all been taken out and the base panel removed, revealing a cavity about four inches deep below it. In the space, about three feet long and two feet wide, there were forty-eight clear plastic bags of white powder.

The phone rang in Tom and Mags's bedroom further along the corridor, but no-one seemed to hear it.

★

Jack sat alone, ashen-faced, in the rear of the police car staring in front of him at the back of the driver's head. Tom was talking to Jo at the bottom of the steps up to the front porch entrance.

"You do realise this is a big mistake, don't you, Inspector? Trust me, my son had no idea that stuff was there. All that locking the door and such – he was worried about the magazines."

"I'm sure the truth will come out very soon," said Jo, with the merest smile.

"When can we see him?" he asked.

Jo checked her watch.

"Give it a few hours," she said. "We'll need some time with him. Say ten o'clock. Bring him some spare clothes, toothbrush, that sort of thing. Just in case we keep him for a while."

Jo went to get into the car.

"By the way, Inspector, how did you get through the gates, and past security?"

"Not my responsibility, sir," Jo replied. "That was taken care of before we arrived. But don't forget that your security people work for the same boss as me. Their orders came from the same source. So please don't think they let you down or anything."

He nodded as she slipped into the back of the vehicle next to his son. Jack turned his head towards him as it pulled away, but his eyes were glazed over and he seemed to see nothing. Tom went back to their room, where Mags was lying on the bed in a state of utter despair. The phone rang again. She picked up the handset and he could hear Katey's voice shouting in panic.

"Mum, oh, Mum!"

Tom took the receiver gently from Mags and pressed the 'speaker' button so they could both share the conversation.

"Katey, what's wrong?" he said.

"It's Jason, Dad. The police came – about five o'clock – and raided the house. They found …they found …" She began to cry, almost out of control.

"Katey, Katey, please calm down," said Tom. "Look, it's all a big mistake. They've been here as well. They've found some stuff in Jack's room."

Katey seemed to pull herself together.

"Stuff? What sort of stuff?"

"You know… stuff."

"Oh, God!" gasped Katey. "So it might be true?"

"What might be true?" asked Tom.

"Well, drugs, of course," she sobbed. "That they're doing drugs. I mean dealing."

"Of course they're not!" Mags almost screamed at the phone. "That's ridiculous! Don't you dare think that!"

"Is Jason there?" asked Tom.

"No, they took him away. And Jack? What have they done with Jack?"

Mags turned onto her side and buried her head in the pillow.

"They've arrested him, Katey."

"Oh, no! Oh, God, no!"

★

Three days later
Week 4; Friday, 17 April…

Daniel Hastings, Senior Partner, and the third generation member of his family in the firm of Hastings and Medforth Associates Ltd, Solicitors, had been awaiting Jack at Guilford police station when he arrived with Jo Cottrell on the morning of his arrest. Tom had called him the moment the car taking his son away had left the house. Daniel had subsequently agreed to represent Jason as well.

It was 9.30 am and he was pacing uneasily around the front sitting room at Etherington Place, where Tom and Mags were seated separately listening to the details of the investigation which lead to the events of three days ago. Daniel was a distinguished-looking figure, tall, slim, with handsome features and slightly greying hair. He was wearing a navy suit with white shirt and red silk tie.

"The investigation got underway around two months ago," he said. "That was after the police had received a number of phone calls from drug users – seven in all – about some dodgy crack cocaine being distributed in the Woking area. All seven, and quite a few others it seems, suffered significant side effects. They gave the names of the dealers responsible as Jake and Jasper, and their descriptions pointed to Jack and Jason, who are on record as known associates of Mickey Kadawe, following the police surveillance of Kadawe the previous year…"

"I bloody knew it!" Tom almost exploded, addressing the comment to Mags. "I've said it time and time again! I thought he'd be behind…"

Daniel held up his hands to stop him. "Hold on, Tom. Kadawe is *not* under suspicion. He was closely observed for half of last year, and the police were satisfied that he's clean. He's a licensed trader, but there was no evidence he'd strayed beyond that. So he's out of the picture; all his previous convictions were as a minor – no point in going down that road."

Mags glared at Tom. "Too bad. You'll have to try and fix him up for something else."

Daniel looked from one to the other before continuing.

"Around three weeks ago, four of the users were persuaded to come forward, and three of them actually provided samples of the substandard goods. These were analysed and confirmed as being contaminated. Also, in the opinion of the examiners, they could have produced the side effects described.

"And I'm afraid it gets worse. The fourth user who came forward claimed to have gone to the home of one of the dealers. He couldn't remember the address, but he described it pretty accurately and picked your house out from a number of photographs he was shown of different properties. He says he had intended to confront Jack but couldn't get in because of security. Instead he threw the bag with what was left of the stuff in it over the property wall. Can't imagine why he did that, but during the search of the grounds here on Tuesday, they found a small packet near the boundary wall. His fingerprints were on the pack which goes a long way towards confirming his story."

"Compelling stuff, I'm sure," said Mags, "but he didn't do this, Dan. I can tell you that for certain. So instead of accepting all this as gospel, you – we – need to be thinking how it was done."

"I totally agree, Maggie, but you should hear the whole story first. No point in trying to work out alternative scenarios until we know alternatives to what."

Mags nodded but said nothing.

"Three of the four separately identified Jack – as Jake – from photographs taken on last year's surveillance. The other identified Jason – or Jasper, as he knew him. The three who didn't come forward after the phone calls, by the way, had all named Jasper as their supplier. There is also CCTV footage of Jack in brief conversations with half-a-dozen known drug users, and a couple of encounters also picked up through police shadowing."

"Christ Almighty!" said Tom, slumping forward in his chair. He turned to Mags. "We can't ignore all that just because we don't want to hear it. Blind denial isn't going to help our son." His voice was rising and shaking at the same time.

"So what's that supposed to mean, exactly? You're not seriously thinking …!"

"Look, hear me out and then we can talk about what we think and what we believe – and more importantly – what we need to *do*," Daniel said. "Arguing amongst ourselves isn't going to help Jack either."

They both became silent and turned back to him.

"On Tuesday, last week, the police received a tip-off from someone – anonymously, by phone – informing them that he had information that drugs were being stored in the homes of both Jack and Jason – Jake and Jasper. That is what prompted the raids earlier this week.

"Two mobile contact numbers provided by all seven witnesses were being operated on a pay-as-you-go basis by two people who had given false names and addresses in acquiring them. DI Cottrell phoned both numbers while they were searching Jack's bedroom. The first call was answered by a DI Waters at Jason's house on a mobile phone he'd just found under the floorboards there. Her second call wasn't picked up but the number was later confirmed as that of a phone hidden in the wardrobe in Jack's room under a panel next to the one where the drugs were. Apparently the phone was switched on but the battery had been discharged. With that phone was a half-empty box of disposable surgical gloves. Traces of the glove material were later found on the phone itself and the packets."

He stopped pacing for the first time and sat down on the end of the sofa.

"That's it; the full story," he said. "That's what we've got to work with – or against, in fact."

They were all silent for a long time.

"So, what do we do, Dan? You make it sound hopeless," Tom said.

"Not at all. Those are the facts of the case so far. *If* they are charged – and in the face of those facts it does seem likely, I'm afraid – a jury has got to believe they could have done it – not just the mechanical means to do it, but the will, the capability, the …whatever. And it's a difficult one to call. The main person in the spotlight will not be just any nineteen-year-old local man; it will be the son of the Home Secretary. And that could have a bearing on the case if it comes to trial, which, as I say, I am pretty sure it will."

Mags gave a little sigh, which was really a suppressed sob.

"And that fact could affect it either way," Daniel continued, glancing at her. "There will be a wave of sympathy for you both, there's no doubt about that. Ellen Gormley wasn't just speaking for the House yesterday, she was reflecting pretty much the feelings of the whole country. So that's good; that could have a knock-on effect with the jury.

"On the other hand, this can work against us. They could see it as a challenge to its impartiality, and that could sway them the other way into the face of that public sympathy. Because they – the courts – know, that the very people who say they can't believe the son of Tom Brown would do such a thing, will be the same ones who, after an acquittal, would say 'well, it was obvious they wouldn't let him be convicted'. And that could be a big problem going forward."

"Jesus, Dan, you're a real comfort," said Mags, standing up and walking across the room to stare out of the window. "You're saying that the judiciary might convict him just to show that there's no favouritism, even though he's innocent."

"No, Dan isn't saying that …" Tom started to respond, but Mags cut him short.

"Isn't that what you just said, Dan?"

"No, Maggie," said the lawyer. "Not exactly. …"

"Okay, what *exactly* did you say, then?"

Daniel hesitated. "Well, firstly, the judiciary can't convict him – only the jury can reach ..."

"Oh, for God's sake, Dan, you know what I mean. Even with the new jury system, the judge can still swing it in most cases."

"Some cases, certainly," he replied. "But I wouldn't say most. Look, Maggie, I'm just trying to lay this out objectively. Just trying to make you see the dynamics of the thing. And please don't tell me you weren't both already aware of them anyway."

"No, you're right," Mags sighed. "But let me tell you something – again. Jack is innocent. Of that I am one thousand percent certain. Right, Tom?" She almost shouted the question at him.

Tom said nothing, but nodded his reply. She glared at him as she continued to address Daniel.

"If you had seen him that night, before they showed us the ... stuff, it was obvious – absolutely obvious – that he had no idea it was there. He was worried about them finding the porno mags, worried because he thought we'd be upset. And when we said it wasn't those they were looking for, it was drugs, he just laughed. He was so thankful because he genuinely believed he wasn't going to be in trouble. Surely you felt that, Tom?"

"Yes, that's right," Tom said. "It was clear he didn't think ..."

"And do they seriously think he would draw their attention to where he was keeping the stuff by clearing everything on top of it out of the way?" said Mags. "What did they think he was going to do – flush the lot down the toilet while they waited outside?"

"I understand that *is* a bit of a sticking point for the CPS. But on the other hand, are people likely to believe that he seriously thought the police had raided the Home Secretary's property at five in the morning to confiscate some naughty magazines. And when I say people, I mean a jury."

Mags snorted. "It's ridiculous. And where's the *circumstantial* evidence, Dan? It's all hard, forensic stuff, nothing vague or questionable. Don't you think that's unusual?"

"I don't think I follow you, Maggie."

"Well, it's all so neat. The calls, the packages, the mobiles, the gloves – all linked and seemingly rock solid. But what about the missing bits? Jack's behaviour – no sign of any change – where's the money? I suppose he spent it on the magazines! And Jason – Katey has hardly left his side over the past God knows how long. Wouldn't she …?"

It was the lawyer's turn to interrupt.

"I really don't think we should pursue that line of argument," he said. "If, God forbid, Jason is convicted, they could use that very fact – that Katey has been with him continuously – to look again at *her* possible involvement. I mentioned this before, Maggie; it's best we leave Katey out of this as far as possible."

"Christ, Dan," said Tom, "you're not saying she's still a suspect, are you?"

"I couldn't say categorically that she *isn't*, although they appear to be satisfied for the moment. What I *am* saying is that convincing the jury that Jason couldn't have done it without Katey knowing, is more likely to put her in the frame than take Jason out of it."

As he finished speaking, his mobile sounded softly in his inside jacket pocket. He took it out and looked at the display.

"I'm sorry," he said, getting up, "but I should get this. It's Amanda – it might have some bearing on the case."

Tom and Mags nodded and Dan walked out into the hall to speak to his assistant. Mags sat down again and they waited for him to return in complete silence. When he did he was shaking his head.

"I'm afraid that was more bad news. The police believe there could be a link between this case and a recent death on the Lawns Estate near Byfleet. About ten weeks ago a young addict died after using some bad cocaine. Forensics said the composition of the lethal dose was very similar to the stuff recovered from Jack and Jason. We requested independent testing of the samples, and that was Amanda with the results. I'm afraid our tests support the original findings. What they *can't* say for certain – and won't be able to prove – is that it came from the same batch. It is statistically possible that there were two similarly contaminated batches on the streets in the same area at the same time. Highly unlikely but statistically possible. Also, there is no obvious connection between the dead user and the seven witnesses who contacted the police – different groups, different markets, so it's unlikely they will put a lot of effort into establishing a link."

Mags sank back in her chair and put her head in her hands. Tom went to her, putting a comforting arm around her shoulder, which she shrugged off. She turned to Daniel, her eyes glistening.

"But if they *can* make a link, Dan …what then? How much worse would that be?"

"Surprisingly enough, Maggie, legally no worse at all. It won't bring any further weight of proof to the charge of trafficking, and that's what we're dealing with. If the charges are proven and the link *is* made to the death, then they could in theory also be charged with unlawful killing."

Mags broke down and slumped forward, this time clinging to Tom as he held her to him.

"But, *but* …" Daniel stressed, "there would be no point in their doing that. The drug dealing carries the higher sentence in this case. The *mandatory* sentence." He looked at Tom. "We are all fully aware of the rationale for certain elements of the NJR, but we're still uncovering the ironies."

Tom turned to glare at him as Mags again shook herself free of his embrace.

Daniel left soon afterwards, Tom walking him to his car and nodding his goodbye with a brief handshake. The lawyer half got into his car, and then stood up, turning to Tom again.

"Look, Tom, this thing about the death," he said. "I didn't want to say it back there, but it *could* have an impact on the case if it comes to light. I meant it when I said it was inadmissible, but we might not be able to prevent the Prosecution from mentioning it. At that point, of course, they will be *told* it's inadmissible. But the damage would be done; it would be in the minds of the jury. We'll try to suppress it, of course, but …" He sighed and looked away. "I'm sorry, Tom. I'd much rather be telling you both not to worry, that everything was going to be okay."

"I know, Dan. Thanks all the same."

★

Three days later
Week 5; Monday, 20 April…

Grace looked up as her office door opened. The man entering, unannounced and unaccompanied, sat down heavily on the chair in front of her desk and leant across towards her. He seemed very agitated and a little out of breath.

"Andrew. Quite a surprise." She looked past him towards the door, expecting to see his usual entourage of security personnel, who on this occasion were conspicuous by their absence. "To what do I owe ...?"

"Just wondered how you felt about this drug business with Jack Tomlinson-Brown, Grace. Any ideas ...thoughts ...feelings?"

Grace hesitated.

"Well, they haven't been formally charged yet."

"No, but we both know they will be; so what do you think?"

"Well, I think it's unfortunate, and I really can't believe ..."

"The reality is," Andrew continued, "this is a massive embarrassment for the Party, whatever the outcome."

"Whatever the outcome?" Grace repeated. "You don't really believe Jack did this, do you? Surely it has to be a mistake. He's going to get off ... isn't he?"

"I don't know whether he'll get off or not," snapped Andrew. "How the hell *could* I know? It's the sort of question I should be asking you. It will be decided in the usual way; nothing we can ..."

"Yes," Grace jumped in with feeling, "but we all *want* him to get off, don't we? Don't you? You sound like you don't give a shit. For God's sake, surely ...!"

"Don't overstep, Grace! I'm just thinking of the bigger picture here. The longer term. There are enough people getting all bristly and wet-eyed on Jack bloody Tomlinson-Brown's behalf. I thought I was going to throw up last Thursday when Gormley made her tear-jerking speech to the House. What the hell was she thinking of?"

"Am I missing something? All she was doing was saying what most of the people in the country will be thinking. That we're all sorry for Tom, after all he's done. What 'bigger picture'? What 'longer term'? I thought we were discussing the fate of the Home Secretary's son. Just why *are* you here, Andrew? I should have known it wouldn't be to show empathy with a fellow human being!"

Andrew was silent for a long time.

"You're right," he said. "I didn't come here to sympathise – or empathise – with anyone. I came to give you *my* feelings about the situation. You see, we are promising the people of this country that we will protect them from harm. We will keep the bad guys away from them until we've got rid of enough to persuade the rest to be good guys. And I think they believe we can do it – so far.

"Now … the bigger picture, the longer term, which, apparently, you have had neither the time nor the inclination to think about. If Jack *is* found to be innocent, it means someone has infiltrated the Home Secretary's home and perpetrated an elaborate frame-up right under the noses of some of the best security personnel in the land. The crème-de-la-crème of the very agencies charged with looking after everybody in the country. At which point that same 'everybody-in-the-country' could be excused for thinking 'how the fuck can they promise to look after us if this happens to the Home fucking Secretary; the very person who has designed the fucking system to protect us'. Sorry about the language, Grace, but you know how these common people talk.

"On the other hand, if handsome Jack-the-lad is found *guilty*, along with his little ethnic pal, of generating a bit of extra cash to supplement the inadequate spends bestowed on him by his rich and beautiful parents, then I believe people will *not* perceive this as a massive breach of security – just the work of a clever little bastard who no-one could have reasonably suspected. In fact, those same agencies of law and order will get quite a bit of kudos for sorting out the ungrateful little shit.

"So now, here's the dead easy question, Grace. Which outcome is best for us – and the country, of course – guilty or not guilty?"

Grace's expression betrayed her mounting horror at what she was hearing.

"Don't look so bloody shocked, Grace. You're not exactly whiter than white when it comes to manipulating justice." His voice was rising now.

"Manipulating justice! What exactly are you suggesting?"

"I'm not suggesting anything, Grace. Heaven forbid. As I said, there's nothing we can do to influence it. Well, there's certainly nothing *I* can do. I mean it would be totally out of the question for *me* to interfere in the process of justice, wouldn't it?"

"Andrew, if you're asking me to get involved with a view to…" she almost shouted at him.

"Grace, I haven't asked you to do anything. I've simply stated, very objectively, the outcome that I believe would be best for the country as a whole. As I said, whichever way it goes, it's a major embarrassment. I just think an embarrassment is enough of a setback, without an attendant crisis of confidence in this government. That's all."

"I'm still not sure. ..." Her eyes suddenly blazed with anger. "This is Tom Brown we're talking about. The hero of the NJR, as you recently called him. And this is how you recognise this man's loyalty?"

Andrew thrust his face close to hers.

"This man! This man! Do you mean *this man* who you've been spying on for me for the past four years? Have you forgotten all those years of pretending to be his strong right hand, when all the time you were feeding back to me every single word *this man* had spoken to you in confidence? I shouldn't be in too much of a hurry to set yourself up as a loyalty consultant, *Miss Goody!*"

Grace glared back at him then dropped her eyes.

"If Jack *is* innocent," Andrew continued, backing off a little, "of course I wouldn't want him to be exiled. But I repeat – it would not be a disaster for *us* – this government – if he were found guilty. I am not suggesting we should – or could – do anything to bring about such a verdict, but neither let us expend any time or energy pushing for a 'not guilty' vote. We should clearly declare our sympathy for the Tomlinson-Browns, but *not* our support. Our support must be for our new system of justice. We have to be transparently objective throughout. Do we understand each other?"

Grace nodded.

"What I will say, though," he continued, "is that if the verdict *is* guilty, then I want the process from that moment fast-tracked to completion. If they have to jump the queue to get them onto Alpha quickly, then I want you to make it happen. Okay? There will be no benefit in having this thing dragged out."

As he rose to leave, he leaned across to Grace again, this time offering his hand. She looked at it for several seconds before standing herself and taking it limply. Andrew smiled.

"Let's not fall out, Grace. We're soul mates, you and I. Haven't you always felt that?"

"It's not official yet," said Daniel, "but the police will be charging Jack and Jason tomorrow. That's the latest they can do it after taking advantage of the full seven days for questioning, and they've let us know their intention in advance."

They were sitting exactly where they had been seventy-two hours ago when Daniel had outlined the case against Jack and Jason to them, and he, as before, was pacing the floor in front of them.

Neither Tom nor Mags were able to speak.

"Nothing's got any worse over the past six days," Daniel went on. "We pretty well knew they'd be charged as soon as we saw the evidence, didn't we? So this isn't a backward step. We'll request bail, of course, but this will be turned down. We have also let them know we will be asking for the maximum six-week extension before the trial. They have indicated that we are likely to be granted just two extra weeks, giving us four to prepare. But that's fine; we'll be ready.

"Our counsel will be Lorna Prentiss. She's very good, excellent record and very happy to take the case, which is a good sign. Barristers with good reputations who can pick and choose who they represent don't readily accept cases they think they'll lose."

They were silent for a long time before Mags spoke.

"So, as a friend, Dan, tell us what we should do now," she said. "Pray, do you think?"

Daniel hesitated before replying.

"I can't see that it would do any harm."

CHAPTER THIRTEEN

Four weeks later
Week 9; Tuesday, 19 May…

The venue for the trial was one of Guildford's new modern courtrooms in the annexe to the previous older courthouse. Its white walls, strip lighting and beech furniture and fittings were a marked contrast to the sombre dark-panelled rooms next door. Jack and Jason were seated side-by-side a yard apart in the dock, separated by an opaque Perspex screen. They were both smartly dressed in lounge suits, Jack's shirt was open-necked; Jason wore a tie.

The judge, Justice Miles Pendle, was a very large and impressive figure, with a round ruddy face and extensive white side-burns. His size was further accentuated by his flowing gown and wig. Even so, as if these attributes were not imposing enough, he chose to break with tradition by standing to address the court.

"Before we start the proceedings, let me say a few words to all present on two aspects of this case. Firstly, one of the defendants is already known to you. At least, his family background is known to you. Hugh Jacob – known as Jack – Tomlinson-Brown is the son of our Home Secretary, Tom Brown. Mr Brown is a man who has deservedly received much acclaim in recent years across the UK and far beyond; someone who has transcended party-political boundaries in acquiring his popularity and a man, you may think, who has made a greater contribution than any other individual to the betterment of our communities. He is someone for whom we should rightly have the highest regard."

Tom heard Mags give a half-sob, half-snort beside him.

"Secondly, the charge – which will be shortly read out – has been the subject of much discussion recently. I am sure you are aware of this and I do not propose at this juncture to further expand on it.

"For these two reasons, the case has attracted much attention in the media over the past few weeks, and we must accept that today, and for the duration of the proceedings, we will all be under the spotlight. This places an even greater burden than usual on those in this courtroom to behave with dignity, restraint and diligence in the pursuit of our decision concerning these two young men. As such, I must warn you all that I will not tolerate any extraneous comments or outbursts, and any person or persons disrupting the smooth running of this court will be asked to leave and forcibly removed if they refuse. I trust that is *absolutely clear* to everyone."

He swept the room with a menacing glare to reinforce his words before sitting down and nodding to the person just to his left in front of him.

"Mr Simpson."

The Clerk of the Court rose to his feet and looked up briefly at Jack.

"Hugh Jacob Tomlinson-Brown, you are hereby charged under the Misuse of Drugs Act with being concerned in the supplying of cocaine, a class A drug. Do you plead guilty or not guilty?"

Jack was staring at the floor in front of him, head bowed, and when he spoke his voice was barely audible. "Not guilty."

The judge leaned forward in his seat.

"Could the defendant please speak up so the court can hear his plea."

"Not guilty," said Jack, only marginally louder.

"Thank you," said the judge, with the slightest of sighs, and nodded again to the clerk.

"Jason Louie Midanda, you are hereby charged under the Misuse of Drugs Act with being concerned in the supplying of cocaine, a class A drug. Do you plead guilty or not guilty?"

"Not guilty." Jason's response was in sharp contrast to Jack's – loud and strong, projecting a clear sense of purpose.

"Thank you," said Justice Pendle and turned to the Crown Prosecutor. "Mr Forsythe, please proceed."

Jeremy Forsythe QC rose slowly to his feet and walked over to where the jury was seated, looking round the courtroom as he did so. The Crown Prosecutor was slim and no more than average height, with sharp features, steel-grey eyes and an air of absolute confidence, which, in spite of his limited stature, made for a commanding presence.

"This is a simple case," he said, addressing the jury. "There are no mysteries, no subtleties, no complex clues to unravel. Yours is a huge responsibility, but on this occasion, we will make your task easier by presenting you with a wealth of evidence pointing clearly in one direction. Over the next couple of days, the testimonies of a number of highly competent and dependable witnesses will lead you unwaveringly towards one irrefutable conclusion – that the defendants standing before you are guilty as charged.

"To set the scene and put those forthcoming testimonies in chronological context, I call to the witness stand Detective Inspector Harry Waters, the chief investigating officer in this case."

A man in a creased grey suit entered the courtroom and walked the dozen or so paces to the witness stand. He stepped onto it and turned to face the jury.

"Inspector Waters," said Jeremy, "could you please share with the court the events leading to our being here today, starting with the first of the phone calls you received."

★

"I wonder if you can help me. I'm trying to locate a friend of mine. She's in her early thirties, about five-foot-five, three-quarters West Indian, very pretty with beautiful hazel eyes."

Jo laughed.

"Is this one of those dodgy phone calls?" she said. "Because if it is you've not mentioned really sexy, great figure and legs…"

"Oh, you know her then? That's very encouraging."

"How are you, David? And what have I done to deserve the call?"

"I'm very well, thank you, and I'm just checking that *you're* okay. When will you be called, do you think?"

"Most likely Thursday, just possibly last witness tomorrow."

"And you're okay about it?"

"Not really, but I don't have to be, do I? It's just a job."

"Sometimes that's the best way to look at things."

"Actually, I was going to phone you later. Can you think of anything significant about the date today?"

David thought for a moment.

"Go on."

"It was *exactly* three years ago to the very day that we arrested a certain John Alexander Deverall in a cemetery in Hammersmith."

★

The spectators in the public galleries fell quickly silent under the critical gaze of Miles Pendle as Lorna Prentiss rose to her feet. The Defence counsel was a large, well-made, handsome woman, an inch taller than her opponent and with almost as deep a voice.

"DI Waters," said Lorna, "how many of the people caught on camera and observed by the police were actually questioned?"

Harry Waters looked slightly uncomfortable. "None, ma'am. But we didn't need …"

"So basically all you have from that line of investigation are images of young people talking to each other in an area of Woking where masses of young people converse every day?"

"Yes, but …"

"No, that's okay, Inspector, just so we know what to expect when the Crown attempts to elaborate; so we don't get our hopes up in anticipation of something meaningful. No more questions for now."

She resumed her seat and looked down at her notes in a gesture of total dismissal. DI Harry Waters stepped down.

"We will break here for lunch," said Miles Pendle. "Be back in your seats by one-thirty prompt."

"Court will rise."

★

"Thank you for the comprehensive technical description of the security arrangements at Etherington Place, Mr Michaels," said Lorna, cross examining. "I am sure that if there are any security experts present or listening in today, they will have found the depth of detail very interesting. But am I right in saying that on the night of the party there was a fault with one of the interior cameras?"

Greg Michaels was the last in Jeremy Forsythe's first parade of 'competent and dependable' witnesses, and the head of the local agency responsible for security at Etherington Place. He was a squat, muscular man with a shaven head and a hard face. He was dressed in a formal suit, shirt and tie.

"Not exactly," he replied. "The lens of the upstairs camera was sprayed with some lotion. So it wasn't a fault with the camera, as such."

"No, I understand that, but it wasn't doing its job for a while is what I mean. Did you check it out?"

"Yes, I went to check it later."

"Later?"

"We didn't want to be heavy-handed at the party – asked not to be, in fact – so we waited until it was a bit quieter and ..."

"Wasn't that a bit of a risk?"

"Not really. The cameras are there primarily to pick up any intruders, not to spy on houseguests. We'd checked everybody in at the gates, searched them, recorded names and all, so we didn't see the problem as a risk."

"What did you find when you checked it out?"

"Well, as I said, someone had sprayed this artificial tanning stuff onto the lens."

"Why would anyone do that, do you think, Mr Michaels?"

"Well, it could have been just for a joke, but more likely to hide the identity of anyone using the bedrooms."

A chuckle went around the gallery and some knowing nods were exchanged.

"But you don't know that for certain, do you?"

"Not for certain, but someone at the party actually told me that was why it was done. And it's happened before at other places I've covered on similar occasions."

Lorna sat down with an inward sigh.

★

Mags was sitting on the far side of their bed with her back to him. Tom could see her shoulders shaking.

"Mags, are you okay?"

She didn't answer for a long time.

"Who was that young man in the courtroom?" she said eventually in a small voice. "I didn't recognise him."

Tom went quickly to sit beside her and put an arm round her shoulders. She stiffened for a moment then all but collapsed against him.

"I don't know," said Tom. "Not our little wolverine, that's for sure."

Mags sat up and stared ahead.

"The truth is he has no notion of self preservation, has he? And it's our fault."

"But Mags, we've done everything we could – for both our kids. If he's going to get through this, he has to stand up for himself. He's nearly twenty years old and …"

"But that's the point," Mags interrupted. "He's spent his whole life in a cocoon; one that we made for him. He's never had to do anything for himself. We've left him totally unequipped to confront adversity of any kind."

★

Week 9; Wednesday, 20 May…

The sun streamed in through the high windows along the wall opposite the judge's dais on the morning of the second day of the trial. The two counsels were conferring as the jury filed in and people settled in their seats in the public galleries. Technicians set up recording equipment and carried out their sound checks for the Legal Live broadcast. The defendants were escorted to the dock and at precisely 10.00 am Miles Pendle swept into the room to start proceedings.

"As you've already heard from DI Waters and his colleagues," Jeremy Forsythe said to the jury, "over a period of ten days, seven users phoned the police all with information about supplies of cocaine, which had caused them to be ill. They also gave descriptions of the suppliers of those drugs. Subsequently, four of these were persuaded to come forward and meet with the police. We have taken statements from all four and I am quite prepared to ask each of them to take the stand. However, as we are tasked with expediting these proceedings, I would like to call just one of these and have the statements of the other three read out to the court."

Miles Pendle nodded and turned to Lorna with the unspoken question.

"I am happy to agree to that, m'lord, with the proviso that any of them can be questioned if we perceive any anomalies or irregularities in any aspects of the statements."

The judge nodded again and turned back to Jeremy. "Proceed."

"Thank you, m'lord. I call William Wade to the stand."

A thin white man in his early twenties walked in, looking round and grinning as he approached the witness stand. He took the stand and gave a little wave to someone in the public gallery. He looked reasonably presentable, albeit uncomfortable, in an open-necked pale blue shirt and light grey suit, the formality of his clothes off-set by a pair of bright white trainers.

"You are William Torstein Wade of Manvers Street, Byfleet?" Jeremy asked.

The witness grinned again. "I guess."

Miles Pendle roared at him from three yards away. "You *guess*! Well are you or aren't you?" He turned to Jeremy. "Mr Forsythe, I hope you are not going to waste the court's time by producing witnesses who are not sure of their own name!"

"No, sorry, m'lord. Please allow me to ask the witness again. Are you William Torstein – *known as Billy* – Wade?"

"Definitely," said Billy Wade, still grinning.

"Thank you, Mr Wade. Could you please tell the court how you came into possession of the cocaine which made you ill?"

"Sure. I got it from that guy over there." He pointed to the dock.

"Which of the defendants do you mean, Mr Wade?" asked Jeremy.

"The white guy – Jake. He was the one."

"And how did he deliver the cocaine?"

"Same as always. Jordan Street in Woking. Round the back of Delaware. Same place, same time every other week. I phone him and we meet."

"Can you remember the number you phone to arrange the meetings?"

Billy grinned again. "You bet, I'd just about die if I forgot that."

He said the number, pausing briefly between each digit, whilst Jeremy checked it against a note he held in his hand. He repeated the number, reading it from the note.

"Let the court know," he said, turning to the jury, "that this is the number of the phone found at Etherington Place on the night of the raid, and that records confirm that calls were made to that number from Mr Wade's own mobile phone."

Jeremy continued. "Tell the court what happened once you had got the cocaine. When you took it."

"Well, I thought I was going to die. I mean, I've had dodgy shit before, but this was different. Head was sort of exploding; puking everywhere; couldn't stand up; pain in the gut like … like …like I'd been poisoned. If my mates hadn't found me …"

"Quite. So what did you decide to do about it?"

"At first I was planning to fix him – well, at least confront him, you know. So I found out where he lived and went and waited for him."

"What were you planning to do, exactly?"

"Not sure, but I was real mad when I saw where he lived. Big posh house in its own grounds, wall round it …"

"Let the court know that the witness has since identified the house as the home of Mr Tomlinson-Brown in Etherington Place. Please continue, Mr Wade."

"Well, I'd got some of the stuff with me and I thought I'd force him to take it – just so he'd know what sort of fucking crap he was peddling."

"But you didn't do that, Mr Wade. What changed your mind?"

"There were security guys there – not sure how many but they kept driving past and one or two would get out of the cars and sort of prowl around. I decided to leave and get him the next time we met. So I threw the bag of stuff I had over the wall into the grounds and fucked off."

"Let the court know," said Jeremy, "that a package containing cocaine was found inside the grounds in the area where Mr Wade said he had thrown it."

Miles Pendle leaned forward. "Before we proceed any further, please spare us the expletives, Mr Wade. We can get the drift without them, thank you."

Billy looked across at Jeremy, frowning in confusion.

"The 'f' word, Mr Wade," Jeremy explained. "Please refrain. Tell us why you phoned the police."

"Well, I still felt like shit a week later and I thought the bastard's not getting away with this. So I phoned. And then they phoned me back a few times, told me he was spreading this dodgy stuff all over the place and would I be prepared to come in for an interview – for evidence, like. In the end I said I would."

"And when you went to the police, were you able to identify the defendant as your supplier?"

"Yes, that's right. I picked him out from some mug-shots they showed me."

"Thank you, Mr Wade."

Lorna rose slowly to her feet shaking her head as Jeremy sat down.

"Mr Wade, I congratulate you on remembering all that story, but you don't seriously think anyone is going to believe it, do you?"

The grin left Billy's face. "It's the truth! Why would I lie?"

"Well, let's see if we can find out, shall we? How long are you claiming that Jake – Mr Tomlinson-Brown – has been supplying you with drugs?"

"About a year – perhaps a bit more. Not absolutely sure but ..."

"And how many times have you been ill using the drugs he's supplied?"

"Well, I think that was the first ..."

"You *think!* You told the court you thought you were going to die. How many near-death experiences have you had? Come on, you must remember."

"Yes, okay. No, it's never happened before."

"So, you *allege* that this man has been supplying you with drugs for over a year with no problems at all; then you get one bad package from him and decide to sell him down the road. I don't believe you, Mr Wade. Dealers with spare capacity are a bit thin on the ground these days with the extra squeeze on them."

"Yes, well you don't know how fucking rough it was ..."

"Language, *please*, Mr Wade," said Lorna, with a condescending smile. "So where have you been getting your supply from for the last couple of months?"

"You can't expect me to tell you that."

"Why not, Mr Wade. Or is it because there is no-one, in fact, and that Jack – or Jake – has never been your supplier either?"

Jeremy Forsythe got to his feet.

"M'lord, I can't see any relevance in pressing the witness to name any other dealers. It was indeed a risk for the witness to come forward anyway, but …"

"Your honour," put in Lorna, "I don't think Mr Wade has any qualms about naming dealers. After all, if he is to be believed, he fingered his long term supplier because of one bad batch. He seems to have little or no loyalty towards his chain of supply. So why should he not name the latest link – unless, of course, there isn't one and his whole story is a fabrication?"

"M'lord," Jeremy spread his arms in a gesture of incredulity, "how can my learned friend possibly draw *that* conclusion from the witness's reluctance to …"

"Ms Prentiss," said the judge, "there are limits to the conjecture we can exercise in a court of law, and I think you are close to those limits. I do not see how Mr Wade's not naming someone whose identity has no relevance to this case can be construed as obstructing the process of law."

"With respect, m'lord, I did not say it did, but …"

"No, not in so many words, but I'd like you to move on if you have anything more to ask this witness."

Lorna was silent for a while.

"Mr Wade, can you recall the times that you met with Mr Tomlinson-Brown just prior to when you received – *allegedly* – the bad package?"

"No, of course not," said Billy.

"You said 'same place, same time', didn't you? So you must know."

"It wasn't always the same day, though. Could have been any day."

"Well, just one day, then. You must remember at least *one* occasion when the actual day sticks in your mind."

"No, sorry."

"Very convenient, isn't it? If we can't establish *any* precise times for your dealings, we can't check out any possible alibis. No chance for the defendant to deny meeting you with any chance of proving it." She turned to the jury. "When you hear the statements of the other three users read out, you may be surprised at how similar they are to each other and to Mr Wade's testimony. I encourage you to make the comparison and consider how four disparate individuals could come up with statements so alike."

Lorna sat down.

★

Grace looked with a morbid fixation at the information on the PC screen in front of her. She had seen it all before, of course. It was nearly six weeks ago when she first received the details of the post mortems carried out on the remains of the two bodies retrieved from the wire. But now she was reviewing them in a different and closer context.

'The corpses of the two men had been on the fence for nine days', said the preamble to the main findings. 'They were mutilated by the constant attention of sea-birds feeding on them. However, the cold conditions helped in preserving enough to determine the injuries received prior to their climbing the superstructure. Also, these injuries seem to point to the reason why they undertook the climb'.

She scrolled down to a summary of the findings.

"Extensive bruising on both specimens where enough skin remained to enable an examination," she read from the report. "Specimen one – stress fracture of left forearm and three fingers on left hand. Damage to right patella. Nose broken and damage to left eye socket. Severe abrasions ..."

She minimised the document and, after a moment's hesitation, clicked on the icon titled 'Conclusions'.

'Both men died from a combination of hypothermia and trauma caused by injuries sustained either in an assault by other inmates or in a fight with each other. There is also evidence to suggest that they were attacked by sea birds whilst still alive, which may have accelerated their dying'.

Grace closed the document and then the file with a feeling of sickness rising in her stomach, and reflected, not for the first time, on the level of fear which would be needed to drive someone with such injuries to make that sort of climb.

★

"Dr Brotherton," said Jeremy, pacing around the area between the jury and the witness stand, "please tell the court the position you currently hold and the work you have carried out for this case."

Simon Brotherton was a tall, thin man in frameless glasses. He had wispy receding hair combed straight back and long enough to hang over the collar of his brown sports jacket which he wore over a check shirt.

"I am Senior Scientific Advisor to NCSRA – that's the National Controlled Substances Research Agency – based here in Guildford. I have undertaken extensive examination of samples of the drugs provided by the users who came forward and those found at both houses, and compared these with each other and with samples from batches confiscated in recent similar cases."

"And what can you tell us about the results of this extensive testing?"

"As far as is possible, I can confirm that the drugs at both locations and those handed to the police were from the same or very similar batches and hence most probably from the same source or sources."

"And what did you find regarding the quality of these drugs, specifically in relation to the sickness described by Mr Wade earlier and in the statements read out in court?"

"The cocaine was significantly contaminated, certainly enough to produce the effects described by the witnesses."

"Thank you, Dr Brotherton. One last question; is it possible that the substance found at the homes of the defendants could have been from the same batch as that which led to the death of Vincent Remus …?"

Lorna was quickly on her feet and shouting. "The Prosecution has no right …!"

"*Mr Forsythe!*" Miles Pendle boomed and turned an admonishing glare on the offending counsel.

"I was merely trying to put into the jury's minds," he responded, with exaggerated deference, "the possible severity…"

The judge cut him short.

"I know very well what you were trying to put into the jury's minds. Let me make it clear to all present. This court is not concerned in any way with the quality of the substances involved, or the consequences – real or suggested – of that quality, *except* in establishing a link between the witnesses and the drugs found at the two addresses. Otherwise, we are *only* concerned with deciding whether the defendants are responsible for selling these drugs, and I take a dim view of anything or anyone that causes us to be deflected from that objective, or who confuses the process of reaching a proper conclusion."

He turned to the jury.

"You are to ignore the last question put by the Prosecution on the basis that it has no relevance to this case whatsoever and I trust," turning back to the barrister, "I shall not have to intervene again to remind you of your duties in this matter."

Jeremy Forsythe bowed his apology and spoke again to the witness.

"Thank you, Dr Brotherton. No further questions."

He resumed his seat.

Lorna rose to her feet.

"Dr Brotherton," she said, "in your opinion, would the symptoms described by the witnesses and confirmed by you normally require treatment – at a hospital, for instance, or by a GP?"

"Not necessarily …"

"But normally?"

"There would be no permanent damage – providing the user got over the initial effects – and that would depend on quite a number of factors."

"Such as?"

"Well, primarily the amount they took, their general health at the time, their living conditions …"

"These people are addicts, Dr Brotherton, with a hard drugs dependency. You wouldn't expect their general health and living conditions to be conducive to fighting off the effect of a toxic dose of cocaine, would you?"

"I must protest, m'lord." Jeremy was on his feet. "We have no specific evidence relating to the health and accommodation of these witnesses. If my learned friend is about to produce some, then, having failed to disclose it to the Crown beforehand, I suggest that it should be deemed inadmissible."

"Like the Prosecution's last question to this witness," Lorna snapped back. "Nothing further, m'lord."

She sat down.

★

Week 9; Thursday, 21 May...

Jo took a deep breath and fixed her eyes on the Prosecution counsel.

"Detective Inspector Cottrell, could you describe for the benefit of the court, the events of the morning of Tuesday, 14th April this year?"

"On that morning, I was in charge of a police raid on the property of the Home Secretary, Tom Brown, and his wife, Maggie Tomlinson-Brown. We entered the grounds of the property at exactly 5.00 am and ..."

"When you say 'we', Detective Inspector, who exactly was with you?"

"Along with myself, a total of twelve police officers, in five vehicles, including four dog-handlers with their dogs; plus one scene-of-crime unit with four personnel. We were prepared for an initial search of the house and grounds."

"Thank you, please go on."

"I knocked on the door and rang the bell, and requested entry into the house. Then ..."

"Were you granted immediate access?"

"Yes," said Jo, a little too quickly. Jeremy raised his eyebrows.

"Really? And who was in the house, and where, when you entered."

"The Home Secretary, his wife and son were all in the hall."

"And then what happened?"

"Jack went up to the first floor and we followed him to his bedroom. He briefly locked himself in his room, saying he was getting dressed. After a short delay, he opened the door and ..."

"How short, would you say?"

"Well, I wasn't actually timing it, but ..."

"Ten seconds? Twenty seconds? A couple of minutes?"

"About three or four minutes, I suppose."

"Three or four minutes. Certainly ample time for him to get fully dressed. DI Cottrell, please tell the court what the defendant was wearing when you first entered the house."

"Just a pair of shorts."

"Shorts?"

"Boxer shorts."

"Boxer shorts. And when you gained entry to the defendant's bedroom, what was he wearing then?"

"The same."

"So he had clearly *not* been getting dressed?"

"Clearly."

"So, what had he been doing?"

"He had removed some magazines from the bottom of his wardrobe and was putting them into a holdall. When I asked why he was doing that he said he was just tidying up…"

"Even though the magazines were *inside* the wardrobe." Jeremy turned to the jury as he spoke to emphasise the point. "Detective Inspector, did the defendant at any time change his story about why he was moving the magazines?"

"Yes, on being questioned later he said he simply didn't want the police to find them."

"Thank you. Please continue."

"The dog started pawing at the remaining mags in the bottom of the wardrobe. That is when I asked the family to leave the room and brought in the forensic team. We moved the rest of the magazines out of the wardrobe and removed the base panel. Under the panel we found forty-eight bags of a substance which was later confirmed as crack cocaine."

"And please tell the court, Detective Inspector, what else you found in the room."

"Under the panel in the wardrobe next to where the drugs had been hidden, we found a mobile phone and some surgical gloves."

"And were you able to establish a connection between the phone and the drugs?"

"I had with me the two numbers we had been given by the people who had contacted the police, so I used my phone to call both numbers. The first call was answered by DI Waters using a phone he had found with the drugs at the Midanda's house. I called the second number but with no response. However, it was later shown to be the number of the phone we had found at Etherington Place."

"Just so there is no confusion, could you explain why your second call was not picked up."

"Yes, it appears the phone had been left switched on and the battery had fully discharged."

"Thank you, Detective Inspector."

Jeremy turned to the jury again, this time with an exaggerated shrug of the shoulders as if to ask if they needed any more convincing.

The counsel for the Defence rose slowly from her seat and smiled warmly at the witness.

"Detective Inspector, in your opinion, when you attended the house that morning, did the defendant's behaviour suggest ..."

Jeremy was quickly back on his feet. "M'lord, we are here to consider the facts, and one person's opinion will add nothing to ..."

"I would point out, m'lord," Lorna interrupted, "that Ms Cottrell has had ten years experience as a detective, the last two-and-a-half at inspector level. Not wishing to embarrass her, she has also recently been identified among the ranks of her peer group as exceptional in her job, resulting in her current assignment to Guildford. I cannot imagine that she has achieved all this without her expressing along the way *opinions of great value* to the course of criminal investigation and, ultimately, justice. And I am surprised," she added, "that the learned counsel should be so dismissive of one of his own key witnesses."

Miles Pendle could hardly suppress a smile at her last remark, as the chastened gentleman sat down with an apologetic look to Jo. "Please put your question, Ms Prentiss."

"Thank you, m'lord. Detective Inspector Cottrell, when you attended the house that morning the drugs were – clearly – already concealed in Jack Tomlinson-Brown's room. There is no question of that; we do not dispute it. Our contention – as you are aware – is that he did not *know* they were there.

"When, soon after arriving," she went on, "you gained access to

179

his room, Jack would have realised – *if* he had known they were there – that he was minutes away from being arrested for an extremely serious offence. *In your opinion,* was his behaviour consistent with someone in that situation?"

"No, it was not."

"So, in your opinion, he did not know they were there?"

"His *behaviour* suggested he didn't know."

"Isn't that the same thing, Detective Inspector? What I think you're saying is …"

"I think, Ms Prentiss," the judge interrupted, "the Detective Inspector has answered your question. You asked for her opinion regarding the defendant's behaviour. I paraphrase – 'was this normal behaviour for someone on the point of being exposed as a serious offender?' Answer; 'no, it wasn't'. That is clear enough. It is for the jury to decide whether that indicator is significant when considered along with everything else. I do not think you need to embellish the point by trying to draw any further conclusions from this witness."

"Thank you, m'lord. In which case may I please ask again my penultimate question, which you seemed happy for the witness to answer, so I can ensure I have not inadvertently confused the court?"

The judge nodded, with a degree of impatience.

"Detective Inspector, in your opinion and experience, was the defendant's behaviour consistent with someone who knew he was about to be arrested for a very serious crime?"

"No it was not," said Jo.

"Thank you. No further questions."

Jeremy Forsythe sprang to his feet.

"If it pleases, your honour, just two further questions to the Detective Inspector."

The judge sighed his assent.

"DI Cottrell, in order to leave no doubt in the jury's mind that I *do* value your opinion," he beamed at Jo and then the jury, "could you answer me this? You told the court how the defendant, Mr Tomlinson-Brown, claimed his hurried clean-up operation behind his locked door was because he was concerned that you would discover certain magazines in his possession. Would you say these publications were in any way extreme in their content, in terms of the level of pornography, I mean? Any disturbing images, for example?"

"No, they were relatively mild."

"*Very* mild, I would say, Detective Inspector. Now, *in your opinion*, is it likely that a highly intelligent young man of nearly twenty years could seriously believe the police would raid the Home Secretary's house at five in the morning to confiscate some lads' mags?"

Jo hesitated before replying. "I would have to say that it is *un*likely, although it would explain why he seemed surprised that …"

"You would say it is *un*likely that he would believe that," the Prosecutor interrupted. "Thank you, Detective Inspector. No further questions, m'lord."

Jo stepped down from the stand, glancing briefly towards Jack as she left the courtroom. Jeremy turned to the Judge.

"I would like to recall Detective Inspector Harry Waters to the stand, m'lord."

★

"Under-Secretary Harding to see you, sir."

"Send him in, please, Kim."

Jonathan Latiffe stood to receive his visitor and leaned across his desk to shake his hand. The Minister of Justice was a huge man, six-foot-three inches tall with broad shoulders and a significant girth. A native Black South African of forty-five years, his tight curls had started to turn grey along with his neatly-trimmed full beard, adding a distinguished element to his impressive bulk. His eyes were deep blue and twinkled with life.

"Lawrence, do sit down," he said.

His visitor seated himself on one of the wing chairs in front of the large oak desk with its green leather inlaid top as Jonathan settled back in his own chair. Kim Lacey, Jonathan's PA, entered the office with a silver tray on which was a cafetiere, cups, saucers, milk and sugar. She placed it on the desk.

"Shall I …?" She looked at Jonathan.

"No, that's okay, Kim, thank you. We'll help ourselves."

She left the room, quietly closing the door behind her.

"So, did they make it?"

"Yes," said Lawrence, "just about. The rail tracks were fixed well in advance, but they had a complete rethink on the plumbing, and especially the toilet facilities. They finished the day before yesterday – full testing yesterday and sailed today. So it was a little bit too close for comfort."

"So what have they done about the toilet problem?"

"Replaced the lot with sealed units and automatic flushes, so nothing can be moved now. They've also adapted the water supply to the cabins so that each individual one can be isolated remotely. I have to say, they've done a brilliant job in the time available."

"And the next lot after this. Remind me when they go," said Jonathan, pouring the coffee.

"Six weeks from now. Thursday 2nd July."

"Okay. Stay close to Nicholson, Lawrence. Useful to have direct access one-to-one. Sugar?"

★

"Detective Inspector Waters," said Lorna, "you have told the court in great detail how the raid on the Midandas' house was carried out on the morning of the 14th of April. Can you now describe Mr Midanda's *behaviour* during the course of the raid?"

"He was clearly shaken and worried," said DI Waters, "as you'd expect under the circumstances."

"Meaning what, exactly," asked Lorna. "What 'circumstances'?"

"Well …" the detective hesitated, looking confused. "Being put on the spot, I mean. Being found out."

"So you don't think a *perfectly innocent* person might look shaken and worried when they are awakened at five in the morning by a dozen police officers crashing into their home?"

She looked across at the jury and gallery, her eyes wide with incredulity, and was rewarded with a few smiles and sniggers.

"I'm not saying that, but…"

"Did Mr Midanda exhibit any surprise when you *tore* up the floor and found the drugs? In your opinion, I mean."

"Well, he …"

"Or did he just say something like 'it's a fair cop, guv?'"

"Well, of course he *acted* as though he was surprised."

"You know Jason well, do you, DI Waters? Met him many times before? Always in trouble, is he?"

"No, I'd never met him previously, in fact."

"So how could you possibly know he was *acting*?"

DI Waters hesitated briefly before answering.

"Well, because of all the other evidence."

"But you were *there*, DI Waters. You have – what – fifteen years experience in CID? I'm sure you can form your own opinions and ideas; you don't need backroom experts to *tell* you what to think, surely?"

Jeremy Forsythe got to his feet.

"M'lord, the witness is giving his *opinions*, as requested by my learned friend. These are, by definition, what he *believes*. If it is not what Defence counsel wants to hear, then that is hardly the fault of the witness if he is answering the questions truthfully, which I am sure this court has no doubt that he is. I suggest …"

The judge turned to the Defence counsel. "Ms Prentiss, please explain what you are hoping to achieve with this line of questioning so we may 'cut to the chase' as it were."

"Yes, m'lord. I simply want to establish that both defendants exhibited the same level of shock and surprise when the drugs were found. I feel that it is misleading for the witness to dismiss the reaction of Jason Midanda as 'obviously acting' when there is no evidence that it was not genuine. That's all."

"Very well. But I think we must understand that DI Waters *was* party to all the 'backroom' – as you call it – evidence before he went to the house. In fact, without that evidence beforehand he wouldn't have gone there at all. I think with that weight of knowledge, plus the discovery of the drugs themselves, we can forgive him forming such an opinion."

He looked down at her, over the top of his spectacles, inviting her to speak. Lorna chose to remain silent.

"So, Ms Prentiss, can we move on?"

"Just a couple more questions, m'lord. *Factual* ones, this time."

Miles Pendle beamed at her and nodded.

"DI Waters, is it true that on the Thursday before your raid on the Midandas' house, the property was broken into?"

"Well, I was not involved with that."

"No, but you can confirm or otherwise?" Judge Pendle stepped in with the question.

"Yes, m'lord, there *was* a break-in at the house."

"Thank you, Detective Inspector," said Lorna. "And is it true that nothing was taken."

"Yes, that's correct."

"It is just possible though, is it not, that something could have been *left* there by the intruders? Some drugs perhaps?"

"M'lord, I really must …!"

"My question," Lorna continued before Jeremy could finish, "was whether it was *possible*."

"Very well," said the judge. "Please answer the question, DI Waters."

"Yes, it is just possible, I suppose. But highly …"

"Thank you, DI Waters. No further questions."

Jeremy was on his feet.

"Just a couple more questions to the witness, if it pleases, m'lord. Detective Inspector, was the Midanda household the only one which was entered on that street on that particular day, and if not, how many others?"

"No it was not. A total of eight houses were broken into."

"Thank you, and how many of those had anything taken from them?"

"Four of them; they just had laptops taken. There were no laptops in the others, including the Midandas'."

"Thank you. No further questions. That completes the case for the Prosecution, m'lord."

DI Waters stepped down.

"Thank you, Detective Inspector," said the judge. "The court will adjourn until 10.00 am tomorrow when we will hear the case for the Defence."

"The court will rise."

Justice Pendle swept from the room.

CHAPTER FOURTEEN

Week 9; Friday, 22 May…

Shortly after 10.00 am, in a packed and expectant courtroom, Lorna Prentiss rose to begin her attempt to save her two clients. They were both dressed smartly, as before, in the same lounge suits and Jack was now also wearing a tie.

"These two young men are well educated individuals from good families," she said. "They have no history at all of ever stepping outside the law; of breaking the rules of our society. Academically, they have demonstrated a high level of commitment to their education and their personal development. Nothing in their behaviour or demeanour over the past weeks and months and years is consistent with the serious crime of which they find themselves accused.

"Where was the opportunity, or the *need*, for such activities? Who are their contacts higher in the chain? Police intelligence is extensive on the sources and suppliers of the types of drugs involved, so why are they unable to make a link between the defendants and a likely source. The street value of the drugs confiscated from both houses was in excess of a hundred thousand pounds. Where did they get the means to acquire them, and where is the money from sales already made?

"No-one has provided answers to those questions. The very proof of their innocence lies in the *absence* of those answers and of any evidence pointing them towards such actions. In fact, the absolute normality of their lives is the most compelling piece of evidence you will hear in the whole of this trial. Today, I will be calling a number of witnesses to testify to that fact and they, I have no doubt, will convince you that the defendants ware simply not capable of perpetrating this crime."

She turned to the judge, who nodded to proceed.

"Call Mr Terry Patterson."

A tall thin man in his late forties with wiry red-brown hair and a long pointed goatee beard took the stand. He wore a purple corduroy sports jacket over a black polo shirt and faded blue jeans.

"Mr Patterson, could you please tell the court your position and places of work."

"Yes, certainly, I am the Higher Education Art Coordinator for the Guildford area and as part of that role I teach at a number of colleges, including Kingfield College in Woking, where Jack Tomlinson-Brown is a student."

"Thank you, and can you tell us about Jack in terms of his time spent as a student at the college."

"I've known Jack now for nearly three years. He is extremely talented – a natural at his chosen subject. I see him three times a week. Jack is a diligent worker with, I understand, an excellent attendance record. He completed and passed the applied A level in Art and Design last year with a double A grade and is currently taking a one-year extension to an A level in Fine Art which, I believe, is his main strength."

"Thank you, Mr Patterson. You are aware of Jack's circumstances, of course. Is there anything in Jack's background or behaviour that would lead you to suspect he was in any way capable of doing what he is accused of doing?"

"I am absolutely certain he could not have done this. In addition to his academic ability he is invariably the life and soul of the class – sometimes a bit too much so," he added, drawing an appreciative smile from Lorna. "There is no way he could be guilty of such a crime."

"Thank you, Mr Patterson. What proportion of your students – approximately – choose to do an extra year once they have completed their A level studies?"

"Oh, very few – probably less than five percent, I'd say. It's quite rare. Most of them can't get out of the door fast enough!"

"So it seems unlikely, doesn't it, if he had such a lucrative, albeit illegal, business going on outside the college, that he would choose to take up his time with more college work?"

"Certainly very unlikely."

"Thank you, Mr Patterson. No further questions."

Justice Pendle nodded to Lorna then to Jeremy to invite his cross examination. The Prosecution counsel rose very slowly and walked forward to stand close to the jury facing the witness.

"Mr Patterson, how long have you been teaching art – not just in your present capacity, but overall?"

"Just over twenty-three years."

"And during that time, I guess you must have taught hundreds – more likely thousands – of students."

"Yes, I should imagine so."

"And how many of those were drug dealers?"

Terry Patterson's eyes shot wide open. "Well, I've no idea. None I should think."

"But you *do* think you would recognise one if you saw one?"

"Well, I'm not sure. But what I can say is that Jack certainly doesn't fit what I would *imagine* a drug dealer would be like."

Jeremy let the statement hang in the air for a few moments. He looked across at the jury and shook his head before speaking.

"I am sure *imagination* is a great asset in art, Mr Patterson, but it's not much use in a court of law, I'm afraid. Let me ask you another question – approximately how many hours a week are you in contact with Mr Tomlinson-Brown?"

"Well, I can tell you exactly. Two hours – that's three periods including one tutorial."

"So, if my calculations are correct, that leaves just one hundred and sixty-six hours every week during which you are *not* in contact with him."

Lorna stood up quickly. "M'lord, Mr Patterson has not been asked here to account for the defendant's movements, but to deliver a character reference, as the Prosecution knows. I believe he has done that very effectively in spite of the attempts to trivialise his testimony."

"I am merely pointing out, m'lord, that Mr Patterson only observes the defendant for a very short period of time each week in a very structured environment and hence ..."

"Ms Prentiss. I take your point," said Miles Pendle, "but I also recognise that of the Crown as well, particularly in relation to the specific circumstances under which the witness has observed the defendant. You may proceed, Mr Forsythe."

"Thank you, m'lord. I have no further questions."

Mr Patterson left the witness box.

"I'd like to call Mr Tariq Shah to the stand," said Lorna.

The man who strode confidently into the room was the diametric opposite of the previous witness in appearance. Below average height, he wore a white shirt under a charcoal grey suit jacket, both items of clothing stretched to their limit by his bulky frame. His thin black hair was combed straight back and held in place by gel.

"Mr Shah, could you tell the court your current occupation and how you come to know Jason Midanda?"

"I am Senior IT tutor at Kingfield College in Woking, and Jason is one of my students."

"Thanks you, Mr Shah. Could you tell the court what you know about Jason, please?"

"Jason Midanda is, quite simply, an exceptional student – the best I have ever taught in over fourteen years in this field. He has an almost uncanny aptitude for the subject and I have no doubt will have a brilliant career in any branch of information and communication technology he chooses. In this, his final A level year, he has also been broadening his experience by taking tutorials with groups of first year A level students and giving talks to the after-school IT club for years ten and eleven."

"Thank you, Mr Shah. Very comprehensive. And based on your knowledge of this young man, do you think it is at all possible that he could commit the crime of which he has been accused."

"I'm not sure it would be accurate to say it was not *possible*, but I would be astonished if it were true, not just on the basis of his academic prowess and his very high earning potential in this field, but because of the person he is, a supportive, caring individual who will always find time to help others."

"Mr Shah, have you had any experience with drug users and dealers in the past?"

"Yes, I used to be a volunteer counsellor for drug addicts with an off-shoot of the Samaritans, working with people who were trying to fight their addiction. I didn't interview any dealers, of course, but you got to know a lot about them through the users – you know, how they would prey on people's dependency."

"So you do have a working knowledge – albeit second hand – of what dealers are like?"

Lorna looked across at Jeremy and then the judge.

"Yes, I think so, and they are nothing like Jason Midanda."

"Thank you very much, Mr Shah. No further questions."

Lorna sat down as Jeremy got to his feet and strolled to his favourite position near the jury.

"Mr Shah, approximately how many hours each week are you in contact with Mr Midanda?"

Lorna looked across at the judge and raised her eyebrows with the unspoken question. Miles smiled down at her, shaking his head.

"I see him every day except Monday" said Mr Shah. "I would say, on average, around eight to ten hours a week."

"Thank you, Mr Shah. No further questions."

Judge Pendle leaned towards Lorna.

"Ms Prentiss, how many more character witnesses are you planning to call?"

"Three more, m'lord. Each of these will be providing testimony on behalf of *both* defendants."

"Very well, please proceed."

The first of these witnesses, Jonnie Denver, the landlord of the Cross Keys pub in Woking, described two friendly, popular individuals who never caused trouble, were never rowdy or difficult or got into fights. Always paid up for drinks without any hassle. Were ideal customers, in fact, and were certainly never seen talking in a clandestine way to anyone else. In fact, he said, the establishment had a strong policy for identifying and banning any dealers who tried to ply their illegal trade on the premises.

"Mr Denver," said Jeremy, on cross-examination. "How many hours a week on average are you in a position to observe the defendants?"

"No idea," said the landlord, "but easily enough to be certain I'm right about them."

Miles Pendle smiled across at Lorna as Mr Denver stepped down.

"I'd like next to call Mr Antonio Rocco."

A heavy-set man in a cream suit and open-necked floral shirt took the stand. His Latin features and dark complexion were accentuated by long jet-black hair which was combed straight back.

"Mr Rocco," said Lorna, "could you tell the court your occupation, please?"

"I am the owner and manager of Rocco's Ball Room, Snooker and Pool Club, in Leatherhead."

"And how do you come to know the two defendants?"

"Well, they are regular customers and I've known them for quite a few years."

"And, in your own words, how would you describe these two young men?"

"Good kids, lots of friends. Polite, courteous, always pay on the spot for drinks and for the tables. Both good players, actually."

"Do you ever have any trouble at your place, Mr Rocco? You know, arguments, fights – that sort of thing."

"Nothing excessive. I suppose I have my fair share. But it's a good, safe place," he added quickly. "We soon sort things out if there's a problem."

"Have either of the defendants ever been involved in any trouble?"

"No, Never."

"Never?"

"Never. That's the truth. As I said, they're good kids. If all my customers were like them, I wouldn't have to use all that Grecian 2000." He pushed his hand back through his hair and smiled at the jury, extracting some laughter.

"Thank you, Mr Rocco," said Lorna, smiling. "Just one more question. Do you have a policy on the dealing of banned substances on your premises?"

"It's simply not allowed, if that's what you mean by a policy. I employ a number of security people part of whose job it is to identify and eject anyone even suspected of dealing in the Ball Room. As far as it's possible to say, it just doesn't happen at Rocco's."

"Thank you. No further questions."

Jeremy rose and walked slowly across to stand next to the jury.

"How many times a week do the defendants attend your club, Mr Rocco?" asked Jeremy.

"It varies. Pretty much every week though; sometimes just once, sometimes a couple of nights. Sometimes on Wednesday afternoons as well."

"And is the club doing well? Are you busy most of the time?"

"*All* the time, actually. Manic most nights. Usually four on each table and punters waiting."

"And how many tables do you have?"

"Four snooker and six pool – ten all together."

"So that's forty people playing and – say – forty more waiting. Would that be about right?"

"Yes that's …"

"And I assume you get quite a lot of custom from people just there to have a few drinks – I mean, not playing at all?"

"Yes, some people just use it as a pub. There's a large lounge area as well."

"So at any one time you might have – would you say – over a hundred people in the club?"

"Easily …but why…?"

"Well, Mr Rocco, it seems to me that the defendants could only ever be a couple of people in a large crowd during their one or two visits a week, rather than people you could observe closely enough and for long enough to make a statement about their character. Isn't that right?"

Jeremy glanced across at Lorna.

"Well, you get a sort of feel for who's okay and who isn't," said the witness.

"A sort of feel," Jeremy repeated, slowly, shaking his head. "Thank you, Mr Rocco, no further questions." He went back to his seat, crossing his arms.

As Antonio Rocco left the stand, Tom sat, head in hands, staring down at his feet, thinking just how light-weight such a defence was sounding against the volume of hard evidence which had gone before.

"Just one more witness, m'lord," said Lorna.

Tom's head shot up and his eyes bulged in disbelief as the name was called out. He looked angrily across at Daniel who had already turned and was waiting to receive his glare. The lawyer nodded to him, vigorously, trying to convey as much assurance as possible. A tall good-looking young man in an expensive sports jacket and designer jeans entered the court room, turning to Jack and Jason with a grim smile and a slight raising of his right hand in a thumbs-up gesture. He took the stand and then the oath.

"State your name, please."

"Mickey Kadawe."

"And could you tell the court your address and occupation?"

"Manston Grange off Grindalls Road in Woking. And I'm the manager-stroke-agent for a number of professional and semi-professional rock artists and bands, including Lilli Bo-Peep, Abattoir Ratts and Chick Eater."

"A very impressive client list, Mr Kadawe, if I may say so," said Lorna. "You know why you are here today – to provide an insight into the lives of Jack and Jason. I am fully aware of your close friendship with both men, but I remind you that you are under oath and should not try to embroider the truth for their benefit. I believe, as I'm sure you do, that the pure and simple truth is all that is necessary to convince the court of their good character." Mickey nodded and smiled at Lorna who continued. "Could you describe in your own words how you come to know the defendants, starting with Jason?"

"Sure, I've known Jay for nearly nine years, since we were both in the same junior school, although in different years. Most of the kids were white and we just sort of came together with some of the other black kids. I always thought of myself as like a big brother to him. And we kept in touch after he got a scholarship for Bishop's and even after ... well ... even after I left school."

"Tell the court why you left the school, Mr Kadawe."

"I was sent to a young offenders' institute after someone got hurt in a fight I was in. I was fifteen-years-old and it followed a number of other convictions for things like theft, disruptive behaviour, fighting – just normal kids stuff, really. I sort of fell apart after my dad went back to South Africa."

"And following your detention?"

"Well, I guess it did the trick. I've not been in trouble since then – that's nearly five years now."

"Thank you for being honest with the court, Mr Kadawe. And during the nine years you have known him, you have always been close to Jason?"

"Yes – and quite literally now, in fact. He hangs out at my house quite a lot – when he's not at college. We play pool; just chill out together really, like you do. And I know he's there when I'm away, because my work takes up a lot of time now."

"And has he ever been in trouble during the time you've known him?"

"Not once. I don't think he'd know how to get into trouble if he wanted to. He's absolutely squeaky clean – probably been a good influence on me." He smiled again at Lorna, who gave a little laugh.

"And Jack, how did you come to meet him?"

"Well, through Jason. One night, we all ended up – the three of us – in an alley together facing off a bunch of guys who were getting at Jay for some reason," he glanced up at Katey in the gallery. "Anyway, we saw them off, and after that me and Jack have been best buddies really. That happened around eighteen months ago, I guess."

"And do you see much of Jack as well?"

"Yes, he stays over at the house at least a couple of nights a week, sometimes three or four, so I see him probably more than I do Jason."

Tom sucked in a breath causing Mags and Katey to look briefly across at him.

"So you see both of them regularly?"

"Just about every day of every week when I'm not working away."

"And you would know if either man was dealing in banned substances – hard drugs?"

Mickey laughed. "It's unbelievable! The whole thing is a farce. I doubt if Jack has ever had a single criminal thought in his entire life. There is absolutely no way he – or Jason – could have done this. Never in a million years."

"Thank you, Mr Kadawe."

Jeremy sprang to his feet.

"Mr Kadawe, I bet you of all people, with your background, *never in a million years* expected to appear as a character witness for the Defence in a court of law. But it's happened nonetheless, hasn't it?"

Mickey remained silent.

"Can you remember how many times you were charged with offences between the ages of twelve and fifteen?"

"No, it's all in the past."

"Twenty-seven times, Mr Kadawe, I'm not surprised you can't …"

"*Master* Kadawe, to be accurate."

"I beg your pardon!"

"Well, at the time I was Master Kadawe, not Mister. It was a long time ago. I was just a kid."

"And can you remember what those charges were?"

"Not all of them individually. I've just given some examples. Ancient history was never one of my best subjects."

"Burglary, mugging, threatening behaviour – to two of the teachers at your school, in fact, on separate occasions – vandalism, assault, stealing a car – twice, supplying drugs – at school! Shall I go on?"

"Please do, it's all water under the bridge as far as I'm concerned. Oh, and by the way, I didn't steal a car twice, I stole two different cars."

There was some laughter in the courtroom and Miles Pendle had a quiet smile behind his hand.

"Well, I'm glad you think this is amusing, Mr Kadawe. If I was either of the defendants I'd be very concerned if you were the best person my counsel could find to give me a character reference." He turned to the jury. "I can only assume that the Defence feels that the witness's presence in that role might generate some sympathy on behalf of the accused. That is the *only* reason I can think of for getting him here."

Mickey's composure suddenly gave way to anger "Look this is fucking stupid!"

Miles Pendle was quick to step in.

"Mr Kadawe, I will not stand for that sort of language in my court! I will refrain from taking any action because of your behaviour so far in the face of the Crown's goading. But I will not allow a repeat, do you understand?"

"Yes, I apologise, your honour," said Mickey. "But what I mean is that the whole thing is ridiculous. You don't know these guys. Jack is the biggest goody-two-shoes in the world."

"Mr Kadawe…" the judge again.

"I bet he's never had an overdue library book. If he spit in the street, he'd turn himself in. *And* Jason. They wouldn't know cocaine from cocoa."

"Mr Kadawe! You will stop right now. You are here to answer the specific questions put to you by counsel; that's all."

"But *he* hasn't asked me *anything* about Jack and Jason. It's been all about me. Hey, I admit I've been a bad boy in the past, okay? But these guys? No way!"

"Your honour," Jeremy said. "I do think this witness should be removed if he can't..."

"M'lord," Lorna interrupted him, "Mr Kadawe has been called as a character witness for the defendants and, whereas, of course, I cannot condone his indiscretion, I think we can recognise his frustration at the questions being put to him by the Prosecution."

"We have every right to challenge a witness's suitability to provide an assessment of another person's behaviour and character. And it seems reasonable to assume that a witness's *own* personal history – recent *or* ancient – would have a huge impact on what he or she regards as *acceptable* behaviour and *good* character. It is for the Defence to draw out the witness's views and for the Prosecution to examine their validity. And I suggest, m'lord, that is precisely what has just transpired. And, furthermore," he added, "it mirrors exactly what the Defence attempted to do – unsuccessfully, I might add – with a number of the Crown's witnesses earlier in the proceedings."

"If it pleases ..."

"It does *not*, Ms Prentiss." Miles Pendle turned to Mickey.

"Mr Kadawe, you may stand down. Thank you for your testimony." He turned to address the jury as Mickey left the witness stand with obvious reluctance. "Mr Forsythe is quite correct in pointing out that he is within his rights to challenge the suitability of the witness and the integrity of his testimony. However, you should *not* be influenced by the last witness's outburst and use of the f-word word. It is, after all, just a word, and one which is in such common use now as to carry very little weight even as a means of emphasis. What you *should* concern yourself with is the sincerity and relevance of Mr Kadawe's observations."

He consulted some papers in front of him.

"Ms Prentiss, am I to understand that you will next be calling the defendants to take the stand?"

"That is correct, m'lord."

Jeremy Forsythe got to his feet.

"Excuse me, your honour, but I had expected that the Defence would be calling Katey Tomlinson-Brown."

Miles Pendle sighed.

"And why would you expect that, Mr Forsythe?"

"Well, for the same reason as the last witness was called. Someone who has been very close to both defendants, being the sister of one and the partner of the other."

The judge transferred the question to the Defence counsel with a raising of the eyebrows.

"I shall not be calling anyone else to the stand except the defendants, m'lord."

"Thank you, Ms Prentiss."

Jeremy Forsythe sat down with a noisy flourish.

"The time is twelve-fifteen. I would normally call a recess for lunch at this time and reconvene in approximately one hour. However, I feel it is important that we hear from both defendants on the same day, and I do not believe we will have time this afternoon. For that reason, I am now calling an end to today's proceedings. Please be back in court for ten o'clock prompt on Monday morning. Good afternoon."

★

Tom pulled into the drive at Etherington Place. Mags got out of the car almost before it had stopped and walked quickly to the house. Tom ran after her, catching up just as she entered the porch. Mrs McGovern, their housekeeper, was waiting for them in the hall. Her eyes were watery and red and her whole body seemed to sag with the weight of her sadness.

"I was going to do dinner for around seven o'clock," she said, in a shaky whisper. "But I could do lunch instead. Just something light."

Mags shook her head.

"Not for me, thank you, Millie."

"You must eat something. It won't help Jack if …"

"*Nothing* is going to help Jack now!" Mags cried, and ran upstairs.

Millicent McGovern broke down herself, covering her face with both hands. Tom put his arms around her and held her to him.

"Everybody's doing all they can, Millie. It's not over yet. I'll try to get Mags to come down, but I'll have some lunch anyway, please. Then you can get an early finish."

He held her until she had recovered her composure and smiled gently as she stepped away from him. He went upstairs to see Mags. She was sitting in Jack's room on his bed, staring at the wardrobe as if the object itself was the source of all her grief.

"Darling, do come and have something to eat."

Mags remained silent.

"Perhaps I should ask Katey to come back," he said. "I'm sure Leila will be alright on her own and I think you need her here – we both need her."

"Did you expect something like this?" she said, turning on him angrily.

"What do you mean?"

"You knew this was coming, didn't you?"

"Knew what was coming? What on earth are you talking about?"

"That night before your speech to the House, you told me you were worried about the children. I asked you if it was anything to do with the NJR, and you didn't answer me."

"I seem to remember that I didn't answer you because I didn't understand the question."

"And then the following day you announced this barbaric treatment for drug dealers – which nobody wants, anyway, it seems …"

"Just listen to what you're suggesting, Mags! You're not seriously accusing me of believing that Jack was dealing drugs, and then pushing for a proposal to exile drug dealers? Or *is* that what you're saying?"

"It all fits, now. That's why you didn't answer me."

"That's why I didn't understand the question!" he shouted. "Because it was based on such a ludicrous assumption! How can you believe that? Perhaps you think I made this change *just* to punish Jack. You know – 'I'll teach the little bastard. I'll send him away for ever!' Is *that* what you think of me?"

He suddenly gave way, slumping to his knees and covering his face with his hands as the tears came. She instinctively started to go to him, and then held herself back. Neither spoke for several moments while Tom struggled to recover his dignity.

"Tell me, Tom." Her voice was just above a whisper. "Do you think he's guilty?"

"I don't know. I just don't know. I really want to believe …"

There was another long silence as Tom finally composed himself and rose unsteadily to his feet, rubbing his eyes.

"I'd like to be alone," said Mags.

"Yes," he said. "I'll see you later."

"No, I mean I'd like you to move into another room. Now. This afternoon."

Tom fought back more tears.

"If … that's what you want."

"It is. Until this is all over – at least."

CHAPTER FIFTEEN

Three days later
Week 10; Monday, 25 May…

Jack entered the courtroom alone. He was pale, hunched, lethargic in his movements and appeared lifeless and disinterested. Lorna Prentiss spoke slowly, as if explaining a difficult concept to a small child.

"Jack, the Prosecution has presented a catalogue of evidence – hard evidence – linking you with the selling of illegal drugs in and around the Woking area. This is your opportunity to convince this court – this jury – that what they have heard from the Crown based on that evidence is incorrect and that you are, in fact, the victim of a malicious deception. Do you understand?"

"Yes." His reply was barely audible.

"You will need to speak up," said Miles Pendle, "so everyone can hear what you are saying."

"You have seen images," continued Lorna, "allegedly of you, which were captured on security cameras in Delaware Street in Woking on a number of occasions earlier this year." She raised her eyebrows, inviting a response. Jack remained silent, his eyes unfocused, head slightly bowed. "Can you confirm that those images were, in fact, of you?"

"Yes." His voice was still not much more than a whisper.

"Mr Tomlinson-Brown," said the judge, "please …"

"Yes!" snapped Jack, his head turning briefly towards him, eyes flashing. There was a buzz of surprise around the room. Lorna continued quickly.

"They showed you meeting with and talking to some people there. Can you explain what was going on?"

"No!" Jack almost shouted his response this time. Even Jeremy Forsythe looked a little uncomfortable.

"What I mean is, could you tell us what happened?"

Jack looked across at her for a few moments before answering. "I just told you, I don't know."

"Mr Tomlinson-Brown," Miles Pendle boomed at him. "This is *your* counsel, putting *your* case to the jury. I strongly advise you to try and help her."

Jack shook his head violently with a noise somewhere between a snort and a sigh. "I have no idea what's going on," he shouted, "so I'm not sure *how* I can help her."

Lorna turned to Miles Pendle. "M'lord, could I request a brief recess whilst I speak to my client?"

"I think that's a very good idea, Ms Prentiss. I am sure when you do you will make him understand just how critical this part of the proceedings is, although I am very surprised as to why it should be necessary to do so. Court is adjourned for thirty minutes."

★

There was a buzz of anticipation as Jack was led back into the courtroom and Lorna stood in readiness to begin.

"Jack, it's very important that you explain satisfactorily to the court the circumstances surrounding the incidents on Delaware Street in Woking where you were approached separately by a number of different people. As you have heard, all those involved were known drug users, so clearly we need to establish why they approached you. Do you understand?"

"Yes, I understand," said Jack.

"Let's start with the most recent incident. This took place just after six o'clock in the early evening of Tuesday 24th March. On this occasion you were observed by one of the investigating team. Do you remember the incident?"

"Yes."

"Can you tell the court what happened?"

"This guy came up to me and said he wanted to deal. That's all."

"What did he mean by that?"

"He wanted drugs."

"What kind of drugs?"

"Hard stuff – crack, heroine."

"How did you know that?"

"They say 'deal' for hard and 'trade' for soft."

"Please tell the court, so there's no misunderstanding, how you come to know the terminology."

"It's common knowledge. The words they use on the street. Everybody knows that."

"When you say 'everybody' you don't mean everybody who uses, deals or trades in drugs. You mean, I think, *all* young people who are familiar with current terms and expressions used on the streets. Am I right?"

"Yes."

"Quite. So what happened next?"

"Next when?"

"When this person approached you in the street."

"I told him to … well … fuck off. I didn't want anything to do with him. I just thought it was mistaken identity. You know, like the rest."

"And what did he do?"

"Well, he got a bit aggressive. Pushed me; I pushed him back; one or two other people round about got involved. Then it all calmed down and he went. Never saw him again."

"Thank you, Jack. You said 'like the rest'. Could you explain what you meant by that."

Jack visibly sagged, as if the effort so far had drained him. He took a long time to reply. Lorna shuffled her notes impatiently.

"Jack …?"

"There were about six others." The words came out like a long sigh. "Same thing. Asked me for drugs. I told them the same – fuck off. That's all I can tell you."

"Why do you think they approached you, Jack?"

"Like I said before. Mistaken identity. They thought I was somebody else."

He turned his head, looking blankly at the wall at the back of the court, as if he'd said all he was going to say.

"But you can assure the court that nothing passed between you and any of these people?"

Jack looked wearily towards her, then suddenly shouted.

"I've just said what happened! How many different ways do you want to hear it?"

Lorna was silent for a long time before speaking again.

"Can we talk now about the night of the party …"

★

Jeremy stayed in his seat for a long time after Lorna sat down. When he rose it was slowly and with great deliberation.

"Firstly, Mr Tomlinson-Brown, let me congratulate you on your command of drug-related street language. I certainly didn't appreciate the subtle differences in terminology. For someone who claims he has never been anywhere near drugs in his life, you seem remarkably well educated."

He swept a look of wide-eyed incredulity around the courtroom.

"You told the court that you believe you were a victim of mistaken identity on the *twelve* occasions you were approached by *eight* different people on Delaware Street. One of those eight approached you …" he checked his hand-written notes "…three times, and two others on two separate occasions each. I'm sure the court will find it hard to believe – as I do – that multiple cases of mistaken identity are likely in such clandestine circumstances. It seems incredible that people seeking illegal substances in broad daylight would be that careless. Don't you agree, Mr Tomlinson-Brown?"

Jack had been staring down at the floor in front of him and looked up quickly at the mention of his name. He said nothing.

"I said, don't you agree, Mr Tomlinson-Brown?" Jeremy repeated.

Jack looked blankly around the courtroom and shrugged. "Don't know," he said.

Jeremy gave a loud sigh and looked across at Lorna with a private, almost apologetic, shrug. He turned back to Jack.

"Mr Tomlinson-Brown, let me recap just *some* of the facts in order to save you having to answer any more unnecessary questions. Eight different *known* drug users approached you asking for drugs over a period of two weeks, some on more than one occasion. Prior to that, seven different people phoned the police, three of whom have since identified you as their supplier. These three are known to have made calls to a phone found hidden in your wardrobe, along with forty-eight bags of crack cocaine. Everything I have just said is *true*. Can you think of *any* context where these facts could apply other than the very obvious one, which is that you are a dealer of Class A drugs?"

Jack said nothing, and his eyes dropped to stare at the floor again.

"The court is waiting, Mr Tomlinson- Brown."

Still no response.

"Mr Tomlinson-Brown," Miles Pendle leaned forward, "are you going to answer the question?"

Jack shook his head but remained silent.

"Let me put it another way, Mr Tomlinson-Brown. If you are claiming – as you have – that you are innocent, can you think of anyone who would go to so much trouble to do you this sort of harm? Anyone who has a grudge against you? Anyone who you have upset or annoyed? Anyone you owe money to? *Anyone?*"

Jack continued looking at the floor and gave the slightest shake of the head.

"One final question, then," said Jeremy. "An easy one. When did you decide to hold the party at Etherington Place?"

Jack shook his head again without looking up.

"Surely you can answer that?" said Jeremy.

"No. Can't remember."

Jeremy shot a glance at Lorna.

"No further questions, m'lord."

★

David was halfway through his forty sit-ups when his mobile sounded with an incoming call. He recognised the number.

"Hi," said Jo. "You sound out of breath. Are you okay?"

"I'm at the gym, and I am certainly *not* out of breath."

"Just the standard heavy breathing like last time, then. Anyway, just wondered if you got to listen on Thursday."

"I did and I thought you were great. Not sure whether Mr Forsythe will think so. He seemed to be having trouble getting you on his side. I doubt if you'll be nominated for witness-of-the-year by the Crown Prosecution Service."

"But it was okay, you think?"

"Absolutely."

"Thank you. And the other reason I phoned is that I'm over your way this Thursday to sign the contract for Brantingham Villas. Bit sad really, like signing my past away, but lucky to get a buyer so quickly, I suppose. I wondered if you were free for lunch."

"That would be great," said David. "We could go to my new local."

★

The courtroom settled after the lunch recess as Lorna rose from her seat.

"You have heard the evidence presented by the Crown allegedly linking you with the selling of illegal drugs in and around the Woking area. This is your opportunity to convince the jury that you are in no way connected with this crime and that you are the victim of a malicious deception. Do you understand?"

"I understand," said Jason.

He projected a very different figure to that of his friend, standing tall and erect in the dock, eyes alert and attentive, as if to ensure he caught and understood every word.

"Could you tell the court, have you ever been approached, directly or by phone, by the witness whose statement was read out earlier and who claimed to be buying drugs from you?"

"Absolutely not."

"Do you recognise his name or those of any of the three users who phoned the police claiming to have bought drugs from you but who did *not* make statements?"

"No, I haven't heard of any of them. I have no idea what's going on. I only know there's a hell of a lot of liars out there and ..."

"Thank you, Jason. Please just answer my questions for the moment. Can you describe what happened in the early hours of the morning on Tuesday 14th April?"

"Well, what happened was exactly what the detective described. There was a hammering on the door at about five o'clock – it scared my girlfriend and my mum half to death. Then they waded in – about ten policemen – and started searching around, mainly in my bedroom. The dog started sniffing the carpet and they ripped it up and found a loose floorboard. They tore that up as well and found this stuff. I'd never seen it before, that's the God's honest truth. I was just amazed! I definitely *wasn't* acting, that's for sure!"

"And have you any idea how it got there?"

"I can only think it was put there during the break-in."

"What was the place like after the break-in? Was there a lot of mess?"

"A bit, not much. There was nothing smashed or anything, just some stuff pulled out of drawers and that – clothes mainly. Nothing touched that you might expect to go – x-Box, DVD, PC, TV and such. They hadn't been moved."

"So none of the sort of items which could have been relatively easy to remove had been taken?"

"No, none at all."

Lorna hesitated. Jeremy rose to his feet to fill the empty few seconds.

"M'lord, I'm not sure where this is taking us. I certainly would not want to curtail the defendant's attempt to support his case, but the court already knows why these items were not taken." He looked down at his notes. "For example, in one of the houses in the same street where nothing was taken, a five hundred pound digital camera was lying on the table and was left untouched. I thought we had established that the thieves were looking specifically for laptops and these were the only items stolen." He shrugged and sat down.

"Ms Prentiss?" Miles Pendle invited a response.

"Well, m'lord, the break-in at the Midandas' is the obvious time for the drugs to have been placed in the house. I am merely trying to establish any clues that point specifically to that taking place. However, I will move on."

She turned back to Jason.

"Along with the drugs which were found in your house, a mobile phone was also recovered. You have been shown the list of numbers that previously contacted that phone?"

"Yes, I have."

"Do you recognise any of the numbers?"

"No, none at all."

"Is the number of the phone which was found in your bedroom at all familiar to you?"

"No, it's somebody else's. Has to be."

Jeremy gave a loud sigh, and Miles Pendle looked questioningly at him. The counsel spread his arms wide in an elaborate shrug.

"Do you have a point to make Mr Forsythe?"

"With respect to my learned colleague, m'lord, I am at a loss as to the point of these questions. The defendant has pleaded not guilty, so he will obviously deny any familiarity with anything incriminating found at his house. However, I will wait my turn."

"Indeed you *will*," said the judge. "Ms Prentiss?"

"I have no further questions, m'lord, but I would point out that the answers given by Mr Midanda are consistent with those of an *innocent* person, as he will remain unless proved otherwise."

She took her seat with a fierce glare towards her opponent.

Jeremy rose from his seat.

"Mr Midanda, can you remember when it was decided to hold the party at Etherington Place?"

"Well, it wasn't exactly *my* party, so ..."

"Let me put it another way; when did *you* first learn about the party? Can you remember?"

Jason paused for a moment.

"Yes, it was when I saw Katey – my girlfriend – on the Saturday before. She'd just asked her mum and..."

"So that would be six days before the party itself?"

"Yes, that's right."

"Now, with you being very close to both Jack and Katey, am I right in assuming that you would know about it before it was *generally* known and certainly before people were actually invited?"

"Yes, I guess you would be right."

"Thank you, Mr Midanda."

He walked slowly from his seat and stood beside the jury, pausing for a long time before he spoke again.

"Mr Midanda, can you think of *anyone* who would want to carry out such an incredibly elaborate scam in order to put you in this position?"

Jason was silent for a long time.

"Well, no, I can't …"

"In fact, can you think of anyone you know being *capable* of such a multifaceted conspiracy involving so many people?"

Jason hesitated again.

"No, I can't, but …"

"Then how can you and your counsel *possibly* expect anyone in this courtroom to believe it? It is, in fact, *unbelievable*, isn't it?"

"No it's not!" Jason shouted his reply. "*I* believe it! I believe it because it *fucking well happened*!"

"I don't think so, Mr Midanda. No further questions, m'lord."

★

Week 10; Tuesday, 26 May…

Tom looked at the clock on his bedside table – 2:37am. He sat up in bed and realised he was sweating profusely. The sheets were wet and his boxer shorts were sticking painfully to him. He got out of bed and paced the room for a long time.

Eventually he lay down on top of the duvet and stared at the ceiling, drifting in and out of shallow sleep. Sitting up, he checked the time again – 5.05. He swung his legs off the bed and reached for his mobile.

"Tom?" Grace's voice was hoarse. "Do you know what time it is?"

"You said phone any time, day or night, remember?" he said.

"Yes, but that was when …"

"I need your support with something. Something that's more important to me than I can tell you … I know we've had our differences recently, Grace, but I hope you'll …"

"Forget that, Tom," she interrupted. "That was nothing, a misunderstanding. We can work that out later. But what…?"

"It's the exiling of the drug-runners. We need to reverse it. Today, this morning! Right now!"

There was silence for a few moments.

"Tom, did I hear you right? It's just after five o'clock, for God's sake."

"No time to lose, Grace. I can be at Westminster in less than two hours from now. I'm going to contact Andrew so that he can get me in front of the House before start of business – immediately after prayers. I need you to go and see him as early as possible and tell him you support this. He'll listen to you. With your help…"

"Tom, it's not going to happen."

"It will if you persuade him. He wasn't all that happy about it anyway. Tell him I've been rethinking the whole thing because of public concern – you know what to say."

"But, Tom, I …"

"Look, by midday, or mid-afternoon at the latest, it will be confirmed that Jack is guilty."

"You mean *found* guilty. Surely you don't…"

"*Just listen, Grace!*" Tom yelled down the phone. "I haven't got time for semantics! It doesn't matter how you say it, does it? I have got to make this statement before …"

"Before when, Tom? The House doesn't sit today until two-thirty, but that's academic, anyway. Andrew hasn't seen you in nearly six weeks. Even if he agreed with you about reversing it, there is no way he's going to let you walk straight back in and make a statement to the House. As I said, *it isn't going to happen!*"

"It will if you have a word with him."

"*No it won't!* Stop saying that! I'll do anything possible to help Jack. But what you want is *im*possible. Don't ask me to do this. Don't set me up to fail you … to fail Jack. That's not fair!"

"Christ, Grace, just listen to yourself! I'm trying to save my son's life, my own life, my marriage, and you're talking about what's fair to *you!*" Tom was yelling.

Grace shouted back. "Your *marriage!* You're asking me to help you save your *marriage?* When all you've done for years is encourage me to *ruin* it!"

"I didn't mean my marriage, Grace, I'm not thinking straight at all. I don't *care* about that. It's Jack, only Jack … Oh, God. You've got to help me. *Please!*"

"I can't do what you ask, Tom. But listen to me. *If* Jack is found guilty…"

"There's no 'if', Grace."

"*Listen to me!* If he is found guilty and even if he is sentenced today to life-exile …"

"He will be."

"*If* all that happens, it will take months for the final stage to be reached. You have all that time to work at reversing the legislation – or proving his innocence. Just think about it. And another thing, how would Jack feel if the worst happens and he looks across and you're not there. He'd think you'd disowned him or something."

"Yes, of course. I couldn't do that."

He ended the call without another word.

★

Jeremy Forsythe QC rose at 10.15 am in a tense, packed courtroom. People were leaning forward in their seats in anticipation and there was a low hum of conversation which ceased abruptly as the barrister swept his eyes around the gallery.

"I will not keep you long," he said, turning to speak directly to the jury. "I am sure, in fact, that you have individually all reached your decision, the *same* decision, in this dreadfully sad affair. I do not propose to go over again the damning evidence given by those honest people who are far more qualified than me to present the details of the case. I can add nothing to the volume of proof you have already heard, absorbed, and will have considered – or *will* consider – in reaching your collective conclusion.

"The Defence, of course, will throw in a few red herrings in an attempt to shake your resolve. That is to be expected in the absence of anything they have of their own which is even approaching substantial. Perhaps a good example of that is counsel's attempt to raise doubts based on the *consistency* of the statements of the four users who came forward to testify – the fact that they were all so similar. Just how desperate must they be to resort to that?" He smiled at the jury. "Usually, on these occasions they are highlighting *in*consistencies – irregularities – between testimonies.

"You might ask yourself why the Defence counsel did not exercise their prerogative to question the three people whose *similar* statements were read out. Was it, perhaps, that they felt their very consistency would undermine the whole argument?

"They have mentioned how much it would cost to acquire the drugs, asking you to accept that it is unlikely that the defendants would have the means to do so. How much *less* likely is it, though, that someone would spend the *same* amount of money just to place the drugs somewhere where they could *never* be sold, where they would have no chance to recoup the cost of purchasing them?"

"They have attempted to discredit the evidence provided by the CCTV and direct police surveillance – trivialising the point that a total of eight known users had approached one of the defendants – some on more than one occasion. You must decide whether you want to simply overlook that – although I doubt if you will.

"The defendants *themselves* could not identify anyone who might want to do them harm – let alone undertake such an elaborate and costly scam involving so many people. And even if they had been able to point the finger – how could the placing of the evidence in the respective houses have been achieved? The Defence says one portion was planted during the break-in at Mr Midanda's house. And they are right – as Detective Inspector Waters agreed – that it is *just* possible. You have to weigh the probability of that being the case alongside the rest of the evidence against them, and ask yourselves how likely it is that someone would break in to eight houses just to plant evidence in one.

"But what of Etherington Place? The Defence points out that there was a party there the day after the break-in at the Midandas'. But we have heard that security was extremely tight on that night, with everyone accounted for – and searched – going in and out of the grounds. And for the rest of the time, well the property is like a fortress – an impregnable castle. Let us recap on what Mr Michaels, the security officer in charge of the property, told us on the first day of this trial."

He consulted his notes.

"The house is surrounded by a wall, eight feet high and with a two-foot-high electric fence on top of it all the way round the perimeter. The only access to the grounds is through a pair of ten-foot high iron gates, the top sections of which are also electrified. These gates are alarmed and can only be opened using a hand-held remote control or by inputting a five-digit code into a keypad at the side of the entrance. The five-digit code, which is changed every seven days, also deactivates the alarm, which is re-activated as soon as the gates are closed.

"Inside the gates, between the perimeter wall and the house itself, at various points throughout the grounds, there are laser censors, criss-crossing the gardens and wooded areas, plus a total of ten CCTV cameras which together cover the whole of the grounds, including the inside of the boundary walls and the outside of the house. The live images from these cameras are monitored continuously by full-time security officers based at a control centre within one mile of the house.

"As to the house itself, there are locks and alarms on all three exterior doors, the inner door of the front porch and all windows. There are four more cameras inside – in the hall, the main living room, the kitchen, which has an exterior door, and one covering the long corridor on the first floor from which there is single access to all the upstairs rooms. As I said before, more of a fortress – an impregnable castle – than a house.

"To achieve what the Defence will ask you to believe would take something magical – and evil. A wicked wizard, perhaps! They will encourage you to ignore the facts and accept the fantasy; and on what basis? That a number of disparate, albeit well-meaning individuals – most of whom are only able to observe the defendants for a few hours a week in a crowd of people – tell us that actually these are two really good, nice, friendly people."

He paused, looking from the jury across to the defendants then back to the jury.

"Well, I have seen little or no evidence of those glowing qualities in this court over the course of this trial."

"Impregnable castles and wicked wizards are the stuff of fairy tales. The question you each need to ask yourself is this … Do I believe in *fairies*… or do I believe in *justice*?"

He beamed at the jury then the public gallery, then walked to his chair and sat down, swirling his gown around him with a theatrical flourish as he did so. He leant back in his seat; arms folded and face set in an expression of satisfied triumph.

There was a murmuring in the public gallery accompanied by nodding heads and knowing looks as the judge looked to the Defence counsel, inviting her to respond. Lorna Prentiss rose from her chair and walked very slowly towards the jury, stopping short and turning to address the court as a whole.

"First, let me forewarn you that I shall not be trying to amuse you with fairy tales. In my opinion, which clearly differs from that of my learned colleague, Guildford Crown Court is *not* a forum for entertainment. It is a place where we should be working together to make sure that one of the most important decisions that we will ever be involved with is the correct one. You," she turned to the jury, "must decide the fate of these two young gentlemen. These are two successful, well-behaved, popular young men, the vast majority of whose lives lie before them. You have the power to decide what sort of life that will be. There can be no more serious responsibility than that.

"Let me start by saying that what was so casually discarded as an impossibility by the Crown is what really *did* happen at Jack Tomlinson-Brown's home in Etherington Place. Someone *did* breach security; someone *did* put the drugs there. It must have happened like that, because the drugs *were* there and the defendant knew nothing about them.

"And similarly with Jason, whose home is as secure as most houses, I'm sure, but certainly *not* a fortress. He won't mind my saying that access to it would be easier, far easier, than the Tomlinson-Browns'.

"Why they have been targeted together, I do not pretend to know. They are close friends; *very* close friends. It is quite conceivable that a grudge against one would manifest itself in action against both, cruelly adding to the hurt and the anguish of each.

"As to how the planting of the evidence could have happened, you know about the party at the Tomlinson-Browns' house just over a week before the discovery of the drugs, and, less than two days prior to that, the break-in at Jason Midanda's home. The Crown has contemptuously dismissed these events as irrelevances, but it's rather a coincidence, you must think, that both properties were, in effect, entered within a couple of days of each other and that the drugs were found so shortly afterwards following a tip-off just *four days* after the party. You have also been told that the CCTV camera which covered the upstairs corridor in Jack's home was deliberately tampered with before or during the party. Another coincidence? I think not.

"The person or persons who perpetrated this callous conspiracy were clever enough to collate a surprising amount of evidence in an attempt to achieve their intended outcome. But one thing he – or she – or they – were *not* able to create is the rationale and background for such a crime. They cannot change retrospectively these young men's characters, their personalities, their clean and exemplary lives. They *cannot* – could *never* – place this crime into the context of their existence up to that date. It simply does not fit; it simply does not make *any sense at all.*

"The world of illegal drug dealing is a hard and brutal one, where life expectancy for the majority of those involved – statistics will confirm – is short, where the risk of violent death is high and where hardened criminals vie for supremacy in dark corners of our society. Take a long, close look at the defendants, ladies and gentlemen of the jury, and decide if they belong to that world. And then come to the only verdict that *does* make any sense at all…

"*Not guilty!*"

Tom and Mags sensed a positive impact in the room, the knowing nods of a short time ago replaced by questioning shrugs to each other by the people around them, their body language reflecting at least a partial acceptance of the argument they had just heard.

"Thank you, Ms Prentiss," said Miles Pendle.

He looked at his watch. "We will take a break now and resume at twelve o'clock precisely."

"The Court will rise!"

★

"Ladies and gentlemen of the jury." Miles Pendle looked even larger and more imposing as his booming voice launched the penultimate act of the drama. "You have a particularly difficult task today. I know all of you have been in this situation before, but today, as I said at the start of these proceedings, there is an added dimension to this case – your knowledge of the background of one of the defendants. Knowing Tom Brown as we do, it is inevitable that we should feel considerable sympathy for him, and for the rest of his family. *However* – and this is the challenge you must meet today – I ask you to put that aside. Only at one stage in your deliberations must you take into consideration the background of either of the defendants, and I will refer to that later.

"You have heard the details of the case, presented by the Crown and the Defence, and the evidence from fifteen different witnesses. You have also heard from the two defendants. There is nothing material I can add to that wealth of information. However, I should like to share with you a few comments and observations following the summing up of the two counsels.

"The Defence, quite properly, has drawn your attention to the fact that, contrary to the picture of impregnability painted by the Prosecution, the household of the Tomlinson-Browns was made *deliberately* accessible for guests attending a party just ten days before the discovery of the drugs and at a time when both parents were away. She also pointed out that one of the security cameras – the very one which monitored the area where the bedroom in which the drugs were found is situated – had been tampered with sometime during the party. The Defence suggests that these facts are enough to raise doubts as to how the drugs came to be in the room. She also asks you to consider that the break-in at Jason Midanda's house so close to the time of the party was more than a coincidence, but in fact was part of a concerted operation to place the incriminating evidence in such a way as to implicate both defendants. The Defence is right in asking you to consider this."

He paused, looking intensely along the line of jurors.

"However, you must place these facts into the context of the overall timescale of the police operation which led to these charges. The seven separate phone calls to the police which activated the investigation in the first place were made within a period of ten days, the last one of these being a full eight weeks prior to the arrests; that is six weeks before both the break-in and the party. During that intervening period – between the last of the calls and the break-in – the two defendants had already been identified by four of the initial callers, all of whom had also provided mobile phone contact numbers which later checked out with the phones found at the two houses. Also during that time CCTV footage and direct police surveillance had revealed approaches made to Mr Tomlinson-Brown by eight known drug users. And finally, as to the party itself, we have heard from Mr Midanda, under cross-examination, that the decision to hold it was made only a few days before the event itself; six days before, to be precise.

"You must ask yourselves the following questions.

"*One*, how probable is it that such an extensive deception, involving so many people and diverse elements, would be carried out, which was reliant to succeed on an opportunity to place these substances in the houses of the two defendants, bearing in mind that if the party had never taken place all that effort could have been a waste of time?

"*Two*, when the opportunity did arise, how likely is it that the planting of the evidence could have been planned and executed at such short notice – five days in the case of the Midanda home, and six in the case of the Tomlinson-Brown's, especially with the latter being subject to such stringent security?

"And *three*, why would anyone have gone to so much trouble if, as the Defence claims, the lifestyle of these two young gentlemen appears, on the surface at least, to be so ordinary and innocuous?

"It is for you to answer these, and other questions, to your collective satisfaction, remembering that if you are in any doubt as to the answers, then you must *not* find the defendants guilty. On the other hand, of course, you may find these questions very easy to answer when you consider them carefully.

"I am sure that you are aware," he continued, "that under new provisions, introduced within the last two months, the selling of certain drugs carries with it a mandatory sentence of the severest kind. Those found guilty of this crime, may be condemned to the status of Life Exiles. That is the law – the *new* law."

He glanced around the courtroom again, this time his eyes remaining on Tom for the most fleeting of moments.

"However, let me stress that this is no concern of yours. I cannot put it more bluntly than that. The resultant sentence, dependant on your verdict, is not your responsibility; it is mine. *Your* job is to decide on the verdict – or verdicts – based on the evidence you have heard. That decision will enable me then to do *my* job. Under the terms of the new regime, you must state, for *each* of the defendants, one of the following verdicts;

"Not guilty, if you feel that the evidence presented clearly indicates that the defendant is innocent of the crime with which he is charged.

"Not proven, if you feel that the evidence presented is

insufficient to demonstrate beyond all reasonable doubt that the defendant was responsible for the crime. Until recently this option has only applied in Scotland, but has been adopted across the UK as part of the new justice reforms. This verdict would apply even if you accepted that there was a strong possibility that he *could* have committed the offence.

"Guilty with mitigation, if you agree that the evidence clearly proves that he is guilty of the charges brought against him, but – and this is where it *is* appropriate for you to consider the defendant's personal and family circumstances – there are understandable reasons which may touch the sympathy of this court, as to why this crime was committed.

"And finally, guilty without mitigation, where you conclude that, not only is the defendant guilty of the crime, but there are no such mitigating circumstances which might excuse his actions.

"Please be clear that you are not required to bring the same verdict for both defendants. You may feel it necessary to differentiate between the two, in spite of their close personal relationship, their common associates and their seemingly parallel lives. It is for you to decide. I do not require a unanimous decision, but I will only accept a verdict agreed by a minimum of ten members of the jury.

"I will now ask you to leave the courtroom to consider your verdict or verdicts. Under the recent Jurors' Charter, let me remind you that you are entitled to reconvene this court in order to ask for clarification of any information received during the presentation of the case or to request any additional data you may feel essential in reaching your decision. Please inform the Clerk of the Court if you wish this to happen. Otherwise, we await your decision forthwith.

"The time is now," the judge glanced at his watch, "12.25. The court will adjourn until at least 1.30 pm, at which time you may all return to your places in readiness for the verdicts which will follow as soon as the jury have completed their deliberations. Ladies and Gentlemen of the jury, please rise and leave the courtroom. Thank you."

The jury rose and filed out through a side door into their anteroom.

"The court is adjourned."

"All rise!"

★

Tom watched as Mags left the room, supported by Megan, and followed by her mother and father – Jack's grandparents – who had been present in court since the previous day. Katey followed them, her arms tightly clasped around Leila Midanda who was crying loudly, her whole body shaking with the agony of unbearable anticipation.

Tom did not move for the whole of the interminably long hour of the recess. His mind seemed incapable of holding on to any rational thought for more than a few seconds as they oscillated, out-of-control, between the extremes of a complete surrender to despair and constructive planning for his change of policy. The overall effect was a waking nightmare of confusion, the sort he experienced in restless sleep during an illness, where problems and challenges whirl with ethereal complexity; ill-defined and unresolved.

He felt a hand on his shoulder. He had completely forgotten the presence of his own parents, who had been seated behind him with his in-laws. He reached up and put his own hand on top of his father's.

No words were spoken.

There was nothing to say.

★

At 1.35 pm the jury filed solemnly in, their heads lowered to avoid making eye contact with anyone in the courtroom. They remained standing until all had reached their places and then sat down together.

"Have you concluded your deliberations?" asked the judge.

The foreman of the jury got to his feet again and replied. "Yes, m'lord."

"And have you reached a verdict for each of the defendants?"

"Yes, we have, m'lord."

"Are the verdicts unanimous?"

217

"Yes, m'lord."

"How do you find the defendant, Hugh Jacob Tomlinson-Brown?"

"Guilty, without mitigation."

Mags slumped sideways across Tom's knees. He held on to her tightly, as much to steady himself as to give her comfort. There was a rustle of activity in the press gallery and Tom looked across. People were frantically tapping their electronic notepads and scribbling with pencils, with one exception; Tony Dobson's eyes were riveted on him, wide, staring and filled with sadness, like tiny mirrors reflecting Tom's own desolation straight back at him.

The judge continued.

"How do you find the defendant Jason Midanda?"

"Guilty, with mitigation."

Leila Midanda's piercing wail was cut short by Jason's shout as he sprang to his feet.

CHAPTER SIXTEEN

Two days later
Week 10; Thursday, 28 May…

The sun shone through the restaurant window onto the two former colleagues sitting across the table from each other. The room was quite busy for a Thursday lunchtime, with all the diners nodding or speaking to David as they took their seats at their respective tables.

"You're quite a celebrity here, aren't you?" teased his companion.

"Yes, rugged good looks seem to be very popular in the village."

Jo laughed. "Do you remember saying to me after Ben Neville's suicide that you wondered what would happen to the farm? I bet you never thought in a million years you'd end up living there – even though it's a bit different now to what it was then. And certainly not having the same room where he shot himself. Doesn't that bother you?"

"Well, I guess I did think about it a bit at first. But I always fancied living on a farm and now at least I've got half a farmhouse. And I've certainly never regretted moving into the village."

She turned and looked out of the window onto Main Street.

"I've always felt guilty about not being here that night," she said. "You know, the night of the 'Meadow Village Massacre', as they called it."

"Yes," said David, "I was never sure whether four deaths legitimately constituted a massacre, but it wasn't the time to argue the point. And anyway, if you add the Enderbys, Emily Burton and Ben to the list of the deceased, I guess it's getting close. But there's nothing for you to feel guilty about; there wasn't anything you could have done. It's not something we could have anticipated and prevented."

"I know, but …"

They sat in silence.

"Anyway, Detective Inspector, what's your point about Jason?"

"Well, what he actually said was," she consulted the note she had in front of her, reading from it slowly, "'No, that's not right, we are in this together, equal partners, a team. That's how it's always been.'"

She continued looking at the note for a few seconds then looked up at David.

"Well, what do you think?"

He shrugged.

"I assume, from the fact that you've asked the question, that this won't be the answer you want," he said, "but it sounds like a confession to me. Well, perhaps not a confession, but a statement made knowing that the truth was out, so to speak. And it seems the judge interpreted it the same way."

"You see, I don't see it like that at all," said Jo. "I think it was just an instinctive expression of solidarity with his best friend. The verdicts clearly implied that the jury thought Jack was the leader and Jason the follower. That Jack was to blame for Jason's predicament. That Jack was the baddy and Jason the victim of his … influence, for want of a better word. Jason just wasn't having it – they were *real* friends; they looked out for each other – and that's what Jason was doing then – looking out for Jack."

"Or it was pride, not wanting people to think he was the junior partner, just a gopher."

"But people don't sacrifice their lives for a bit of pride, David. The point is, can you remember any criminal, on the point of going down, sparing a thought for anybody but himself – or herself? It would have made sense if he had got the *same* verdict as Jack and had leapt to his feet and said, 'it wasn't me, it was that bastard! He was going to stop me seeing Katey if I didn't help him!' or something. You know what I mean, don't you?"

"Yes, I do," he replied, thoughtfully. "But I'm not sure what all this has to do with anything."

A tall, gangly young man in black trousers and polo shirt walked over to them holding a pen and note-pad.

"Ready to order yet?"

David turned to him, eagerly picking up the menu.

"Not yet," said Jo, without taking her eyes off David. "We'll call you over when we're ready."

"Okay, any more drinks?"

"No thanks," snapped Jo.

"Same again, please, Tommy," said David, smiling at him.

"Right, David."

"Hey, Jo, this is my local," he chastised, gently, as the waiter left. "Don't upset the staff. They'll be putting something into my scampi and chips. Not that we'll ever get round to eating."

"Sorry, David," Jo relaxed a little. "Just let me share a couple more thoughts with you."

"Go on," he said.

"Well, the users who gave evidence. They were the ones who came forward – four out of the seven who initially phoned in. Now, neither of the ones the police saw talking to Jack on Delaware, nor any of the six caught on camera approaching him were actually picked up and questioned, because the police couldn't find any of them. Right?"

"My brain must have shut down, Jo; because I'm afraid I don't know what you're getting ..."

"Well, if there was a set-up."

David smiled and shook his head.

"Bear with me – I know it's a massive 'if' – but *if* there was one, then you could have two groups of people. One lot – the main actors – to turn up and give the evidence and another lot – the extras – just to walk up to Jack in a place where there's a good chance they'd be on camera or were being watched. Then the second lot fade into the background, out of sight, can't be found. The police ..."

"That's you," said David.

"Not really me," countered Jo. "I only got the shitty bit remember? Not the investigation. Anyway, the police don't mind so much – they're supposed to be fast tracking and they've got four in the bag anyway. That's more than enough to get the message across."

"And I would agree with them."

"Yes, but why, when the police knew all of these people, could they not find a single one. They had addresses, knew where they hung out and who with. But no sign of them anywhere."

"Well, you've explained that, Jo. They didn't *need* them."

"Even so, it's not as if they didn't *try* to find them; they just didn't try very hard. I just think you'd expect *one* of them to be at home – or where you thought they'd be – when you called, *unless* they'd been told to make themselves scarce. And *before* NJR, I don't think we'd have been satisfied if we hadn't picked at least a couple of them up."

"But it's *not* before NJR, Jo," said David, leaning forward, "and think about the scale of this conspiracy of yours. Someone would have to take an enormous bloody risk in casting all these characters – from the most unreliable and unpredictable pool of acting talent in the country. Seven phone-ins *then* eight spotted by CCTV and the police. Even if the three no-show phone-ins were part of the eight, that's a minimum of" – he paused to work it out –"twelve people involved in the scam. That's hard to believe. Then there's the big mystery of how the drugs were planted – at Jack's, I mean; it's not difficult to work out how it could have happened at Jason's. The party was the only opportunity, but how could that have been anticipated – given that it would have to be an integral part of the plan? Pretty much the core of the plan, in fact."

"I know, I know. But I keep seeing Jack at the house at the time of the raid. Even allowing for the fact that it was 5.00 am, and he was probably half asleep, and that you'd expect someone who was devious enough to pedal crack these days to be able to deceive people by acting the innocent, et cetera, et cetera … Even allowing for all that, I find it hard to believe he knew the stuff was there. And the magazines. I don't think for a microsecond he thought that's what we were looking for. It was just that he knew we'd find them if he didn't get them out of the way, and that might embarrass or upset his parents. If he knew the drugs were there, you'd expect him to pile stuff *into* the wardrobe, not draw our attention to the hiding place by clearing it away. God forgive us, David, but what if we've made a terrible mistake."

"What about an appeal? Is that going to happen do you think?"

"Well, they can't appeal the sentence, because that's mandatory, and they can only appeal the verdict if new evidence is presented."

They were silent for a few moments.

"Look," David said, "why don't you eat something? I'm sure you'll feel a lot better afterwards. I know I will."

Jo snorted a laugh, and looked up with a smile of resignation.

"The weird thing is, you know, I do actually *want* to believe they're guilty. The alternative is too painful to consider. I keep reassuring myself of the two biggest arguments against there being a set-up. One – why would anyone go to all that trouble to frame two people who don't seem to have a single enemy in the world between them? And, two – the fact that someone would have had to come up with better than a hundred grand to kick-start it."

"Well I agree with your first point," said David, half-reading the menu, "though I guess the police must have considered that the target might not have been Jack so much as his dad. Someone teaching Tom Brown a lesson by getting at his son. Although it wasn't intended to put him in exile, of course, because it all started long before the new sentencing law was in place. But if that was the case then you could get your mind a bit more easily round the complexity of the set-up. You know, if big league villains were involved. They'd be able to put a lot of pressure on the players without having to get close enough to the action to put themselves at risk. Or what about political opponents, trying to discredit the family, or soften the NJR."

Jo started reading the menu but put it down again.

"They did give both of those some thought, but the fact that Jason was involved as well sort of scuppered that theory. Including him in any sort of set-up would have added an extra level of complexity that just wasn't necessary. And point two?"

"Point two. Well, the police never recovered the bulk of the stuff that killed that young guy – somebody Johnson, wasn't it? So it was still out there. But once it was known to be lethal, then the whole batch would have become next to worthless. Anyone in the know, finding out where it was and who'd got it, might have been able to take it off their hands for next to nothing."

"Jesus!" Jo gasped, turning a few heads at nearby tables. "Why the hell didn't the Defence pick up on that?"

"They probably did," said David. "But there was so much other incriminating stuff around. And I did say '*might*' have picked it up for next to nothing, not '*would*'. And what is 'next to nothing'? Five grand? Ten? It's only small potatoes compared to the original value, but it's still a big spend for a long-shot chance of success and with no way of getting your money back. You know, I think I will have the scampi. What about you?"

"Vegetarian lasagne," said Jo.

David breathed a sigh of relief and turned to attract Tommy's attention.

★

"Is it okay?" They'd hardly spoken for nearly twenty minutes.

Jo looked up. She had been pushing her food round the plate but had eaten very little.

"Yes, it's fine, thanks," she answered apologetically. "Just not all that hungry."

"I'll finish it for you, if you like," said David, who had emptied his own plate some time ago.

Jo smiled. "Still as helpful as ever, I'm glad to see," she said, pushing her plate over to him. "I'm not very good company, am I?"

"Someone once told me 'don't expect too much on a first date, then you won't be disappointed'. So I'm fairly cool about this, providing there's a next time."

"So this is a date, is it?"

"Well, you should know. It was *you* who asked *me* out."

"Yes, I'd like to do this again," said Jo. "I just wish I could get this off my mind."

A few minutes later, David pushed his second empty plate aside and leaned forward.

"Listen, don't misinterpret this as support for your conspiracy theory, but how about this for an idea?"

★

"They'll be taken to an intermediate location," said the woman, "the redeveloped Bull Sand Fort in the Humber Estuary."

Tom and Mags were seated together on the sitting room sofa. Opposite them, across the low table on which Millie had placed a tray with four cups and saucers and coffee, tea and biscuits, sat their two visitors in the wing chairs which normally occupied a position by the window. Delia Tremlett, Senior Judicial Advisor was a large

224

woman in her mid forties. She was confident and business-like and was doing most of the talking. Gemma Gray, her assistant, was small and slight, about ten years younger, with a thin, serious face set in a permanent frown.

"This is a designated stopover establishment," Delia continued, "for those awaiting final posting. Places in exile are limited at present to the single off-shore facility." She looked at Tom as if for confirmation. "So waiting time at present will inevitably be longer than for the final-state plan, when full accommodation will be available."

"And when will they be moved to this fort place?" asked Mags.

"That will be on the 10th June, in thirteen days time."

"What!" Mags leapt to her feet. "Don't be ridiculous! You can't give us less than two weeks with him."

"I'm sorry, but that's ..."

"That's what?" Tom was on his feet as well. "Don't tell me that's the norm, because this is virtually the first time."

"For drug dealers, yes," said Delia. "But we already have five groups of prisoner-exiles, including the two already on Alpha, and we have not been notified of any changes in procedure or timeframe for this new offence."

Mags turned on Tom. "So it's you again!" she shouted, and looked for a moment as if she would storm out of the room. Then her whole body sagged and she subsided back onto the sofa.

★

Tom drummed his fingers on the desk as he tried to come to terms with the news of Jack's early departure.

His office at Etherington Place had originally been a dressing room off the large bedroom in the west wing of the house where he had been sleeping for most of the past two years. He had converted the room some time ago into a good-sized office by incorporating a box room next to it. It had a large antique walnut desk, a luxurious tilt-and-swivel chair in burgundy leather, and book cases lining two of the walls. There was a door in each of the other wood-panelled walls, one into the bedroom and one onto the corridor. The period feel of the room was offset somewhat by the six spotlights set in the high ceiling.

He sat in silence for a long time, then picked up the desk phone.

"He's not available, I'm afraid," said Shirley, as soon as his call was answered.

"Is he deliberately avoiding me?"

"I couldn't possibly comment on that, Home Secretary," she answered, unmoved by his agitation. "I know he's very busy, and I'm sure he intends getting back to you. But your continuing absence has put an extra …"

Tom slammed down the receiver, regretting it immediately. He phoned again. Shirley picked up straight away but said nothing.

"Listen, Shirley, I'm sorry about that. And I'm sorry that I've not been around and everyone has had to work harder. But please cut me a bit of slack. You have no idea what …" His voice broke slightly, enough for Shirley to pick up on it.

"I'm sorry, too. Really I am. For Jack; for everything. But …" She paused. "Listen, Home Secretary, I'd get the sack if the PM found out I'd told you this. But he is a bit reluctant – well, let's say, hesitant – to speak to you, because he knows what it's about. And it's not that he isn't sorry about what's happened, it's just the bigger picture, you know, the wider implications." She paused again. "He says it's impossible to do what you want right now and for the foreseeable future. So, yes, I guess he is avoiding speaking to …"

"It's not impossible! It's perfectly possible!" shouted Tom. "In fact, it's what people want! What have I done to make him so…?"

Shirley remained silent, not saying any more.

"Shirley," he said, calmly, after a few moments, "thank you for telling me that. I do really appreciate it. It's the first bit of kindness I've been shown for what seems like a very long time. I won't forget it and, of course, the PM will never know you told me. Hopefully he'll tell me himself when he gets round to it."

"He will, Home Secretary. I promise I'll get him to speak to you very soon. I hope we can save Jack."

"Thank you, Shirley. Bye."

Tom slumped in his a chair.

'I hope we can save Jack.' Shirley's words echoed in his mind for a moment as he wondered how Andrew came to know what he wanted to speak to him about.

Week 10; Friday, 29 May…

They arrived at the visitors' reception in the holding centre just before 10.00 am. The room was large and airy, with several full planters colourfully decorating the area along with a small central fountain. The dozen or so armchairs around the walls looked comfortable and welcoming. The atmosphere of calm seemed at odds with the grim purpose of their visit.

Katey and Leila Midanda were already there. Katey flew into her mother's arms and then into Tom's, clinging and sobbing, close to hysteria.

"She's been wonderful, simply wonderful," said Leila in a small voice. "I couldn't have managed without her. I don't know what I…"

Mags put her arms around her. Leila was a tall, handsome woman in her late thirties with a round face and bright eyes. She wore a pale yellow trouser suit which accentuated her smooth ebony skin.

"Listen," said Tom. "We must get ourselves together for Jack and Jason's sake. God knows what they must be feeling, but we won't help them by falling apart. We must try to be strong for them."

That was as much as he could bring himself to say, but it had a stabilising effect and they had all managed to compose themselves by the time two prison officers entered the room a few minutes later.

"Good Morning, I'm Emily Parker, Senior Prison Officer, and this is Prison Officer Jools Gorton."

She stepped forward and shook hands with all four of them, addressing them individually as she did so. She was of average height with a sturdy figure and kind, friendly smile. Her dark hair was pulled back into a ponytail. Jools followed her along the line, also shaking their hands. He was almost a head taller than Emily, very slim, with a pleasant, boyish face.

"Follow me, please," said Emily, raising her arm to indicate the way. "We'll explain what the arrangements are in a few moments."

She led them down a whitewashed corridor, with Jools bringing up the rear. At a T-junction, they stopped.

"Mr Midanda this way, please," said Emily indicating to the right.

"Give Jack my love," said Katey. "I'll go with Leila to see Jason, but tell him I'll see him soon."

They followed Emily as Jools walked past Tom and Mags, leading them off to the left without speaking. Ahead of them, another female officer was waiting next to a long table near a heavy metal door with a combined handle and keypad, which faced them at the end of the short passageway. On the wall above the table was a large monitor screen. She stepped forward, extending her hand to greet them.

"Good morning, I'm Phoebe Barnes, Prison Officer."

Phoebe was almost a carbon copy of her senior colleague; same height and build and with a ponytail, except that her hair was blonde.

"I'm sorry, sir, madam," she said, "but we have to do this. Could you leave your bag on the table, madam, and both empty your pockets. Everything, please. That way we can raise the glass panel in the room, if you wish."

They complied, showing no emotion. With some embarrassment Phoebe took a hand-held metal detector from a bracket on the wall and passed it over Mags as quickly and unobtrusively as possible before passing it to Jools who did the same with Tom.

"Jack is in there," said Phoebe. "There is another prison officer with him at present and a glass panel which separates them from the part of the room you'll enter into. Once you are inside and seated, we will leave the room and the panel will be raised so you will be able to... get closer if you wish. However, we shall be monitoring the meeting, visually and aurally. Do you understand?"

"Yes, I understand," said Mags. "I don't understand *why!*"

Phoebe looked at Tom for support. He nodded to her but said nothing. Mags was entitled to her anger, he thought; it was a relief to hear her express any feelings at all.

As Phoebe turned to open the door, Mags grabbed his hand, interlinking their fingers and squeezing tightly. Her nails dug into the flesh between his knuckles so that he momentarily winced with pain. They followed the officer into the room with eyes impatiently seeking the first sight of their son for nearly seventy-two hours. He was wearing blue jeans and a white hooded top over a black tee shirt and was seated on a basic wooden chair behind a glass screen, which reached from floor to ceiling and across the full width of the room.

The prison officer was standing in a formal 'at-ease' position just behind him. Jack's face was without expression and only his eyes moved as they entered, turning to look at them without any hint of acknowledgement or recognition. Tom could feel the whole weight of Mags's body transferred through the grip on his hand as she fought to steady herself.

Phoebe indicated for them to sit down on two similar chairs, which faced their son through the screen. They sank, rather than sat, onto them and she nodded to her colleague on the other side of the glass. He removed a key from his pocket, inserting it into a small control box on the wall, and turning it through 90 degrees. Then he pressed and held in a mushroom shaped knob next to it and the glass panel slowly lifted through the ceiling of the room, finally disappearing altogether.

Both officials turned to leave, the one who had been with Jack through a second door on his side of the room. Phoebe turned back to them as she left.

"You have just over an hour," she checked her watch, "until eleven-thirty. If you wish to terminate the meeting before that, just indicate to the camera up there." She pointed to the wall above the door. "There will, of course, be other opportunities to visit Jack. You can all leave your seats, but please be aware that we shall be observing you throughout the session as I explained."

She closed the door behind her.

For several seconds no one moved. Jack's eyes were still on them but continued to show no emotion, as if he was unsure what to expect. Then Mags flew out of her chair, throwing her arms around him.

"Oh, Jack, Jack, darling …" she cried, her tears soaking his shirt. Tom followed, wrapping his arms around them both. Jack succumbed, his head dropping into his mother's hair, and his own tears flowed.

They stayed in that position for a full minute, gently rocking back and forth as finally their shaking shoulders came to rest. Jack stiffened and pulled away from them, his face a blank mask again. He looked from one to the other and then relaxed a little.

Tom and Mags backed away to their own chairs. They each tried to pull them closer to Jack, but found they were fixed to the floor. Jack remained still, only his eyes moving, now flicking round the room looking everywhere but at his parents.

"Darling, are you alright?" Mags asked.

Jack's eyes fixed on her, widening. Then he began to shake. It was a few moments before they realised he was laughing, silently and maniacally, until he seemed almost out of control. He broke the silence with a great guffaw.

"*Alright! Alright! …* Never been better, seeing as you're asking. Three meals a day; don't have to tidy my room – well there's nothing in it to tidy, come to think of it – daytime television, which features me and Jay most of the time, by the way and, guess what, in a couple of weeks I'm going on holiday – for ever! *Of course I'm not fucking alright!*"

He crumpled forwards and doubled over, his chest almost falling onto his knees. They both went to him. He straightened up and clung to Mags.

"Mum I'm sorry. I shouldn't have said that."

"It's alright, darling …darling Jack," she said. "It was a stupid question. I didn't know what to say."

"It's okay, Mum. I understand."

He pushed Mags slowly away, still holding her gently by the shoulders at arms length.

"I'll tell you what you can say," he said, looking from one to the other again. "You can say you believe I'm innocent."

"Jack, we *know* you're innocent." Mags spoke almost before the words were out of his mouth. "We never, for one minute, doubted it."

Jack's expression hardened again.

"I want *him* to say it!" he snapped, turning to his father.

The coldness in Jack's voice and eyes was enough to stay any immediate response from Tom.

"*Well?*" Jack's voice was fiercely demanding of an answer.

"I have great difficulty believing you had anything to do with this, Jack. I feel …"

Mags turned to stare at him in disbelief.

"*Great difficulty believing?*" said Jack, his voice shaking with fury. "Well, you're a man who's used to overcoming *great difficulty*, aren't you? So, let's hear it, Father. Let's hear the conclusion you've had *great difficulty* reaching!"

Mags looked at her husband as he again struggled with his reply.

"It's of no consequence, Jack," he said. "We love you – so much. That's all that matters to us; whatever you have or haven't done is not important."

"It's fucking important to me! I just want to know what you think. Can't you stop being a politician for a minute and just be my father. There'll be plenty of time in the future to be a politician; you've only got a few days left to be my father!"

The tears welled in Tom's eyes.

"Jack, I …"

"Too late, Dad; I wouldn't believe you now anyway. You had your chance. You *have* to think I'm guilty, don't you? Otherwise your whole new super-duper fucking justice system's a crock of shit! Right?"

He leaned forward again into Mags's arms.

"I'd like to be alone with you, please, Mum. I want him to leave."

Mags turned to Tom. She nodded to him with an expression that said, "Go, it will be alright." He rose from the chair and shuffled towards the door, which was opened by Phoebe as he reached it.

Tom stepped outside the room. The two officers were seated at the long table facing the screen showing the scene inside. Phoebe glanced at him with a look of disgust, which contrasted starkly with her unspoken sympathy of just a few minutes ago. Jools ignored him completely. As his mind reeled, he was suddenly aware of familiar voices. Mags and Jack were talking and – of course – as well as observing, they were hearing every word.

"Can I listen … and watch?" he asked.

Phoebe nodded.

"If you're sure you want to," said Jools.

He stood behind them facing the screen.

"You must understand, Jack, your father loves you so very much," Mags said, her voice tiny through the speaker. The monitor showed her moving in her chair.

"Maybe he does," Jack said, "but what I need more than that is for him to *believe* me. I'm finished, Mum, finished. How long do you think I'll last on one of those off-shore things? A day? A week? The one source of any comfort I had to look forward to half-an-hour ago was my parents stating, loudly and clearly, that they knew I hadn't done it. That would have given me something positive to take away with me. Knowing that you knew I hadn't let you down."

Mags began crying again. "Oh, Jack, please let him come back in. I'm sure …"

"It's too late, Mum. I knew *you* would believe me. I never doubted that for a moment. But I guess I always wondered…"

He broke down himself again and they held each other tightly in silence for a long time. Tom turned away and leant against the opposite wall of the passageway, his forehead resting on his folded arms, oblivious to his audience and with tears running and dropping to the floor. He heard Mags' voice again and turned back to the screen.

"Please let your father come back in, Jack. I know he won't if you don't want him to, but I think you should."

Jack remained still in his mother's embrace for a long time, and then gave a single nod of his head.

"Is that yes?" asked Mags.

Jack nodded again, without speaking. Phoebe rose from her chair and opened the door, inviting Tom to enter without looking at him.

"Ten more minutes," she said.

He stood just inside the door as it closed behind him. Mags looked across at him and smiled through her tears. He walked quickly across the room and put his arms around them both.

"We've ten minutes left," he whispered. "Until next time," he added. "And I do believe you, Jack, I really do."

Jack sat up. When he spoke, it was to Tom, and his voice was cold again.

"Well, if that's true – I mean if you *really* believe that I'm innocent, then it goes without saying that you must also believe that someone is guilty of setting me up. And, with time running out, I expect you are currently bringing to bear all the resources at your disposal in order to find them. And that being the case, then I won't keep you, Father. Best you leave right away and get on with it before it's too late."

Tom sat back down on his chair.

"I'm doing what I can. Please believe me. I'm sorry if I let you down today. Your mum is right, though. I love you very much."

No-one spoke again until the door opened and Phoebe entered the room.

"Time's up, I'm afraid," she said, adding, "until tomorrow, of course."

Mags had continued holding Jack and now she slowly stood up looking very unsteady. Tom rose from his chair and stepped over to them, taking Mags's hand again and placing the other on Jack's shoulder.

Jack tilted his head sideways so it lay briefly on his father's hand. It was the smallest of gestures. Mags bent down to him again and placed her arms around his neck, kissing him gently on the forehead.

"Until tomorrow," she said.

Jack suddenly looked up.

"Where's Katey?" he asked.

"With Jason and his mum," Mags replied. "She sends her love and said she'll see you soon."

He nodded. "It had better be *very* soon," he said, almost to himself, as they left the room.

★

"Hello, Home Secretary? It's Phoebe here, Prison Officer at Guildford. Excuse me for calling you at home, but …"

"How did you get this number?"

"Mr Mackay let me have it. He said you wouldn't mind."

"That depends," said Tom. "Is it Jack? Is he alright?"

"Yes, sir, but he has asked if he could see you separately at some time. He seems to want it kept secret from the rest of your family. Perhaps you can give me a time, one morning perhaps in the next couple of days…"

"Did he say what it's about?"

"No, he's just mentioned it now; he said it was private."

"I see," said Tom, absently.

"I really think you should say yes, sir."

"Oh, of course," said Tom. "I was just wondering why – I mean

– it having to be kept secret from … and all. Look, I won't say tomorrow, because I don't want to leave my wife on her own just yet. Possibly the day after. Would you explain that to Jack, please? So he doesn't think I'm just putting him off. I know he worries about his mum, like I do, so I'm sure he'll understand."

"It would be better if I could tell him *definitely* the next day, sir. It would be good for him to have something certain to be thinking about."

"Okay, definitely the next day," said Tom. "What time's best, do you think?"

"As early as possible. Could you make it, say, eight o'clock?"

Tom thought for a moment.

"That's fine," he said, ending the call.

He heard the front door close. Looking out of his office window, he saw Mags get into her Range Rover and drive off.

★

It was almost 5.00 pm. Jo was planning an early start to the weekend which she had arranged to spend with her friend in London. Someone's outline appeared behind the frosted glass door of her office.

"Come in," said Jo, before they had chance to knock.

Detective Constable Shana Whitlock entered, closing the door behind her and leaning with her back against it.

"Hi, Shans," said Jo. "You look very furtive."

"Sorry, I know you're trying to get a flyer, ma'am, but there's someone here to see you."

"Well? Who? Not Leonardo di Capprio!? Oh for God's sake, that guy won't take 'no' for an answer …"

Shana smiled.

"Do you seriously think I'd be in here telling you if it was? I'd be out there with him, claiming I was you." She became serious. "No, but it is someone you might want to see. In fact, I'm not sure it would be a good idea to avoid …"

"Okay, okay, I give in. *Please* tell me who it is …"

"Maggie Tomlinson-Brown."

Jo looked at her, wide-eyed.

"Are you sure? Well of course you are. I didn't mean that. I mean … what does she want?"

"To see you, that's all she'd say. Oh, except could she see you somewhere more private, so she doesn't have to walk through …?"

"Yes, of course," said Jo, thinking about the circumstances of the only time they had previously met. "Is she angry? How does she seem?"

"Very keen to see you," said Shana. "You could use the Chief's office now he's gone. I could bring her up the back stairs. She's waiting outside."

"Okay. I'll go there now and wait."

Her reaction to seeing Mags was one of shock and disbelief. Jo was sure she would not have recognised her if they had been the only two people in a lift together. She still had the same stunningly beautiful presence, but her face was thinner and her expression reflected the desperate agony of recent weeks. Even so, she was composed and surprisingly gracious, given Jo's role in the current plight of her son. She shook her hand and thanked Jo for seeing her. They sat down, facing each other across John Mackay's desk.

"This is completely off the record, Detective Inspector, so please hear me out. I absolutely promise you that I will not repeat anything we talk about today to another living soul. Unless you want me to, of course."

Jo nodded slowly. Mags hesitated, as if choosing her words carefully.

"I know for absolute certain that my son is innocent."

She spoke very slowly and paused after the statement. Jo took a sharp intake of breath.

"You would expect me to say that, of course," she continued, smiling thinly, "so nothing unusual there. However, what would be much more unusual is if *you* believed he was innocent as well."

Jo's stomach did a little flip.

"I don't suppose it really matters one way or the other what you believe," Mags went on. "You catch the bad guys – *suspected* bad guys – and hand them over with the evidence for someone else to decide what to do with them. That's what you've done in relation to this particular case; and done it well, I believe. Certainly my husband thinks so. But that doesn't mean that the right verdict was reached in that courtroom on Tuesday, does it?"

"Mrs Tomlinson Brown …"

"That's such a mouthful," Mags smiled again. "Please call me Maggie."

"I was not the investigating officer on the case. In fact, I was not even part of the investigating team. I …"

"That's the reason – well, one of the reasons – I wanted to see you." Mags went on. "Not the *main* reason, I have to say. The main reason is that I think you might share my feelings about Jack's innocence. Not with the same absolute conviction, of course, but certainly with some strong doubts."

Jo's stomach flipped again as Mags continued.

"You were there when the stuff was found. You saw Jack before you found it; you observed his reactions afterwards. You must have believed he had no idea it was there."

She looked into Jo's eyes, searching for some sign of agreement.

"Go on," she said, blankly.

"And then in court," Mags continued, "when you were questioned, it seemed to me you wanted to say more than you were allowed to – or say it more *forcefully* than you were allowed to. You wanted to say that if he had been guilty, there was no way – *no way* – he would have behaved like that. The more I go over it in my mind, the more I feel it."

Mags watched her steadily, their eyes locked. Neither spoke for a half a minute. Jo broke the silence.

"You said something about my not being the investigating officer being the other reason – or something?"

"That's right," said Mags, relaxing her gaze. "You were one step away from the action. You can take a detached view, with no axe to grind. I couldn't ask you if you had been the officer in charge."

"Ask me what, Mrs Tomlinson-Brown?"

"Maggie, please," said Mags.

"Ask me what, then, Maggie?" Jo leaned further forward. Mags clasped her hands together on the desk in front of her.

"I want you to find who it was who set up my son before it's too late," said Mags, her now small voice wavering in a hoarse whisper. Her composure left her as her true feelings surged to the surface.

Jo instinctively reached across and clasped Mags's hands in hers.

"Mrs ... Maggie," she said softly. "Even if you were right in what you say, they can't re-open the case without further evidence. You must know that, with your legal background. There's nothing I ..."

"I'm begging you, Detective Inspector. Somebody *must* do something. *Please!*" She was shaking now, tears falling. "It wasn't your case. You said that. So you could express concern at how it was handled. Say you're not satisfied – or something. Anything! Some day the truth *will* come out. Jack – and Jason – *will* be shown to be innocent. I just want it to be in time. Don't you?"

CHAPTER SEVENTEEN

Two days later
Week 10; Sunday, 31 May…

Tom arrived at the holding centre at 7.35 am for his meeting with Jack, feeling a little easier in his mind. The previous day his son's behaviour had been more stable, with none of the mood swings of the first visit. He was struck by the complete absence of any traffic, until he realised that it was Sunday. He was not even surprised that he hadn't known what day it was, each one now simply representing an equal step in the terrifying count-down.

When he entered the room, he saw that the glass screen had been lifted out of sight and the prison officer with Jack was already activating his door in order to leave. Tom noted that the room seemed to get larger with each subsequent visit as he became accustomed to its confines.

Jack was wearing the same clothes as on previous days, baggy jeans, black tee shirt and loose hooded top. It was clear as soon as Tom entered that he had a specific agenda. There was no exchange of pleasantries, and he was stiff and awkward when Tom went to embrace him. They sat facing each other on the chairs, Tom leaning forward, encouragingly, Jack in a neutral upright posture.

"I just wanted to chat through a few things," he said. "You know, make sure I've got some memories right." Tom was aware that his voice sounded mechanical, as if he had carefully rehearsed what he was saying.

"Yes, of course…" Tom began.

"A shame really that such private things have to be listened to by complete strangers," his voice rising to emphasise the point to those observing outside, and turning as he spoke to stare accusingly into the camera.

"For example," Jack went on, "you know when you were operating behind enemy lines; you must have felt scared at times about what would happen if you were taken alive. Terrified, probably; I've read a lot about the sort of things they did to members of the Special Forces that they captured."

"Well, there were a lot of different 'theys', Jack. Not all of them …"

"I mean the really bad ones. The ones that *did* do those things."

"What about them, Jack?" Tom asked. "What exactly do you want to know?"

"I guess they're wondering that as well," said Jack, nodding towards the camera. "Careful what you say, Jack," he added in a child-like voice. "Don't want to confuse them, do you?"

He laughed loudly, without humour.

"Just tell me, Jack. You wanted me to come and see you on my own. Well, I'm here, and Mum doesn't know, like you asked. So what is it?"

"I'm just interested in your time in the Special Forces." He was back to the script again, generating the words rather than articulating them. "How you coped with the prospect of capture and all that would follow."

"It was part of the job, I guess. I don't even know whether I ever did think about …"

"When you were right there, knocking on Heaven's door."

Tom went cold. Jack started singing, swaying from side to side.

"What … exactly?" Tom stammered.

"It's just a song, Dad," Jack went on. "But it must have been a comfort all the same."

"Another time, another place," said Tom, his voice shaking, "and another person. Not really for …"

"But a concept that's transferable, surely?" Jack was sounding more like himself now. "You know what I'm saying, don't you?" he added.

★

Phoebe escorted Tom from the building and returned to the screen on the wall where she and Jools had observed his meeting with Jack.

"What was all that about?"

"Haven't a clue," he said. "Let's run it again."

He pressed the start button on the recorder and they settled down to watch the replay.

"Perhaps he's just a Dylan fan," he added.

They watched it through and then sat in silence for some time puzzling over the conversation. Phoebe eventually spoke.

"I think we should get Em to watch this and then take it upstairs; let the Chief and the shrink have a look. Probably just the meanderings of the mind of a lost soul. But they can decide that. We'll add it to this morning's meeting with both parents, and then they can look at them together." She checked her watch. "They'll be here in less than an hour."

★

It was just after 9.15 am when he arrived home. Mags was getting up from the morning room table. He could see that she had eaten a reasonable breakfast for a change – there was an empty cereal bowl on the table, two empty eggshells and the remains of some toast. It was encouraging, though surprising, to see her taking her first meal in weeks at such a time.

"Are you ready to go?" he asked.

She looked up at the kitchen clock.

"Fifteen minutes," she replied, and walked past him out of the room.

★

Jack was leaning back on his chair, legs spread out in front of him looking somewhere between relaxed and indifferent. They both embraced him awkwardly and sat down.

"How's Megan?" he asked, mentioning her for the first time and without much feeling.

"She sends all her love," said Mags. "She's desperately sorry she can't see ..."

240

"It's okay," he interrupted.

The time went quickly. Mags did almost all the talking, while Tom looked blankly down at his clasped hands, turning over in his mind his earlier conversation with his son. It seemed a lot longer ago than just two hours. As they rose to leave, Jack looked intently at his father for some sign or guarded words of understanding. Tom produced neither.

"Everything cool, then?" said Jack, looking from one to the other but his eyes finally resting on Tom again.

Mags flashed Tom an enquiring look and then turned back to Jack.

"Sorry," she said. "I'm not sure I understand ..."

"Just man-words, Mum." Jack gave a little laugh. "No specific meaning, eh, Dad?"

"That's right," said Tom. "Just between us lads."

As they left the room, Jack was singing again.

★

David Gerrard was watching a DVD when the doorbell rang. He pressed the 'Pause' button on the remote; Lee Marvin froze on the boardwalk and Liberty Vallance's death sentence was reprieved, at least for the time being. He opened the front door. The attractive young woman outside held up an envelope.

"Delivery for Private Detective Hercule Gerrard of *deux* Neville Farm Fold." She pronounced it 'Gerrar', with emphasis on the second syllable.

David smiled. "Come in, Jo."

He led them through to the kitchen-cum-dining room and they sat down across the table from each other.

Jo looked round in admiration.

"Very clean and tidy," she said. "I *am* impressed, unless of course you simply don't *use* the kitchen."

"Not today – yet. Just been for my Sunday lunch at the Dog, actually," he said, patting his stomach with both hands. "I can get served there straight away when I don't have somebody with me."

Jo laughed, then looked round again, this time with a frightened expression on her face.

"Is this the room?" she said in a whisper.

David leaned across to her.

"Yes," he whispered back. "Right where you're sitting now."

"Ugh!" Jo gave an exaggerated shudder. "I thought it was cold in here. Is it haunted do you think?"

"Well if it is I'm too insensitive to see anything. And this isn't the room, anyway, in fact. It's upstairs where the bathroom and box room are now. So unless you want to spend a penny, you'll be safe enough."

"I can't promise," said Jo, smiling. "Anyway, I bet you didn't expect me to change my mind; not in a million years?"

"Not in a billion," said David. "Well, I certainly didn't expect a personal visit. I thought a phone call or perhaps an email."

"Better this way. No audit trail or whatever. As long as there are spies and secrets, I reckon there'll always be a paper industry. So you *did* expect me to change my mind?"

"I thought it was somewhere between just possible and highly likely."

Jo laughed.

"Why did you offer to do this?" she asked. "Not that I'm not grateful, obviously."

"Because I'd like to help you put this behind you. I don't think we'll find anything, but you have better instincts than anyone I've ever worked with, so it's worth a look. Anyway, it's your neck on the block if anyone finds out you're sneaking around trying to undo a conviction. So why are *you* prepared to do this? You weren't the investigating officer; you're not responsible for the end result."

"Yes," she said, "it *is* my neck on the block and I think someone has just inadvertently loosened the guillotine. I had a visitor on Friday afternoon. Maggie Tomlinson-Brown, no less."

David listened without speaking as Jo described their meeting.

"So, to answer your question about why I'm doing it, it's because I *have* to; because I promised to. And anyway, if I didn't, I'd always wonder if I should have."

David shook his head. "Not good," he said. "Puts a lot of pressure on you, doesn't it?"

"Well, no more than before, really. I mean, my mind was already some way down that road."

"Yes, but that was just *you* checking things out. For Jack's mother, it's so much more than that. I know which way you're leaning at the moment, but I think it's much more likely that you'll satisfy yourself that they're guilty than convince yourself that they're not."

"Well, I'm not sure I agree …"

"I know that," David interrupted, "but *if* you were to satisfy yourself it was the right conviction, then that would be enough for you; but it sure as hell won't be enough for Mrs T."

Jo didn't reply, showing in her face the first sign of doubt.

"I'm just saying," David went on, "that it would be better for you if you didn't have the responsibility now of meeting Mrs Tomlinson-Brown's expectations. Finding the truth isn't the measure of success any more – now, it's freeing Jack. The goalposts have moved big-time and that's what I mean by it putting pressure on you."

"So do you think I should have refused to help Maggie?"

David thought for a long moment. "Yes, I do," he said, finally, "but I doubt if *I* would have done."

Jo smiled and they were both silent for a while.

"So, what have we got?" he asked. "But before that, can I get you a drink – tea, coffee, Southern Comfort?"

"Nothing for me, thanks," said Jo. "Starting my first assignment as a Fart tomorrow – in Leicestershire. Got to get there for an early start in the morning, so can't stay long. But I'll take a rain-check on the moonshine for the next time I come."

She opened the envelope and emptied its contents onto the table. There was a collection of documents and several glossy A4 photographs of a thin, slightly-stooping white man of average height, showing him face-on, side-face, some with him wearing a hood and four very grainy CCTV stills in which he was talking to a tall, good-looking young man in a street somewhere.

"This is one of the guys caught on camera; known to the police, but … well, impossible to find, apparently. I'm afraid it's too risky going after any of the ones that came forward. They'd be easy to contact but they were guaranteed police protection for a period after the trial. Can't have you being picked up by the filth for harassing people. Think of your pension. Anyway, they'd obviously been very well briefed and it's not likely to be easy to get them to change their story."

"Except that they could have been telling the truth, of course. You now seem to be coming at this from the point of view that it was definitely a set-up."

"No, but we have to assume that it *might* have been, or there's no point in doing any of this?"

David thought for a moment and then nodded. "So what have we got?" he asked again.

"One Lawrence Harvey Newhouse – known as Laser – aged thirty-one; unemployed, serial user, both soft and hard; since the amnesty, as far as we know, just soft. Twelve separate convictions for theft, including aggravated robbery with an offensive weapon – twice – a screw-driver each time. One ABH, in addition to these cases, making unlucky thirteen overall. Lives in Cobham, officially, but dosses all over the place. Four of the offences, including the ABH, took place in Central London, in or just outside a tube station. Done time twice, short stretches, each of six months."

"Six months for ABH?"

"Pre-NJR. And it was one of his earlier offences; also some mitigation; self-defence, provocation, six-of-one – that sort of thing."

David sighed. "Carry on."

"Address and phone number of the place in Cobham where he's registered for benefits." Jo handed David a single sheet of paper. "The property isn't in his name, not surprisingly. It's a small guesthouse run by an elderly aunt or something. The Nook, Ivygreen Avenue. Apparently he's very rarely there, although he's seen fairly frequently near the rail station."

"I wouldn't have thought there'd be much action in Cobham," said David.

"Well, none of the action has actually been *in* Cobham – at least none that's come to our attention. Two of the four incidents at tube stations have been at Waterloo, which is where the main line from the town links with the underground. Most of the other incidents have been close to stations on that line. So he seems to spread himself around – or along – when it comes to his day job."

"Jason lives in Cobham, doesn't he?"

"*Used* to live there, you mean," said Jo. "Yes, Copley Road, on a small estate on the Byfleet side. I doubt that's significant, though. As I said, this guy, Laser, is hardly ever there, according to his aunt, so it's unlikely he and Jason have ever met. There's a big age difference as well."

David went through the pile of papers on his table, studying the photographs and sifting through the documents to check what Jo had brought him. They were mostly copies of official notes from statements and interviews relating to his earlier offences, plus printouts of investigating officers' reports. He went back to the CCTV images and studied them for a long time.

"So that's handsome Jack-the-lad Tomlinson-hyphen-Brown. What a waste. What a terrible waste."

"You're absolutely right there. He's beautiful; just about perfect. And remember, I've seen him in just his boxer shorts."

"So, where am I most likely to find this Laser?" asked David.

"Look," said Jo, leaning forward and placing her hand on his. "You will take care, won't you, and not get involved in a scene or anything?"

"Jo, what a hurtful thing to say," he said, frowning in mock surprise. "You know me; I'll be virtually invisible."

She smiled across the table at the massive human frame in front of her.

"And just how are you planning to achieve that? Borrowing Harry Potter's invisibility cloak, are you?"

David smiled back.

"Let me worry about how; you just tell me where."

"I wish I knew," said Jo, withdrawing her hand. "I guess you could ask his aunt. She might be able to point you in the right direction, though she's much more likely to call the police, of course. Perhaps the railway station at Cobham might be the best starting point. That's where he's known to hang out fairly regularly. At least there, if you're seen, you could be waiting for a train. Not that you *will* be seen, of course, being invisible and all that."

"You're right, that would be the best place to start. I could just be waiting for someone off the train," said David. "In fact, I would be, wouldn't I? Do we have a timescale on this? I mean, when are they due to start their passage?"

"The Wednesday after next, but I guess we have until just before they get shipped to Alpha. In practice they'll be retrievable until then and that could be some time. There's enough ahead of them in the queue to fill the first platform and then they've got to get the second facility in place. I'm guessing, then, it could be up to a year or more. So I suppose there's no rush from that point of view. But you know how it is. This story will pass quickly and soon no-one will care – except the families, of course – and me …"

"And me," added David. "I'm in it as far as you are now."

"Sorry," said Jo, putting her hand back on his and squeezing it gently this time.

"No need to be sorry," he said. "My idea, remember?"

She smiled at him, and then frowned as she withdrew her hand again. "All this depends on your not being too expensive, of course," she added.

"I'm *very* expensive," he said, "but you get what you pay for."

"Seriously, I don't want you to be out of pocket for this. I can put stuff through on miscellaneous expenses, I guess. You know, fuel, rail fares, stopovers, whatever."

"You can't do that," said David. "You're a police officer, not a member of parliament. And this case is closed, don't forget. In my day, you had to at least show which case the expenses applied to."

"Same now," said Jo. "But it's still in pursuit of the cause of justice," she added.

"Tell you what, if I find myself short, I'll let you know. Otherwise, we can discuss finances later. Okay?"

"Okay." She got to her feet. "And now I must love you and leave you."

"But apparently not in that order," said David.

She laughed, kissing him on the cheek.

He showed her out and waved goodbye as she drove off. Then he turned and swaggered purposefully back to the lounge to finish off Liberty Valance.

★

"I'm sorry about the short notice, but I need you to attend an emergency meeting in my office at 7.00 am tomorrow morning – Monday. This is regarding some information, which has just come – today – through Ruby's area, relating to hostile colonisation of the redundant rigs in the North Sea. If the information is correct, then – worst case scenario – we have potentially a very significant threat to national security. We need to discuss this with the utmost urgency. See you tomorrow morning."

Tom left the same message for Andrew, Grace and Jonathan.

He phoned Jenny, getting through to her voicemail.

"Hi, Jenny. Long time no hear, but just to let you know I've got a meeting in my office tomorrow morning – Monday – at seven o'clock. Hopefully, we can catch up with stuff after that. Look forward to seeing you."

Finally he called his driver.

CHAPTER EIGHTEEN

Week 11; Monday, 1 June…

The gravel outside crunched at 5.25 am as Paul eased the car as quietly as possible up to the front door. Tom turned and looked up briefly towards Mags's bedroom as he walked across to it. He thought he saw the curtains twitch.

Paul Webster mumbled an incoherent greeting, accompanied by a loose salute, as was his custom.

"Morning, Paul," said Tom, "how are you? Long time, no see."

"I'm fine, thank you, sir. And you … I'm so sorry about … you know …it must be …"

"Thank you, Paul," said Tom. "Do you think we can make it for six-thirty?"

"No problem, sir. There shouldn't be much traffic at this time."

He closed the door as Tom settled into the back seat, slumping down.

"Seat belt, please, sir," said Paul, as they turned into the lane, the second car slipping in behind them.

★

Jo's alarm woke her at 6.30 am in the small B&B in Enderby which would be her home for the duration of her assignment. Just about right for a leisurely breakfast and an unhurried start to the day, she thought. The place was only a few minutes drive away from the Leicestershire Constabulary's headquarters where she would be attending her first briefing at 8.00 am.

She was just about to step into the shower when she heard the ring tone on her mobile.

"Hello, DI Cottrell."

"Hi, Jo. It's Maggie. I'm sorry to phone so early. I was planning to leave a message. Can you talk now?"

"Well, I'm naked, actually, and I've got the shower running – just about to get in – but if it's a quick one …"

"Well, that depends on what you've got to tell me. You said you'd keep me informed."

"And I will, Maggie, if and when I have something to tell you. It was only Friday, remember, when you asked me to look into it, and I did say I would do my best, but … well, you know."

"Yes, I'm sorry. I don't want to be a pest. But, it's a week on Wednesday he gets moved out – I'm not sure I told you that on Friday…"

"You didn't tell me, but I knew anyway."

"After that, I guess we'll never see him again."

"Listen, Maggie. Just so you understand, there is virtually no chance that anything is going to happen in the next ten days. You'll have to come to terms with that, I'm afraid."

"Oh, God!" Mags gasped.

"*But,*" Jo went on. "*But* … Jack – and Jason – will be in the system, on passage and accessible, up to the point they step onto the transfer vessel. At this point in time no-one knows when that will be. I wouldn't like to even hazard a guess. But it will be a lot – a *lot* – later than a week on Wednesday. I can't even begin to imagine how you must be feeling, Maggie, so if it sounds insensitive asking you to be patient, then I apologise. But that's the way it is."

There was no reply from the other end. Jo could hear Mags breathing deeply.

"Listen," said Jo, after a long silence. "I'm freezing here. I must get into that shower."

"Yes, of course," said Mags in a small voice. "I know I'm being a nuisance, but you're all I've got, my only hope. I don't suppose you can tell me what it is you're doing. I mean, *how* you're looking into it."

"You're *not* a nuisance, Maggie, but you're quite right, I can't tell you. And it's not me, actually; it's someone I know who I believe is our very best chance."

★

Tom checked his phone again for messages as the car pulled up at Number 2 Marsham Street. Surely someone should have replied to his voicemail yesterday, he thought, coming as it did out of the blue like that; at the very least confirming their attendance, but much more likely with urgent questions as to the nature of the threat. As he approached his office he noticed the door was slightly ajar. He knocked gently before pushing it open. Andrew was sitting in Tom's chair and facing him across the desk. Tom looked round the room for the others.

"Morning, Andrew," he began, "you're here bright and ..."

The look of open hostility on the prime minister's face stopped him in his tracks. His countenance was anything but bright.

"Look, Andrew, I'm sorry it's so early, but ..."

"The time is not the problem," Andrew boomed. "The *problem* is that pathetic message I received yesterday after nearly six weeks of complete silence. I'm not sure what to do about someone of your seniority who tells ridiculously transparent lies in order to get his own way." He paused as if to let the statement register. "So, come on, prove me wrong. Shock me with this potentially cataclysmic security issue. And then perhaps you can explain to me how the information managed to 'come through Ruby's area' as you put it, without Weller knowing anything about it herself. I realise communications in the Home Office haven't been exactly world class recently, but ... Well, let's hear it."

Tom sank into one of the chairs in front of his desk. He looked across at Andrew.

"Look, I've been trying to get to speak to you for the last couple of weeks" he said, "but you wouldn't get back to me. No-body would. I was desperate; I had to do something if there was even the smallest chance of saving Jack ..."

"Saving Jack," Andrew repeated, shaking his head. "So not, quote, because of public concern, unquote, after all? Well, what a surprise."

Neither man spoke for a long time. Tom slumped further in his seat, his head sagging forward, like a schoolboy who had just been found guilty of lying to his headmaster. Then suddenly he snapped out of it. He sat up, leaning forward across the desk, his eyes flashing with anger.

"You don't know what it's like," he said. "You make the rules, but you don't play the game. If *you* had kids, if it was *your* son, you might be entitled to play God and decide who lives and who dies. But as it is …"

"*Me* play God!"

"Yes, that's what I said. I'm going to pull this off, with or without your cooperation. I'll swing the whole fucking country if I have to. You'll see who the people want to lead them!"

Andrew sprang up from the chair, sending it careering backwards on its castors into the wall behind him. He towered over Tom looking for a moment as if he was going to reach down and grab him.

"My *cooperation*! You arrogant bastard," he yelled. "You're out of your fucking mind. How dare you sit there and say *I'm* playing God. *You*, who have started believing that you *are* God. A few weeks ago, I sat in that very chair on the morning before the debate discussing with you whether we should hold back on that piece of legislation! You sat here with that smug, smarmy expression of yours and said, 'Nah, they'll get used to the idea'. And afterwards, when God knows how many people were urging a rethink, not a murmur of hesitation, not a hint of a doubt, not a word of compromise left the golden larynx of this most wonderful of men. Absolutely typical, predictable reaction – Tom knows what's best for *everybody*. Trust Tom. He's charming and charismatic, after all. He *must* be right."

Tom half rose. Andrew reached forward and pushed him back down onto the chair. Tom jumped up and gave Andrew a shove in the chest that caught him off balance and sent him staggering backwards a few steps so that he dropped onto his chair again.

"Don't you put your hands on me!" hissed Tom "You don't have any of the equipment necessary to push me around. I'm not Jackie Hewlett or one of your fucking puppets."

Andrew opened his eyes wide then threw back his head and laughed.

"Not one of my puppets! Not one of my puppets! That's hilarious, that is!"

Tom was trembling.

"What the hell do you mean by that?" he shouted.

"I mean, that's *exactly* what you've been for – what – six, seven, eight years now? A bloody good one, admittedly, but a puppet just the same. Hey, what's the big deal? You're famous … and popular. And now that Andy Pandy's finally retired, you might even get your own TV show; with your own signature tune. 'Tommy Brown is coming to play, la la la la la lah la…'"

He laughed again.

"Given that everything that's happened was *my* idea," said Tom, "my *own* idea – I wonder how you come to the conclusion that *I'm* the puppet and, presumably, *you're* the puppeteer. I'd bet that most people in the country – the world, probably – see it the other way round. All you did was agree with everything I said, and did whatever I asked. You've got a strange idea of how the puppet business works."

Andrew smiled at him.

"To be honest, Tom, I don't think *you* have any of the equipment to understand, so I'm not even going to try to explain it to you. But just so there's no misunderstanding about the plan for today, let me be absolutely clear. There is no meeting. I've spoken to the others and told them not to come; just to carry on with what they had already scheduled for today.

"There will be no reversal of the policy relating to drug dealer sentencing. Not yet, and probably not ever. Latest opinion polls show a definite movement towards public acceptance of the measures, in spite of their awareness of Jack's own predicament. From an initial seventy-thirty split against, we've moved almost to parity. And that's down to you, Tom. Well done. Your absolute intransigence on the matter in that first week or so seems to have paid off. And, I admit, this time you did it all on your own. No strings pulled by me – except, if anything, in the other direction.

"And finally, I need you to decide how you want to proceed in terms of your current position. And let me be clear on this as well. Continuing as Home Secretary is not an option, nor is moving to another post in Cabinet at any level. In fact, I would ideally like your resignation as a member of parliament as soon as possible; that way I won't need to formally suspend or remove you. You have forced my hand; I'm not so much of a bastard that I would otherwise choose to do this right now, but I can't have the integrity of this government put at risk by the destabilising effect of one man on a very personal crusade. What has happened with your son is regrettable, but the fallout from it has already hit our ratings. It's just a small dip, admittedly; two percentage points and we're still way ahead, of course. But it's significant in that it's the first reversal in over three years and it's down one hundred percent to you, and your family."

"That's okay," said Tom. "Pretty much *all* of what's happened in the last three years is one hundred percent down to me. I was the one who got us up there."

Andrew shook his head.

"I'll miss this element of surprise, Tom. The way you can always push back the boundaries of arrogance just when I think it's impossible for you to go any further."

"Arrogance or whatever, Andrew, it's served you well. Do you really believe you'd be where you are without me?"

"There you go; surprising me again. But you have a point, Tom. You played your part, dangling there on the end of your strings, along with Grace and Jackie and – well – any number of people. And, yes, you were the main mover and shaker. But you would never make a half-decent Home Secretary; not in a million years – a million terms, even. You made a really telling comment in your interview with Hanker. You said something like, 'it's a Pareto analysis; you tackle the biggest thing first, then when that's sorted, you move onto the next biggest thing'. The perfect summary of the way you work. One thing at a time."

There was a long silence. Tom chose his words carefully and spoke quietly.

"Well, Prime Minister, you've given me a lot to think about today. However, I can tell you right now that I shall certainly *not* be resigning and I doubt if you'd be stupid enough to sack me. I've got some very influential friends in the media, as you know. They'd be delighted to tell the country how traumatised I am to be kicked out at a time of such personal suffering by the very man I've put into 10 Downing Street. That's how it will read, whatever *you* believe is the truth. Now, if you'd please get out of my fucking chair, I've got some phone calls to make."

The senior man rose from the chair slowly, the smirk frozen on his face but a sudden feeling of uncertainty betrayed in his eyes. As he stood up, he snapped into an exaggerated military salute, his raised hand shaking theatrically against his temple.

"Permission to whistle *Colonel Bogey* on the way out, *sah!*"

He marched stiffly past Tom and out of the room, pausing briefly at the door.

"We've achieved a lot together, Tom, you and I. Think how much more we could have accomplished if we'd actually liked each other."

Tom sat motionless, looking across the desk at the vacated chair. He checked his watch – 6.58 am. He moved round to his own chair so that he was facing the door.

The minutes passed.

No one came; just as Andrew had promised.

At 7.15, he picked up the handset and phoned Mags, leaving a message when – as he expected – she didn't answer. More minutes passed. He checked his watch again. Still only 7.35; he had a long time to wait, and he was not going to spend it in an empty office.

He left the building and walked the few hundred yards to Balmaha. At 9.00 am, he made his call. The woman on reception was very helpful, and at 9.15, he left the apartment and flagged down a black cab.

★

Tom was shocked all over again at the thin limbs and drawn features of his friend as he got up slowly from his chair to greet him. His conscious memory of Jad was of the robust, dashing companion of his military years and even though he had witnessed his physical decline in recent months, his mind's eye still preserved this chosen image.

"Hi, Jad, how are you? Stupid question. I ..."

Jad's expression was a reflection of his own, and Tom could see the impact of his own weight loss and haggard appearance in his friend's eyes.

"Better than you, ol' pal o' mine." Jad's voice was a hoarse whisper. He paused for a long time. "Tom, I'm so sorry about ... I don't know what to say ... I should have got in touch, but ..."

254

"It's okay, Jad."

"I know I must be the worst Godfather in the world, but I've always felt close to him, you know."

The two looked at each other in silence, both breathing heavily. They each moved forward and embraced.

"I've done nothing for him in his entire life," Jad continued as they stepped apart. "I just wish I was out of here and then maybe ..."

"Actually, I came here to ask for your help; and advice. There may be time yet to do something."

★

David Gerard called for a paper on the way back from his visit to the Alpha Male Grooming Emporium in Cullen Hall. Before starting to read it, he checked his landline for messages. There was one from his daughter.

"Hi, Dad. Linny here. Just to let you know that we'll be away for ten days from tomorrow – that's Tuesday. Back a week on Friday. Caz has got to use up some hols carried over from last year before the end of the month. We're going to the Lakes. Doing a bit of walking. Take care. Love you. Bye."

David smiled. Linny and her husband, Caz, had recently moved to Earlsfield in Wandsworth, a short commutable distance from their work in the Capital. He started to text her to 'have a great time' and then stopped as an idea came to him. He called her instead. She answered immediately.

"Hi, Dad!"

"Hi, Gorgeous!"

"Did you get my message?"

"I did. It sounds great, though I can't remember Caz asking permission to take my daughter away."

"No? Well, I definitely told him to."

They laughed.

"I'll have to have a word with that little rascal," said David.

"He's not little, Dad. He's six-two. He only looks little next to you."

"Whatever. Anyway, I want to ask you a favour. I've got a job – some security consultancy work – in and around Cobham for the next week or so. Would it be possible, seeing as you're away, to stay at your place?"

"'Course, Dad. But you could have stayed anyway. I hope you know that."

David looked at his reflection in the mirror over the fireplace; at the shaven head, at the colourful tattoos on his forearms and round his neck – albeit temporary ones he could remove using the small bottle of special solvent which came free with the make-over – at the clip-on earring with its dangling cross. He wondered if his daughter's invitation would have survived the shock of his new image.

"Yes I know I could, but I never thought about it until I picked up your message. You sure it's okay?"

"Of course it is. Listen, why not come tonight and stay over. We would love that and …"

"Sorry, Linny, but I can't make it tonight. What time are you leaving tomorrow?"

"First thing. Trying to get a flyer before the worst of the M25. Leaving around five. Probably better if you're not here. We'd only wake you up, I guess."

"Perhaps I could stay to welcome you back. You could show me all your photographs and if that didn't work, Caz could beam me to sleep."

Linny laughed.

"That would be great. So make sure you plan to stay over the Friday night we're back. You've still got your key? Not forgotten where you've put it or anything?"

"Look, I'm only fifty-six. You're not suppose to start forgetting things until you're at least sixty."

"Really?"

"Really. By the way, what did you say your name was?"

★

Week 11; Tuesday, 2 June…

David arrived at 23 St Herbert Street – a medium-sized Victorian terraced – just after noon. He was relieved to see that there was no-one around.

He pulled off the road onto the paved area in front of the house – previously the front garden – grabbed his hold-all from the back seat and rushed into the property. He was starting to think that the two parts of his brilliant plan might not fit comfortably together. His new image, calculated to give him an air of menace in any confrontation with his quarry, might prove to be something of a liability in a tranquil London suburb. He wondered what the neighbours would think of a very large, shaven-headed, tattooed individual suddenly replacing a friendly young couple in their street. A couple who, it might seem, had disappeared without trace overnight.

He settled into his temporary accommodation, laying out his clothes and placing his toiletries in the bathroom. He checked the fridge and noted that Linny had left him enough milk, eggs, bacon and spread to last him a good few days. In the freezer compartment there were also several ready meals for the microwave and a couple of loaves of bread, one of which he removed and placed on the worktop to defrost.

He changed into black jeans and a tight black tee shirt, flexing his chest and arms in front of the mirror to test the effect. Satisfied, he picked up his leather jacket and peered out of the front door, looking up and down the street before rushing into his car like an escaping bank robber.

★

"Bon soir, Cherie."

"Hercule! Quelle surprise! 'Ow goes eet?"

"I'm just phoning to let you know I'm staying at Linny's – moved in earlier today – just in case you were planning to drop by my place with wine and flowers. It's in Earlsfield, on the Cobham line into Waterloo. How's that for a piece of luck?"

"That's great. I feel a bit sorry for Linny, though."

"No need, she's, on holiday in the Lake District, but thanks a lot, anyway."

"Then I'm definitely *not* sorry for her. Have you done anything yet? A bit early, I guess."

"Just a bit, but I've been to Cobham, checked around the railway station for likely dealing places – no obvious ones, as you would expect – but found the guest house where Laser's aunt lives. Not asked around at all yet. Planning to do that tomorrow at the stations along the route. Very exciting, all this."

"Great, keep me posted. How's the invisibility cloak working?"

"I tell you, you wouldn't see me if I was standing right behind you."

Jo laughed.

"Well, just be careful, anyway. Speak soon."

★

Week 11; Wednesday, 3 June …

Before they left the holding centre, Mags spent a few minutes with Jason while Katey went to see her brother.

Tom waved Emily to one side.

"Could I have a word in private, please?"

"Of course." Emily smiled and waved him towards a door off the reception area and they seated themselves across the table in a small interview room.

"Look," said Tom, "I wonder if I can have another one-to-one with Jack. Could you arrange that? I just want to put everything right between us. I don't want to look back and think of things I should have said. I'm sure you can appreciate that. And I know Jack will feel the same."

Emily hesitated. "Well, as you know, sir, such a meeting would normally only be allowed at the request of the prisoner."

"Well, ask him!"

"But …" Emily continued, still smiling sweetly. "I really can't see a problem. Frankly, I've never understood why that rule applies; it seems nonsense to me," she added. "What about tomorrow afternoon? Three-thirty?"

"Yes, thank you," said Tom, a little sheepishly. "That would be ideal."

★

Emily watched them leave the building then picked up the phone.

"Alison Anders speaking."

"Hi Chief, just to let you know, father and son have another meeting arranged for tomorrow – Thursday – three-thirty – just the two of them again. After the weird conversation they had last time, thought you might be interested in listening in; perhaps Doc Wallis as well. Did you come up with anything about 'Heaven's door', by the way?"

"Not yet," said the Chief. "Still looking into it. Obviously some connection with the father's years in the armed services, but there's nothing jumps out. I'll definitely come down and listen in tomorrow though, and I'll ask the doc."

★

"Right," David said. "The story so far, day two." He was stretched out on Linny's sofa with a large malt at his elbow and his clip-on earring in his pocket. "I have spent the whole of the day – well, pretty much – travelling between Waterloo and Cobham – backwards and forwards. Did you know you can get a daily saver ticket for £10.80 that gives you unlimited journeys…?"

"That's absolutely fascinating," interrupted Jo. "And I've made a note of it, so you don't have to keep the receipt. Now, can you tell me – was it worth it? What did you find out?"

"You know, you can be very pushy sometimes. Anyway … around most of the stops I managed to locate some user action – nothing major, just soft legit stuff. I waved the photos of Laser around and five people at three different stops identified him, though none of them could – or would – say where I was likely to find him. They all confirmed, however, that Laser's patch – or perhaps 'stretch' is a better word – is along the railway like we thought, but none of them had seen him for quite some time."

"Did you check at the guest house yet?"

"I didn't want to knock on the door and risk frightening her so I phoned instead."

"No, I can understand that. An elderly lady answering the door to someone she can't see; a disembodied voice asking her awkward questions – very scary."

"Look, I think you're taking the invisibility thing a bit too literally. It's my new street-fighting-man image that's a bit … well, I'll show you next time I see you."

"Can't wait. So what did you find out?"

"Well, I asked if she knew where her nephew was – said I was a friend who'd arranged to meet him last night and was wondering why he hadn't turned up. She hadn't seen him for nearly a week, but – very encouragingly – is expecting him any day to pick up the benefit payment she's just collected for him. So tomorrow, I'm bound for Cobham and a stake-out at Chez-le-Nook."

"And how does your new image assist you in the hunt?"

"So far it's worked pretty well. The biggest challenge is getting back into Linny's without causing a panic. I keep thinking about that scene in *Frankenstein* where all the villagers are marching to the castle carrying flaming torches to burn the place down and kill the monster. I've put the fire extinguisher next to the front door just in case."

Jo laughed.

"Good luck tomorrow. Keep me posted. Oh, and please be careful."

"I will. Night."

"Night."

CHAPTER NINETEEN

Week 11; Thursday, 4 June ...

Jack was wearing just his tee shirt and jeans, having discarded the fleece. He looked thin and frail; his fair hair was uncombed and flat to his head and his whole body seemed to have sagged.

"Before we start, can I see Katey again afterwards?" he asked.

The door opened briefly and Jools popped his head in.

"Will do, Jack. We'll extend the session for ten minutes or so."

Mags thought how very young he suddenly looked, and how vulnerable.

"Are you eating, Jack?" she asked, tentatively. "You don't look as though you are."

He took a long time to reply.

"Not much," he said. "Can't see the point, really."

"What about exercise?" Mags realised she was asking obvious, basic questions for the first time.

There was another long silence.

"We have access to a gym and there's an exercise yard. Been out there a few times just to see Jay." He looked intensely at her and then Tom. "But, as I said, what's the point?"

"Jack, we haven't given up you know. Where there's life ..."

"There's shit happening!" Jack completed the sentence for her. "You carry on hoping, Mum. Do it for both of us, because I'm not sure I ..."

He stopped, as if he had simply shut down; as if a switch had been thrown inside him. He stared intensely at her for a time, his eyes gradually softening. Finally, he gave her a smile before turning to Tom.

"So, how are things coming along, Dad. Making progress, are we?"

"I'm doing what I can," said Tom.

"Well, I guess you'll keep me posted."

Most of the time they sat in silence, but the atmosphere became more relaxed. As they left, he shook hands briefly with Tom and then hugged Mags closely to him for a long time. When they broke off the embrace, his eyes were full of tears.

"Take care, Mum. And please, I want you and Dad to stay friends. You love each other. Everyone knows that. You must take care of each other. Promise me that."

Mags broke down and Tom could feel his own eyes filling up.

"Of course we will, darling," she said, choking out the words. "Of course."

As they left the room, Jack shouted out to the prison officers.

"Is Katey coming? I need to see her."

"She's on her way, Jack," said Jools.

★

David had not seen a soul for two-and-a-half hours; which made it all the more remarkable that the first person he did see was the one he was looking for.

A thin, stooping figure in the same shabby hooded top he had been wearing on the CCTV images, scurried furtively up to the front door of The Nook on Ivygreen Avenue. The houses on both sides of the road were small semi-detached dormer-bungalows with reasonably large and neat front gardens and narrow drives. The guesthouse was a conversion of a pair of semis into a single dwelling with a porch added in the middle to form the entrance. The front gardens had been paved to provide off-road parking for up to six cars behind a low brick wall with an iron gate opposite the porch for pedestrian access.

Turning the knob and finding the door locked, Laser hammered impatiently with the knocker, looking anxiously around him as he did so. David, watching from his car a hundred or so yards away, guessed that someone had told him there was a big guy looking for him. Lawrence Harvey Newhouse was decidedly uncomfortable.

His aunt eventually opened the door and he almost pushed her over in his haste to get inside.

★

He had a decision to make. It was two hours since Laser had gone into the house and by now David knew there was a good chance he would have seen him waiting in the car.

He started the engine and drove along Ivygreen Avenue, passing The Nook on his left without looking at it, and accelerating fiercely to give the impression he was leaving the area. He turned first left fifty yards beyond the house, and then made two further left turns, taking him round behind the guesthouse and stopping just before he reached Ivygreen again.

He got out, threw the hi-vis jacket he'd been wearing onto the back seat and walked quickly towards the avenue, positioning the clip-on ring on his left ear as he went.

★

Tom sat at his dressing table and opened the small padded box, which held his grandmother's locket and chain. Taking it out, he opened the large oval-shaped pendant and removed the two small photographs of his grandparents, carefully replacing them with a picture of him and Mags in one side and one of Jack and Katey in the other. When he had finished, he looked at them for a long time before his grief overwhelmed him and he sobbed, loudly and uncontrollably.

He got up and put on his sports jacket, placing the locket in the left side pocket and checking for the fifth time the small envelope in the right one. Then he strode from the room, down the stairs and out to his car. He looked at the dashboard clock – 2.40 pm – and eased down the drive and out through the slowly opening gates.

★

As David approached Ivygreen Avenue on foot, he heard the metallic clang of a gate closing. He quickened his pace, looking left as he

263

reached the corner. Laser was heading towards him along the avenue, half-walking, half running and looking back over his shoulder, checking there was no one following him. When he turned to the front again, the two men were no more than five yards apart.

Laser stopped, eyes bulging at the man blocking his way. David moved forward quickly, reaching out and grabbing his left arm just above the elbow.

"It's your lucky day," said David. "You're obviously in a big hurry, and now you've got a lift."

"Look …I …" stammered Laser.

"Plenty of time to talk in the car," said David, increasing the pressure on his arm and turning to walk him the short distance back to where he had parked.

When they reached the car, David spun him round to face it, pushed him hard up against the passenger door, and checked his pockets.

"Lost your screw-driver, Laser?"

"Wha…"

David could feel him trembling, and when he opened the door and shoved him roughly into the seat, he looked as though he was going to burst into tears. David slammed shut the door and went quickly round to get in the driver's side. He grabbed Laser by the chin and twisted his head round towards him, leaning across until their faces were only inches apart.

"Listen, son," he said, "I have no intention of hurting you – none at all – providing you cooperate, tell me what I want to know, and do exactly what I ask you to do. But if you *don't* cooperate, I promise you I'll break every bone in your body, finishing with your neck. Understood?"

"I haven't done anything."

"Understood?" David shouted.

Laser gulped and nodded.

"Say it!"

"Understood."

"Good boy," said David, releasing his chin and slapping him hard twice on the cheek in acknowledgement. "Now put your seat belt on."

David started the engine and pulled away. He drove out of the residential area to where the road passed through fields before reaching an abandoned builders' yard. There were still piles of old bricks, timber and breezeblocks lying around the crumbling walled perimeter, but the extensive presence of buddleia and thistle was evidence to its disuse.

He pulled in to the yard, turning sharp left and parking out of sight of the approach road against the boundary wall, close enough to prevent Laser from opening the passenger side door. He switched off the engine and took his mobile from his jeans pocket, pressing the mode button a couple of times and placing it in the hands-free console.

"Okay, Laser, we can do this one of two ways. Either we can sit here in comfort and you agree to everything right away, or I can introduce you to some of the materials round here – bricks, stones, blocks and such like – until you do. Personally I don't mind either way, so you decide. What's it to be?"

"I'll do whatever you want," whined Laser. "I mean … just tell me. And then you'll let me go, right?"

"Well, let's see how we get on before I start making promises I might not be able to keep."

Laser looked blank. "Who are you?" he asked. "What am I supposed to have done?"

"I want some information. You share it with me now, and then with the police afterwards. Okay?"

"The police? What information?"

David continued to stare at him.

"Just ask me," said Laser. "I'll tell you whatever you want to know. I haven't done anything wrong."

David thought about the thirteen convictions, but said nothing.

"Look," said Laser. "Just tell me who you are and what you want."

"I work for this man, see. I tell you, Laser, he's a fucking vicious bastard. He scares the shit out of me – and I don't scare easily." David prodded him hard in the chest. "Know what I mean?"

Laser nodded jerkily.

"He's a sort of …healer, I suppose you could say. He makes people feel better. At least he supplies the *stuff* that makes them feel better. He's the guy who gets it into the country to the dealers, who get it to the pathetic little people like you. With me so far?"

Laser nodded again.

"But he likes to know the score on the ground. You know, who's doing what on which patch. Not that he *cares* all that much, but he just wants to know. Now you're thinking, why bother himself about that so long as he gets his money. Fair point, Laser, I'm glad you brought that up."

"But, I ..."

"Well, it's the pride he takes in his work, I suppose. Being completely on top of everything; knowing the business, understanding the market; who the really big players are and who the little shits are who are trying to muscle in and poach the big guys' customers."

Laser opened his mouth to speak.

"Don't worry, Laser, no-one's suggesting you're *that* type of little shit. That type of little shit needs brains and bottle. But that's where I come in. Think of me as a sort of market researcher. Okay? And I know that some time back you approached a new kid on the block – well, he's very much *off* the block now, as it happens. All I need you to do is tell me who put you on to this guy, and what sort of stuff he was dealing. Couldn't be easier, eh?"

David took a brown A4 envelope from the storage pocket of the driver's door and pulled out one of the CCTV stills. It showed Jack speaking to someone who had his back to the camera.

"That's you, right?" he asked. "Not the good looking one; the little toe-rag with the hood."

Laser looked wide-eyed at the image. "Where'd you get this?" he said.

"Oh, it's not you then?" said David, with feigned surprise and biting sarcasm. "Mistaken identity, is it? Well, I do apologise, Lawrence, old chap. I guess you'd better go then." He grabbed Laser's chin again, this time forcing his head back against the side window "*Is it you or not?*"

"Yes, yes... "

"Then what the fuck does it matter where I got it?"

"Okay, okay. It's just that I couldn't be certain. I've got my back to the camera."

"Well, let's make absolutely sure, then," said David, releasing him. He removed the other three stills all of which showed Laser's face, one with the hood down.

Laser looked from one to the other and nodded.

"Where was this?" asked David.

"Delaware Street – in Woking."

"And do you know who this guy is?" David pointed to Jack.

"Yes," said Laser, in a whisper.

"And you know what's happened to him?"

"Yes."

"Put away for ever. And fucking good riddance, because he must be one of the new little shits I was talking about. We don't know him; never even heard of him before all this came out. And you don't get the continuity with these bit players, Laser. Unreliable. A quick fifty grand and they're gone."

He replaced the photographs in the envelope.

"So, tell me, Laser, is he your usual dealer?"

"No, I only saw him twice."

"And what did you get from him? What was he selling?"

"Fuck all. Well, to me, anyway. I asked him about the stuff and he told me to fuck off. I showed him some big notes; he didn't even look at them."

"That was the first time?"

"Both times. Second time I thought he was going to stick one on me – or in me. I just did what he said and fucked off. Quick."

"What stuff did you ask him for?"

"Ex and Speed, that's all."

"And Brown, and Snorkel, and Crack."

"No, none of that. Don't do that any more."

"Really? Says you. Okay, what happened?"

"As I said, nothing, like he didn't know what I was talking about."

"You're not shitting me, Laser?" said David, reaching across and grabbing the front of his fleece. "I'm a human lie detector, you know. Never wrong. I'll know if you are."

"Then you'll know I'm telling the truth, right? Why would I lie about it? The guy's fuck all to me, anyway. Little rich bastard got what he deserved."

"So who's your usual source, Laser? Give me the name of someone I do know."

"Oh, come on. You can't expect me to tell you that."

"Okay," said David, with a shrug. "What would you like to start with? A couple of bricks or that fucking big plank over there?"

"Look, I've answered your questions. You said I could go when I …"

"Are you as fucking stupid as you look?" yelled David, grabbing him by the throat. "This isn't a freaking quiz show. You don't get to answer two questions so you can come back in a week's time for the next round. This is life or death, Laser. *Your* life or *your* death! Do you understand?"

"Yes, yes, okay."

David relaxed his grip but kept his hand in place under his chin.

"Now, I'll ask again. Who is your usual source?"

"Sammo. Sammo Sampson. I don't know what his real first name is; everybody just calls him Sammo. And he's legit, anyway."

"So why didn't you want to tell me his name?"

"I don't know – just habit, I guess."

David released him.

"Let's see those pictures again," said Laser.

David took them from the envelope and handed them over. Laser shuffled through them, selecting one and showing it to David.

"There," he said, pointing at the still.

It was the image with Laser face-on to the camera with his hood down. Across the street on the very edge of the frame, a figure facing a shop window was at that moment looking over his shoulder at Jack and Laser.

"That's Sammo?" asked David.

"Yes, that's him."

"So what was he doing there when you were checking out this new guy? I would have thought Sammo would be well pissed off with somebody selling on his patch."

Laser thought for a moment. "Yes, it's fucking weird, actually. It was Sammo who put me on to him. I went to him for the usual and he said he'd subbed to this new guy."

"Subbed?"

"You know, like he'd got himself a partner, and I had to go to him this time – well, from now on, he said. So he took me to this place and we stood around for ages – where he is in the picture, across the street – and waited for him. And this guy – that guy," he pointed at Jack, "came along. I thought Sammo would take me over and, like, introduce us. But he just said 'there he is, go see him', or something."

"Just like that?"

"Yes."

"You're right," said David. "That *is* fucking weird. Did you ask him why?"

"No, man. I was desperate for the stuff. As long as I got it from somebody. It's only now that I've thought about it – and another thing; I had to wait until the guy had come so far down the street before I approached him. Like there was a special place where he did his trade."

"So when this guy told you to fuck off, why didn't you tell him Sammo sent you?"

"He said not to. 'Just go and ask, like it was me', he said."

"So you left him and went back across to Sammo?"

"I went back to where I'd been waiting with him, but he'd disappeared, slipped away. I guess he must have only just gone because he's in the picture there. I tell you, I was really pissed off. It was early next day before I found him and told him about it."

"And what did he say?"

"He said he didn't know what had gone wrong. He'd been told everything was cool with this guy. He said perhaps he thought he was being followed, so just played it dumb."

"But that wouldn't matter if he was legit, would it? And you said same thing happened the second time?"

"Sammo said it had all been sorted for next time, but, yes, same thing – 'fuck off!' – only he seemed to really mean it this time, so I didn't push it at all."

"And that was it? Nothing else?"

"I went to see Sammo again and he said something was screwed up big-time, and told me to lie low for a few weeks. He'd get the stuff to me in the meantime and tell me when it was safe to come back out again. That's what I did. It was only last week he told me all clear."

"If this was all legit stuff, Laser, why all this ducking and weaving in the shadows, going into hiding for weeks? It's all supposed to be out in the open, right?"

Laser raised his eyebrows in disbelief. "Now you're shitting *me*. The only thing that's changed is you don't get done for selling the soft stuff. It's still a fucking war zone on the streets between the dealers, *and* the traders. You know that."

★

Tom arrived at the Holding Centre just after 3.15 pm, in plenty of time to prepare for his meeting with Jack. After five minutes he was all set. He screwed up the small envelope, dropping it onto the floor of the car, and replaced the first aid kit in the glove compartment. Closing the driver's door gently and with great deliberation, he turned and walked towards the reception area.

He stopped briefly on the steps outside before entering, breathing deeply.

★

David removed the keys from the ignition and his mobile from the hands-free console.

"Don't move an inch. Right?"

He got out of the car and sent a text to Jo. 'Know you're a busy girl. Call when you can. Important.'

He paced up and down for a few minutes, occasionally glancing at Laser, who seemed to be frozen in the one position, eyes looking straight ahead. When it was clear Jo would not be calling right away, he eased himself back behind the wheel,

"Okay, so far so good," said David. "Just a couple more things, then I'll try and call the boss again. Who's the big guy behind Sammo?"

Laser looked shocked.

"I don't know," he said.

"Laser, Laser, Laser," David said, shaking his head. "And just when I thought you were going to make it. What a pity. That nice old lady back there is really going to miss you."

"Sammo'll fucking kill me."

"He *might*, I guess. But I'll *definitely* kill you if you hold out on me. So you decide."

David opened the glove box and took out the replica Gloch 17 pistol. He pretended to dust it down with his hand.

"Long time since I used this," he said. "It'll make a nice change."

"I don't know his name," said Laser. "They call him 'Duke' or 'The Duke'. I think he lives in Woking but I'm not sure where. I've never met him, honest. Never even seen him."

"So how do you know him?"

"Sammo's always threatening me with him. You know, if I complain about the price going up or if some of the stuff's real shit or late or whatever. He says he'll tell the Duke and he'll come and talk to me about it. Sammo's shit scared of him, you can tell."

"And you've never seen him?"

"No."

"So you don't know what he looks like?"

"No idea. Don't know anything else. Honestly, mister, and I don't want to." Laser's voice had changed to a whine. "Please can I go now?"

David picked up the mobile and pressed one of the keys. Laser looked at the phone, wide-eyed, as he heard their voices played back.

"Don't worry, Laser. This is insurance against you choosing to clam up later or change your story. But first, we're going for a little ride."

He copied the postcode on the back of the CCTV image into the satnav on top of the dashboard, and gave it the habitual tap with his forefinger.

"Fasten your seat belt."

★

"What's this, sir?"

Emily Parker dangled the locket questioningly in front of him. Her usual friendly expression had been replaced by a hard, accusing glare.

"It's a locket, what does it look like?"

"Okay, let me put it another way. Why is it still in your jacket when Phoebe asked you to empty your pockets … sir?"

"Look, it's just an old memento of his great grandmother's," Tom said. "Something Jack asked me to bring for him to take away. What harm can it possibly do? He's not going to bloody hang himself with it, for Christ's sake. Look how thin the chain is!"

"That's not the point, is it? If you wanted to take this to Jack, then why not ask?"

"Well, I ..."

"And where does it stop, sir. The rule is – *nothing* goes in. Not *my* rule, sir, *your* rule – indirectly, anyway."

Phoebe and Jools watched anxiously as the tension mounted.

"If we let *you* do it, Home Secretary ..." Emily continued, opening the locket and checking the photographs inside.

"Look," said Tom, "Emily, isn't it? Well, Emily, I'm going to pull rank here," he forced a smile. "I'm taking this in for my son. You'll have to wrestle me to the ground to prevent that, and whereas under different circumstances such action would be more than acceptable, I beg you not to try it today. And I promise, I will take full responsibility for this deviation from procedure."

Emily bristled.

"Actually, Home Secretary, you *may* take it in to Jack. But not because you've pulled rank, as you put it, but because *I* have decided you can. Now, could you turn out your pockets again, please, so we can be sure you're not hiding anything else?"

Tom pulled his trouser pockets inside-out while Emily searched his jacket again.

"Thank you, Home Secretary," she said, handing it back to him along with the locket. Jools scanned Tom again with the metal detector as he put his jacket back on, placing the chain in his right hand pocket.

"Jack's waiting," said Emily.

Tom's heart was pounding as Jools reached over, punched in the four-digit code and opened the door. Emily took out her mobile as he entered the room.

Jack rose from his chair as his father entered. The central glass screen was raised and Tom stepped forward to embrace him. Both men were shaking, a fact not lost on the three POs watching from outside. Clicking heels sounded in the corridor as Alison Anders walked up to join them, taking a chair at the table in front of the screen.

"They seem really agitated today," said Emily. "Little wonder, I suppose. Getting so close …"

★

"Everything okay, then?" asked Jack. They sat down.

"Yes." Tom's voice was faint enough to prompt Jools to turn up the volume on the wall-mounted microphones.

"You've got it?"

"I've got it."

★

"Anything on Heaven's door yet?" Emily asked.

"Might get lucky," whispered Alison, without taking her eyes off the screen. "Judy's tracked down one of the Home Secretary's old Special Forces buddies. They're a nightmare to find; they never release their real names to the public, you know, even when they're getting a medal or something, or after they leave. Anyway, some guy called McNaughton, regular member of his unit, I believe. She's left a message and asked him to get back to her as soon…"

Jools interrupted. "Sssshhh… please, ma'am."

"Sorry."

★

Tom took out the locket, holding it in front of him and slightly to the side. He appeared to be opening and shutting it, and cleaning it with his fingers. Jack looked intently across at it.

"This is what you asked for," said Tom, his voice wavering. "For if there are really bad times; it might help."

Jack looked momentarily confused. Tom handed it over to him.

★

"Now I think about it, do you ever remember him asking for a locket?" Jools said.

"What do you mean?" asked Phoebe.

273

"Well, when you found the locket he said that Jack had asked for it. I don't remember him asking for anything, do you?"

"Well, no, but we've not been here for every visit."

"No but we've heard the recordings, seen the transcripts. Nothing comes to mind. Here, let's see."

He turned to the PC on the table and brought up the file containing the verbatim transcripts of all Jack's meetings with his family. He clicked on Edit, then Find, typed in 'locket', and clicked on Find Next.

"'Search item not found'," he read from the screen. "No mention of a locket."

"Try ... pendant," said Phoebe.

Jools went through it again.

"No."

"Chain?"

"No."

Alison was looking at the PC screen now.

"What did he call it – a 'memento'?" said Jools, typing it in. "No, not that either. I don't think he's asked for anything like that."

"Then what ...?"

★

Jack opened the locket slowly with a sharp intake of breath. He remained silent for a full minute, staring at it, eyes wide and moist. Tom had slumped back in his chair. He rallied, sitting upright and speaking firmly to his son.

"At least it will always be there, Jack. Hopefully you won't need it, but ... nice to have a reminder of the ...the ...times ... good times ..." His voice was breaking; he couldn't continue and slumped back again.

★

Alison's phone rang. She checked the caller on the display.

"It's Judy," she said. "She'll leave a message."

★

"The thing is" – Jack was speaking now, slowly and calmly – "this will never get back to my room. They'll take it off me as soon as you leave." He paused, still staring at the locket. "I do really appreciate what you've done, Dad. It must have been just about the worst thing I could have asked of you … But you did it and, as I say, I'm very grateful." He looked up at his father. "And I want you to know that I do love you, more than I can say. I've always been so proud of you." He paused and shook his head slowly. "You know, I can't stop thinking about those two guys on the wire. Judge's nephew, one of them, wasn't he; most likely singled out for what his uncle stood for. So imagine – the Home Secretary's son. Shit, what will they do to me?"

★

"Answer it, *please!*" Judy pressed the speed-call number again. She got up from her desk and left the office, heading for the holding area. Still no answer. She started to run, kicking off her high heels and racing along the corridor as she tried again.

Third time lucky.

★

"*What!*"

Alison, was still half-listening to the conversation in the visiting room as Judy breathlessly gave her the information she had just received from ex-Major Anthony McNaughton. She leapt to her feet.

"*Christ!*" She turned to her three colleagues. "Get in there! *Now!*"

She led the way, dropping the phone as she reached for the door handle.

★

Jack took the tiny glass capsule from the locket and placed it in his mouth. Tom's eyes widened with horror. He sprang to his feet, although it felt as though he was moving in slow motion; and the shout seemed to take an age to pass through his lips.

275

"No-o-o-o-o!!"

Jack's eyes were pouring tears.

"I want to die with someone I love, Dad. I'm so sorry."

Tom reached across to him.

Jack bit down onto the capsule.

The door crashed open behind him and people burst into the room; Voices were shouting, some were screaming.

He grabbed his son, forcing his fingers into his mouth. He could already feel the convulsions shaking his body.

"No-o-o-o!" Another voice; he recognised it as his own.

Hands gripped his shoulders, trying to pull him away. He held onto Jack tightly with one arm, flailing behind him with the other, catching someone hard and high on the head. He heard them fall to the floor with a cry of pain.

"Jack! Jack!" The same voice again, screaming now.

Someone was forcing their arms between him and Jack, trying to prise them away from each other. A young man, shouting into his face.

"Let go, sir! Let me see him! Please!"

"Get off him! Leave him alone!" He yelled back at him, freeing one arm again and pushing his hand into the young man's face, clawing at his eyes. The man turned his face away, still trying to force them apart.

More people were grabbing his shoulders, trying to pull his arms away. He tried to shrug them off.

"Get away! Get away from him!"

He needed both arms now to hold on to Jack; he could feel his body arching backwards and stiffening with the poison. He was not going to let go. He was *never* going to let go of his son. They couldn't make him. He gripped him, harder and tighter.

Then he was free of them. He sensed the young man standing motionless by his side. He could hear sobbing behind him and heavy running footsteps in the corridor outside.

And then, for a long time, there was nothing else in the world except his son, clutched to his chest as he knelt on the metal floor of their last meeting place.

CHAPTER TWENTY

"Tom, leave him, please," said John Mackay, eventually. "I'm afraid there's nothing you can do. Let the doctor see him. Please."

Slowly he released Jack and as they lifted him away, it was Tom who slumped to the floor, as if he was the one being supported. John helped him back on to his chair again, standing in front of him as he did so to block his view of the medical staff working on his son.

Several uniformed police officers had by now sealed off the corridors leading to the room and were preventing anyone entering or leaving the building. A forensic team was already in the reception area waiting to be summoned to what they had been informed was a crime scene. The four prison officers were sitting in a state of shock at the table outside, where events were unfolding on the screen in front of them; but no-one was observing any more. Judy was slumped on the floor with her back to the wall, crying openly. Alison and Phoebe were trying to comfort Emily, as she described, for Alison's benefit, the incident with the locket. Jools was sitting motionless, staring into the middle distance, occasionally dabbing at the scratches on his cheek with a moistened tissue.

Twenty minutes later, the paramedics left the room pushing past them with the trolley with Jack's body on it. Emily turned away as the others stared at it in horror and disbelief. Shortly afterwards, John Mackay emerged, looking pale and tense.

"The doctor's looking after the Home Secretary for now," he said. "Your office, please, Chief Anders."

"Yes, sir."

They walked off together, leaving the three prison officers

anxiously looking at each other wondering what was to follow. Ten minutes elapsed and the Chief Superintendent returned alone, seating himself at the table on the vacant chair. Judy got unsteadily to her feet and Jools got up from his own chair so she could sit down.

"I need to officially inform you," John said, "that there will be an immediate internal enquiry into what happened this afternoon, and you will all be required to assist as key witnesses. I suggest – no, I *instruct* – each of you to take time out right now to separately record your account of the Home Secretary's visit with his son today, whilst it is fresh in your mind, starting from the point at which you each had your own first contact with him. Judy, I'd like you to do the same for your call with Major McNaughton. Do you understand what I'm asking – and why?"

"Yes, sir." In unison.

"*Unofficially*, Officer Parker, I don't think any human being in the world would have decided other than to let Mr Brown give the locket to his son. You examined it first, I understand, and at that stage it contained nothing but the photographs. From what I can gather – although he is currently not in a fit state to communicate clearly – he had concealed the capsule between the base of his thumb and the palm of his hand, fastened there by a piece of sticking plaster. It would have been virtually undetectable unless you checked all ten digits individually, and even then there's no guarantee that you'd realise what it was. It would have been relatively simple for him to slip the capsule into the locket before passing it over.

"So, although it would be wrong of me to anticipate the outcome, I am confident the enquiry will not find any evidence of negligence. I think you can all pretty much depend on that, but we must go through the process – for all our sakes. Okay?"

They all nodded, relieved and grateful.

"What was it that he took, sir?" asked Phoebe.

"A suicide pill – kill-pill, death-pill, L-pill – whatever. Most probably liquid potassium cyanide, to act that quickly. The sort of thing given to spies in wartime and, in some instances, Special Forces operating in areas where being taken alive is ... well ... let's say, not advisable."

"But how could he do it, sir?" said Jools. "How could he just hand that thing to his own son and watch him ..."

"Let's not be too hasty to judge, Officer Gorton. From what the Chief tells me, his reaction to Jack taking the pill suggests he had no idea he planned to use it there and then. You were in a good position to see that. But we'll have to wait until he can be properly questioned."

"And 'Heaven's door', sir," Emily spoke for the first time in half an hour. "What's the significance of that?"

The Chief Superintendent turned to Judy.

"Major McNaughton told me it's the name Tom Brown's unit had for the pill," she said. "Not a term used generally in the Special Forces, just one adopted by their own small group."

"And something he must have talked to Jack about," said John.

His composure briefly left him and he shook his head in sadness.

"It's the timing I find hard to come to terms with," he went on, half to himself. "If Judy had got that call yesterday – or just five minutes earlier; if the Chief had answered her phone the first time ... That's not a criticism, by the way, but ... well, we might have prevented this."

"Except Jack wouldn't have seen that as a good thing, would he, sir," said Jools. "This is how he wanted it. Just before he took the pill, he mentioned the two guys on the wire on Alpha; particularly the judge's nephew and what happened to him. And I reckon he was right. God knows what they would have done to Jack, with his dad being the reason they were out there."

The Chief Superintendent paused as if absorbing what Jools had said.

"I guess that's true," he said, with a deep sigh. "And the Home Secretary would have known that, too, of course."

He turned to look at the screen, which showed Tom still slumped in his chair, the doctor kneeling beside him.

"I'd better get back in there."

★

David drove along Delaware Street. It was a typical suburban, supermarket-era thoroughfare; formerly a busy local shopping centre, now comprising a string of estate agents, cafes, amusement arcades, charity shops and dubious takeaways. At 4.30 pm there were relatively few pedestrians around.

They crawled along, Laser directing, until they reached the place where he had waited with Sammo. David double-parked and got out, his huge frame and intimidating appearance discouraging any complaints from the following motorists faced with the prospect of easing round his car through the infrequent gaps in the oncoming traffic. He crossed the street to the spot where Laser said he had approached Jack. Standing in the same place, David checked the walls above the shop windows on both sides of the street and easily picked out the CCTV installation which had recorded Laser, Jack and Sammo.

He turned back to the car. Laser was still there, but looking furtively across at David, as if weighing up his chances of making a break for it. David slipped back into the driver's seat and pulled away again taking a couple of left turns to head back towards Cobham. A few minutes into the journey his phone sounded. He pulled over to the side of the road, pressing the answer key so he would not miss the call. Removing the keys from the ignition he got out and walked round the car, leaning up against the passenger door.

"Hi there," he said.

"Hi," said Jo. "First chance I've had to call. Sounds like you've got news."

"News *and* Laser," he said.

"Wow! Do tell."

"Well, it seems Laser was put up to asking Jack for drugs, though he claims it was only soft stuff. Jack told him to get lost – I'm paraphrasing to save your delicate ears – so he reckons no deal was done. What's also interesting is that he was told a very specific spot to contact Jack – right where the camera would get them."

"That sounds like progress, don't you think? Not bad for a pensioner."

"I've just added a nought to my invoice for that remark, young lady. Anyway, Laser's supplier – the one who set up his meeting with Jack – is one Sammo Sampson, and the guy behind him is someone they call Duke, or 'the Duke'. Any bells ringing?"

"I know Sammo, but never heard of Duke. Actually, I think Sammo is legit now," she said. "At least I thought he was. He was a beneficiary of the amnesty; got a license out of it for the soft stuff. I'm pretty sure he's not doing the sort of gear we found at Jack's."

"But we know that Laser *used* to take the hard stuff, so if he's had a relapse that would explain why Sammo put him on to Jack."

"Hey, whose side are you on? We're trying to clear Jack, not ..."

"I thought we were looking for the truth, and what I just said is the best fit with the facts so far. We're not going to get to the truth, Jo, if we just blindly assume that Jack is innocent and try to fit all the facts to that."

"Okay, point taken, but why was it so important, then, for Jack to be caught on camera with a known – albeit ex – hard drug user?"

"That I can't answer yet. But I'll carry on reeling you in whenever you get ahead of yourself. We're nowhere near proving anything yet, let alone a set-up. This joker isn't capable of setting up a deckchair, and if Sammo is really just a legit street-trader, it has to be Duke or beyond if you're right. And even then, it could be just one dealer trying to stitch up another, you know. That's much more likely than the framing of an innocent."

"Yes, I know, but it's new evidence – the fact that Laser was *told* to speak to Jack and in a very specific place – under the gaze of the security cameras. That's the best we could have hoped for from Laser and it might be enough to put the brakes on for an appeal. Right?"

"Possibly, but not automatically. It will have to be weighed against the mass of evidence on the other side. Anyway, the question is, what exactly do we do with the info and, more importantly right now, its source? He's sitting in the car, probably thinking I'm getting instructions on how to kill him."

"You're not planning to, I assume," asked Jo.

"It's not Plan A," said David. "But I'm worried about getting hold of him again if we need him. You're the boss, so tell me what to do."

"What about threatening to kill his auntie if he disappears? How much does he like her?"

"Christ, Jo, I didn't bring you up to think like that! Mind you, that's exactly what I was planning to do, and in the meantime I'll send you the recording of our little chat."

"Hold it! Got another call. Need to take this. I'll get back to you as soon as I can. Oh, and well done, Hercule."

"Merci, ma petite."

★

Jo ended the call from Shana and ran to the ladies room, falling onto her knees in the nearest stall before throwing up violently into the basin. She flushed it away and stayed there for a long time, her arms around the seat and her head hanging over the bowl, tears splashing into the water. The sickness and despair had drained her almost to the point of sleep, when a hand on her shoulder made her start.

"Jo – ma'am? What's wrong?"

It took her a few seconds to remember where she was, mainly because Detective Sergeant Seb Carter should not have been in there. Seb had been assigned to her team as her number two. He was around five years younger than Jo, not much smaller than David and with a handsome, boyish face and easy, relaxed manner.

"Seb, what on Earth are you doing in here?" she asked, in a faint voice.

"Just checking on you, ma'am. I saw you rush in here and – well, you didn't come out. That was about twenty minutes ago."

"Twenty minutes! Christ!"

Jo struggled to her feet, helped by Seb.

"Just felt sick," said Jo, recovering enough to feel embarrassed. "Been sick, actually."

"Do you always cry when you feel sick?"

Jo turned and looked in the long mirror over the washbasins. Her face was streaked with mascara and her eyes were red with crying.

"Give me a couple of minutes, Seb. I'll be right out."

"I was just coming to get you anyway," he said. "Dot-com wants to see you."

★

It took a long time for Tom's mind and eyes to clear and for his surroundings to come back into focus. He looked around. He was

282

sitting in a wing chair in John Mackay's office. John was standing by his side, a hand on his shoulder, and crouching in front of him was a small, thin man in a white jacket and rimless glasses looking anxiously up into his face.

"I must get back to Mags," Tom said. "Oh God, poor, poor Mags. She doesn't deserve this."

"We'll drive you over," said John.

"Thanks, but it's better if I tell her. I'll go on my own."

"I'm afraid I can't let you do that, Tom. You can tell her yourself, of course, but for one thing, you're in no condition to drive, and also, more to the point, you are now formally in police custody. I should caution you really, but there'll be time for that later."

Tom turned to look at him through his glazed and bloodshot eyes.

"What? What are you talking about?"

"I'm sorry, Tom, but you are now officially helping us with our enquires. As you know – or you'll realise when you are in a fit state to think about it – what happened today will likely prove to be a crime; helping someone in custody to take their own life. Please don't make me go into it now. Just accept the need for our being with you. Believe me, I am trying to be as sensitive as possible about this."

"Sensitive! Well, thank God for that, Chief Superintendent. I can't even begin to imagine what you're like when you're *not* being sensitive!"

"Tom," said John. "I have said many times during the last hour or so how terribly sorry – devastated – I am about what has happened, and how desperately I feel for you. Maggie is not the only one who doesn't deserve this. But I have to do my job. It's what you expect of me. Things are bad enough, aren't they, without you kicking out at your friends? Let's just say, for now, that I'm giving you a lift home. I've got to come with you – I'm afraid you have no choice in the matter – and you're right, you must get back to Maggie as soon as you can. So let's go now, together."

★

"Right, Laser, all you have to do now is answer one more simple question, and then you can go – for the time being. Okay?"

283

"Okay," replied Laser.

They were back again in the builders' yard, parked in the same place.

"Where can I find Sammo?"

"Why do you want ...?"

"I need to find out who this Duke is. Unless, of course, you can now suddenly remember yourself; which could make me think that you were lying to me before."

"No, I don't know him, honest."

"Which means Sammo will have to tell me, right? So – I'll ask you again – where can I find Sammo?"

Laser looked David up and down.

"Okay," he said. "But promise you won't say it was me who told you?"

"Of course not, Laser," said David, smiling. "Look, after today, and all you've helped me with so far, we're almost best mates, you and me. So just tell me. Okay?"

"Best place is where we've just been – Delaware; where he was standing in the picture. He's there for an hour or so some time between six and nine most nights. Not every night, but that's where you can usually get him."

"What about tonight?"

"Don't know for sure, but probably. Don't fancy your chances of sneaking up on him though, unless you can shrink a bit."

David smiled.

"I don't have to sneak, son," he said. "People just freeze with terror when I get anywhere near them."

"Yes, I can believe that."

They both gave a brief laugh.

"The thing is, Laser, I'm going to need to see you again very soon. So I'm wondering – do we arrange to meet somewhere, or do I tie you up and keep you in the boot. What do you think?"

"Look, just say where and I'll be there."

"Okay, at your aunt's place then, where I picked you up today."

"Yes, that's fine."

He reached for the door handle. David grabbed the front of his fleece and pulled him round towards him.

"You haven't asked me when."

"Oh, yes. When?"

"Tomorrow morning – ten o'clock."

Laser nodded.

"Now you promise me you'll be there, don't you?"

"Yes, sure."

"Well that's good, Laser. So if I call tomorrow and Auntie Nookie says you're *not* there, then I'll know *she's* lying, won't I, because you've promised? And I don't like people lying to me, so I'm going to give her a really bad time. Know what I mean? Do you like your auntie, Laser?"

"Yes, she's more like a mother to …"

"So if anything happened to her that would make *you* more like an orphan, wouldn't it? But, hey, what am I talking about? All you have to do is be there at ten tomorrow and she'll be fine. Okay?"

Laser gulped, audibly, and nodded.

"As I said, Laser. I reckon you and I could be really good mates when all this is over. Till tomorrow then."

He released his fleece and Laser slipped quickly out of the car. Then he stopped and looked back at David. He nodded and ran away.

★

Wesley W Wallace sat behind the desk in his large office. The detective superintendent was in his early fifties; tall, slim and with square shoulders which he pulled back to provide the clue to an earlier military background. His face was thin, but with handsome chiselled features under thick steel-grey hair cut very short.

"So it appears I'm going to lose you already, Jo," he said, after telling her about Jack. "Mr Mackay can't live without you, it seems. Understandable, under the circumstances. He's going to be tied up with the internal enquiry. Nasty business for him."

"Can you tell me what happened, sir?"

"Only that Jack apparently took a poisoned capsule during a visit by his father. John couldn't tell me much more than that yet, but he's going to call back when he can. In the meantime, it appears his father is being held by the police."

"What? The Home Secretary? He's under arrest?"

"It seems Mr Brown might have smuggled the capsule in to his son, although please be aware that isn't official yet. The internal enquiry will focus on how it happened, I expect."

"But why would he help his son take his own life? I'm afraid I just can't believe it."

"I think the answer to that question is fairly obvious if you stop to think about what's already happened on Alpha. Anyway, I'd like you to start tying up any loose ends and hand everything over to DS Carter, so he can brief your replacement. I'm really sorry to lose you, Jo. I sincerely hope we can work together again. I'll certainly be asking for you personally if the need arises."

"Thank you, sir."

★

Mags was downstairs at the window of the front sitting room and saw them as they drove through the gates. She realised the car was a police vehicle from the uniformed officer in the driving seat and for a few hopeful moments, as she hurried to the front door, she wondered if this could be Jo Cottrell with some news for her. Instead, she was instantly shocked at the sight of her husband's face as he got out of the car, a picture of tension and despair.

"What?" she gasped. "Tom, what's happened?"

He grabbed her, pulling her to him, as if trying to hold her as close as possible, not wanting to look at her face.

"Darling Mags," he sobbed. "It's Jack. He's ... he's ..."

"*No-o-o-o!*" Mags screamed, finishing the sentence for him in her mind. He held her as tightly as he could, but she pushed him away, looking up wide-eyed in horror.

"He's dead ... Mags, I'm so sorry" he said, speaking words she could barely hear. She felt herself falling against him and everything receded quickly into darkness.

★

Kim Lacey was waiting for Jonathan in the Commons Lobby when he left the Chamber.

"Sir, this message was left for you by Chief Constable Mills."

"Thank you, Kim."

He read it quickly and stepped into one of the rooms off the Lobby facing onto the Inner Court. He called Grace on her office landline.

"Grace, have you …?"

"Yes. Eddie phoned me as well." Her voice was hoarse and strained. "I called Kim straight away – told her not to interrupt you in the House. Didn't want to drag you out and start a lot of people guessing."

"Does Andrew …?"

"He's still in Paris. I haven't tried to contact him yet, but we'll have to do it fast. Can you imagine if it gets to him via one of the other delegates?"

"I don't like to think. I'll speak to him. I'll have Shirley get him right now."

"Okay." She dropped the business tone and her voice was filled with sadness and regret. "God, Jonathan, what must Tom be feeling now, I can't even begin to imagine. Poor Jack; he was such a lovely young man."

"And Maggie," said Jonathan. "Poor woman. Did you hear what happened? Eddie didn't give any details."

"Jack took a capsule, apparently, that Tom seems to have taken in with him. Like he used to carry himself, I guess, when he was in the SBS. They're not releasing any details to the press other than the fact that Jack died. I'm meeting with Eddie in a few minutes. He's on his way from Guildford. Listen, you get in touch with Andrew and I'll get back to you after Eddie's brought me up to date."

"Right. I guess we'll need a press release tonight as well. Should it be us or the police?"

"Probably both. Ask Andrew what he thinks and I'll check with Eddie."

★

The prime minister made no attempt to hide his annoyance at being interrupted during what he described as 'a crucial debate at which his attendance was imperative, and without distractions'.

"We have to distance ourselves from Brown, Jonathan, just as soon, and as far, as possible. We need a press statement tonight – with all the usual 'regrettable, tragic, etc.' – but making it clear that I had already asked for his resignation and was waiting for him to confirm. It must not be seen that we failed to recognise and to deal with a loose cannon in the government. We might take a ratings hit from the Tom Brown fan club in the short term but, trust me, we need to be – and be *seen* to be – as hard-as-nails on this one. Have you got that?"

"With respect, Prime Minister, I think including the fact that you have asked the Home Secretary to resign in a statement which will essentially be the news of his son's death, will look very bad indeed. We have no need with an initial statement to say anything at all other than Jack has died. There seems no point at all in using it as a vehicle to defame his father."

There was a long silence.

"Very well. Do it your way tonight. I'll draft a statement for when it *does* become clear that Brown has lost the plot – my guess, tomorrow at the latest. Just one thing though, Minister. I expect unflinching support from my Cabinet at times when the credibility of this government comes under threat. Send me a copy of the statement before it goes out."

He hung up.

The phone rang less than a minute later.

"And I want that little black friend of his on the next shipload to Alpha. I don't want him hanging around a minute longer than necessary as a magnet for public sympathy. Get Goody onto it. She can do stuff under the radar that you wouldn't be able to do."

The phone went down again.

★

Looking around, David estimated that he was probably twice the age of the next oldest person on Delaware Street. He was standing in a shop doorway, scanning the milling crowds for the man in the CCTV image. Hispanic-looking, longish dark hair, medium height, average build, casually, but tidily, dressed, – he thought he had a fairly good picture of him in his mind after staring at it for ten minutes before starting his search. However, presented with the tide of similarly aged and dressed individuals ebbing and flowing before him, he wasn't so sure.

His mobile rang. He checked his watch as he answered the call – 7.35 pm.

"Hi, Jo. I was beginning to get worried about …"

"David, something terrible has happened."

"What? Are you okay? You sound …"

"It's Jack. He's dead!" Her voice broke and David could hear her sobbing quietly.

"Christ! How?"

"Not got all the details, but it seems he took some poison."

"Poison? But how …"

"That's the worst part. It's not official, but it seems Tom Brown gave it to him. God, it's just too awful …" She broke down again.

"Where are you?" he asked.

"Newport Pagnell services. On my way back. Where are you?"

"On Delaware. Desperately seeking Sammo," he said. "Or at least I was. What now?"

"I've been thinking about that. There's still Jason. I feel like we'd be abandoning him if we didn't carry on, especially when there's even the smallest chance that we're on to something. On the other hand, it could make it even worse for Maggie if we uncover anything now, when it's too late. Perhaps we should leave it."

"I don't think so, Jo. As far as I'm concerned this was to help *you* get to the truth, in which case there's absolutely no reason to stop looking. Nothing can bring their son back now, but I'm sure Mrs T would still like to clear his name if possible and – more than anything right now – save her daughter's boyfriend."

"I'm glad you said that, David. Let's carry on. You're way ahead of where I thought you'd be by now. Do you think I should phone Maggie now? Just to say how sorry I am."

"Why not wait until you get back. And you just take care driving home."

"Yes. I'll phone later. I'm alright now. You take care as well."

"I will, and I think my next appointment has just turned up. Speak soon."

★

Philippa Symes looked up from her monitor on the news desk in front of her and spoke into the camera.

"We are just getting news in of the death of Jack Tomlinson-Brown, the son of the Home Secretary, Tom Brown, at the Guildford Holding Centre earlier today. We will shortly be going over to Westminster for a statement by James Landish, the Government Press Secretary. That's in just a few minutes."

Across the bottom of the screen, the moving message reinforced her words. 'BBC News 24: Breaking News – Home Secretary's son dies in Guildford Holding Centre whilst awaiting passage to exile.'

News channels across the UK, Ireland, Continental Europe and the US and Canada were carrying the same bulletin in anticipation of the press statement. At 8.10 pm, James Landish faced the cameras from behind the lectern on the pavement in front of the Home Office Building on Marsham Street.

"Ladies and Gentlemen, Mr Andrew Donald, the Prime Minister, is at present at a meeting of the G20 group of nations leaders in Paris. He has asked me to read you this statement from him:

'It is with the deepest regret that I must inform you of the death this afternoon at 3.40 pm, at the Guildford Holding Centre, of Jack Tomlinson-Brown, the son of the Home Secretary Tom Brown and his wife, Maggie Tomlinson-Brown. The police are currently looking into the circumstances surrounding the incident and at the moment are not in a position to provide any further information. As more details emerge from their investigation, I will, of course, ensure that they are communicated to you in full at the earliest opportunity. In the meantime, I know you will join me in extending our prayers and sympathy to the family and friends of the deceased and wish them strength in what has already been an exceptionally difficult time for them.'"

James Landish looked up from his notes.

"That is the statement in full, and as this comes directly from the prime minister himself, I am sure you will respect the fact that I am not in a position to add to it. Thank you."

He turned and walked up the steps into the building.

Grace and Jonathan looked down from the second floor window overlooking the scene. In spite of the Press Secretary's closing remark, the crowd of reporters predictably shouted their questions until the doors closed behind him. Once he was out of sight, they turned to each other, exchanging comments and gestures which reflected their excitement at the story, but conveyed none of the sympathy they had been asked to extend to the bereaved.

"Andrew would have made a good reporter," said Jonathan, absently.

Grace turned to look at him.

"No feelings, just reactions."

"I think you're being a bit hard on reporters," said Grace.

They laughed briefly.

"I still think you should have cleared the statement with him, like he asked" said Grace.

"Seemed to slip my mind," said Jonathan.

They both smiled and sat in silence for a long time.

"What about Midanda?" asked Jonathan, eventually. "You know, about his jumping the queue?"

"Oh, just ignore that," said Grace. "Andrew will probably forget he even mentioned it, but I'll smooth it out anyway."

★

"At 3.40 pm precisely today, Mr Hugh Jacob – known as Jack – Tomlinson-Brown died whilst in custody at Guildford Holding Centre. A full investigation into the circumstances of his death is already under way and we will keep you informed of any developments. We extend our sincere sympathy to the family of the deceased, and in particular, his father, Mr Tom Brown, the Home Secretary, his mother, Maggie Tomlinson-Brown, and his sister, Katey. Our thoughts are with them at this extremely difficult time.

"Thank you."

Edwin Mills turned and walked back through the gates of New Station Yard.

★

Sammo hesitated on the pavement immediately in front of where

David was standing and then, glancing up at him, hurried on twenty yards or so, and settled down to wait.

David didn't move for several minutes, during which time Sammo shot him a few anxious looks. Eventually, David left his doorway and walked quickly up to him.

"Got a problem with me, Sammo?" he said.

"How do you know me?"

David grabbed his arm, gripping it tightly.

"I thought I just asked *you* a question," he said, clenching his teeth.

"Okay," said Sammo, with a sneer. "Answer to yours is 'no, I don't have a problem with you'. Now, your turn. The question was – how do you know me?"

Sammo was no bigger than Laser, and not much stockier, but considerably better dressed in designer jeans and an expensive-looking polo shirt under a light-weight Barbour jacket. And, quite clearly, David thought, he had a lot more bottle. Either that or a couple of minders watching over him from close by.

"Duke sent me to get you," said David.

Sammo's expression changed.

"The Duke," he said, wide-eyed and in a small voice. "What does he want?"

"He wants to see you; that's all I know. As I say, he sent me to get you."

"Where is he?"

"He said you'd know; I haven't a clue. He just phoned, told me where to find you and said 'go get him'. I'm the new guy, see, so I reckon he's still testing me out. Doesn't give me much info. But that's okay, because I'm not sure about him either. Doesn't do to rush in to new business partnerships. Right?"

"You don't look much like a trader," said Sammo.

David gave a laugh.

"Right on, Sammo. Security and dispatch, that's me. And today, I'm collect as well. Shall we go?"

He gripped Sammo's arm a little tighter and set off to where he had parked his car. Sammo pulled back.

"How do I know you're who you say you are?"

"I haven't told you who I am, Sammo. But you don't need to know. Duke wants me as low profile as possible for now."

He looked David up and down.

"Low profile! Christ, you're not much fucking good at that part of the job, are you?"

"Look, Sammo, I've been really nice about this so far. But I'm losing my patience now. I don't know about you, but I'm not in a hurry to get on the wrong side of the man. So one way or the other, I'm taking you to him – upright or horizontal – I don't give a shit which. So you decide, before I give all these toe-rags round here a quick demo on how to motivate people."

Sammo walked along, looking curiously up at him.

"I think it's you who wants to see the Duke," he said. "Not the Duke who wants to see me."

They turned into a quieter side street away from the shops. Grabbing the front of Sammo's jacket, David lifted him off the ground and slammed him against the wall. The few people close to them retreated to a safe distance before turning to watch the action.

"Listen, you fucking insignificant little wanker!" David hissed through his clenched mouth. "I don't give a fuck what you think, or whether you think, or whether you live, or whether you die! Duke didn't say anything about delivering you alive; just to deliver you. *Okay?*"

"Right," said Sammo, his face contorted with pain.

David lifted him a couple of inches higher then threw him down onto the pavement. Sammo moved to get up but David grabbed him again, hauling him to his feet by his hair. Sammo's hand went into the inside pocket of his jacket. David grabbed his wrist, holding his hand inside the coat. He swung him round to face the wall and crushed him up against it. This time Sammo slumped to the ground without any assistance, eyes half-glazing over. David reached inside the jacket and removed a switchblade knife. He pressed the catch on the handle releasing a serrated six-inch blade, which snapped into position.

"This for your day job, Sammo? Sharpening pencils?"

He closed the knife, slipping it into his back pocket, then hauled Sammo to his feet again and dragged him down the street, now almost running. David rammed him into the passenger seat of the car. Sammo was groaning in pain with his arms wrapped around his chest as if holding his ribs in place.

"Okay," said David. "Where to?"

Sammo looked across at him. His eyes were watering and when he opened his mouth to speak, the words would not come at first. David reached behind him and took out Sammo's knife, clicking open the blade.

"I hadn't planned to give you this back yet," he said, "but if you're going to go quiet on me."

"You've broken my fucking ribs!" said Sammo, finding his voice. "You fucking bastard!"

"That's a shame," said David, "but your fault. Just tell me where to take you, so I don't have to break what's behind them."

It took several moments before Sammo could speak again, during which his eyes never left the knife, which David waved like a windscreen wiper in front of his face.

"Just off Grindalls Road," he said. "Know it?"

"Like I said, I'm new around here. You direct me."

"Listen, I got a car just round the corner," Sammo was breathing a little easier now. "I'll go see the Duke. I'll tell him you found me and …"

"No, no, no," said David, closing the knife again and dropping it into the driver's door storage pocket. "I have to take you. That's the deal. Duke's instructions, not mine. So let's go."

Sammo hesitated, wincing and holding his ribs again.

"Okay, straight ahead."

★

David and Sammo looked across the street at the large detached house with its name in stained glass in the arched window above the double front doors; a name David thought was vaguely familiar. The house itself looked a little run-down and in need of a face-lift, but there were cheerful sounds coming through the partly opened sash windows from the brightly lit rooms inside.

"Is this it? The Duke's place?" asked David.

"Yeah, this is it. You coming in?"

"No. Done my job. I'll just wait here to see you get in alright. There are some rough characters around, you know. Wouldn't want to see you get hurt."

Sammo turned to David with an expression of pure malice. He got out of the car and walked round it and across the street towards the house. David lowered the window.

"Hey, Sammo, you might need this. Just in case Dukey-boy wants some pencils sharpening."

He threw the knife across the street. Sammo picked it up and looked back at him with the renewed courage that came with the weapon. David casually lifted the replica Gloch so it was just in view, pretending to examine it and passing it from hand to hand as if checking its grip and weight. Sammo pocketed the knife, turned and walked up the three steps and into the house.

David drove on and did a three-point turn at the end of what was a short cul-de-sac before returning to stop in the same place opposite the house. He reached behind him under his seat and took out the retirement present he had received from his colleagues at Parkside station. It was one of his favourite possessions, an item whose full description it had taken him some time to memorise; a Panasonic Lumix 15-mega-pixel digital camera, with 24-times optical zoom.

He lowered the passenger side window and took a photograph of the name above the door. The flash automatically activated in the fading light. He checked the time – 8.55 pm – and settled down to wait, the camera trained on the double doors, and the car engine running.

The front doors burst open and Sammo shot out and down the steps, obviously propelled from behind. Following him closely was a tall, good-looking, dark-skinned young man – David guessed Somali or mixed ancestry – wearing a tee-shirt and jeans. He was clearly very angry and considerably anxious as well. He looked up and down the street.

"Are you fucking stupid, or what? Where is he?"

"There!"

Sammo pointed across at David and the man looked straight at him. The camera clicked rapidly three times, the attendant flashes temporarily confusing the subject. David slipped the car into gear and turned the corner onto Grindalls Road. He stopped at the first opportunity to check the shots he had taken. The images were crisp and clear.

★

David picked up the A3 and raced back to St Herbert's Street. He attached the camera to his laptop and downloaded the images into a file, including the picture of the house name. As the camera screen had shown, they were clear and well-defined. He wrote a brief email to Jo and attached the file. Then he phoned her mobile.

"Hi," he said. "Feeling okay?"

"Not really, but I'll be fine."

"Did you phone Maggie?"

"Yes, but no answer. Hardly surprising. I left a message. Are you okay? Where are you?"

"Back at Linny's. And I've got a present for you. A photo of Dukey boy."

"Wow, you do move fast for an elderly detective. Where did you get it?"

"Outside his house. It's called Manston Grange; it's on Sharp Street, off Grindalls Road in Woking."

He heard her gasp.

"Say that again," she said.

"Manston Grange, on Sharp Street, off Grindalls …"

"Oh, my God! "

CHAPTER TWENTY-ONE

Week 11; Friday, 5 June …

"I *am* sorry, sir," said Jo, "but I wasn't sure what to do. The case was closed; I was moving to Leicester; there was obviously very little time, what with their starting on passage next week." She paused, swallowing before she continued. "In fact, as it turned out, there was less time than I realised – than any of us could have realised."

John Mackay had been staring down at his hands clasped tightly together on the desk in front of him. Then he looked up at Jo, seeming to snap out of his melancholy.

"The weight of evidence is so damning, Jo. You cannot begin to imagine how much I wanted us to be wrong, hoping we'd find nothing, that it would all prove to be a big mistake. But it *wasn't* a mistake, because with all the different strands of evidence, even if you did uncover some sort of set-up, that wouldn't prove that Jack wasn't a dealer. It's much more likely to be one dealer setting up another than…"

"The framing of an innocent?" added Jo.

"Exactly," said John. "I mean, just let's recap your conspiracy theory. You're saying that Kadawe, knowing that Jack frequented Delaware Street, sent a string of users to approach him in view of the CCTV cameras so we'll suspect he's a dealer. Kadawe – this is your theory – would bank on the fact that, because we regularly trawl images from that area, we were bound to see him. Well, for a start, *why* would he do that?"

"If you mean why had Mickey got it in for Jack and Jason when they all seemed to be very close friends, I haven't a clue. But if you mean in the context of a conspiracy why would he do it, well, as part of an accumulation of evidence. If we can now establish links between Mickey and the guys who actually came *forward* ..."

"If there *are* links."

"Well, we have *definitely* established one between him and one of the guys caught on camera with Jack. And remember, it's more than a link, sir, it's a loop. Jack to Laser, Laser to Sammo, Sammo to Kadawe, Kadawe to Jack. If we can trace some more of these guys back to Kadawe, then surely there's a real chance Jack was set up. And Jason."

"But if Jack and Jason were into drugs, then you'd *expect* them to all to know each other, whether they're dealing soft or hard. Jack's standoff with Laser on Delaware could have been because Laser was after the soft stuff and Jack wasn't into that. That fits a hell of a lot better with everything else we know, *including* the type of stuff we found in his room, than with a complicated conspiracy. And let me remind you that we watched Kadawe for seven months last year, on suspicion of illegal drug dealing – *and* small arms dealing, as a matter of fact – and we came up with nothing. Zilch with a capital zero."

Jo remained silent, deep in thought.

"Okay," said John, "so let's go back to the other 'why'. Motive. Why would someone go to that much trouble to frame two of their best friends?"

Jo shrugged.

"What is Kadawe's background, sir?" said Jo. "Family and such like."

John reached down and took from a drawer in his desk a battered manila file with an elastic band stretched to its limit holding it together.

"How much do you want to know?" he asked. "You heard quite a lot from the Prosecution's cross-examination at the trial. This is all stuff I collected myself when we were doing the surveillance. Lots of detail about personal history."

"I *would* like to know about his background if possible," said Jo.

"No problem," said John. "All this stuff's on e-file," he tapped the folder, "you can access it yourself; but I can give you a whistle-stop tour if you like."

"Yes, please."

John put the file back in the drawer.

"Well, I suppose it's quite a sad story, really. Mickey Kadawe is of dual ancestry – African-Asian – although the identity of his biological father is unknown. His mother, Idabel Matal, was recruited in India by a multinational food company with a small operation in Middlebank, Johannesburg. She moved there, on her own, to be their IT Manager, They set her up in the best part of town – top end of market – walled executive estate; she must have thought all her Christmases had come at once. What?"

Jo was smiling.

"Just fascinated that you know all this stuff by heart, sir – oh, and she probably didn't celebrate Christmas. Sorry, didn't mean to be impertinent."

"No, it's a fair point about Christmas; and I know all this stuff because, as I said, I collected it myself and spent half of last year going over and over it during the surveillance period. Anyway, a long story short – or shorter anyway – Idabel was attacked and raped one night on returning home from work and as a result got pregnant. Her beliefs wouldn't allow her to consider an abortion so she had to have the child. The gardener on the estate – a Black South African – looked after her; they became romantically attached and married just before she gave birth. The man's name was Milton Kadawe and the baby – Mickey – took his family name.

"That might have been a happy ending to a traumatic year, but the neighbours on the estate didn't like living next door to a poor Black African and they were forced to move away."

"That really is sad," said Jo. "Poor woman. And poor man, as well."

"Actually, that's not the sad bit. They moved to a much more modest place close to where Milton's family lived in a small township called Bonjwane – or something like that – just north of Jo'burg and, it seems, they were very happy there for the next ten years. Mickey thrived at school, and they added two daughters to their family. Then Idabel, who, apparently, was exceptional at her job, was offered a promotion to a senior IT position at the company's European Head Office in Leatherhead. A dream come true – it must have appeared at the time – but that's when it all started going wrong – or soon afterwards, anyway."

"So where are his parents now?"

"Not here, that's for sure. It seems Idabel and the children settled well in Leatherhead. Idabel got a further promotion within a year and the children – all three of them – did well at school. The problem was dad. Milton couldn't get a work permit and although he didn't *need* a job – Idabel was earning more than they'd ever dreamed they'd have – this was a guy who'd worked long hours – manually, outside – all his life since leaving school at fourteen. He must have gone stir crazy being at home all day."

"I bet their garden looked nice, though," said Jo.

John snorted a laugh.

"Yes, I bet. But it clearly wasn't enough to keep him occupied because after two years they separated and Milton went back to Bonjwane."

"That is such a shame," said Jo. "And after the sort of fairy-tale start they had."

"Well, Idabel was interviewed by the police a few times soon after he left, because that's when Mickey started getting into real trouble, and she said they had made a commitment to each other – she and Milton – to get together again some time in the future back in South Africa."

"People do that, though, don't they," said Jo, "when they split up. They pretend, to soften the blow – for themselves and particularly if there are children. Or am I wrong? Did they get back together?"

"Well, I can't say whether they're together now, but that's not where Idabel went when she left the UK. Anyway, Milton's leaving turned out to be life changing for Mickey. He was just thirteen years old and getting in with some bad kids. His close bond with Milton had been keeping his life in balance, but once he'd gone – well, you heard it all in court."

"So what of Idabel and the girls?"

"Idabel did really well – within four years of moving over here she'd got the company's top IT job in Europe. The girls as well – did great at school and had lots of friends in the neighbourhood. But Mickey spent very little time at home. Even so," John looked thoughtful for a moment, "I got the impression that he still had a lot of affection for his family. Visited them fairly regularly; always took flowers for his mum when he did – at least every time we saw him go there."

"So what happened? You said she left the UK?"

"Yes, she was head-hunted by a huge conglomerate back in India. Offer she couldn't refuse, I guess. Anyway, she went back home, taking the girls with her but leaving Mickey behind. He was just six weeks short of his eighteenth birthday. Thing is, though, she bought four tickets for the flight. She must have hoped – and had *reason* to hope – that he would be going with her – or at least there was a good chance he would."

Jo didn't speak for a few moments.

"You're right, sir. It is a sad story. But how did Jack and Katey get involved with him."

"Through Jason – he was a friend of Mickey's since junior school. So Katey got sucked in first, through her relationship with Jason. As for Jack, pretty much as Mickey described in court. One evening, Jack and Jason were playing pool at Rocco's Ball Room in Leatherhead. Jason left first to get a taxi to Cobham; Jack finished his drink, left about five minutes later and found Jason in an alley surrounded by a gang of five yobs threatening him and telling him to stay away from Katey. Jack was about to wade in and probably get done over himself when Mickey turned up at the other end of the alley. The swift change in odds from five-against-one to five-against-three must have caused them to think again, because they ran off.

"It was Tom Brown who told me that, in fact. When we started the surveillance on Mickey and realised that Jack and Katey were spending so much time with him, we told Tom, and that's when he told me the story. I think he wanted to believe that what Jack felt was just gratitude rather than real friendship."

"Interesting, story, sir, and one hell of a coincidence, don't you think?"

"What do you mean?"

"This Rocco's is in Leatherhead; Mickey lives in Woking, and he just turns up at the critical moment to save Jack – and Jason. What an amazing piece of luck, or something else."

"You're starting to see conspiracies everywhere, Jo. Mickey goes to Rocco's from time to time, so it didn't stand out as anything other than a lucky coincidence. I think they were just fortunate that he was passing and tipped the balance. There's absolutely no reason to believe it's anything other than that."

"Possibly," said Jo.

John was silent for a moment before he spoke.

"Look, Jo, I wanted you as part of my team because your Chief Constable felt that, among many other things, you had exceptionally good instincts. And I need you applying those in the right place." He held up his hand as Jo started to speak. "So what I'm prepared to do is sanction you looking further into this, but on your own – not with any outside help, which means you've got to call off your hound-dog. And the reason I'm agreeing to that is because I'm *convinced* that there is no set-up, no conspiracy; and I'm equally convinced that if you apply yourself objectively to the task, you will reach that same conclusion."

"Thank you, sir, I'm really …"

"However," interrupted John, "that does *not* mean that I'm re-opening the case, so, for the time being this is just between you and me, which means you don't go interviewing people; you just trawl the records for now. You will need an awful lot more than Mr Gerrard has uncovered to date for me to take seriously any suggestion of a set-up. Okay?"

"Okay, sir. Thank you."

"I am sure that Tom and Maggie believe Jack was innocent, but ultimately, I'm afraid they will have to accept the unthinkable, and the sooner the better. I would hate to raise their hopes even for a short time only to have them dashed again. So this is completely unofficial, otherwise it could get back to them. Okay?"

"Okay, sir."

"Keep me posted," said John. "That's all – for now."

He stood and offered his hand as Jo rose to her feet.

"Good to have you back, Jo, even though the circumstances couldn't have been any worse."

"Good to be back, sir."

★

David pulled over to the side of the road to take Jo's call.

"Poirot ici."

"Bonjour, Hercule," said Jo. "Just had a chat with Johnny Mac. He seems to think that what we've got reinforces, rather than casts doubt on, Jack being guilty."

"But he didn't convince you?"

"Well, no, of course not." She paused. "Although I have to say he did make a good point."

"Which is?"

"Well, if Jack *had* been a dealer in that area, then Sammo, Kadawe, Jason and Jack – they would have all known each other, anyway. Right?"

"That's right. In fact, I'm not sure the link to Kadawe has any real significance at all. For me, the main points of note are the way Laser was introduced to Jack – this 'don't tell him I sent you' stuff – plus the fact that Jack – according to Laser – didn't seem to know what was going on. Those are the only causes for any doubt in my opinion."

"I understand what you're saying, but I just *feel* Kadawe's involved in some way."

"Okay, fair enough. Anyway, what next? I'm on my way to Auntie's right now to renew my acquaintance with Lawrence H Newhouse."

"Well, the other thing I need to tell you is that I'm banned from working with you, so you're not to get involved any more. Mackay said I can dig around in the records but that's all. So you're on sabbatical for the time being."

"On full pay?"

"I think I can guarantee there'll be no reduction in salary."

David laughed.

"Okay, I'll tell Laser he's got time off for his good behaviour yesterday. And look, Jo, don't let this get to you. I know you feel you've got some obligation to Maggie, but if Johnny Mac – and the justice system – are right, then the sooner the better for her and Tom Brown to get to grips with the fact that they didn't know their son as well as they thought. Your promise to Maggie was to look, not to find."

"That's another thing the Chief said, that it was important they get over it as soon as possible."

"Great minds, you see," said David.

"That description clearly doesn't include me," said Jo. "Oh, and he also said something like 'whatever you do don't tell Maggie you're looking'. I paraphrase but that was the gist. That made me feel *really* bad – like I was deceiving both him *and* Maggie." She sighed. "Tell you what; let me treat you to dinner as a thank you. I could do with cheering up and you're the best at that of anyone I know."

"Why, Ms Cottrell, what a lovely thing to say …"

Jo laughed. "You see, you've started already. What about next Thursday?"

★

Three days later
Week 12; Monday, 8 June …

Katey reached into the pocket of her jeans, taking out the crumpled piece of paper John Mackay had given her, one of two letters found in Jack's room at the Centre when it was cleared following his death. She was sitting in front of the window in her bedroom at Etherington Place, looking out over the extensive wooded garden area at the back of the house. She remembered how, when they were very young, she and Jack would chase each other through and around the trees, and how it always ended with Jack jumping out at her and making her cry. She smiled, also recalling that it never stopped her wanting to carry on with the game.

She read the letter again, although by now she knew the words off by heart.

'To my beautiful sister Katey

'When you read this I will have left you for ever. I am so sorry for the pain this will bring. But I beg you to try and understand why. You will be thinking what a coward, leaving Jay to face his exile alone. I don't blame you, but please understand I did it for him as much as for my own escape from suffering. He is the best friend I ever had. The way he stood by me in court was proof of that. It was an amazingly brave thing to do. And I know he would have always stood by me in the future and that is why I could not go with him to Alpha. If we had gone together he would have been treated the same as me and God knows what that would be like. What they would have done to me. To both of us.

At least this way he will be able to lead whatever passes as a normal life out there. If there is a chance of a real life, Jay has all the qualities and toughness to make one happen for him. That is as long as he has no baggage to bring him down. So please be generous in your thoughts for me and what I have done. Think of it as me just getting rid of Jay's baggage for him. Please help him to understand.

'I love you, Short-one. Look after Mum and Dad. They love each other, you know. Please try to make them realise that.

'Jack'

Katey's sadness was mixed with a feeling of relief that the understanding of his motives brought with it. She could remember him now with the unmitigated love she had held for him all her life.

★

Week 12; Tuesday, 9 June …

In spite of the attempt to avoid public attention, hundreds of wreaths and bouquets of flowers had been placed along the route of the short journey between Etherington Place and the modest little church of St Gilbert's in Weldon-in-the-Vale.

The mourners alighted from the convoy of sombre limousines as the coffin was removed from the hearse. After the short solemn walk down the aisle, the pall bearers gently placed it on the stand close to the altar and stepped back to fade into the recesses of the church. Mags and Tom, clinging to each other, followed them at the head of the congregation and took their places at the front.

St Gilbert's was a typical small village church, with lines of chairs instead of pews, and flowers provided by local residents of the village on the window ledges and around the font. It was the Tomlinson-Browns' usual, if infrequent, place of worship.

The funeral was a private affair, attended primarily by family members along with a few invited friends, including Tony Dobson, George Holland, and John Mackay. Jackie Hewlett, Jonathan Latiffe and Jenny Britani sat together at the back of the church, uninvited but not unwelcome. Also at the service, sitting on either side of Katey, were Megan and Leila Midanda.

At the end of a harrowing thirty minutes during which scarcely a single voice could be raised to sing or join in the spoken prayers, Tom walked slowly to the front, turning to the congregation to pay his tribute to his son.

"There are no words that can dilute our torment on this day. There is no consolation in the knowledge that a wonderful human being has been spared that fearful final crossing into the unknown. There is nothing … nothing … that will cheer us.

"We must try to take strength from the Reverend Alan Gillis's words; draw what comfort we can from the belief that God has accepted our child into Heaven where he may live forever. And as for his earthly journey, at the end of it, in spite of this sensation of unbearable grief, our overwhelming feeling must be one of gratitude; thankfulness that we have had the privilege of sharing that journey with him. For it is far better that we suffer this pain now than to never have known him at all."

He turned unsteadily to face the coffin.

"Our Jack. Our little wolverine. The words have not been invented yet that can express how much we love you; how much we will miss you; how deeply and unwaveringly proud you have made us for each precious moment of your life. We will think of you every second of every day of every year for as long as we live. And our love and pride will endure undiminished."

A loud gasp jerked his whole body and he seemed momentarily incapable of moving. Then he reached out to the coffin and his knees buckled. He collapsed into a kneeling position beside it. His two brothers rushed from their seats to help him.

Mags got there first, driven by a protective instinct which was out of her control. She crouched behind him, her arms wrapped tightly around his shoulders and chest, hugging him to her, exactly as she had done when he had his last nightmare.

★

Week 12; Wednesday, 10 June…

The door to the room stood open and the two guards waited respectfully outside for them to say their last goodbyes.

"You know what, Katey; I don't think this is the end for you and me. I can't believe it is; I *won't* believe it is. In spite of what is happening, where I'm going … Somehow, I *know* we're going to meet again, and then it will be forever. You and me, like we always said, just as it's meant to be. I'm not just saying that, Katey; I really do believe it. And I want you to have faith in that, too."

He looked deep into her eyes. The expression on his handsome, ebony face reinforced the words, his own eyes shining with a desperate hope and drinking in his final mental picture of the beautiful girl he held in his arms.

"You'll do that for me, won't you? If you believe it, it will happen. Say you will, and just trust me."

"Oh, Jason, I will, I will, I will …"

He pulled her to him again and they clung to each other for the last two minutes of their life together. Then they kissed passionately and Katey withdrew, backing away from him out of the room as his shape became increasingly indistinct through the torrent of her tears.

"Believe, Katey," he said, "and it will happen. Hold on to that."

★

Along with six other detainees, he was escorted, handcuffed, into the back of the prison transit vehicle. The windowless passenger compartment had a row of four seats along each side, facing inwards. The individual seats were separated from their neighbours by two-foot deep floor-to-ceiling panels.

The seven prisoners were strapped in with conventional seat belts, which were then locked in place preventing any movement from the seats or contact with other passengers. One armed prison officer sat with his back to the bulkhead watching the group, out of reach of the two nearest prisoners' seats. On this occasion, one of these was unoccupied; Jason was in the other.

Outside, the rest of the five-vehicle convoy manoeuvred into position in readiness for the journey; at the front, a police motorcycle, followed by two police cars, sandwiched between which were the transit vehicle and a smaller van carrying the prisoners' personal belongings.

As they pulled away from the Centre for the twenty-mile drive to Heathrow, Jason looked across at the vacant seat and thought about the letter Katey had read to him and about his final statement to the court which many people believed had sealed his fate. As his sense of loneliness grew, the gesture now seemed worthless and naïve.

The journey took fifty-five minutes during which time no one in the transit vehicle spoke, including the two officers in the driving compartment. The motorcade eventually stopped and, after several minutes, the back doors opened letting in more of the sound of revving aircraft engines close by. The driver and his colleague released the first prisoner, who was led away by two other guards into a prefabricated single-storey building. One-by-one they followed, joining a larger group of around fifty inside, all of whom were given a drink of coffee or water, and a package containing a sandwich, a piece of fruit and a cereal bar.

Jason looked round the room at his travelling companions, an assortment of young males varying in age from eighteen to mid-twenties. Different in size, shape, colour and background but all with expressions of hopelessness and disbelief. They were seated theatre-style, still handcuffed, facing the end of the room, where a senior officer strode onto a small stage to address them.

"In a few minutes, you will officially start your passage into exile. We shall be boarding a flight which will take you to Humberside Airport at Kirmington in Lincolnshire. From there you will go by coach to the port of Immingham and then by boat to Bull Sand Fort. Unlike on Alpha, security guards will also be present on the fort, but this experience of simulated segregation is designed as a first step in the preparation for your final destination.

"At every transfer stage you will each be accompanied by two officers, both of whom will be armed and authorised to use their discretion in reacting to any problems of disorderly behaviour or violence. Please, let's not have any bravado, which may lead to someone getting hurt.

"The flight will take around forty-five minutes and as you will not be allowed to leave your seats during that time, should anyone need to use the toilet, they should go now. Please raise your hand if you do."

Almost all of the prisoners raised their hands and were shown to a line of WCs at the side of the room. The doors were closed when they entered but opened by the guards after a couple of minutes had elapsed if the prisoner had not re-emerged. A few were caught squatting and their privacy quickly restored.

Then they were taken out, again individually, to a waiting 737 in black livery with the words 'Prisoner Transfer' barely visible in a dark grey lettering along the fuselage.

At Kirmington, the prisoners were escorted onto two separate coaches – around thirty on each, all handcuffed to rails on the backs of the seats in front of them – with half a dozen armed guards assigned to each coach. From there they were driven to a secure quayside area in Immingham dockland where they boarded the large motor launch to take them to the imposing steel and concrete WW1 fortress which had been redeveloped to provide its occupants with a gentle sampler of the isolation to come.

Bull Sand Fort was the larger of two similar structures, the other being Haile Sand Fort. It was situated one-and-a-half miles from shore off Spurn Point, the narrow spit of land which stretched across the Humber estuary mouth from the northern side. The four-storey, sixty-foot high edifice was originally designed to accommodate four 6-inch – and later, 12-inch – guns, and 200 troops whose job, along with their comrades on its sister fort, was to protect the Humber ports from naval attack during the two world wars. The guns, in fact, were never fired in anger, although the forts continued to be occupied by the military until the mid fifties. Now they were subject to Grade II Listed Building status and, somewhat ironically, Bull Sand Fort had been used for a period as a drug rehabilitation facility.

The launch docked and the prisoners disembarked.

CHAPTER TWENTY-TWO

Week 12; Thursday, 11 June …

Tom awoke from a shallow sleep at 6.30 am. He went downstairs to the kitchen, making himself an instant coffee, nibbling absently at a piece of dry toast, and contemplating, with a further sinking of the heart, the day which lay ahead of him.

He showered, shaved, dressed and waited for the police car to collect him and take him, still under house arrest, to give his evidence to an investigative committee from PIRA – the Police Internal Review Authority, the NJR's successor to the Independent Police Complaints Commission – which was handling the internal enquiry into Jack's death.

★

Mags waited until Tom had gone before going down to the kitchen. She took the letter from the pocket of her robe. She had carried it on her person since the moment it had been handed to her by John Mackay. Unfolding it, she read it for the hundredth time.

'My Darling Mum

'Please, please, please forgive me for what I have done. This must seem to you the most sickening way for me to repay the infinite love and kindness you have given me all my very fortunate life. I don't know how it came to this. I swear to you that I am innocent of any wrongdoing, although I know that you never believed it anyway, that not for a moment did you waver in your faith in me. That has meant so much to me during these final weeks.

'The reasons for what I did I explained in Katey's letter and I beg you to understand. Not only could I not face the prospect of the inevitable violence and intimidation awaiting me in exile, but I could not make Jason a target for such treatment as well. I had to give him a chance. I do hope Katey accepts this. Please try and help each other understand, and forgive me.

'As for Dad, it is obvious that you love each other and the worst thing for me would be that you let what has happened drive you apart. I want you to help him with what must be the most unbearable feeling of guilt. It would have been so much easier for him to refuse to help me. It must be one of the most selfless things a father could do for his son.

'Please show him this note if you wish. I have not left him a separate letter. When I see him today for the last time, I will thank him and tell him how much I love him. You are the most marvellous parents in the world. And you are meant to be together, for ever. Promise me you will be.

'Goodbye, my most beautiful and caring mum. I love you so much.

'Jack'

★

George Holland sat in the waiting room drumming his fingers on the arms of the wing chair and wondering why he'd been kept waiting for so long. He was dressed for his meeting later in Whitehall in a modern blue suit with narrow lapels, matching tie and a cream shirt. His neat goatee beard was trimmed very short.

"Mr Holland."

He looked up to see Jad's consultant smiling down at him. She was a tall, handsome woman in her mid forties, wearing a white overall pulled in by a belt at her narrow waist.

"Could we talk in here?" she said.

She ushered George into a small interview room and they sat facing each other across the table.

"I'm afraid you won't be able to see Mr Deverall today, Mr Holland. He's deteriorated very quickly over the last few days. It was expected, of course, but I think the news about his Godson has

311

probably accelerated the decline. He's getting very near the end now. I'm very sorry."

George was shocked into silence. He thought how much his friendship with John Deverall meant to him, coming after his despair over Irene. The one fresh thing in his life; the symbol of a new existence; and his partner in building a platform for the future.

It took a full minute before he could speak.

"Does this mean I won't … I mean, was that the last time – last time?"

"Not necessarily. We expect him to rally again … maybe. But it's very unlikely he'll get back to how he was before. As I said, it's very close now."

George slumped forward, his elbows on the table.

"Look, I'll tell you what I'll do," said the consultant. "Let me have a contact number, and when he's well enough to receive visitors again, I'll let you know. You'd need to get here quickly, though. He's likely to be more down than up for his remaining time." She waited for a response from George that was not forthcoming. "That's the best I can do, Mr Holland," she added.

George nodded, took his wallet from his inside jacket pocket and handed over a business card.

"Try the mobile first," he said. "Unless I happen to be in London for a meeting like today, it will take me the best part of two hours to get here, so please let me know straight away. I don't want to miss saying goodbye." His voice broke on the last word. He stood up quickly and started to leave before turning back briefly to shake the consultant's hand.

"Thank you," he said.

"I really am very sorry, Mr Holland."

★

Tom was interrogated by the panel of three investigators for six hours with just a forty-minute break for lunch. He couldn't face eating anything during the recess, taking only some painkillers with a glass of water for a thumping headache. By the middle of the afternoon session he had started to feel faint and was conscious of becoming less spontaneous with his responses to their questions.

The committee spent most of the post-lunch period probing the source of the capsule. They clearly disbelieved his story of its being a relic of his Special Forces days, reading him a submission by a Professor of Toxicology who was very definite that such a poison could not be that instantly effective after a period of nine years.

"It seems rather pointless you asking me questions if you're only going to believe the answers you want to hear," Tom said, finally giving way to his anger. "And anyway, I think you're stepping outside your terms of reference. Your task, as I understand it, is to examine the apparent breakdown in the internal security procedure at this Holding Centre and *not* to challenge me personally. I shall be responding to questions about the source of the capsule – which *I have already admitted* to bringing into the Centre – as part of the criminal prosecution I will be facing. It seems to me that you are confusing the two issues and if this line of interrogation persists, I'm afraid I shall have no alternative but to leave the interview."

The head of the committee was a very large man in a mid-grey suit, which seemed a little tight for him, and a white shirt and dark blue tie. The other two members of the committee – a man and a woman – were small and slight by comparison, and their contributions to the process seemed to reflect their lesser physical stature. They hardly spoke at all but spent their time nodding vigorously as if to reinforce their colleague's questions and taking pages of copious notes, even though the interview was being recorded.

The large man sighed.

"Home Secretary, it is not our intention to cause you any further anxiety or distress after what you have had to contend with during the past week. But we must consider all possibilities or we would not be doing our job properly. One of those possibilities is that you acquired the capsule from an *internal* source, and this line of questioning is designed to eliminate that scenario for the benefit – if I can put it that way – of the staff at the Holding Centre, which I think you will agree certainly *is* relevant to this committee's remit. *And furthermore ...*" he held up his hand as Tom made to interrupt, "we cannot ignore the expert opinion of one of the country's leading authorities on toxicology."

There was a long silence.

"However," said the man, "we'll leave it there for now. But we may return to this again. Thank you, Home Secretary."

As he was driven home, Tom's thoughts went back to the meeting with Jad, and he wondered how soon, if it had not happened already, his visit would come to light and yield its obvious conclusion about the source of the capsule.

★

The house was quiet. Tom found Katey in her study upstairs working at the computer. She turned and smiled at him as he poked his head round the door.

"Hi, Dad. Tough day?"

"No worse than I deserve, Princess," he said. "Thank God I've got you."

"No more than you deserve, Dad," she said, smiling again.

She stood and they embraced, holding on to each other for a long time.

"Listen, Katey," he said. "I'm going to need your help – I mean *more* of your help. I want you to get Mum and come down to the front sitting room in," he checked his watch, "ten minutes. That's five-fifteen. I have to talk to you both about … what happened. It can't wait any longer. Okay? Oh, and I'd like to see you separately afterwards, please."

Katey's face started to crumple as her self-control wavered. Tom pulled her tightly to him again.

"It'll be alright, Princess. Really," he said. "Honestly it will." He moved her gently away from him still holding onto her. "Go now. Please."

She ran off, like a little girl, wiping her eyes.

Tom went downstairs to wait for them. He was standing looking out of the window as they entered the room together. They were holding hands. Katey smiled at him whilst Mags refused to meet his eyes, staring towards the sofa where she went to take a seat, pulling Katey down beside her.

"Mags," he said.

There was no response.

"Mags, please."

Katey gave her a nudge. "Mum, this is really difficult for Dad, for all of us. Remember what Jack said …"

Mags snatched her hand away.

"That's between me and Jack," she said. "Just me and Jack."

"What did Jack say?" asked Tom, addressing the question to his daughter.

"Don't say anything," Mags snapped at her. She stared down into her lap.

Katey shrugged helplessly at Tom.

"Perhaps later," she said, taking back Mags's hand in both of hers. "Go on, Dad."

"Look, just tell me." Tom's voice was raised.

"Dad, tell us what you have to. You said it couldn't wait any longer. And, Mum, you better listen to what he has to say. Right?" There was an edge to her voice now, like that of a parent trying to deal with two sulky children.

"Yes," said Tom after a brief silence. "Right … okay."

Katey nudged Mags again, harder this time. Mags looked up and across towards Tom, her eyes cold and neutral, seeming not to see him at all.

"Mags, please," he said. "For Katey. *Please.*"

Her eyes came to focus on him.

"For Katey then," she said.

He sighed and pulled the wing chair closer to the sofa.

"As Katey knows, today I've been to …"

"I know where you've been," Mags interrupted. "You've been telling the police how you helped kill our son."

Tom slumped back in the chair. Katey leapt to her feet.

"You take that back!" she screamed at Mags.

"Alright! Alright!" cried Mags. "I take it back."

Her eyes had dropped again and she stared at her hands, clasped tightly together on her knees.

"Katey, I'm sorry," she said. "I didn't mean to upset you."

Katey sat down on the sofa again, this time well away from Mags with her back half-turned to her.

"Look," said Tom. "Let's just get this over with. It's clear then that *you* know what happened when I went to see Jack that last time."

He directed the statement at Mags, and then turned to Katey without waiting for a response. "What about you, Princess?"

"Well, I guess so. Jack left me a letter."

"A letter? Saying what?"

"Well, explaining why he did it."

"How could he write a letter explaining *why*, when he didn't even know *if*?"

"Well, that's obvious, isn't it?" Mags volunteered, taking them both by surprise. "He would write the letters beforehand and leave them in his room. If he didn't get the chance to … to … do it, then he would have just destroyed the letters."

"Yes, of course," said Tom. "You said letters. There was more than one?"

"Yes, one for me and one for Mum."

"And me? Did he leave one for me?"

"No." Mags's reply was cruelly succinct.

"But he explained why in Mum's letter." Katey was quick to add.

"Well?" He looked angrily at Mags.

"He said he just couldn't be bothered," she sneered back at him.

"Mum!" Katey was on her feet again. "I don't want to take sides in this unless I'm forced to, but if you carry on like this…"

Mags looked away, apparently unmoved.

"Right!" said Katey "If that's the way."

Mags turned back to Tom.

"He said in his letter that he would be telling you personally what he wanted to say when you met, so he wouldn't need to write to you." She looked at Katey. "Okay? Satisfied?"

No one spoke for a while. Katey sat cross-legged on the floor close to her father's chair. At last Tom broke the silence.

"Look, I just want you both to understand what happened in the visiting room that day. If you know already, then that's okay. But there's going to be a press statement about what happened – what I did – what Jack did."

His head dropped onto his chest as he choked on the words. Katey reached across and squeezed his hand.

"Tell us, Dad. We're listening."

He sat up again, his eyes glistening.

"I just wanted you to hear it from me first."

He stopped, looking across at Mags.

"Go on," she said, meeting his eyes more gently this time.

He spoke quickly at first, desperate to get it over with.

"I had a meeting with Jack – just the two of us – at his request. He asked me about providing him with ... a way out. You know, if things got really bad. It made me feel sick just to think about it, but what could I do? What would you have done? It was the very last thing that any of us could do for him."

He stopped, panting with emotion, and turned his head away to hide the standing tears. It was a full minute before he could continue. Mags and Katey waited in silence. He continued in little more than a whisper.

"I managed to get the stuff to him in Granny Brown's locket. I handed it over and ... he just ... took it out of the locket and ... put it in his mouth. I had no idea ... I didn't think he'd ..."

The surface tension of his tears gave way and they rolled slowly down his cheeks.

"I reached across to him," his voice even softer now, barely audible, "it was too late ... he died in my arms."

His whole body sagged, drained of strength.

Mags and Katey looked at him wide-eyed with shock.

"You mean ... you were actually with him when ...?" said Mags.

He looked across at her. In her expression of horror he thought he detected, briefly, signs of sympathy and understanding. Then she rose from the sofa.

"Thank you for telling us," she said, reaching out her arm to Katey, inviting her to take her hand.

"I'll just be a minute," said Katey, and Mags walked quickly from the room.

Neither spoke for a long time. Katey shuffled round, still in her sitting position, so she could face Tom and take both his hands in hers.

"You poor thing," she said, followed by more silence.

"How was it for Jack?" she asked, eventually, in a small voice. "Was it ... very bad? Did he suffer?"

The question jerked Tom out of his trance.

"No, darling," he said. "Not at all. It was over in a second. He wouldn't have felt anything."

"Perhaps it is best," said Katey. "For both of them, like Jack said."

She took his letter to her out of the pocket of her jeans. It was crumpled and ragged, more like a piece of cloth. She handed it over to Tom. He read the note in silence.

"Listen," said Tom, "you need to go to your mum and see that she's alright, and I want you to look after her. And also, you need to get back to college as soon as possible." He held up his hands when she tried to protest. "Katey, you are going to be a great lawyer. Everybody thinks so – *knows* so. That's what Jason will want you to do, won't he? Correct me if I'm wrong."

She thought for a moment.

"Yes, you're right, of course. Perhaps the week after next. I will … definitely. But what do you mean, you want me to look after Mum? That's your job. You told me half an hour ago that everything would be alright."

"And so it will, Princess. But she needs time and space without me. Surely you can see that."

Katey thought for a moment.

"If you say so. But where will you go? Are you going back to work? Will they let you?"

Tom sighed.

"I can't go back, Katey. Tomorrow morning, I shall be appearing at Guilford Magistrates Court to be charged with a criminal offence. I guess you must have known that was coming. Either that or you're grounded until you catch up with your homework. Then I'll go on to SW1 and stay there. But we'll keep in touch, you and I. Let's talk every day, by phone. Call me whenever you like, and come to see me. But please don't leave your Mum on her own in the evening or overnight. Not for a while …"

"Not until you come back."

"That's right. It won't be long. You do understand, don't you? You and I have just got to be really good friends again. I couldn't stand it if I lost that."

"You won't, Dad," she said, in a whisper. "We'll *always* be friends now, you and me. And Mum will come round. She loves you. I'm sure you know that."

"I hope so."

He rose from the chair.

"You'd best go and check that Mum's okay. See you later."
She reached up to kiss him then left the room.

★

Jo burst through the door of the Thonburi Thai Restaurant in High Street, three minutes late and with an apologetic expression already in place, and peered round the softly-lit room. Her search eventually reached the huge shaven-headed man in the corner booth, and she averted her eyes quickly as she realised he was staring straight back at her with a sly smirk on his face. She eased herself up onto a stool at the bar, turning her back to him. After ordering a tonic water and settling herself to wait for her dinner date, she became aware that the man had got up from his seat and was heading towards her.

The man stopped behind her. Tight black T-shirt, black jeans, black leather jacket, stubble, and earring.

"You're late!"

A familiar voice with an unfamiliar growl. Jo spun round.

"Oh, my God!" she shrieked.

Everyone in the restaurant turned to look at them. Then Jo started laughing.

"What on Earth? You scared the life out of me!"

He leaned a long way down to whisper.

"Sshhh… I'm under cover, remember?"

"And this is your idea of being invisible, is it?"

She laughed again and looked him up and down.

"Have you grown?"

The two-inch heels of his cowboy boots placed his earring at approximately the same height as the picture rail which ran round the four walls.

"Only a bit. Anyway," he did a camp 360-degree twirl, arms spread outwards, "what do you think?"

"I think we'd better take a seat before someone calls the police."

They went to the corner booth and sat down. Jo smiled across at him.

"Actually, you look absolutely great."

"Go on, you're just saying that."

319

"No, you really do. And I hope you're not going to ditch the new image just because you're fired. Well, laid off, anyway."

David shook his head.

"What happened to the sabbatical on full pay? Have you found someone cheaper? We can haggle if you like."

Jo looked serious.

"No, it's just that John Mackay is *not* going to re-open the case. As far as he's concerned there's no reason to. Says it's just a strange encounter on Delaware described by an unreliable witness, stacked up against a mountain of police evidence pointing to a solid conviction. And when he puts it like that – in the cold light of day – it sounds perfectly reasonable."

"So you found nothing more?"

"I spent the last six days, including the weekend going through the police records for the five other users caught on camera with Jack, plus the two observed through police surveillance and the four who came forward and gave evidence at the trial. Details of convictions, appearances as witnesses in other cases, medical files – including any emergency hospitalisation and programmed treatment for addiction – and incidents where they had been picked up and not charged. There seemed nothing to link any of them directly to Mickey Kadawe."

"Massive job."

"Yes, massive job, particularly for a weekend. Good thing, of course, is that since the amnesty all the legit ones are on PROLIST. That cuts it down a hell of a lot. All dealers had to disclose the names of their customers to become Licensed Street Traders and get on the police register. Makes the links a lot easier to find – which makes it all the more conclusive, of course, when you *can't* find a link."

"What about Sammo? Any links to him are sort of links to Kadawe, aren't they?"

"Well, including Laser, four of the six captured with Jack on CCTV were Sammo's customers. That doesn't mean, of course, that Sammo necessarily *sent* the other three to meet with Jack; and, even if he had, Jack may or may not have sold them drugs. And given John Mackay's point that dealers and traders in the same area would all know each other, well … it all adds up to nothing really."

"I wish now that I'd pressed Sammo about Laser's meeting with"

Jack on Delaware, but at the time I was desperate to get to the Duke."

"It wouldn't have made any difference, and I reckon that was the right thing to do at the time." Jo paused for a moment, choosing her words. "And I'm starting to think that there really isn't a conspiracy in this anyway."

David's eyes widened.

"What about this feeling of yours that Kadawe must be involved? You seemed pretty sure before."

"Well, it's all the wasted days looking, I guess. And even if there *was* a set-up, as you yourself said, it fits just as snugly with Jack *being* a drug dealer as with him *not* being one – perhaps even more so."

"And I still believe that's true," said David. "Something my friend Laser said – it's still a war zone on the streets between the dealers. I guess sometimes we choose to believe that genuine progress had been made, rather than just the legalising of a free market still backed up with threats and violence. But I also think it's important that you get closure on this; that it's not hanging around in your head. So if you do want any more help, then let me know. I mean it. We did a good job as far as it went, didn't we?"

"You mean *you* did a good job."

"Well, yes, but I didn't like to say that."

She laughed again.

"Let's eat," she said.

He waved to the waiter who shot across the room with a couple of menus and the wine list, before retiring a short distance, poised for a quick return.

"Tell you what," said David. "I've never been served as fast in my life as I have this last week."

Jo's mobile sounded. She checked the screen for the caller's ID.

"My toy-boy," she said, putting the phone back into her shoulder bag. "I'll call him later."

David raised his eyebrows. "Your what?"

"Detective Sergeant Sebastian Carter. My number two at Leicester. He called me a couple of days ago, just to ask how I was – he *said*. Anyway, he went on to ask quite a lot more than that and I'm meeting him in London for a weekend soon. Separate rooms, of course," she added, with a serious frown. "At least to start with."

"Well, I'm shocked *and* shattered," said David. "And I always thought – you and me – you know, with you always asking me out ..."

"Well, I shouldn't worry too much, because I can't see anything coming of it," she said. "Nothing ever does. And I don't see Johnny Mac approving of it either. But Seb's ever so nice and he looked after me really well when I was there. Even so, I mean, he's *only* a sergeant," she added, with mock disgust. "What could we possibly have in common?"

"Well, I know what he's got in common with *me*," said David. "He seems to think the world of Jo Cottrell."

"Aw, thank you," said Jo, and she patted his hand.

"And if it doesn't work out," he said, "and you decide it would be great fun making a complete fool of a much older man, then ... well, you know where to find me. And based on recent experience, I think I can guarantee getting you the fastest food in the UK wherever we eat."

★

They left the restaurant at around 10.30 and David walked Jo to her car a hundred yards or so down the street.

"Are you back in Meadow Village?" she asked.

"No, still at Linny's. I promised I'd be there when they got back – that's tomorrow. So I thought I'd stay there this week. Bit like a holiday, really."

They stopped at Jo's car.

"What are you going to tell Maggie?"

"I'm going to tell her I'm still looking – which I will be doing, through the records. I'll carry on until Johnny Mac tells me to stop. And while there's a chance, however small, that I might find something, I don't want to dash her hopes. Even so, I feel a bit of a coward for not being more honest with her, I suppose, but I need to think about what to say." She paused, and then looked up at David. "Do you think I'm being a coward?"

"Not at all. I'd do the same – take my time and be as gentle as I could. And who's to know – something might just turn up."

She smiled. "Thanks, David. You always say what I want to hear – well most of the time, anyway."

CHAPTER TWENTY-THREE

Week 12; Friday, 12 June …

Mags was sitting in her office-cum-studio, dabbing distractedly at a canvas on an easel near the window. The room mirrored Tom's own office in the other wing – a converted dressing room extended into a small bedroom. This was where she carried out her work for the family businesses and for her campaign activities. In the little spare time she had, she pursued her passion for landscape painting, mainly in oils and acrylics, so there were always five or six unfinished works dotted around the room.

She was wearing a loose open-weave top, which looked suitably like an artist's smock. Her hair was pulled back and held in place by a wide blue band which exactly matched the colour of her calf-length leggings. She appeared thin and pale, but Tom wondered at just how beautiful she looked all the same.

"Just to let you know, Mags," he said, almost choking on the words, "I'm moving out for a while, going to stay at …"

"SW1, yes, Katey told me," she said, without looking up from her task. "I wondered if you were going to mention it."

"I just thought it best …"

"Yes, it is. I would just like to be informed, that's all. Like about what happened this morning, for instance."

"Well, exactly what we expected to happen. I was charged with – you know what. I pleaded not guilty …"

Mags looked up from her painting. "How can you be not guilty? I mean of supplying the capsule?"

"Dan's advice. I can change the plea before the trial, but in the meantime it means I can extract myself from professional life with some dignity – if that's possible now. He said if I pleaded guilty it would precipitate an automatic and immediate surrender of my political status. I didn't know that; I guess I should have."

Mags looked away again. "And when is the trial?"

"In five months; on the 3rd November."

She turned back to him.

"That's a long time to be dragging this out. What happened to the NJR's fast tracking policy? Doesn't it apply to the people who came up with it?"

"You're right, it is outside the guidelines. It was scheduled later to allow any media interest to fade away. It wasn't my doing but I'm glad, if only for Katey's sake."

Mags remained silent and resumed her painting. Tom stood watching her for a long time before speaking.

"Mags, I thought … you and me … I mean, after what happened at the funeral. The way you …"

"I've been going over that in my mind. I really don't know what came over me."

"Look," he said. "I'm hurting too, you know. I've got the guilt as well as the pain …"

"Yes," she snapped, spinning round on him as she spoke, "and I'll make sure you never …"

The expression in his eyes stopped her words, and Tom saw her own eyes soften, as a feeling of sadness briefly replaced the anger. Then she turned back again to the easel.

"Take care," he said, and left the room.

★

Tom arrived at Vauxhall Bridge Road at just after 1.00 pm, parked in the underground garage and took his holdall, suitcase and laptop up to the apartment. Before unpacking anything else, he set up his laptop in its docking station on the glass and chrome dining table in the semi-circular living room, whose floor-to-ceiling windows provided a 180-degree sweeping view of Westminster and beyond. He then typed a letter of resignation to the prime minister. It was as stark and impersonal as he could make it without being unprofessional. He sealed the envelope and tucked it into the gilded frame of the mirror over the console table, feeling a sense of relief, albeit tempered by the thought of Andrew's delight at receiving it. Then he carried his bags into the master bedroom to unpack.

Afterwards he drove out to his constituency home in Marlburgh, parking his car outside and walking along Westbourne Avenue to the Party office. Sitting behind the desk-cum-counter in the reception area was a smartly dressed girl in her mid-twenties with short spiky red hair. She almost jumped to her feet as he entered and looked at him wide-eyed with alarm.

"Mr B-B-Brown," she stammered. "I didn't expect …"

"It's okay, Zara," he said, with a reassuring smile, "I didn't expect to be here either. Is Jenny around?"

"Y-yes." She pointed behind her. "Through there. Shall I tell her that …?"

"No, I think I can just about find my way."

"I know, but …"

"It's okay, really."

Tom walked through reception into the large inner office, which was empty. The premises were too big now for his small constituency team of three full-time and two part-time staff. The place had been initially selected to accommodate his project team of between twelve and fifteen people when he was in Opposition. Along the left-hand side of the area was a line of four smaller rooms. The one on the far right was his office, and at the opposite end was the one that had been Grace's. The middle two were used for meetings and at present had been converted into one by opening the folding partition between them.

He could hear someone in his office. He tapped gently on the half-open door as he stepped inside. Jenny was dressed in baggy jeans, a loose top and trainers and was kneeling in front of the oak sideboard, the bottom drawer of which was pulled out as she transferred its contents into a plastic container at her side. She turned to the door at the sound of the tapping. Her expression changed to the same look he had just seen on Zara's face and she rose quickly to her feet.

She was crying.

"Oh … Home Secretary … Mr Brown …"

She broke down completely, leaning against the sideboard for support. Tom went across to her, turning her to face him and holding her closely against him.

"Jenny, Jenny," he said. "Whatever is the matter?"

"I'm so sorry," she sobbed, "so sorry."

"Sorry for what, Jenny, you've nothing to be ..."

"For everything, *everything*! For Jack, oh, poor Jack, poor you."

She stopped, shaking almost uncontrollably. Tom held her until she was calm and still.

"And for this," she added. "For all this."

She half-turned, still in his embrace, and swept her arm around the room. "For what they've asked me to do to your office, to *our* office."

"What have they asked you to do?"

"Well, clear it out ready for ..."

She stopped again, not wanting to continue, but more composed now. Tom released her slowly, keeping one arm round her shoulders, and looked around his former place of work.

"That's okay, Jenny. I came here today to ask you to do the very same thing."

"Oh, no!" She turned into his arms again.

"It's alright. There's no choice, Jenny. Let's sit down."

Jenny took her usual seat at his desk and Tom pulled his own chair round to the front so they could sit together. He reached across and took her hand in his.

"Look, I'll bring you right up to date with where I am," he said, "on one condition."

"Okay," she said, in a small voice. "What's that?"

"You make us both a cup of coffee first. Now do you think you can do that without scalding yourself?"

She smiled "I'll try."

Tom walked around his former domain, looking first into Grace's office and then the main area, noting all the small personal items which had made it such a happy place for him to work. The posters on the walls – a lot more of pop stars and sporting heroes than there were of Party and campaign propaganda – small ornamental touches to work stations – miniature soft toys, novelty pen holders and decorative magnets.

This is where it *really* ends, he thought – right here, right now. Not with a letter to his boss, but with the last moments he would spend in the place which had been the launch pad for his meteoric political career. From retiring SBS colonel to Home Secretary in just over seven years – an impressive trajectory, he used to think, and similar to that of his military ascent through the ranks. But he knew now that it was almost pedestrian compared with the angle and speed of the catastrophic free-fall he had just experienced.

He was brought out of his trance by Jenny emerging from the kitchen with a tray containing a cafetière, two mugs and a small milk jug, a welcome display of normality. She placed it on the desk and took her seat. She smiled across at him.

"No biscuits, I'm afraid," she said. "I finished the last and haven't got round to …"

"That's okay."

She squeezed down the plunger of the cafetière and filled both their cups.

"Thanks," said Tom, adding some milk and taking a sip. "Now, where was I?"

"You were holding my hand," she said, sheepishly.

"So I was." He laughed and took hold of her hand again. "You're good for me, you know, Jenny. Whatever happens, we won't lose touch with each other. I promise. I want us to carry on being friends. That's if it's okay with you, of course," he added.

"Of course it is," she said.

"So," he sighed. "Down to business. Here's where we are." He drew in a deep breath. "Today I officially became a criminal – or more accurately, I was charged with a criminal offence. I've been released on bail pending trial on the 3rd November – five months from now."

She swallowed and shook her head, the tears appearing in her eyes again.

"And the charge? Assisting a prisoner in taking his own life. My only son, Hugh Jacob – known as Jack – Tomlinson-Brown."

They sat in silence for a long time before Tom could continue.

"Jack had asked that I help him to – let's say – prepare for a way out if necessary. I smuggled a capsule into the holding centre for him and he took it there and then while I was there. I had no

327

idea he was going to do that. I don't know what I thought looking back …"

He took a deep breath. Jenny was crying again.

"Anyway, that's about it, Jenny. I pleaded not guilty – but I *am* guilty – it was just a technicality so I stayed in control of when and how I left office. Because you can see, can't you, that it's simply not possible for me to continue under those circumstances? Anyway," he added, looking around the office, "it seems Mr Donald is well ahead of me in terms of closure."

"He told me a couple of days ago that you wouldn't be coming back," said Jenny. "I didn't want to believe it, but … And that's why you made me jump – I wasn't expecting you. I was just making sure none of your personal things would get lost in the changeover when someone new arrives."

"Well, I really appreciate that, Jenny. But what about you? Have you had any assurances about your job?"

"Only that I'll be kept on and be able to apply for any vacancies. I can understand it, I suppose. Whoever replaces you, well …they'll want to appoint their own PA just like … you … appointed … me." She stumbled over the words.

"You'll be fine," said Tom, who realised that he was still holding her hand. He gave it a squeeze and released it. "I guess I'll retain enough credibility to give a meaningful reference. And as I said – and I mean it – we'll keep in touch. Anyway, let's get to work!"

After they had finished sorting through the rest of his personal effects, Tom walked back for his car and pulled it in to the small car park behind the office. They just about squeezed two of the three containers into the limited space behind the seats and put the other on the front passenger seat itself. Then he went back inside.

He kissed the receptionist briefly on the cheek, tasting the salt of her running tears.

"You take care, Zara, and thank you for everything."

Back in his office, he gave Jenny another long hug and felt her body gently shake with her silent sobbing.

"Hey, cut that out," he said. "You'll set me off in a minute."

They eventually stepped away from each other.

"Oh, just one thing," said Jenny, anxiously. "I don't know whether I'm supposed to tell you this, but Grace asked me to let her know if you came to the office. To be fair, I think she just wanted to speak to you, probably to check how you are. Is it okay with you if I tell her? Now that Zara has seen you, it might be awkward if ..."

"No, that's fine," said Tom. "You must let her know. No problem at all."

"Also, she said for me to find out where you were staying. I don't have to tell her that, of course."

"No, that's okay as well. I'm staying at Balmaha for the time being. Hey, perhaps she's thinking of offering me a job. What do you think?"

"Well if she does, and you need a PA ..."

"Then I'll be in touch right away. You have my word as a gentleman."

They laughed again, and Tom left, placing a final kiss on Jenny's cheek.

★

Tom thought about staying in Marlburgh overnight and travelling back to London the following morning, but watching the news coverage of the enquiry and his appearance in court, he thought better of it. People would quickly realise he was there – they would see his car outside and the lights on in the apartment – and he could just imagine how quickly the crowd would gather. Well-wishing constituents he could deal with – just about – but not a media siege.

Before leaving he phoned Katey.

"Hi, Princess. Did you see the news?"

"Yes," she replied, in a small voice.

"Any reaction there yet?"

"A lot more reporters here now. About three times as many as the vultures who've been here all week. Not nice for Mum; not that she's planning to go out or anything."

"Look I don't like to ask you to do this, but could you just go to the gates and tell them I'm at my constituency home in Marlburgh. That's the gospel truth at this precise moment. I'll be heading back to SW1 in around half an hour, but they don't need to know that. Just don't answer any questions. Are you okay to do that?"

"Yes, no problem. What about you? Are you alright?"

"I'm fine. Tell you what; I'll call you when I get there."

"Oh, by the way, George phoned. Mum spoke to him but he said he'd like to talk to you as soon as possible."

"Right. I'll phone him on the way back."

"Okay. Drive safely. Speak later."

Tom put timers on the table lamp in the living room and the standard lamp in the dining area, set to switch on at 7.30 pm and off again at 11.00. He looked out onto the avenue to make sure there was no-one around outside yet, then left for Balmaha and relative anonymity in the populous refuge of central London.

★

Week 12; Saturday, 13 June …

Tom dropped the last of the empty envelopes into the waste paper bin next to his chair and looked at the pile of letters and circulars on the table in front of him that he'd filtered out from the mountain of mail he'd been sifting through. He logged off on his laptop before closing it and pushing it away from him. He checked his watch – nearly three o'clock. It had taken him around five hours to catch up, but there again, he reminded himself, he'd been making it spin out for as long as possible just to fill the time.

He put the stack of opened mail into the top drawer of the sideboard and opened a new bottle of Glenfiddich. He poured himself a large one, added a dash of highland spring water from a bottle in the fridge and took his first drink on to the balcony.

★

Week 12; Sunday, 14 June …

Tom was awoken at just after 10.00 am by the sound of the doorbell. He looked round, totally disorientated, his memory not best served by his being in the one room in the apartment that he very rarely entered. The ringing stopped, and he turned over on his side. Then it started again and didn't stop.

He stumbled to the front door of the flat, squinting at the small monitor screen next to it. It showed the person who was pressing the bell outside the main entrance at ground level. Just about the last person he expected to see. He closed his eyes tightly then looked again, as if he might be mistaken. Then he rushed into the en-suite of the master bedroom and looked at himself in the mirror. The image was what he expected – a complete mess. The bell was still ringing. He went back to the door and spoke into the intercom.

"Hi, Grace. What brings you here?"

"Are you okay?"

"Not really, Grace. Late night – well, very early night actually, but lots to drink and …" He hardly recognised his own voice; it was hoarse and squeaky.

"Are you going to let me in?"

"Not sure I want you to see me like this, to be honest."

"Oh, for goodness' sake! Look, I'll sit quietly and avert my eyes until you're decent – or you've done whatever you need to do to yourself. Come on, Tom, letting yourself go isn't going to help anyone, you know. Think of Katey."

He paused for a moment.

"Just give me a couple of minutes, then you can come in and wait while I get a shower."

"Look, can't you just let me in?"

"A couple of minutes."

He went through to the living room, looking into the bathroom as he passed and recoiling from the stench. He had a hazy recollection of making an emergency visit to throw up during the night and had failed to flush the toilet. The smell turned his stomach. He went in and flushed it, turning his head away, then rifled through the floor cabinet for a de-odorising spray, emptying it into the room and closing the door behind him.

Grace was ringing the bell again.

In the living room he quickly cleared the chairs and sofas of papers, and the tables of glasses and the almost empty whisky bottle, before rushing back to the front door.

"I'll leave this unlocked. Make yourself comfortable; I'll be about ten minutes."

He activated the lock on the main doors downstairs and fled into the en-suite shower room.

When he joined Grace in the living room, she was sitting, perfectly relaxed, on one of the black leather sofas. She was wearing a loose, very short, patterned dress over black leggings, and sling-back sandals. Her hair was held back from her face by a grey silk buff pulled down in pirate fashion on her head. Her heavy-rimmed week-day glasses had been discarded in favour of contact lenses. She wore very little make-up, and, as always, the overall effect was dazzling.

"Coffee?" he wheezed.

She reached across to the occasional table next to the sofa and held up a mug.

"Been there, done that," she said, smiling. "But please, be my guest."

Tom gave a twisted smile in response, not yet feeling totally in command of his limbs and features. He dropped heavily in to one of the armchairs, stretched and yawned.

"Oh, sorry," he said. "Rough day yesterday."

"Yes, I heard. Jenny phoned. Told me about the magistrate. Then the Press release, and clearing your office. Actually, that's why I'm here. One of the reasons."

He looked across at her, blinking his eyes to focus.

"What's why you're here?" he said.

"I'm here to accept your resignation."

Tom stared at her.

"As I said, that's one reason. The other was to check whether you were okay. Well, as okay as you can be, I suppose."

"Really," he said, without expression, his voice back to normal. "I wonder why I find it easier to believe your first reason."

"Okay," she said. "Andrew did ask me to see you as soon as possible and persuade you to do what he called 'the right thing'. I was going to do it next week, but … well, to be honest, Tom, I don't see that you really have a choice given…"

"Why did he send *you*?" Tom snapped. "You're rather a big girl now to be running errands for people, even the mighty Donald."

Grace looked down at her hands, clasped together on her lap. She spoke sadly.

"He seems to think we have a special relationship. A few weeks ago I would have said he was right."

Tom was silent and still for a moment, then he got up and went over to the mirror, taking the letter from the frame.

"Here," he said, handing it to her as she looked up.

"What's this?"

"My resignation. I was going to give it to Andrew tomorrow morning, but now, thankfully, I don't have to see him."

She took it from him, frowning.

"Are you sure you don't want to take it?"

"Absolutely sure. You'd be doing me a great service." He sat down on the sofa, a couple of feet away from her. "Like you've always done," he added, with a sigh.

They looked at each other without speaking for a long time.

"Would you like to talk now about my second reason for coming, and our special relationship? Not that we have one, of course, you couldn't have been clearer about..."

"I'd like to talk about that very much," he said, softly. "But not now."

"Why not? I ..."

"Because I wouldn't be sure if you weren't just softening the blow, so to speak. Whether you actually meant it. Tell you what – leave now, with what you came for, and come back again – soon. Tomorrow; the next day – to talk about our 'special relationship' when you don't want anything else. Okay?"

She screwed up her eyes as if trying to read his mind.

"Alright," she said, "but only if you promise to get some decent coffee."

"I promise."

He smiled and walked her to the door. She turned back to him, kissing him lightly on the cheek.

"Until ... whenever," she said.

He closed the door behind her and went back into the living room, noticing for the first time the red message indicator flashing on the house phone. He picked up the handset and followed the menus to his messages. There were six from Katey, four last night, the first at just before ten, and two from earlier that morning.

He checked his mobile – nothing on the display. Of course, there wouldn't be; he had switched it off yesterday morning to avoid unwelcome callers. Katey would certainly have tried that too. He didn't bother to check, knowing how concerned she would be. He phoned her straight away.

"Dad! For Christ's sake, where have you been? I've been worried sick!"

"I'm so sorry, Princess. I fell asleep really early last night. Must have slept through the phone ringing."

"And this morning?"

"Slept through it again."

"I tried your mobile."

"Switched off, I'm afraid. Look I'm really sorry."

There was silence for a while.

"Well, just as long as you're alright."

"I am, honestly. How's Mum?"

"Okay, actually. She's done a really good painting. First for ages. Therapeutic, I suppose."

"And you?"

"I'm okay too." She paused. "Look, Dad, I have to tell you, I phoned Jenny when I couldn't get hold of you, so she'll be worried as well now. You'd best call and tell her you're okay. And … you're not going to like this – I also got in touch with Amazing Grace this morning after I'd got no answer again. She said something about checking that you were okay – so you'd best call her right away or she'll be turning up at the door. Sorry – I just didn't know what to do."

Tom laughed.

"That's okay, Katey. Just think of it as pay-back for all the times I've phoned round your friends when I didn't know where you were, and the hard time you always gave me when I did. Now you know what it's like."

"Yes well don't let it happen again," she said. "And, another thing, I want you back home here just as soon as possible," she added, with real feeling.

"Just as soon as possible," he said. "Better make those calls. I'll phone later. Love to Mum. Bye."

"Bye, Dad."

Tom replaced the receiver then checked the message log again for the time of Katey's second call that morning – 9.25 am. Assuming she called Grace immediately after that, then she had got round to see him in about thirty minutes.

He realised he felt very good about that.

Week 13; Monday, 15 June…

The aide knocked on the large white door and poked his head inside to announce the arrival of the prime minister's 7.00 am appointment.

The Study in 10 Downing Street is a light and airy room with pale pastel-coloured walls above a dado rail and white wood panelling below it. The large white cabinets around the walls and between the three large windows are packed with books behind glass doors with a metal diamond lattice. Lighting for the room is provided by a number of table and floor lamps and a single ornate gold chandelier with seventeen shaded candle lamps.

At one end of the room is a circular meeting table with eight chairs. At the end closest to the door where Grace entered, Andrew was sitting in one of the four wing chairs positioned round a small rectangular table in polished walnut. Just to the left of the door the portrait of Britain's first woman prime minister looked down on him from above the white marble fireplace.

"Come in, Grace." He waved her to sit down on the chair next to him.

The PM was as alert and bright as ever, in spite of the hour. His suit was immaculately pressed and his white shirt looked crisp and gleaming. The knot in his old Etonian tie was, as always, perfectly symmetrical. Grace wondered, not for the first time, if he ever slept at all.

"Morning, Andrew. Thank you for seeing me so early, but I was so excited at being the first person to give you a Christmas present."

She handed him the envelope. Andrew removed the letter, briefly scanned it and tossed it onto the table. He looked at her with penetrating eyes.

"Time to move on, Grace," he said. "The age of the all-conquering Charismadon is behind us now and we mere mortals must take over. In a few years no one will believe that such a creature ever existed. His legendary arrogance and smarm will be a thing of the past and …"

Grace got up, turned away and walked out of the room.

"Keep talking, Andrew," she said, over her shoulder. "You might even be able to convince yourself of all that. But a word of advice – don't waste your time trying to persuade anyone else."

★

"At seven o'clock this morning, I received a letter of resignation from the Home Secretary and Member of Parliament for Princes and Marlburgh, Mr Tom Brown. In his letter, he conveys his regrets at having to take this action but feels that under the circumstances, his position is untenable and that any attempt to pursue his official duties would be an embarrassment to his Party and this government. Mr Brown was charged three days ago, at Guildford Magistrates Court, with materially assisting in the death of a prisoner, his son, Jack Tomlinson-Brown, who was awaiting passage to exile."

Andrew looked directly into the camera and paused, projecting a feeling of utter dismay for the benefit of the watching millions. Then he looked down again at the sheet of paper on the lectern in front of him and continued.

"I fully understand the reasons for his tendering his resignation – noble reasons, typical of the man – so I have accepted it, albeit with a feeling of great reluctance and a heavy heart. And I should like to take this opportunity to express my personal sadness at the harrowing events which have led to this eventuality and, at the same time, thank Tom Brown for his enormous efforts – and unmitigated success – over his eight years as a Member of Parliament with this Party, including the past two years as Home Secretary. He will go down in British history as one of a very small and select band of politicians who, almost single-handedly, brought about quantum change to our society.

"I am sure I speak for everyone in sending Tom, and his family, our very best wishes for their future, and to him personally, our eternal gratitude."

Andrew nodded to all parts of the crowd of reporters, then turned and walked back through the door of Number 10, thinking how different the statement was from the words he would have liked to use, and how pleased he was to get it out of the way.

CHAPTER TWENTY-FOUR

Week 13; Tuesday, 16 June…

"So," said Tony, settling himself in one of the huge armchairs in the living room. "What's all this about and why the urgency?"

Tony Dobson was a youthful thirty-two, average height, slim and with a pleasant, friendly face. Five years ago he had been one of Tom's greatest critics during his formative, angry years as a local reporter. But as his stature as a journalist grew, their mutual respect for each other had passed seamlessly into genuine friendship.

"It's that gang outside," said Tom looking out through the floor-to-ceiling windows and craning to see the large group of reporters and several cameras arrayed in a semicircle outside the main entrance to Balmaha. "The doorbell rang just after eight this morning and every five minutes or so since then. I worked it out – that's about a hundred rings so far. I thought I'd be safe for a bit longer – didn't realise so many people knew about this place."

"Ah, news travels fast once the hunt gets under way," said Tony. "It's like twitching."

"Well, I'm getting a bit twitchy right now. I know I need to speak to those guys – *you* guys – as soon as possible. I heard what they were saying to you down there – about me milking the press when it suited and running from them now – and they're absolutely right; I do have a duty to talk to them. The problem is, I don't know how to go about it. I'm nothing now – not even *part* of anything. No one to sort out a press statement, media conference or whatever for me. I need your help with this, Tony, or at least your advice. I'm happy to give you an exclusive – whatever you want."

Tony held up his hands to stop him.

"Hey, I'm here as a friend, Tom, not a reporter – so let's not talk about exclusives. If you want me to set something up, then I can do that, no problem. I'll tell them to come back, say, tomorrow, or Thursday – whenever you say, at whatever time you like and wherever you want to do it – somewhere on the Embankment might be better than round here. More space along there, and no point in giving your address away to the half-dozen people who still don't know it."

"Is it that easy?"

"Sure, they'll go along with that; actually being invited will make them feel good enough to give you some space."

He gave Tom a wide smile, returned with considerable relief.

"So," Tony went on, "I'll go down and get rid of them if you just tell me when and where, while you put the kettle on. A bit much having to actually *ask* for a cup of tea when I'm going to all this trouble."

Tom shrugged his shoulders and smiled.

"Right then," he said, "let's say ten o'clock Thursday morning and … how about down on Millbank – Riverside Walk Gardens? Can you do that?"

"No problem."

"Great," said Tom. "And you did right to choose tea, by the way;" he added, as Tony left the room to end the siege. "My coffee's come in for some criticism recently."

★

Week 13; Wednesday, 17 June…

"Hi, Shirley, it's Tom Brown here."

"Home Secretary! This is a surprise. A nice surprise, I mean. I don't mean a shock or anything …"

Tom gave a little laugh.

"Thank you, Shirley. Still working hard to cover for an errant senior minister?"

Shirley was silent for a moment.

"I shouldn't have said that. I guess at the time I didn't know what to say."

"That's quite alright, Shirley. I was only teasing, anyway."

"And I really *am* sorry that the prime minister didn't call you after I said I would get him to. I've been thinking about what might have …you know. I did try. Really I did …"

"That's okay, Shirley. I know you did and I'm grateful. And I'm sure it wouldn't have made any difference. Anyway, how are you? Oh, and by the way, I am no longer the Home Secretary – or anything else, in fact."

"I know, but, it still sounds right to … Anyway, I'm fine, thank you. But really sad about your resigning."

"Well, I'm very touched, Shirley," said Tom, "And I really mean that. I feel like I've made a new friend. And if I'm right, I'd like you to do two things for me."

"Yes, okay, anything."

"Well, firstly, could you arrange for me to speak to the prime minister this afternoon, and secondly, do you think you could call me Tom?"

Shirley gave a little laugh.

"I'm not sure which of those will be the most difficult, Home Sec… You see what I mean?"

They both laughed.

"Actually, I think you might be in luck. Hold on, please." There were a few moments of absolute silence. "Putting you through."

"Hello, Tom." The words were not so much spoken as sighed.

"I know you're busy, Prime Minister," said Tom, "but I just wanted to let you know out of courtesy that I shall be speaking to the press tomorrow morning at ten o'clock. I doubt if what I have to say will be quite so eloquently expressed as your announcement about me on Monday, but I can guarantee it will be more sincere. Oh, and I look forward to receiving your *formal* reply to my letter. I assume that, until I do so, I am still the Home Secretary. See you in the House tomorrow after my press conference."

He hung up, then poured himself a small Jack Daniels and sat outside at the balcony table with his laptop in the warm afternoon sun to run through the notes he'd made for his meeting with the Press. Half an hour later, he was interrupted by the sound of the doorbell.

He checked the monitor screen and pressed the door release for the main door at ground level, then stepped onto the landing to greet his former colleague. Jackie Hewlett looked as pleasingly attractive as ever, in a smart close-fitting jacket and skirt, which showed off her slim figure and legs to great effect. They kissed, cheek to cheek, and Tom escorted her onto the balcony, somewhat embarrassed that it was through the very untidy master bedroom, and left her briefly to get another shot glass and the whiskey bottle.

They chatted easily, sipping their drinks, for the best part of an hour before lapsing into a relaxed and comfortable silence. Jackie nursed her glass and looked out over the gleaming vista of the Capital.

"I'll never forget how supportive you were, Tom, that time when Lucy went missing. You were right there at my side all the time."

"It was only a couple of hours, Jackie. It was the least any friend would have done."

Jackie turned to him. There were tears in her eyes.

"But it meant such a lot. I just wish there was something …"

"You're doing it right now, Jackie." He reached across and held her hand. "You're right here with me when I most need a friend."

She smiled and they lapsed into silence again for a while.

"You know what, Tom; I don't know whether I want to carry on without you …"

Tom squeezed her hand.

"You'll be okay, Jackie, and we'll keep in touch, I hope?"

"Of course we will, but you won't be there all the time any more and I always felt safe with you around. You know, from Andrew and …well … Grace, if I'm honest about it."

"Grace? Why, what has she done? I wouldn't have thought you'd have much contact."

"I don't. It's something I can't really put my finger on. I just get the feeling that Andrew has some kind of hold over her, and because of that anything you say in front of her goes straight back to him. I'm probably paranoid."

"You're one of the least paranoid people I've ever met, Jackie. But I can't really see …" His voice tailed off.

"I'm sure you're right," said Jackie. "It probably is just me."

"No, I was just wondering …"

He was interrupted by the bell ringing again.

He went to the door and checked the screen.

"It's Grace, would you believe it?" he called through to Jackie, and then spoke into the intercom.

"Hi, Grace," he activated the entrance door lock, "come on up."

She beamed at him mischievously in the entrance to the apartment, holding one arm behind her back.

"A little something, just in case," she said, revealing and shaking a jar of Columbian roast coffee beans. "Didn't quite trust you to do the right thing."

He forced a smile, taking the jar from her.

"Jackie's here," he said

"Oh, how lovely," said Grace, her features set in a smile, but her eyes freezing over. "I hope I'm not interrupting anything."

"No," he said. "Please, go on through."

She set off for the living room.

"No, through here," he said, waving her into the bedroom. She turned to him with a quizzical expression, her eyes as wide as she could make them.

"Are you *sure* I haven't come at a bad time?"

"Straight through onto the balcony," he said, recovering enough to be annoyed. "I'll get you a glass."

"I'll wait here until you get it."

"You could come back later, if you prefer," said Tom.

"Oh no, I'd like to watch, if that's okay?"

He got the glass and they joined Jackie. Neither woman spoke for several moments, eyes locked and expressions glacial. Grace sat down on one of the two available chairs positioning it so that she and Tom were facing Jackie across the table.

"Jackie."

"Grace."

"Well, now we all know each other," said Tom, turning to Grace and holding up the bottle by way of invitation.

Grace nodded and he filled the shot glass, pushing it across to her. They sat in silence for some time staring out over the panoramic view.

"Anyway," said Jackie, "I'll leave you to it, Tom. I didn't realise you had an *important* meeting."

"No, don't go," said Tom, turning to Grace. "I'm not sure why Grace is here, actually."

"No, Jackie's right," said Grace. "You do have an important – and *private* – meeting."

Jackie drained her glass and got to her feet.

"I'll see you very soon, Tom."

She walked away through the bedroom without another word to Grace, Tom following behind her. At the door she turned to him and spoke loudly enough to be heard on the balcony. "Shame about the interruption; such a pity we couldn't have taken that further. We must pick up where we left off next time. Take care, Tom. See you very soon."

They hugged each other this time.

Tom stood for several moments, gathering his thoughts before returning to the balcony. Grace had moved her chair so she was now facing his.

"So," said Tom, picking up the bottle and refilling Grace's glass. "What's important and private enough for you to make the effort to come round again?"

"Well I said I'd come back."

"Three days ago. The idea must have slipped your mind once you'd left with what you came for?"

"Oh dear, we *are* feeling sorry for ourselves. Well, actually this has been the first chance I've had. Some of us have still got jobs, you know; which reminds me," she went on, reaching into her shoulder bag to retrieve an envelope. "His Unholy Mightiness asked me to give you this." She passed it to him.

He held her eyes as he took it from her, thinking about his interrupted conversation with Jackie. She raised her eyebrows in a gesture of innocence.

"I've no idea what it is."

"No, I bet you don't," said Tom. "Quite the little Postman Pat, aren't we?"

"I don't know what you mean," she said. "Anyway, Postman Pat's a man, isn't he? Do I look like a man to you?"

She turned directly towards him in her chair and crossed her legs theatrically, causing her skirt to ride up high round her thighs. Tom let his gaze dwell for just a moment, and then looked up into her eyes again.

"So you're telling me that you didn't know this is Andrew's letter accepting my resignation?"

"Is it?"

"And that he's rushed it over here with you because I've just told him I'm holding a press conference tomorrow and will be assuming I'm still the Home Secretary until I receive this?"

He waved the envelope at her.

"You told him that!" Grace laughed. "Oh. I wish I'd seen his face when ..."

"Don't piss about with me, Grace. You came here on Sunday to ask for my resignation on Andrew's behalf; then nothing for three days – no phone calls or anything – and suddenly you turn up with his acceptance letter just a couple of hours after I've threatened to make things awkward for him if I didn't get it. I know I can be naïve and idealistic at times, but I'm not all-out stupid!"

"No you're not," she said. "So you can work out whether that's the only reason I'm here."

She slipped down further in the chair so that her skirt rode up even higher. Tom got quickly to his feet and turned away from her, leaning on the rail of the balcony and looking out over the river.

"I'm not sure what your motives are, Grace. If you want me to shag you, that's fine. I can do it now, I suppose – no worries about 'how will it look?' and all that. Broken marriage anyway – just about – no working relationship between us, so no conflict of interest or whatever. But you only come when Andrew sends you. He's probably told you to get laid in my apartment so he can publicly denounce me as a ... whatever!"

"You're getting paranoid, Tom," said Grace. "But could we go back to that bit about you shagging me?"

"No."

"No?"

"No! Not now; not today." He turned to face her. Grace was sitting upright in the chair again and had pulled down her skirt. "I would like to believe that you want more from me, Grace. I mean, why wouldn't I? So let's try again. Come back *another* time, just for me, nothing else. And let's see what happens."

She sighed, and then smiled, rising from her chair and walking up close to him.

"Okay," she pouted, "so here's a test of your resolve and

patience. I'm going to the US tomorrow on a four-week diplomatic assignment. If anything comes up in the meantime, do you think it can wait?"

She placed her hand against the front of his trousers.

"I think so," he said, his voice faltering a little.

"If you're not sure, I could stay," she said, pressing her hand against him more firmly.

"I *am* sure." He stepped to one side. "Anyway, I've got to get to work on my Plan B."

"Plan B?"

"Yes, now Andrew has accepted my resignation, I'll get started on my campaign to fight for the vacant seat in Princes as an Independent. What do you think of that?"

"Well … good luck," she said, and then smiled again. "But what if you get in? Wouldn't we have a sort of working relationship again? I wouldn't like anything to get in the way of… you know?"

"Don't worry; I'll make sure I major on something else. Improving the postal system, perhaps, so I can free up more of your time."

She smiled, and walked through the bedroom to the door of the apartment. She turned and wrapped her arms around his neck, kissing him softly but reaching between his lips with her tongue. He walked her down to the ground floor entrance, this time shaking her hand and kissing her briefly on the offered cheek.

★

Back on the balcony, Tom's thoughts turned to Mags and a feeling of guilt suddenly overwhelmed him. Not for what had just happened with his former colleague, but because he was here, away from the scene of so many harrowing memories; with the real prospect of a new life, one completely detached from his previous existence. Mags and Katey were at home, with reminders of Jack all around them, reinforcing their loss and locking them into their prison of despair. He had escaped and just left them to it. The only linkage to his late son in this new world was the name on the bottle he was reaching for to pour his next drink.

Week 13; Thursday, 18 June…

The sound of his mobile woke Tom. He scrambled to find it on the bedside table, knocking his half full shot glass and wristwatch onto the floor.

"Yes," he rasped.

"Where the hell are you?"

"Tony? What's wrong?"

"What's wrong? I've got half the fucking world's press here waiting to do sound-checks!"

Tom squinted at the display on the phone; '09:38'.

"Oh, shit! I'm sorry, Tony. I overslept."

"Overslept? You sound like you had quite a lot of help. Please don't tell me you're not up yet."

"Okay, I won't," Tom groaned, "but you've just happened to hit on the truth. I'll be there in …"

"Twenty minutes? Because that's how much time you've got. Look, whether you're here or not, the cameras will start rolling at ten and the story will be just as big. 'Tom Brown fails to turn up at his own press conference.' Maybe even bigger."

"Can't you delay them for half-an-hour?"

"You know how these things work, Tom. All the major news channels have got live airtime scheduled for this. There'll be people getting up at five and six in the morning in the US to hear you. What do you think they'll do – show repeats of South Park?"

"I'm moving, right! I'll be there just as …Jesus!"

"What's wrong now?"

"Like I said – I'm moving. God, I feel like shit. I'm not going to make it for ten, Tony. Half-past, that's the best I can do. Tell them I'm not well. It'll be the biggest understatement they'll get to report this year."

"Okay," said Tony. "I'll tell them now and just perhaps they can reschedule the airtime. But ten-thirty – no later – or I'll go live at that time with the truth."

"Which is?"

"You're too pissed to talk to them."

"Look, why don't you just tell them that now …"

"No, Tom, I'm sorry, I shouldn't have said that. God knows, you're entitled to drown your sorrows. I was just concerned about you, wondered if you were okay. I'll hold them off. They don't call me Alamo Dobson for nothing, you know."

"Thanks, Tony; I'll get there as soon as possible. I owe you."

"I'll collect, don't you worry."

Tom staggered around the bedroom looking for his press statement. He remembered taking it off the printer sometime during the evening but it had been lost somewhere between the balcony and the bedroom. Or maybe the living room, he thought, finding the first whiskey bottle empty on the balcony table. Did he take the papers through when he went for the second bottle?

Without any more time to waste on the search he went into the bathroom and made a poor and ill-advised attempt at a wet shave, cutting himself under his chin. He abandoned the task and went back to his bedroom in search of a tissue, picking up his watch from the floor and deciding there was no time for a shower.

He dressed hurriedly, putting on his suit over the boxer shorts and shirt he had crashed out in the previous evening. He pulled on socks and shoes, and grabbed a tie from the rack in the wardrobe, trying twice with the knot before leaving it loose and untidy after the second attempt. He checked his watch again – 10.20.

He fumbled, optimistically, with his car keys, dropping them onto the floor and kicking them under the dressing table in frustration. He couldn't have driven, anyway, he knew, and set off unsteadily down the staircase and out onto Victoria Bridge Road launching himself into the traffic to stop a taxi and almost colliding with a cyclist he had failed to see in the inside lane.

He all but fell out of the taxi a couple of minutes after 10.30, and the media group watched in disbelief as he patted his pockets looking for money that wasn't there to settle the fare. Tony rushed across and paid the driver, and Tom turned slowly and dizzily round to face the gathering.

There were audible gasps of astonishment as he mounted the small stage in Riverside Walk Gardens and clutched the lectern for support. The trickle of crimson which was still clearly flowing from beneath his chin was causing a stain to spread along the collar of the crumpled shirt. His hair was uncombed and he had failed to tie the lace of one of his shoes.

He looked around the sea of faces, blinking his eyes into focus and attempting a smile which was more like a crooked grimace.

"Ladies and gentleman of the press …"

Tony stepped up beside him. "Just a moment, Tom, let's get the mike sorted first."

He clipped the radio mike onto his lapel as Tom gave a loud, unnatural laugh which ceased abruptly as the pain shot through his head. He turned to Tony.

"Are we on camera yet?" It was supposed to be a whisper but was loud enough for all to hear. They exchanged baffled and worried looks as Tom straightened up again and Tony stepped slightly to one side.

"Ready to roll," he said. "Give Mr Brown his cue."

"Ladies and gentlemen of the press," said Tom, his eyes glazed and rolling. "I just want to say …thank you. That is, thank you for coming here today and … for everything else. You know, like reporting all I've done over the years. Because without you, there would be no Tom Brown. And without no Tom Brown … I mean … without Tom Brown, there would be no New Justice Regime. Just remember that."

He wagged his finger limply at the group. No one was taking notes.

"And I want to thank everybody for their support at this difficult time. Well, not everybody – but I won't say any more about that. I'll just say this; I didn't want to resign, because now I've got nothing. *Nothing*. But … well … you know how it is."

He was breathing heavily, struggling with his balance.

"I haven't decided what I'm going to do next. There's one or two things, I suppose but – well – whatever. But I'll keep you all informed as and when – if anyone's still interested."

He laughed again, looking round the sea of blank faces. Then he seemed to slip and gripped the lectern tighter.

"I'm okay," he snapped at Tony, who had taken a step forward to support him. "Just fine." He turned back to the reporters. "Now, any questions? Just ask away, that's what I'm here for."

There was a general shaking of heads, except for one reporter at the back. A young woman with short blonde hair, wearing a pink jacket and black trousers held up her hand. Tom didn't see her but Tony stepped up beside him.

"Over there," he said, pointing.

"Clara Lewis, Network Thames," she said. "Mr Brown, in the light of what has happened, do you have any regrets about extending the expulsion provisions to drug dealers?"

There was a deathly hush as the whole group of reporters turned to look at her in disbelief. Tears sprang to Tom's eyes. He caught them with the thumb and forefinger of one hand. There was a long silence.

"Oh, yes," he said, his voice barely audible. "Most definitely, yes."

He turned and stepped down from the stage.

*

Tom went into the bathroom, seeing himself in the mirror for the first time since he had staggered away from it earlier to find a tissue to deal with his cut. His eyes filled briefly with tears again at the depressing sight in front of him, before he splashed water onto his face and went into the bedroom to change his bloodstained shirt. He picked up the half-empty bottle of whiskey and joined Tony in the living room.

"Could I ask you two big favours, my friend?" said Tom.

"Go on."

"Firstly, don't say anything to me about what just happened, at least for the rest of today. Suffice to say, I'm really sorry. You deserved a lot better. Okay?"

"Okay. And the other favour?"

Tom held up the bottle.

"Stay and help me finish this. That way, I'll only drink half of what's left. If you go. I'll drink the lot."

Tony thought for a moment.

"On one condition. We eat first, and drink later. Okay?"

"Okay."

★

Week 13; Friday, 19 June…

Tom read again the text he had received from Andrew the previous evening.

"Really enjoyed your press conference. Good luck with the campaign."

It was not until now that he realised its implications and thought back to his conversation with Jackie two days ago. He hadn't mentioned his plans to contest the vacant seat in his statement to the press. Only one person in the world had heard him state that intention.

CHAPTER TWENTY-FIVE

Four days later
Week 14; Tuesday, 23 June…

John Mackay's agitation contrasted sharply with his relaxed and smiling demeanour at their first meeting exactly nine weeks ago. He had, uncharacteristically, discarded his uniform jacket and loosened his tie and was pacing backwards and forwards, covering the full distance between the large bookcase at one side of his office and the windows overlooking New Station Yard at the other. Even more unusually, his jacket was roughly draped around the back of his chair rather than arranged neatly on its padded hanger on the coat stand. Jo was sitting on one of the two wing chairs in front of the desk watching and listening intently.

"I – *we* – need to get closure on this, Jo. Today – right *now*, in fact. If Gerrard went round intimidating *all* the witnesses and came back from each with what he got from Newhouse, I *still* wouldn't have enough to reopen the case. There's nothing – and there would *still* be nothing – to indicate anything except the usual on-the-street jostling for positions."

"Yes, sir, I do see that, but …"

"It's the '*but*' that you've got to lose, Jo. Nobody doubts your instincts and your intentions, but there comes a point where *judgement* must take over from them. You don't have an axe to grind, a position to protect. I don't understand what is driving you, other than your feeling at the time you made the arrest that he didn't *seem* to know the stuff was there. But if he's devious enough to peddle crack in the current climate, feigning shock and horror to give himself time to think would be a piece of cake."

"I do understand, sir. I guess I'm just …"

"*And*," John continued, "something we've hardly mentioned; what about his performance in court? Not a lot of shock and horror – or denial – there, was there? A guilty man resigned to his fate if ever I've seen one."

Jo sighed. John sat down and leaned across towards her, resting his elbows on the desk.

"Look, Jo," he spoke quietly now, "I want you back on board one hundred percent. Heather Rayburn told me about your issue with the Enderbys. How you reacted to their drowning; feeling that you were responsible for allowing them the chance to leave their home and take their own lives just after you'd told them they might lose their son again. It wasn't your fault, as I'm sure you've come to realise, but I can understand how it might have seemed that way at the time."

Jo was staring at him now, eyes wide.

"But this is different…" John went on.

"You bet it is, sir," Jo interrupted. "I don't see any connection at all. On that occasion it *would* have been avoided if I'd acted differently. That's a *fact*. If I'd just put a watch on them …"

"It's not about the incident itself, Jo." John held up his hands to stop and reassure her. "I'm talking about the *reaction*. On that occasion, as I said, I can understand how it got to you. But you're a fringe player in this, and yet, increasingly over the past couple of weeks or so, you've been letting this get to you in much the same way. You seem to have assumed the responsibility for Jack and Jason's situation – taken on the blame for their fate. *They* are to blame, Jo. *They did it*, as far as it's possible in this life to be certain of anything. You have to let go."

Jo didn't speak.

"Look," said John. "I'm going to tell you something that only two or, perhaps, three people know. That's me, Tom Brown and, just possibly, his wife. When they made the statement in the House about the sentencing of drug dealers, I phoned Tom Brown in an attempt to persuade him to think again. I actually tried to talk him out of it. Can you believe it! I couldn't tell him *why*, of course, because even at that stage, prior to the drugs being found, we already had enough on Jack – and Jason – to make a case against them. That was bad enough *before* the announcement, but suddenly I was faced with the distinct possibility that what we were about to do could result in one of my best friends losing his son forever. And that's exactly what happened, although not in the way anyone expected. Not my fault – but that doesn't make it any easier.

"It was unprofessional of me to speak to him at all, of course. In a conflict of interest like that you should always put the personal issue aside and do what you're paid to do. And it was a waste of time, anyway, as you know. So I failed twice – made the wrong decision, professionally, *and* failed to carry it through. So when it comes to feeling responsible, DI Cottrell, I'm in the gold medal position and you've not even qualified for the final."

Jo didn't speak for a long time.

"I'm sorry, sir," she said, "I guess I didn't realise just how close … Okay, no more 'buts'. There's nothing I want more than to move on from this – really. And I appreciate your concern about me and for giving me time out to plough my own furrow, as it were."

John was silent himself for a few moments. Then he leaned back in his chair.

"Good," he said, suddenly more relaxed. "I know you can't just throw a switch and turn it off."

"No, sir, but I *can* start to rotate the knob on the dimmer."

John laughed out loud. "From what I've heard about him, that sounds like pure Gerrard."

Jo smiled. "I'll take that as a compliment."

"Something else you should know that I didn't share with you before. When we set up the surveillance on Mickey last year, we had what we thought was rock solid evidence that Manston Grange was the centre of an illegal drugs market. We assumed, because of his background, that Kadawe was the main man – the centre of the activity; the hub of the wheel. As you know, we watched him, pretty much day and night, for seven months; and got nothing.

"We called off the operation, went back over all the information we'd collected beforehand and *still* couldn't understand how we could have got it wrong. So we kept a watchful eye going forward and, lo and behold, Jack and Jason – as Jake and Jasper – came onto the radar. We'd been seeing the Grange and Kadawe as pretty much one and the same entity. It seems certain now, that we were looking in the right place but at the wrong person."

Jo was silent for a long time.

"So why didn't you share this with me before, sir?" she said, eventually.

John got to his feet and started pacing again.

"I didn't tell you because I secretly hoped – almost prayed – that you *would* find something. I desperately wanted you to be right and all the rest of us wrong; even though it would have been a massive embarrassment to us and now, of course, too late for Jack."

He turned to Jo.

"But you can't find what isn't there, even if you look for ever."

★

Jo walked out through the main gates to a small park a couple of streets away where she sat on a bench overlooking the duck pond. She gazed absently at the rippling water stirred by a gentle breeze, then took out her phone and clutched it tightly on her lap for a long time. Eventually she looked down at it and scrolled through her list of contacts.

★

Week 14; Wednesday, 24 June...

For a long time, the dishevelled figure sat on the parapet above the central arch of Vauxhall Bridge, his feet swinging over the side above the Thames. His hair was uncombed, and his clothes creased; the collar of his sports jacket was turned inwards and the tail of his crumpled shirt was half sticking out at the back. People passed by within a couple of feet of him, pretending he wasn't there, not giving him a second glance.

It was hardly surprising then that no one recognised him. If they had looked more closely, they might have noticed that the clothes were expensive, and the face under the mop of hair and behind the stubble was strikingly handsome, with pale-blue, intelligent eyes.

The man looked down at the water forty feet below, churning in the wake of a passing launch, and wondered what it would be like. He was a strong swimmer; he could make it downstream to the flood barrier and back – easily. So, he wondered, would an instinct for survival override his objective? Would his first mouthful of water throw some sort of switch in his mind and activate a natural bid to stay alive? After all, he thought, it wasn't like jumping from a high building or cliff, where the leap itself was the terminal movement. Once *that* step was taken, what followed was inevitable; as certain as Heaven's door.

He looked up and across to the Palace of Westminster, with the sun glinting on its golden highlights, and thought about the man who had delivered a landmark speech to the House on a Wednesday exactly thirteen weeks ago. A man who he realised no longer existed; who had somehow mutated into something else, something worthless. He looked down at the water again and eased himself slightly forward.

"Are you okay?"

He turned quickly at the sound of the voice. The girl was tall and slim, with long, straight, white-blonde hair. With the bright sun behind her he couldn't make out her features, and just for a moment he thought he recognised her. But, of course, he knew it couldn't be her. She hadn't been in touch for some time now; except for just the one text last night.

"I'm fine," he said to the girl.

"You're sure?"

"Yes, honestly."

"Okay." She smiled.

He watched her walk away, and then shouted after her. "Thank you!"

She looked back and gave a little wave. He took his mobile from his jacket and read the text again.

'Mum needs you very much NOW!'

He shook his head. Wrong, he thought. Whatever it is, I would only make it worse.

He turned to look along the bridge where the girl had gone. He couldn't see her. Could it *really* have been his daughter, he wondered, reaching out to him in his troubled mind?

He sat deep in thought for a full minute without moving, thinking about the girl. Then he swung his legs back over the parapet, dropped on to the pavement and walked off the bridge.

HOTEL ST KILDA

The story continues in…

LOST SOULS

PROLOGUE

"Just like in the movies."

The young man seated on the bench spoke the words out loud to himself. He was of medium height and average build, with longish dark hair; and casually dressed in designer jeans, tee shirt and a short, tan leather jacket.

He looked around the nearly-deserted park and across to the shining lake where a mother and her small child pitched lumps of bread at a squabbling group of ducks in front of them. Until now, except for one elderly lady walking her border terrier a hundred yards or so away to his right, they had been the only visible signs of humanity in the tranquil grassy oasis close to the town centre. He wondered how many times he'd watched this scene play out in spy films and TV dramas. The only thing that was missing was a rolled-up newspaper under the arm of the man who was approaching him. Instead, he was carrying a small day-pack, which he removed from his back and placed between them on the bench as he sat down.

The new arrival was tall, in his early thirties, with handsome chiselled features and dark, close-cropped hair. He was formally dressed in an immaculate charcoal grey lounge suit, pale blue shirt and navy-and-grey striped tie. He also wore a pair of soft leather gloves.

"Sorry," said the first man, with a smile which was close to a sneer. "I've forgotten the password."

The newcomer said nothing but fixed him with an intense stare from behind his dark-tinted glasses. The first man broke the uneasy silence.

"I mean, this is a bit John le Carre, isn't it?"

The stranger raised his eyebrows in surprise, still remaining silent.

"Yes, some of us do read things other than the back page of *The Sun* in case you're wondering. Anyway, why didn't the big guy come himself?"

His companion looked momentarily confused, and then smiled thinly.

"You needn't concern yourself with the chain of command."

He nodded towards the bag. The first man unbuckled the single strap, lifted the flap and peered inside. He let out his breath loudly.

"What if I say no?"

"Then there'll be five instead of four."

He closed the flap again, fastening the strap and slumping back on the bench, legs out-stretched in front of him.

The stranger raised his eyebrows again; this time with a question.

"Okay?"

The first man nodded, nervous now. It was a long time before he spoke again.

"When?"

"Down to you. But a week today I'll expect to have read all about it. Then we meet again. I'll let you know when and where."

He got up from the bench, leaving the day-pack and walking away without another word.

ACKNOWLEDGEMENTS

Once again thanks are due to the many people who contributed in different ways to the production of this book.

To those who provided me with factual information for the first book and especially David Monks and Alan Isherwood who have answered more of my queries for *Heaven's Door*. In particular, I thank Richard Latham for giving up his time to provide me with an invaluable insight into the home of the British parliament. In addition to the essential information it yielded, the experience itself was such a memorable one.

To all the people – friends, acquaintances and strangers – who have purchased *Catalyst* and provided me with such encouraging feedback, which has spurred me on to complete this second volume.

To my publisher, Matador, for making the whole experience of creating these books such an enjoyable one, and in particular to Rosie Grindrod and Amy Statham, not only for their assistance with each step along the way, but also for their patience, both in responding to what must have been the most basic and obvious questions, and in watching deadlines pass by like ships in the night when I failed to get materials to them on time.

To Gary Smailes of Bubblecow – again – for his detailed editorial critique and invaluable advice following on from this.

To my family for their ongoing interest and encouragement, and above all to my wife, Carol, for her unstinting support and for continuing to endure my feeling sorry for myself when things were not going as planned – which happened quite a lot.

MICHAEL KNAGGS was born in Hull in 1944. He moved to Thurso, Caithness, in 1966 to work as an Experimental Officer at Dounreay Atomic Power Station, and relocated to Salford in 1968 to complete a degree in Chemistry. From 1970 up to his retirement in 2005, Michael worked for Kellogg Company – the global breakfast cereal manufacturer – latterly as Human Resources Director with responsibility for pay and benefit policy across the company's European organisation.

He lives in Prestwich, Manchester, with his wife, Carol. Their passion is hill-walking and they undertake at least one long distance walk each year. They have two children and two grand-children.

Reviews of

CATALYST

Draws you in and doesn't let go until the final page

A stunning debut. The plot line is intriguing and the characters are
believable and easy to identify with. If crime with political machinations
is your thing then Catalyst ticks all the right boxes. Knaggs can certainly
hold his own among his peers in this genre.

Devious thriller

Just when you think the book is reaching a conclusion it takes a devious
twist that keeps you guessing to the end.

Great read

A great read with lots of twists and turns. Excellent descriptions that
bring it to life. Could not put it down.

Interesting and enjoyable tale from a new author

A great read and an excellent debut novel. I found it to be well written
and I look forward to more from this new writer. If you like thrillers
with a political edge you will find this a good read.

Captured my interest early on

I really enjoyed reading this debut novel... I was captured immediately
and found the book to have a thought-provoking theme. It kept me
interested throughout... Now I am looking forward to a sequel... or
there will be a riot!